MRS HUDSON AND THE LAZARUS TESTAMENT

By Martin Davies

Mrs Hudson and the Spirits' Curse
Mrs Hudson and the Malabar Rose
Mrs Hudson and the Lazarus Testament
Mrs Hudson and the Samarkand Conspiracy
Mrs Hudson and the Blue Daisy Affair
Mrs Hudson and the Christmas Canary
Mrs Hudson and the Capricorn Incident
Mrs Hudson and the Belladonna Inheritance
Mrs Hudson and the Kensington Clairvoyant

MRS HUDSON AND THE LAZARUS TESTAMENT

MARTIN DAVIES

Allison & Busby Limited
11 Wardour Mews
London W1F 8AN
allisonandbusby.com

First published in the United Kingdom in 2015 by Canelo.
This edition published by Allison & Busby in 2026.

A CIP catalogue record for this book is available from the British Library.

10 9 8 7 6 5 4 3 2 1

ISBN 978-0-7490-3366-8

Printed and bound in Great Britain by Clays Ltd. Elcograf S.p.A

EU GPSR Authorised Representative
LOGOS EUROPE, 9 rue Nicolas Poussin, 17000, LA ROCHELLE, France
E-mail: Contact@logoseurope.eu

CHAPTER ONE

An Incident in Baker Street

Death came to Baker Street on a day when spring was in the air and the flower girls were weighed down by the weight of so many early daffodils; a day so bright after the darkness of winter that it made me forget the state of my street-splattered skirts and think instead of happier days to come, when the evenings would lengthen and the sun would finally vanquish the deep, foul-smelling mud through which the hansom cabs lumbered.

Indeed, had it not been for that day's unusual mildness, I might never have noticed the man who, in the days that followed, so often occupied my thoughts. Had there been snow in the air once again, as there had been the day before, I would have been trudging homewards with collar up and eyes down, intent on nothing but a hasty escape from the elements. But a morning of sunshine had wrought a change in the city. Pale clerks stepping from their offices paused to look up at the clear sky and blink at it, while elderly gentlemen held their heads a little higher and noticed the pretty faces of the shop girls, and seemed to wonder if it might not almost be time to dispense with the extra layer of wool worn close to their skin. And I too found the sunlight uplifting. The light picked out the gleaming panes of every window and the shining brass-work of every front door, and turned my thoughts towards cherry blossom and magnolia.

And then, as I waited to cross the road, I noticed the man with the watch in his hand. He was a gentleman of some sixty years, well dressed in tweeds, with a trim figure and hair that had greyed only at the temples. He had paused beside me, on the edge of the kerb, and his repeated glances across the road suggested that we shared a destination: for his eye was clearly seeking out the blue front door behind which Mr Sherlock Holmes pursued his famous career and where, under the tutelage of his formidable housekeeper, Mrs Hudson, I was responsible for the polishing of the floors, the cleaning of the plate and the dusting of just about everything.

My curiosity was aroused by this coincidence and I looked at the gentleman more closely. Here, it seemed, was someone on whom the better weather had *not* had a calming effect. Judging by his air of agitation he appeared to be in a great hurry to cross the road, and he made repeated attempts to do so, frequently stepping a foot or so off the kerb, only to be driven back by the rush of carriages that persisted, almost without pause, in both directions. As each attempt was thwarted he would look down at the small silver watch he held in his hand in the way of a man late for an appointment, and at first I wondered whether his anxiety was simply that of a punctual man delayed. But his distress seemed too great for that, and I realised his urgency must stem from some inner perturbation, for when he looked down at the object in his hand, I saw that it was not the *face* of the watch he referred to so constantly. Instead, he would flip the timepiece over in his palm and study the back of it, before looking up again and searching wildly for a break in the traffic.

Intrigued by this, I might perhaps have spoken to him had he remained there longer, but before I could think of uttering a word he had stepped forward once more and this time he made a desperate dash into the gap between two carriages. Had he continued forward, trusting to speed and luck, he might perhaps have achieved a safe passage to the other side, but in his fraught state it seemed all judgement had deserted him. With the oncoming horses almost upon him, he hesitated. Then, realising his danger, he tried to go on, but his feet slipped from under him on the treacherous cobbles, and before he could even cry out he had been struck by the thundering bulk of a carriage horse. The blow sent him tumbling headlong to the ground and under the wheels of a speeding victoria that was coming on apace from the other direction.

It was a hideous sight to behold, and for a fraction of a moment it seemed the street stood still, its clamour extinguished. Then the silence shattered, and amid the screams and the confusion and the shrieking of horses, I was the first to reach the fallen gentleman. I knew he could not live, for I had seen the whole weight of the carriage pass over him, his chest crushed beneath it. But when I reached him, although there was already blood on his lips, there was still a flutter of life in his frame, and I dropped to my knees beside him in the filth, intent on lifting his head clear of the mud. As I cradled him like that, with the crowd beginning to gather around us, he opened his eyes and gazed at me in confusion.

'Elsie?' he asked in a whisper, his eyes glazed and his breathing uncertain. 'Is that you?'

'Hush, sir,' I replied, still supporting his head with one hand while with the other I tried to loosen his collar. 'Elsie's not here yet. I'm sure she'll come soon, sir . . .'

'I love her,' he murmured. 'But I never told her. I should have said so long ago . . .'

And with that his eyes closed and his breath seemed spent. Above me I could hear a policeman shouting for a doctor, and the voice of a coachman raised in panic: 'He just ran out! He just ran out . . .' Below me, the mud-stained face had turned grey.

Somewhere beneath my fingers I could still feel a very faint pulse, but I knew the end was coming. I had just begun to straighten, sure that his suffering was over, when his eyes opened again and this time they were clear and focused. I saw a movement of his hand and realised he was trying to beckon me closer. So little breath was left to him that he could barely speak, but when I placed my ear close to his lips the words were unmistakeable.

'Tell . . . Mr Holmes . . .' he gasped, 'I have seen . . . a dead man . . .' He paused and I could see a look of panic in his eyes as he gathered himself for one last effort. 'I have seen a dead man risen from the grave . . .'

And with those words I felt the life go out of him, felt it in my hand behind his head and in my fingers on his neck, felt it even where my knees pressed against his side on the cobbles. Like a candle pinched out.

Before I allowed the sobs to rise in me, I reached down and gently closed his eyes.

I remember little of what happened next. I have a recollection of being lifted to my feet, and of hushed voices comforting me while a doctor arrived and told us what we already knew. Then, while I was still weeping into my handkerchief, I was aware of a policeman leading me towards a plain four-wheeler that had pulled up against the opposite kerb. I was dimly conscious of the fact that it was a very grand vehicle, but it bore no insignia or markings to indicate who sat inside. As I approached it, a door was opened and an elderly gentleman with enormous white whiskers leant out of it.

'Very good, constable,' he nodded. 'Come now, quickly, she's beginning to shiver. That's right. Good work.'

I found myself almost lifted into the carriage where I was immediately wrapped in a blanket that smelt of tobacco and sandalwood soap. It was not an unpleasant smell and, comforted by the warmth, I found myself taking notice of the gentleman who had come to my rescue.

Even in my befuddled state, his face looked familiar. He must have been seventy years or more in age, but his hair was still thick and grew in a great unruly white tangle. In conjunction with those luxuriant whiskers, the effect of so much hair was to make his head appear of enormous size, like a lion's, and it seemed impossible that the small top hat on the seat beside him could ever be made to balance on such a great mane. His expression was stern but not unkind, and as I waited for him to speak he reached out a rather mottled hand and patted my fingers.

'There now. Nasty business, but all over. You did everything you could. I saw it all from here. You were very brave. Now tell me, girl, do you have a name?'

'They call me Flotsam, sir.'

'Very good. And do you have an address, Flotsam? My driver will take you home at once.'

I indicated the blue front door visible through the carriage window.

'I live just there, sir,' I told him, 'and I ought to be getting back. Mrs Hudson will be expecting me. I'm supposed to be dusting.'

The gentleman seemed to take a moment to digest this information.

'But those are the rooms of Sherlock Holmes, are they not?'

'Yes, sir. And Dr Watson's.'

'Well, well,' he smiled. 'Something of a coincidence. Now come, child, take my arm while I help you down those area steps.'

And that is how Sir Percival Grenville-Ffitch, KG, KCB, KCMG, renowned statesman and confidant of princes, came to enter our house in Baker Street, not through the front door as he had planned, but directly into Mrs Hudson's kitchen, and on a piece of business quite different from the one that had brought him hastening to Baker Street that morning, directly from the Palace.

* * *

I have seldom seen Mrs Hudson flustered, and if the unannounced appearance in her kitchen of one of the greatest men in the realm in any way surprised her, she certainly gave no sign of it. She simply nodded politely in the direction of Sir Percival, then turned her full attention to me, her hands and her forearms still white with flour from the morning's baking.

'Goodness, Flotsam,' she exclaimed, bustling across the kitchen, dusting her hands against her apron. 'I've never seen you so pale. No, don't talk now. Come, let me get you into this chair . . .'

For the better part of a minute she took no notice at all of our visitor while she busied herself about me, chafing my hands and feeling my forehead until she had satisfied herself I was in no immediate danger. Only then did she turn to our guest.

'I perceive that we are in your debt, sir,' she began. 'If you would take a seat at the table here, perhaps I might offer you some refreshment? I can promise you a very fine glass of Madeira.'

Sir Percival replied with a rather curt bow.

'I fear not, madam. Your young charge's plight has already diverted me from business of the most pressing nature. I am sure she will be able to give you a full account of events in due course. Now, if you will excuse me . . .'

But instead of completing his sentence and turning to go, he seemed to halt in utter astonishment.

'Good lord!' he exclaimed, his tone quite changed, his eyes on the object now cradled in Mrs Hudson's hands. 'By Jove! That's a bottle of the Morley Madeira! Why, I believe there are only a dozen cases left in the country! And most of those are in Lord Grimsby's cellars, behind enormous padlocks. Only the other day I tried to get hold of some for the visit of the Papal Nuncio and was told it was unobtainable at any price . . .'

And as if overwhelmed by the vision before him, Sir Percival sank down into the chair Mrs Hudson held out for him.

'Yes, sir, it is rather rare nowadays. Fortunately his lordship is good enough to send me a bottle or two every now and then, as a token of his regard. I was once able to assist his lordship in a small matter concerning his favourite niece, an Austrian dancing master and a missing pastry cook with expensive tastes.'

Sir Percival frowned, as if struggling to recall something. 'Let me see, madam . . . Did I hear that your name is Hudson? Why, of course! You were housekeeper to the Fosdykes during that business with the French governess and the Mexican revolutionary! I remember young Fosdyke once hinting that you were the only person who really knew the whole truth of that affair . . .'

Rather than blush, Mrs Hudson merely pursed her lips and shook her head.

'I'm afraid discretion was never young Mr Fosdyke's strong suit, sir. His father, of course, was a very discreet man. Now, if you would allow me to pour you a small glass . . . The knack with the Morley is never to decant.'

It says a great deal for the unique qualities of the Morley Madeira that Sir Percival allowed himself to put aside affairs of state for a full five minutes while he enjoyed the glass Mrs Hudson placed in front of him. During that time he chatted with surprising animation about the Fosdykes and their circle, and seemed to quite forget the peculiarity of his circumstances. It was only when Mrs Hudson cleared her throat and looked rather pointedly in my direction that he rose hastily to his feet.

'My apologies, madam. This young lady requires your attention. And given the unfortunate events she has witnessed, it is really unforgivable that I should be forgetting myself in this way. Besides, I am not in Baker Street by coincidence. I have urgent business with Mr Sherlock Holmes. I have come to request an interview at his earliest convenience.'

'I'm afraid Mr Holmes is not at home today, sir, although we expect him back this evening.'

'Very well. Pray inform him that I shall return at eight o'clock. And please be sure he understands that it concerns a matter of unparalleled national importance. International importance, even. It is absolutely vital that we are not interrupted.'

It was not until our visitor had left us that I was free to pour out to my companion the full story of what I had witnessed in Baker Street, and in doing so I found myself once more blinking back the tears. I was no stranger to death. No one who had ever called the dark backstreets of London their home could be unfamiliar with the sight and smell of the dead and the dying. But there was something in the terrible unexpectedness of the scene I had witnessed that left me badly shaken. That a gentleman so full of energy, so visibly wracked by strong emotion, should be suddenly and brutally undone by such a small misjudgement was hard to comprehend. And then there were his last words: his intimation of an undeclared love, and his perplexing message for Mr Holmes . . . These things made it no easier to put the horrible incident from my mind.

And Mrs Hudson, for all her famous fierceness and efficiency, did not make the mistake of making me try. Instead she let me talk, still wrapped in Sir Percival's cashmere blanket, while she busied herself with the kitchen chores that my arrival had interrupted. There was something very soothing about her calmness as she moved around me, from one point to another, creating order and neatness wherever she went. For all her bulk, she moved lightly, and the strength in those great, floury forearms was perfectly complimented by the remarkable deftness of her fingers. When I told her of the dying gentleman's message for Mr Holmes, the housekeeper paused in her progress and raised an eyebrow.

'How very puzzling,' she mused. 'We shall certainly make sure that Mr Holmes is informed of it. But how easy it will be for him to discover the gentleman's meaning is hard to say. Unless the poor man has shared his story with someone else, I fear it may now remain untold.'

I nodded forlornly. 'And then there's Elsie, ma'am. He told me he loved her. But he never told her of his feelings. I'd like her to know what he said, ma'am. I'd like her to know that he thought of her at the end.'

Mrs Hudson placed a reassuring hand upon mine. 'Indeed, Flottie. We must try our best to find her and tell her. It is the least we can do. Constable Dobson may be able to tell us a bit more about the unfortunate gentleman. Tomorrow we shall catch him when he goes off duty and tempt him in for a slice of my rich Dundee. Now,' she went on, producing a feather duster with a flourish, 'I think you'd better have a little lie down. We need to keep you warm while the shock passes. And if I'm to get the gentlemen's rooms ready for their return, I'll need to look lively. After all, we have an important guest tonight, and whatever Mr Holmes might think, I don't believe that Sir Percival Grenville-Ffitch will be at all amused to be offered a seat still covered with our gentlemen's scientific investigations into the different textures of nail clippings.'

Mrs Hudson's advice proved sound, for on lying down in my little cupboard-bed, I fell quickly into a soothing sleep. When I awoke, blinking and slightly disorientated, I found the kitchen transformed into an oasis of heat and light. In the streets outside, the warmth of the day had waned with the sinking sun, and the muffled faces of passers-by testified to the night's sharp edge. There would be another frost. But in Mrs Hudson's kitchen the fire was burning high and the smell of brandy punch crept from the stove and tiptoed softly to where I lay.

'Strictly for the gentlemen,' Mrs Hudson cautioned me sternly, 'though perhaps a small sip later on will do you no harm after what you've been through today. Now, Flottie, your supper's on the table and you need to get it down fast because Mr Holmes will be home any minute and Sir Percival will be calling soon after that. So if you don't want to go hungry, you'd better jump to it.'

And jump I did, wiping the sleepy dust from my eyes and pulling on a clean apron in less time than it took Mrs Hudson to taste the punch and to tip some more coal on to the fire. And it was as well that I hurried, because even before the remnants of my supper had been cleared from the table we heard the sounds of the gentlemen's return. It was only by darting up the stairs two at a time that I was there to greet them in the hallway.

If I had not already guessed how quickly the weather had turned, one glance at the two of them would have told me. Both looked pinched and pale, and Dr Watson was clapping his hands and stamping his feet rather grumpily.

'Really, Flotsam,' he puffed, 'it's damnably cold out there! We've been an hour in a freezing cab from Kennington, and I tell you I was within an inch of jumping out and taking refuge in a public house. I haven't been able to feel the tips of my fingers since Vauxhall Bridge.'

'Come now, Watson,' Mr Holmes admonished him with a smile. 'You are a sight too modest. Any man who can survive an Afghan winter as you have done can endure an hour or two of London in March! Even so, there is some small basis for your complaint. There is a decided chill in the air.' He shrugged his cape from his shoulders with a flourish.

'Please, sir,' I piped up, 'Mrs Hudson has left a veal pie and some hot brandy punch in the study for you. She said you'd be cold after spending all day crouching in that attic.'

Mr Holmes permitted himself another smile. 'You hear that, Watson? The woman's a gem! Is there anything else, Flotsam?'

'Yes, sir. Sir Percival Grenville-Ffitch will be calling at eight o'clock, sir, on a matter of unparalleled international importance.'

'Will he, indeed?' Mr Holmes consulted his watch. 'Well, Watson, we've just enough time to change our clothes and to sample Mrs Hudson's punch. I daresay it will prove another trifling case of ministerial indiscretion, but a man of Sir Percy's standing at least deserves a hearing. Any other messages, Flotsam?'

I hesitated, not sure how to explain. 'Well, sir, there was a gentleman knocked down by a carriage earlier today, just outside our door. He was coming to see you, sir. Oh, sir, he was hurt terribly badly! But he did manage to say something before he died, sir. He said to tell you about a man risen from the grave. It seemed very important to him, sir.'

'Dear me, Flotsam, how very unpleasant! But all too common nowadays, I fear. Unfortunately nothing will change until the pedestrians of London can be made to understand that a four-wheeler travelling at fifteen miles per hour is not a handcart that can be brought to a halt on a sixpence!'

'But what about the message, Holmes?' Watson asked, rubbing his moustache vigorously as if to warm it up. 'Sounds a bit rum.'

'A man risen from the grave?' Mr Holmes shrugged. 'That could signify any number of things, my friend. Remember, since you've taken to publishing those little reminiscences of yours, we've had a constant stream of religious cranks and evangelists at our door. And, I fear, without further relevant data, the precise meaning of this gentleman's words will never be known to us. Even so, it sounds like an ugly episode . . .' He handed me his hat and gloves, then patted me reassuringly on the shoulder. 'Flotsam, perhaps Mrs Hudson would be so good as to find out if there's anything to be done for the poor man's family. I know Watson here will tell me we must do what we can for them in their distress. Now, Watson, lead on! That veal pie awaits!'

But while the gentlemen made their ablutions that evening, the first knock to disturb us was not Sir Percival's, but instead a rather timid tap on the kitchen door which was quickly followed by the appearance of Mr Rumbelow the solicitor, a rotund and respectable gentleman whose professional dealings had more than once brought him into contact with our establishment, and who over many years of acquaintance had come to hold Mrs Hudson's abilities in the highest regard. Indeed it had been through Mr Rumbelow's intervention that we had first come into Mr Holmes's service, something for which, ever since, the gentleman had seemed anxious to make amends.

'Ah, Mrs Hudson!' he began, blinking a little in the light. 'What an evening! Quite winter again, I do believe. Ah, and young Flotsam too! Good evening, good evening. So warm in here! The most welcoming room in London, I always say. I trust I do not intrude at all, Mrs Hudson?'

'Not at all, sir. Let me take your coat. You catch us at a quiet moment.'

Rubbing his hands and puffing contentedly, Mr Rumbelow sank into his accustomed chair by the hearth.

'I hope I find you well, Mrs Hudson?' he began, removing his spectacles, which had begun to steam up in the warmth. 'Excellent! Excellent! Always in such good health! You are an example to us all.'

He began to rub the lenses with his handkerchief while searching for words to continue.

'Mrs Hudson, I confess that this is not entirely a social visit. I was passing, you see, and it happens I have a little matter that I wish to lay before you. Nothing serious, you understand. No, it could hardly be called that. Indeed I hardly like to trouble you with it. But your advice would be very welcome. Oh, yes, very welcome indeed.'

'Of course, sir.' Mrs Hudson eased herself into the chair next to mine. 'If there is anything at all that Flotsam and I can do to help . . .'

Mr Rumbelow beamed at both of us in turn.

'You see, Mrs Hudson, I have received letters from a fellow attorney, an individual I know from my school days who now has a country practice in the north of England. He is aware that I am acquainted with Mr Holmes and has asked me to assist him with an introduction. It seems that he has been handling the lease of a house in his neighbourhood and the situation is causing him a great deal of anxiety.'

Mrs Hudson raised an eyebrow. 'Go on, sir. I imagine it is something beyond the usual business of contracts and curtilages that is troubling him.'

'Indeed so, Mrs Hudson, indeed so. It seems the new tenants – a young American couple, I believe – have been subject to certain disturbances . . . Noises in the night, and that sort of thing. Well, I can't say I'm particularly surprised at that. In old houses a few creaks and groans are to be expected. But my friend Verity appears to be taking the whole issue very seriously. I've always thought him rather a dry old stick, even as a young man. Never one for youthful frolics. But now he's behaving very strangely. The tenants are currently in London and he is insisting they consult Mr Holmes about the matter. If you will forgive a colloquial expression, Mrs Hudson, it is as if something has put the wind up him.'

My companion appeared to enjoy the colloquialism very much, for her eyebrow twitched a fraction. But she quickly composed herself and her reply was seriousness itself.

'So how can Flotsam and I advise you, sir?' she asked.

'Well, Mrs Hudson, you know Mr Holmes better than anybody. Do you think he would be very annoyed to be bothered with something so trivial?'

The housekeeper and I exchanged glances.

'It has to be said, sir, that Mr Holmes can be rather short with callers he considers frivolous. And if this were to be yet another would-be client claiming to be haunted . . .'

Mr Rumbelow grimaced and returned his spectacles to his nose forlornly. 'Quite so. Quite so. You confirm my fears. And yet Verity is extremely insistent, and it is difficult for me to refuse him his request. After all, we once learnt the bassoon together.'

Mrs Hudson rose, her manner purposeful, and I saw that the hands of the kitchen clock were but a few minutes short of eight o'clock. 'If you cannot persuade them otherwise, Mr Rumbelow, then I suppose the couple in question must take their chance with Mr Holmes. If he is made to understand that he is seeing them purely to oblige you, then I'm sure he might be persuaded to remain civil for at least a few minutes. Don't you think so, Flottie?'

Our confidence seemed to raise Mr Rumbelow's spirits, for he stood up looking much relieved.

'Once again I am in your debt, Mrs Hudson. You have taken a weight off my mind. After all,' he concluded, allowing Mrs

Hudson to help him back into his coat, 'for all that I value an old friend like Verity, I wouldn't much care to be the one putting to Mr Holmes his theory that a dead man is haunting the moors . . .'

CHAPTER TWO

The Missing Viscount

To my great surprise, Sir Percival Grenville-Ffitch did not return to Baker Street at eight o'clock as he had promised. Instead when I scurried to answer the door that evening, I was greeted by the sight of a slim young gentleman in evening dress with a neatly waxed moustache and a rather impatient look on his face. He wore his coat draped over his shoulders and had used the brass head of his cane to rap upon the door. When I opened to him, he greeted me with a rather sardonic lift of the eyebrow, as if to say that after waiting so long he was surprised to have been answered at all.

'St John de Lacey,' he announced, airily, 'for Mr Sherlock Holmes. Please take up my card and tell Mr Holmes that I have come as Sir Percival's representative. He has been detained at the Admiralty by the First Sea Lord. A little business in the Balkans. I don't suppose it will amount to much.' The young man began to pull off his gloves, working each finger loose in turn in a way that suggested the task was rather more important to him than the delivery of Sir Percival's apologies. 'To tell the truth, Sir Percy was intending to postpone his visit and call in person tomorrow, but I assured him I was quite capable of acting in his stead. Now, do please show me up, there's a good girl. I'm supposed to be meeting a young lady from the opera and I have no intention of keeping her waiting.'

The study into which I ushered this elegant gentleman bore no resemblance at all to the disorderly workplace Dr Watson and Sherlock Holmes had left behind them that morning. While I'd been sleeping, Mrs Hudson had wrought her magic. All their papers and experiments, their collections of peculiar and disturbing criminal artefacts, and all the general detritus left behind by two careless bachelors, had been tidied away. The shutters had been closed and the lamps lit, and the fire blazed a welcome. Its brightness was reflected in the shining leather of the armchairs, and the overall effect of the firelight was to wrap the room in a soft and confidential glow. It was a room to invite confidences, and one which had heard many strange secrets.

A little distance from the fire stood a tray of amber-filled decanters, and next to these stood Dr Watson, apparently contemplating the merits of a second glass of brandy-and-shrub. Mr Holmes, his face half in shadow, lounged against the mantelpiece, watching him with a smile, his pipe unlit in his hand. Both men, however, looked round in surprise when Mr de Lacey was announced. They had clearly been bracing themselves for the rather more commanding presence of Sir Percival and were disconcerted by this sleek replacement.

My curiosity was aroused too, and mindful of Mrs Hudson's instructions that I should be close at hand if needed, I did not retreat far; in fact, no further than the small cupboard-room opposite Mr Holmes's study, the room in which Mrs Hudson stored the silver. There, I thought, I could make myself useful with some polishing while simultaneously waiting to see if the gentlemen required anything further; a plan only slightly influenced by the fact that the door of Mr Holmes's study tended to hang open a little, allowing someone who happened to be in the silver cupboard a very fair view into the heart of the room.

On taking up my position, I saw that our visitor was stretched in the larger of the two armchairs, drawing on a slender cigarette.

'. . . So as Sir Percy's personal assistant in this matter, I fear you will have to accept me as his replacement,' he was concluding, his tone making it clear that any suggestion of humility in his words was for form's sake only.

'I am sure we will do our best to oblige both Sir Percival and yourself,' Mr Holmes replied rather shortly. 'Now, sir, perhaps you can explain to us the nature of your visit. The message we received suggested that it was a matter of considerable urgency.'

'It certainly is, Mr Holmes. Whitehall's all abuzz about this one. I was the envy of the Club when they heard I'd been assigned to it. Quite the biggest plum in the pie, as it were, and setting branches atremble at the very top of the tree. Happily, the commission I have for you is a simple one for me to explain. Whether you will find it so simple to perform remains to be seen.'

He paused for another drag on his cigarette and ran his eye over the detective appraisingly.

'You will of course be aware of the sensational disappearance last year of Viscount Wrexham, the only offspring of the late Lord Beaumaris?'

Even from where I stood, I could see the detective's eyes grow cold.

'I am certainly aware of it, sir. Just as I am aware that the great brains of Scotland Yard, despite the failure of their own investigations, did not think fit to consult me in the matter. It is now nearly five months since the Viscount was seen alive. If your visit here is a belated request for assistance in the matter, I fear I must decline.'

A long plume of smoke was exhaled gently into the air between the detective and his companion.

'You're absolutely right, Mr Holmes. Those asses at the Yard have made an unholy mess of the thing. But what can we do?' He favoured Mr Holmes with a weary shrug. 'The public pays for them, and the public expects them to be of use occasionally. To be honest, if we'd thought it possible they could fail to find their man, we'd have called you in at once. But locating a Viscount of flamboyant character and striking looks who goes missing practically on the doorstep of the Reform Club . . . ? Well, really, Mr Holmes, it should hardly have taken an expert in deduction to find the fellow, should it? One or two sharp-eyed bobbies should have been sufficient.'

Mr Holmes continued to eye him rather frostily. 'Perhaps I wasn't clear, Mr de Lacey. Five months ago I might have made a difference. But it is now rather late to begin such an investigation.'

'Don't fancy it, eh?' He leant forward to stub out his cigarette. 'I thought that might be the case. It appears the late

Viscount's disappearance is a pretty tricky conundrum after all.'

'The late Viscount?' The great detective's eyes were suddenly alert again, ablaze with new interest. 'He is dead?'

Mr de Lacey nodded, his eyes still meeting those of the detective.

'We fear so, Mr Holmes. A few weeks ago a body was found on the banks of the Thames, just below Rotherhithe. Frightful sight, it was. Unrecognisable in its decay. Of course I took the precaution of keeping my distance, but the doctors say it must have been in the water for at least four months.' Mr de Lacey shuddered. 'All the clothes were gone, even the boots, but I'm told that's not uncommon. Apparently there are resourceful folk out there who scavenge the river for their living. The police think the corpse probably came ashore months ago, and in a better state. It would have been stripped then and pushed back in. The better the quality of the garments, the greater likelihood that not a stitch would be left. And short of chancing upon a man in Rotherhithe with the Beaumaris crest on his under-garments, there's not much we can do about it, is there?'

Mr Holmes looked at him carefully. 'By what means, then, have you satisfied yourselves that the body is that of the Viscount?'

'Well, Mr Holmes, we can't be sure. But the measurements of the corpse fit the Viscount's, the doctors say the age is right, and the teeth suggest a gentleman. And then a man came forward who'd found a ring in the mud, not very far from where the body washed up. I'm told by people who know these things that if the corpse-robbers had dropped it at the scene of their crime, since then it would have moved up and down the river with the tide to much the same degree as the corpse. So finding it where we did isn't such a surprise. And there was no question about the ring. Undoubtedly the Viscount's. He'd been wearing it the night he disappeared.'

'I see.' Mr Holmes's eyes were suddenly expressionless again, closed and guarded. 'So, Mr de Lacey, the Viscount disappeared but has – possibly – been found. I'm afraid I'm still unclear why you have come to seek out Dr Watson and myself.'

'Mr Holmes . . .' Now there was no mistaking the seriousness in the young man's voice. 'We are asking you to attempt the impossible – to follow a trail that must now be cold as the grave, to follow it into every corner, down every twist and turn of its route. The police were merely asked to find a missing person. You are being asked, for the sake of the nation, to trace every movement of Viscount Wrexham from the last time he was seen until the moment he entered the river – what he did, who he spoke to, what he said to them. The facts I can lay before you are few, I fear. As I say, it appears an impossible task, and that is why we have come to you. The Home Secretary himself has declared we have no other hope. And let me assure you, Mr Holmes, there is a great deal at stake. Far more than the death of the Viscount. We can do no more than beseech your assistance.'

For all Mr de Lacey's languorous manners, it was a stirring appeal and I could see that the great detective was moved by it.

'What do you say, Watson?' he asked, turning to his friend,

who had been listening intently, his brandy and shrub almost untouched.

'Well, Holmes, if the Home Secretary has asked for you in person . . . Dash it, Holmes, if any man can do the impossible, you can! I say you should take the case.'

Sherlock Holmes turned back to his visitor, and even from my hiding place I was sure I could detect a gleam of pleasure in his eyes as he shrugged. 'You see, Mr de Lacey, my friend here demands it. Now, tell us more about the Viscount. If I remember rightly, he went missing at around the time of his father's death?'

'Yes, Mr Holmes. Shortly before. His father, Lord Beaumaris had returned from overseas a few days earlier, a very sick man. He'd spent most of his life travelling in the Orient, and of course his health was ruined by it.'

'Came back to see his family, I daresay,' Dr Watson put in. 'I've seen it often. There's nothing like dying to put people in mind of their loved ones.'

'Possibly so, Dr Watson,' Mr de Lacey conceded, 'but his lordship was estranged from his son and had no other family. Prior to the time of his death, he and the Viscount had not spoken a word for over twenty years.'

'I see . . .' Dr Watson murmured. 'Always makes me sad to hear of that sort of thing. Got on rather well with my old man myself, you see, though I can't deny he had his share of strange habits. He used to hiss quite loudly whenever a parson walked past. So Lord Beaumaris and the Viscount fell out, did they?'

'They did, Doctor,' our visitor confirmed, twisting one end of his moustache with just the tiniest suggestion of impatience.

'Although perhaps it would be more accurate to say that they were simply men of very different tastes.'

'Viscount Wrexham . . . Let me see . . .' Dr Watson scratched his head. 'Didn't I read he was a bit of a gambler? You know, a high-roller, a turf-traipser, a Newmarket nobby, whatever it is they call them nowadays.'

Again our visitor nodded.

'That would be to state the case mildly, Doctor. From his youth onwards the Viscount was pre-eminent in sporting circles, and also, I should say, in all the other pastimes that are so often associated with the turf – a string of mistresses of dubious reputation, half a dozen breach of promise suits, and countless rumours of drunkenness and debauchery on a lavish scale. He filled Hawthornden with hangers-on of all kinds – tip-touts, race-readers, work-watchers, gin-skimmers, horse-doctors, and every sort of dubious character – not to mention an ever-changing array of young ladies whose morals were not, at a guess, of the finest. From the age of eleven it's said he never missed a day at Ascot or Newmarket, and his Derby Day parties were infamous. When a filly of his triumphed over the Prince of Wales's horse on Derby Day, it's said the Viscount celebrated by dressing his latest mistress in the Royal Colours and cavorting with her in front of all his guests on the grand staircase at Hawthornden.'

'Outrageous!' Dr Watson declared fervently, his brow furrowed as if trying very hard to imagine the scene. He was prevented from further musings on the subject, however, by the impatient tapping of Mr Holmes's pipe upon the mantelpiece.

'This is no doubt fascinating to students of the turf, Mr

de Lacey, but I'm sure you have not ventured out on such a cold night simply to indulge in society tittle-tattle. Perhaps your time would be better spent if you told us a little about the circumstances of his disappearance.'

'Forgive me, Mr Holmes,' his guest went on. 'But I fear there is little to tell.'

Mr de Lacey pulled a silver cigarette case from his pocket and offered its contents to his hosts.

'Viscount Wrexham was in Ireland examining bloodstock,' he went on, 'when word reached him that his father was dying in London. It seems he returned immediately on hearing the news. Perhaps he had some fondness for the old man after all. Or perhaps he travelled in anticipation of inheriting the title. It's hard to say.'

Our visitor took another long draw on his cigarette and then leant back, slowly exhaling the smoke towards the ceiling, before resuming his narrative.

'He arrived at his father's house in Randolph Square to find Lord Beaumaris barely conscious, but witnesses at the bedside say the old man was able to say a few words to him. We know that the Viscount then left the house. He said nothing as to his destination, merely stepped out into the square. And from that moment, the trail is lost. We don't know where he went or what he did. His valet reports that he never returned to his rooms in the Albany. Neither his social acquaintances nor his turf associates ever heard from him again. You will have seen the posters all over London, Mr Holmes, and his picture in the papers. You'll be aware that he was a distinctive looking man, famous for wearing his hair down to his shoulders. In his youth, of course, it was blond; latterly it was grey, but just as long, and just as distinctive. Yet even so, no witnesses have come forward. Nothing certain was heard of him until his ring was found in the Thames mud. It's as if he simply vanished into the ether.'

In the long silence that followed these words, I could see Sherlock Holmes standing very still, his arm against the mantelpiece, apparently absorbed in the study of his pipe. This almost trance-like state clearly unnerved our visitor. I saw him glance across at Dr Watson who stirred himself out of his chair and began to recharge the glasses, helping both himself and Mr de Lacey liberally to the contents of the decanter.

'So, what do you say, Holmes?' he asked as he went about the business. 'Baffling, eh? The fellow simply disappeared. For all your genius, I don't see what can be done now. We could advertise for witnesses, of course, but I daresay the police have already tried that. What do you think?'

Very slowly, the pipe was lowered and the detective's eyes were raised.

'What do I think, Watson? What do I think? I think we are still waiting for our guest here to come to the real purpose of his visit.' Turning to Mr de Lacey, he went on. 'Really, sir, you surely cannot expect us to act upon the half story. Are you prepared to tell us the rest, or shall we bid you good evening and say no more about the matter? The choice is entirely yours.' And he began to replace his pipe on the mantelpiece in such a way that suggested the interview was drawing to a close.

'I'm sorry, Mr Holmes, but I fail to understand you. I have explained to you the circumstances surrounding the Viscount's disappearance, and of course the police reports will furnish you with more details. If there is anything further I can do to be of assistance, you have only to ask.'

Mr Holmes bowed stiffly. 'If that is all you have to say, our business is at an end. If however, you are prepared to answer some obvious questions, then I may yet agree to act on your behalf.'

'What questions are those, Mr Holmes?'

'Why is the disappearance of the Viscount of such national importance? Why is a man of Sir Percival's stature concerned with it? Why is Whitehall abuzz over the death of an obscure and bankrupt Viscount whose interests have never extended beyond the gratification of his own appetites? Sir, you have told us what you want us to do, but you have not told us why. There is clearly a great deal more to this affair than you are prepared to share with us.'

Mr de Lacey rose to his feet then, his face pale and his eyes glittering with indignation.

'Mr Holmes, you must see that this matter concerns some very important people. If I were able to say more I would have done so. As it is, you must realise that I represent Her Majesty's government and I am acting on the authority of the Home Secretary himself. There are clearly things that men of such standing know which cannot be spoken of to all and sundry. I would ask you to respect that, sir, and to accept my assurances that no information relevant to your task shall be withheld. You are requested to assist us by establishing the Viscount's final movements. The reasons for this request do not concern you. Do I make myself clear?'

Mr Holmes faced this barrage without flinching, his expression unchanged, and when his visitor had finished speaking, his lips curved into a dry, humourless smile.

'Yes, Mr de Lacey. You make yourself clear. Now if you will excuse us, Dr Watson and I are busy men who do not lack for clients; clients who are prepared to place in us their *complete* confidence. Good evening to you, sir.'

And with that, to my astonishment, the interview was ended. All that was left was for me to show Mr de Lacey to the door. He left the study stiff and silent, his face white with indignation, and said nothing to me as I helped him into his coat and handed him his things. It was only after he had stepped, rigid and angry, into the night that I realised something had fallen from his coat pocket and was lying almost hidden in the corner of the hall. On investigation, I found it to be a book, and as I ran out to return it to its owner, I couldn't help but notice the title. I confess it surprised me greatly. Mr St John de Lacey had seemed to me the sort of modish gentleman whose personal interests were unlikely to extend far beyond fine claret and Cuban cigars. I would certainly never have expected him to have an interest in theological writing, and still less in a learned and rather dense-looking volume entitled grandly *The Miracles Explained.*

CHAPTER THREE

The Man With Two Watches

The following day I rose early. Mrs Hudson had always said I was resilient and after a good night's sleep the horror of the accident I'd witnessed had already begun to subside a little. My sympathy for its victim, however, was, if anything, even greater than before, and I was determined to do what I could to convey to the absent Elsie the dying man's last words. On emerging into the kitchen, I was greeted by the sight of Mrs Hudson seated at the table, examining the household accounts. She and I had sat up late the night before, talking through the events of the day until the warmth of the fire and the housekeeper's soothing words had combined to lull me into sleep; but there was no sign of a late night in Mrs Hudson's face as she greeted me that morning and her voice rang out with its accustomed energy.

'Ah, Flotsam,' she began. 'Your timing is perfect. I need you to run an errand for me. Mr Tenderly the butcher has two pounds of the best Old Spot sausages waiting for us at Smithfields. Straight from the Stope Abbey estate, he tells me, and not a better sausage in the land. And sausages aside, you'll be pleased to hear that I've already had a word with Constable Dobson. He's going to drop by when he comes off duty to tell us what he knows about the poor gentleman who died yesterday.'

'Oh, thank you, ma'am!' I replied, greatly cheered by the prospect of her assistance. 'And tell me, ma'am, do you think Constable Dobson will know anything about that other matter? About Viscount Wrexham disappearing, I mean?'

Mrs Hudson eyed me sternly. 'Now, Flottie, that really doesn't concern us. Even Mr Holmes has declined to act in the matter, and while I daresay Sir Percival will be back in due course, I think right now we'd do better to concentrate on the dusting.'

'But, Mrs Hudson, ma'am, don't you want to know what happened? It seems the Viscount just vanished into thin air.'

She nodded absently, her head already back in her books. 'A great many people vanish in this city, Flottie. This one just happens to be a Viscount. Now, about those sausages. There's no time for dawdling, remember, because we've the beds to change and the floors to polish and you're expected for a lesson at Bloomsbury Square at three o'clock sharp.'

I hadn't forgotten. Even the events of the previous day hadn't put it out of my mind, for I always looked forward to my visits to Bloomsbury Square. They were part of Mrs Hudson's dogged campaign to improve my education, and my tutor was none other than Mr Rupert Spencer, nephew of the Earl of Brabham and a young gentleman with a great knowledge of the modern sciences. It seems he had demonstrated this passion for experimentation at an early age by once attempting to mix mud pies on the floor of Mrs Hudson's kitchen. The upshot of this had never been made completely clear to me, but it had certainly engendered in the young man a very healthy respect for Mrs Hudson. Whatever his own view on the subject, when she decreed that he should be the one to teach me the sciences, he had clearly felt it prudent to comply.

Hence my weekly visits to Bloomsbury Square, calling at the front door like a lady, always in my best clothes, with my hair pinned up by Mrs Hudson with such surprising elegance that I would be left looking in the mirror in astonishment at the transformation she had wrought. In the course of these visits, as well as learning how to take tea in good company, I absorbed so much knowledge of subjects from natural history to navigation that Mrs Hudson prophesied from the very first that I would one day make a scholar.

That day, my errand to Smithfields complete and a great deal of scrubbing and tidying successfully accomplished, I arrived in front of the big house in Bloomsbury Square as the clock was striking the hour. The door was opened to me by Reynolds, the butler, an old ally who greeted me with a wink.

'Mr Spencer is not yet returned,' he told me gravely, ushering me into the grand hallway, 'but we expect him shortly. Miss Peters, however, is in the library, and is awaiting your arrival with some eagerness. Miss Peters, you should be warned, is in a state of high excitement.'

This warning, however, was unnecessary, for before I could reply an excited shriek had rung out down the hallway.

'Flottie!' a voice cried and there could be no mistaking Miss Peters. 'You angel! Just in time! I need you desperately!'

Hetty Peters, it should be explained, was the Earl of Brabham's ward and my chaperone during these weekly bouts of learning. It was a role she approached with a great deal of enthusiasm. 'After all,' she used to say, 'two hours looking at Rupert's profile is rather a treat, Flottie. Sometimes I think I might swoon with pleasure simply from looking at him, and swooning with pleasure when someone is droning on about beetles is really quite astonishing, don't you think?'

I recalled these words with a smile as Reynolds and I approached the library door.

'The cause of Miss Peters's excitement is something of a mystery, miss,' Reynolds explained a little anxiously. 'I can only tell you that twenty minutes ago Miss Peters rang and asked for glue.'

'Glue?' I replied, disconcerted.

'Yes, miss, although she declined to inform me why she required it. I confess the request caused me some embarrassment. Nothing in my many years of service has ever indicated the correct way of serving adhesive paste on formal occasions. In the end I chose to present it in a jam pot. On a salver, of course. But I am far from convinced that a gravy boat would not have been more appropriate. The possibility of confusion during the enjoyment of the scones is most definitely a concern.'

I reassured him that I would do my best to steer Miss Peters away from the glue when the tea was brought in, and then paused while he announced me.

'Yes, Reynolds, of course it's Flottie! Who else would it be? Now do tootle off and stop looking so anxious. Now that Flottie's here everything will be right as rain, I promise.'

To my surprise, I found Miss Peters kneeling rather prettily on the floor, examining an enormous and elderly-looking tome. On seeing me she leapt to her feet and welcomed me with a fond embrace.

'But whatever is the matter?' I asked, our greetings over. 'Reynolds tells me you've been asking for glue.'

'Well, to tell the truth, Flottie, I have. Although I rather think there are different kinds of glue, and I've no idea which sort I need. Reynolds asked me an awful lot of questions about it, but I couldn't tell him why I needed it, I just *couldn't*.'

'But why ever not? What have you done?'

Miss Peters sighed and looked despairing.

'Well, Flottie, you know how much Rupert loves all these dusty old books of his . . .' She indicated the walls of the room, which were lined almost to the ceiling with impressive-looking volumes of great age. 'And you remember that he made me promise never to touch any of them ever again after the business with the magnifying glass?'

I nodded very seriously.

'Really, he was absolutely beastly about the whole thing,' she went on, her voice still a little hurt. 'After all, if that particular book was so precious he shouldn't have left it lying around, should he? Besides, it was such an *old* book. It must have been terribly out of date. And of course the whole thing was simply an accident. Rupert must have known I didn't mean to set it on fire.'

For a moment she paused to reflect upon the injustice of it all, then brightened and carried on.

'Anyway, Flottie, I've been very good and haven't touched

his books ever since. To be completely truthful, I haven't really felt very tempted. But then last night, at the Strutherington's ball, Rupert was being absolutely hateful. He spent hours and hours listening to old Mrs Strutherington going on about the time the Luddites smashed her grandfather's mangle, even though we've all heard that story hundreds of times. Besides, I don't believe it's true anyway. I'm not sure there *were* any Luddites when mangles were invented, and even if there were, I'm sure they would have found much better things to smash. I mean, really, Flottie, if you wanted to turn back the whole tide of scientific progress, you wouldn't start with mangles, would you? You might as well smash top hats or French pastries.'

She paused for breath and I seized the moment to remind her of the Strutherington's ball.

'Oh, yes,' she went on, regaining her thread. 'Well, Rupert was being so painfully dutiful, talking to the hosts and being all dull and polite, and the Bradshaw boys were terribly attentive to me all evening. One of them was flirting quite outrageously, although it's difficult to be sure which one because they look so similar and have almost no personality at all. But when I told Rupert how handsome I thought they were, he just smiled and told me he thought they had too much time on their hands and ought to join the Indian Civil Service. Anyway, in the end one of the Bradshaw boys took me out onto the terrace and gave me a rose he'd pinched from one of the big displays, and do you know what Rupert said when I told him? He just said that the terrace must have been rather cold for that sort of thing, and why did I think the Bradshaw boy had chosen such a funny-coloured rose? And you know, Flottie, the annoying thing is that it *was* rather cold out there, and the rose he'd chosen was a rather gruesome apricot colour which clashed terribly with my gown . . .'

'And Rupert's books?' I put in quickly, seizing my opportunity.

'Well, Flottie, with Rupert being so horrible, I decided I was going to press the rose and keep it. After all, it would serve him right if I did fall in love with the Bradshaw boys, or one of them at least, although of course everyone knows they're going to marry the Carstairs twins, because Mrs Carstairs has made up her mind and so the poor old Bradshaws simply don't stand a chance.'

'Hetty,' I replied as calmly as I could, trying to keep a note of horror from my voice, 'you didn't decide to use one of Mr Spencer's rare editions as a flower press, did you?'

'Well, you know, Flottie, I did. They're all jolly heavy and perfect for that sort of thing, and after he was so unfeeling about the rose it seemed somehow poetic. So I came down here and chose the biggest book I could find, but when I pulled it down it was much heavier than I expected, and . . . well, I dropped it, Flottie. Except I didn't drop all of it. The cover somehow ended up staying in my hand . . .'

Her gaze directed me to the floor, where the volume she'd been studying so intently still lay, looking very old and very valuable. Its aged, brown boards, however, were some distance away, resting on a small Louis XIV table.

'He'll never forgive me!' Miss Peters whispered, her voice hushed in dread as she contemplated the destruction she'd caused. 'Flottie, we *must* mend it before Rupert wants it next . . .'

I approached the book in some trepidation and turned its pages so that the title page faced upwards: *Domestic and Funerary Ceramics of Mesopotamia and the Holy Land.* At least that didn't sound like a book Mr Spencer would be referring to very frequently. And I was relieved to see that the pages themselves did not seemed to have been creased or damaged by their fall.

'The really annoying thing,' Hetty went on, her spirits reviving, 'is that it's not at all a good book, Flottie. I was just looking at it when you came in and, believe me, it's an absolute stinker. I mean, the author might have known a bit about old pots but did he really need to go on about them for quite so long? It's simply the most convoluted and tedious thing I've read in my life. Worse than Browning. I bet no one's ever read all of it, not even his mother. And she probably tried really hard to enjoy it. Mothers can be funny like that.'

'I don't think glue's the answer,' I told her gently, my scrutiny of the damage complete. 'But there's a bookbinder on Dover Street. If we can just put the book back on the shelf for now, I'm sure he'd be able to call discreetly and make the repairs.'

Miss Peters considered this carefully. 'Well, I suppose we *might* get away with it. I could tell Reynolds he's a new curate who's calling to ask for money for fallen women. New curates always do that sort of thing. I think fallen women must be part of their training. Does this bookbinder *look* like a curate, do you think?'

Unable to answer that, I contented myself with assisting Miss Peters in returning the volume to its original position, the damage temporarily concealed. Only a minute or so later

Rupert Spencer entered the room, followed by Reynolds with the tea tray.

'Hello, Flotsam!' he greeted me warmly. 'What's Hetty up to? Reynolds says she's been asking for glue.'

'Really!' Miss Peters exclaimed. 'Can nothing be a secret in this house?' She drew herself up to her full height and favoured Mr Spencer with a look of frosty hauteur. 'Besides, sometimes a young lady requires glue, doesn't she, Flottie? It is one of the Mysteries of Our Sex. A true gentleman would not refer to it.'

And with this cryptic utterance, she smiled happily and took a seat by the tea things.

'Milk or lemon, Flottie?' she asked with great serenity.

It was while we were taking tea that I dared to bring up the subject of Viscount Wrexham. Mrs Hudson may have been taking no interest in his disappearance but I found it far more difficult to ignore such an intriguing mystery.

When I mentioned the Viscount's name, Mr Spencer paused, an almost translucent ham sandwich halfway to his lips.

'Wrexham? He was the chap who vanished, wasn't he? I read about it at the time, and you still see the posters up in places.'

'Did you know him at all?' I asked.

Mr Spencer shook his head. 'Not really. I'd seen him around the place a few times. Getting on a bit now, but a striking fellow, like a figure from the Regency with all that long, flowing hair. But I've never spoken to him. My uncle came across him at Newmarket once or twice, I believe, but they moved in rather different circles.'

Rupert's uncle, known as the Irascible Earl on account of his temper, was a pillar of polite society. It didn't surprise me that he and the Viscount were not intimate.

'They certainly organised quite a search when he first disappeared,' Mr Spencer went on. 'I suppose the establishment gets jumpy when it starts mislaying Viscounts. It gives the anarchists ideas.'

He smiled. Mr Spencer had very brown eyes and when he smiled they crinkled at the edges. 'I remember exactly what my uncle said when he heard about him disappearing though. He gave that little growl that he gives when he thinks someone is trying to put something over on him, and said that, from what he knew of the fellow, there was probably more to it than met the eye.'

Shortly after that, the tea things were cleared away and Mr Spencer continued his explanations of the stars and the planetary system. But I took care to store away the Earl's remarks about the Viscount's disappearance, determined to examine them more closely as soon as I had the chance.

Nothing else of note happened during my visit until Reynolds came to show me out. To my surprise, at the front door he drew me discreetly to one side.

'Ahem,' he began, as if about to broach a subject of some importance. 'I wondered, miss, if you would be so good as to give Mrs Hudson a message? Please tell her, if you would, that James, the footman, is extremely keen on Turkish Delight.'

And I confess that my journey home was not spent, as it should have been, rehearsing the order of the planets or the timings of the equinox, but wondering why on earth Mrs Hudson might want to hear about a young footman's taste in confectionary.

* * *

Unfortunately my curiosity was not to be satisfied immediately, for on arriving in Baker Street I found the housekeeper absent, on a visit to old Mr Pomfret, a long-standing friend of hers who had once been valet to Lord Ullswater. Mr Pomfret had retired from service after his lordship's death in the Red Sea tragedy, and had opened a shop in Chelsea from which he sold fine spices to the kitchens of the gentry. He was now well into his eighties and left the commonplace transactions of the shop to his son, but Mrs Hudson would still visit him from time to time to order cardamoms and cloves, and to listen to the old man's tales of exotic travels in Lord Ullswater's service. She returned from this visit in excellent spirits and received Reynolds's message with a thoughtful nod of her head.

'Turkish Delight, you say? Well, well. I must say I'm not greatly tempted by it myself. I shall suggest to Reynolds that he discourages the young man. Now, how were things at Bloomsbury Square?'

Resolving to return to the mysterious subject of James and his taste for Turkish Delight at a later date, I contented myself with repeating Mr Spencer's remarks about Viscount Wrexham. Mrs Hudson listened to these without apparent interest, but she did allow the corner of one eyebrow to flicker a little above the horizontal when I told her of the Earl's verdict on the disappearance. She showed no interest in pursuing the subject, however, but instead began to busy herself around the kitchen while recounting one of Mr Pomfret's stories about sandstorms in Samaria.

This tale was interrupted by the arrival of Constable Dobson, just off duty and eager for fruitcake. Mrs Hudson hastened to make him comfortable, with hot water for his feet, cake in large quantities and a generous portion of Cheshire cheese to accompany it. His tea was served extremely strong and in a pint pot. Constable Dobson was an enormous man who suffered greatly from bunions and we allowed him a few minutes of appreciative foot-soaking before we felt it right to engage him with questions.

The information he had for us about the previous day's incident was enlightening but also disappointing, for it contained no mention of anyone called Elsie. The unfortunate gentleman, it seemed, was one Albert John Swan, an Englishman by birth who had for many years been resident in the colonies. Investigations by the police and the telegraphic assistance of the authorities in the Cape had established that Mr Swan's early years were spent in service in the Home Counties before he decided to try his luck in South Africa. There, through hard work over many years, he had succeeded in making his fortune.

'A very prosperous gentleman, by all accounts,' Constable Dobson told us. 'Seems he did well in the grocery business, providing little things from over here to homesick settlers. You know, Eccles cakes, Shrewsbury biscuits, Bakewell puddings, that sort of thing. Very lucrative, it was. By the time he retired last year it seems he had a fine home in Cape Town and an estate in the country. But you know how it is, ma'am, I reckon home was still calling him, because when he retired he declared he was travelling back here for a lengthy stay.'

The constable shook his head and wriggled his toes. 'It often happens like that in my experience, ma'am. You can't beat home, can you? I said to my wife only this morning, "Bessie,"

I said, "you can keep your Calcuttas and your Cape Towns. There ain't nothing I've ever heard of in either place to make me happier than I am right here."'

'A sentiment that does you credit, Constable, I'm sure,' Mrs Hudson told him gravely. 'They say contentment is the most enviable of all talents. Now tell us a little about Mr Swan's personal circumstances. Did he have a wife and family?'

'No, ma'am. I'm told he was a widower. They say he married a rich woman – the daughter of Spotford, the ships' biscuit tycoon – but his wife died last year. There's a second cousin in Johannesburg who inherits the lot.'

Mrs Hudson raised an eyebrow. 'Caroline Spotford, the daughter of Sir Charles? I remember reading of her marriage many years ago.' She gave me a meaningful look, then turned to other subjects. 'Do we know when Mr Swan arrived in London, Constable? Had he been in the country long?'

'Only a few days, ma'am. He had travelled here from Marseilles after spending the winter in the south of France. He arrived in London last Monday and checked into Brown's Hotel. Which proves he wasn't short of a bob or two. They say Brown's is one of the best.'

'A fine establishment, yes,' Mrs Hudson confirmed, 'though not entirely to be trusted with shellfish. So, did Mr Swan indicate to anyone what his plans here might be, Constable?'

'Not really, ma'am. Although when he arrived he told the manager that he had some personal business in the north and would be spending a few days there. In fact yesterday was the day he planned to leave. His bags had been sent on to the station yesterday morning and he set off to follow them on foot, it being such a fine day.'

Mrs Hudson's eyebrows met for a moment in a fleeting frown.

'Do you have any idea which London station his bags were sent to, Constable?' she asked.

'To Kings Cross, I think it was, ma'am, though I can't remember exactly where he was headed after that. The train ticket was in his wallet when he died but it wasn't a place I'd particularly heard of.'

'King's Cross, you say?' Mrs Hudson continued to look thoughtful. 'For an active gentleman to walk from Brown's to King's Cross is not surprising. But for him to end up in Baker Street . . . Well, it represents a very considerable detour. Do you know what time his train was due to depart, Constable?'

'I believe he was catching an eleven o'clock train, ma'am. He'd checked with the boy at reception to see if he had time to walk and still catch it.'

Mrs Hudson pursed her lips again. 'Then by the time he arrived in Baker Street, he had already missed his train. Am I right, Flotsam?'

'Yes, ma'am,' I nodded, wondering if perhaps that was why he was looking at his watch so often.

In reply Mrs Hudson rose and moved slowly over to a pile of un-ironed linen that lay beside the sink. 'It would seem that something must have happened to Mr Swan between Brown's Hotel and the station to make him change his mind about catching that train. And whatever it was, it was sufficiently pressing to bring him, in a state of some agitation, to Mr Holmes's front door.'

'And what might that have been, do you think, ma'am?' the constable asked, interested enough to lay down his cake for a moment.

In reply Mrs Hudson said nothing. She simply looked at me.

'I can answer that, Constable,' I said quietly. 'You see, Mr Swan told me what he'd seen. He said he'd seen a dead man risen from the grave.'

For a fraction of a second, Constable Dobson looked disconcerted, but then the smile returned to his face and he nodded.

'I daresay he did, young Flotsam. But we've got to remember them's his last words. Folk say all sorts of things when their time is nearly up, what with strange lights and the like. Anyway . . .' he paused to brush some substantial crumbs of fruitcake from his moustache, 'Whatever it was that brought him here, we can't deny that he stepped out under that carriage by mistake. No mystery there, I'm afraid. Mind you, there was one other thing I was going to ask about . . . I almost forgot.'

The constable began to fumble in the pockets of his uniform. 'I have it here somewhere,' he went on. 'I've been asking house to house if anyone recognises it. Someone dropped it at the scene yesterday and it wasn't noticed in the confusion. I only found it after the body'd been taken away. Ah! Here it is! A gentleman's watch . . .'

I gasped when I saw it, for I recognised it at once. 'But, Constable,' I cried, 'that's *his* watch. Mr Swan's. I saw it in his hand. He was checking it over and over again.'

'Mr Swan's, you say?' Constable Dobson looked at me dubiously. 'I don't think so, miss. I fear you're mistaken. Mr Swan's watch was still in his waistcoat pocket when we found him. I noticed it particularly when we sorted his effects because it was keeping good time and I wondered how the wheel of the carriage had missed it. And looking at the thing rationally, miss,' he added proudly, 'it's hardly likely that a gentleman would need to carry *two* watches, now is it?'

'But I'm so sure!' I insisted, taking it from his hand. It had an unusual case, a silver so dull it was really a gun-metal grey.

'And what's more, miss,' the constable went on in a kind voice, 'there's writing on the back. And they're not Mr Swan's initials, now are they? No, miss, much more likely some gent has dropped it in the mud while trying to help.' Slowly I turned the timepiece in my hand, just as I had seen the dead man turn it the day before. Constable Dobson was right. They weren't Mr Swan's initials. They spelled something altogether different:

R.I.P.

I passed the object to Mrs Hudson, but not even the warmth and reassurance in her face could prevent a shudder running through me. *Rest in peace*, I thought. It seemed the business of Mr Swan and his last words was not going to be a simple one after all.

CHAPTER FOUR

An American Visitor

'Mr Swan's wife,' Mrs Hudson announced, as we bustled out of the house the following morning, 'was not a pleasant woman. I knew her a little when she was still Caroline Spotford, and she had a very bad reputation below stairs. She was once very spiteful towards a scullery maid of my acquaintance, and I can assure you it was not an isolated incident.'

It was another bright day, but cold and blustery. The housekeeper paused to tighten the strings of her bonnet against the wind.

'That was many years ago, of course,' she went on, 'before her marriage. I don't think I've heard her name mentioned since she and her father moved to South Africa in the wake of the Spanish weevil affair, but there's one thing I'd be prepared to wager: that no one ever had reason to know her as *Elsie*.'

It was a little after nine o'clock and our destination, Mrs Hudson had informed me as she'd hurried me out of the house, was Brown's Hotel. My companion was clearly in determined mood and we made our way there at the best pace the crowded pavements would allow. There had been little opportunity the previous evening for us to discuss Constable Dobson's visit, for only a minute or two after he had taken his leave our two gentlemen had returned, triumphant, from their vigil in Kennington.

'The case is closed, Mrs Hudson!' Dr Watson had announced proudly, slapping his thigh with pleasure. 'As soon as the fellow received the note Holmes had concocted, he set about trying to drown the cat. Of course, that proved everything. Fortunately we were suitably positioned to seize the blackguard and save the feline. It's the smartest piece of work I've seen for a long time. Holmes, you are a genius!'

'On the contrary, my friend. I did no more than apply simple logic. Once one had understood that the jewel thefts were intended to divert attention from the missing pets, and not the other way round, the solution was obvious. Now, Mrs Hudson, there was some talk of cold partridge and burgundy. And please bring up the newspapers for the last three weeks, and the cards of all our callers. Watson and I have some work to do! We must decide which case should occupy our attention next.'

Mr Holmes's enormous enthusiasm for that task had not flagged until after midnight, and until that hour his constant demands kept us both busy, running out for navvies' tobacco or supplies of brown ale, or brewing large quantities of Turkish coffee, all of which were consumed enthusiastically while Dr Watson dozed in his armchair.

The following morning, however, the two gentlemen were required at Lambeth police station, and Mrs Hudson seized her opportunity with alacrity. No sooner had Dr Watson and

Mr Holmes left the house than she was guiding me into my coat and up the area steps.

'Come on, Flotsam,' she urged, 'we can talk as we go, and time is of the essence. We have a little experiment to perform.'

'Will it help us find Mr Swan's Elsie, ma'am?' I asked hopefully.

'I can't honestly say for certain, Flottie. But it may help us understand a little more about Mr Swan's last hours. Now, tell me, Flotsam, what do you think of Mr Swan's two watches?'

I considered the problem as we hurried along, Mrs Hudson cutting out such a brisk pace that sometimes I had to skip a little to keep up with her.

'Well, ma'am, perhaps he was afraid his own watch might not keep good time and he was anxious about missing his train?'

Mrs Hudson looked at me a little askance. 'I suppose he *might* carry a spare watch in such circumstances, Flotsam. But generally speaking gentlemen don't. They simply carry a reliable timepiece. And we know Mr Swan's other watch kept good time, remember.'

A thought struck me and I looked up at Mrs Hudson hopefully. 'Well, perhaps he didn't set off with two watches, ma'am. Perhaps he'd seen the other one in a shop on the way to the station and bought it that morning.'

'Very good, Flotsam!' Mrs Hudson gave an approving nod of her head. 'That's certainly quite possible. And that's what we're going to find out today.'

We reached Brown's Hotel at a little before ten o'clock and paused by its smart front steps. There Mrs Hudson pulled out her own watch and began to study it intently.

'Are we not going in, ma'am?' I asked when she showed no sign of moving.

'Oh, I don't think so, Flottie,' she replied, her eyes still on her timepiece. 'I'm prepared to believe what Constable Dobson told us about the evidence of the hotel staff. In fact I stepped out earlier this morning to have another word with the constable, just to check a few details. Now, I think we can be on our way . . .'

She returned her watch to the depths from which it had come and looked about her.

'It was at this precise time that Mr Swan set out from Brown's to walk to King's Cross Station. We know from the boy at the desk who gave him directions exactly which route he planned to take. The boy even provided him with a simple map, so I think we can assume that Mr Swan did not wander from the route by accident. And he told the boy that, although he was eager to walk, he was a little anxious about missing his train, so I think we can also assume that he wasn't in the mood to indulge in any spur-of-the-moment detours. Now, how fast do we think a fit gentleman of sixty would walk?'

And with that we set off again, retracing the dead man's steps towards King's Cross. The streets were busy but not impossibly crowded, and despite the gusting wind it was good to be out. London was still revelling in the first touches of spring, with good humour in the air and brighter colours in the shop windows. It was as if the city was shaking itself from a long winter's sleep.

From time to time we would adjust our pace at Mrs Hudson's insistence.

'He was worried about that train, Flottie, so would probably have speeded up a little as he went. And for this experiment I want to be sure we are walking at least as fast as he did.'

I was under strict instructions to keep my eyes open for anything resembling a watchmaker's or a pawn shop, and occasionally we would pause and peer down side streets, to be sure of noticing any such shop that might have caught Mr Swan's eye. These stops apart, it seemed to me that our pace was a brisk one and I was sure Mr Swan wouldn't have walked so fast. More than once we had to step into the street to overtake slower walkers, gentlemen who themselves were walking fairly briskly to their places of business. And after every few minutes Mrs Hudson would again consult her watch.

Finally, when we were about two thirds of the way to the station, she held up her hand and called a halt.

'I think this is far enough, Flottie. I don't think Mr Swan came any further.'

'How's that, ma'am?' I asked, still a little out of breath.

'Because we know precisely what time he arrived in Baker Street, my girl. And if he'd gone on any longer in this direction, he wouldn't have had time to walk all the way to Baker Street as well.'

She waited for a moment while I digested this, then gave a little shrug.

'Of course, it would only be right to point out that he could have caught a cab to Baker Street. But you saw him arrive on foot, and if he'd taken a hansom, he'd have been dropped safely on our doorstep and would never have had to cross the road. So, Flottie, for now let's assume he discovered something between here and Brown's Hotel, something that made him change his mind about catching his train. And whatever it was, I don't think it was the purchase of a watch, because we haven't passed any place where he might have acquired such an item. I think we can be confident he had the second watch with him when he set out that morning.'

'But might he not perhaps have changed his mind about walking from the hotel, ma'am? If he'd caught a cab from somewhere near Brown's he would have arrived at the station with plenty of time to browse the pawn shops near King's Cross.'

Mrs Hudson nodded. 'You're absolutely right, Flottie. Even though we know he was determined to walk, he could have done just that. Or he could have seen the watch in a shop window *after* he'd diverted to Baker Street. Or he could have simply found the watch lying in the gutter. But for now all these things strike me as less probable. Now tell me, Flotsam . . .' She looked at me, her eyes twinkling. 'Why might one man be in the habit of carrying another man's watch?'

'Because he's been entrusted to deliver it somewhere, ma'am?'

The housekeeper pursed her lips. 'Perhaps it's easier to think of it the other way around. When is it common for one man's watch to be presented to someone else? And in what circumstances would that person treasure it so much that they would carry it with them routinely, wherever they went?'

With a shock, I grasped her meaning.

'When it's a keepsake, ma'am. If someone dies . . .'

Mrs Hudson nodded sombrely, there in the sunlit street, while the unnoticing crowds jostled around us.

'And what were the gentleman's last words, Flottie?'

There was no need for me to recall them. They rose to my lips instantly, heavy with portent.

'I have seen a dead man risen from the grave.'

Mrs Hudson smiled then, and took my arm gently. 'Come, Flottie,' she said. 'Let us be consoled by one thing. At least we can have a guess at the dead man's initials.'

Although there were chores aplenty waiting for us at home, we did not return directly to Baker Street. Mrs Hudson, perhaps deciding that I'd had rather too many horrors that week, whisked me off to the tearooms in the park, where I was fed cinnamon toast washed down with hot chocolate so thick it seemed a great effort to stir it. After that we took a turn around the pond and watched the ducks, while Mrs Hudson told me tales of her childhood in service. For a time I quite forgot about Mr Swan, and it was only when we had left the park behind us that my thoughts returned to the missing Elsie. Mrs Hudson must have seen the shadow pass across my face for she gave my arm a squeeze.

'I daresay, Flottie, you'll be thinking we're no closer to delivering Mr Swan's last message. I'm afraid none of the things we've been speculating about today have helped with that. But I see no reason why a more traditional approach might not yield results. I thought this might be a good place to start.'

She fished a folded piece of paper from her bag and handed it to me for my inspection.

Acquaintances of the late Albert John Swan, once of Sussex, latterly of Cape Town, South Africa, are invited to make themselves known to Rumbelow & Rumbelow, Solicitors, at the address below.

'I'm afraid I can't guarantee that will be successful, Flotsam, but if you approve, I suggest you take it round to Mr Rumbelow's offices straightaway. He will know the best publications in which to place it. Meanwhile, I shall go home and make a start on the fire irons. I'm not expecting the gentlemen home till the evening, so you've plenty of time. Now, off with you! And give Mr Rumbelow my regards.'

With those instructions ringing in my ears, I set off at a scamper towards the hushed and oak-panelled offices where Mr Rumbelow spent his days wrestling with all matters legal. There I was greeted by a gangly young man with pimples who informed me that he thought Mr Rumbelow was *in conference* but that he would inform the gentleman of my arrival. I settled down to wait on one of the leather chairs that smelt of wood smoke and old tweed, but before I'd even had time to study the portraits of three earlier and equally round-faced Rumbelows, the young man had returned with his employer's compliments and his request that I should step into his office.

Mr Rumbelow's inner sanctum had something of the atmosphere of a very fine gentleman's club. There was a desk in it, it is true, and Mr Rumbelow invariably sat behind it, but somehow your eye always drifted to the soft leather armchairs and the ancient law books about the walls, or to the Regency decanters brimming with aged, amber sherry.

On this occasion, however, I noticed none of these things. I didn't even take particular notice of Mr Rumbelow as he came forward to greet me, because seated opposite him, perched neatly and elegantly on the edge of her chair, was one of the prettiest women I had ever seen. I saw at once that hers was not a classical beauty. She had none of the fine-boned prominence so admired by artists, nor any of that aristocratic refinement that has its roots in dress and grooming. Hers was simply an intense loveliness, a serenity of face and evenness of features that made me smile without knowing why and brought me stuttering to a standstill on the edge of Mr Rumbelow's fine Persian carpet.

'Ah, Flotsam,' my host began, his voice warm with welcome. 'Thank you for joining us. You are just the person we needed. This is Mrs Summersby. Mrs Summersby, this is the young lady I was telling you about. Mrs Summersby,' he explained, 'is renting Broomheath Hall in Cumberland through my old acquaintance George Verity. We were just discussing whether or not it would be advisable for her to consult Mr Holmes over the, er, happenings there.'

'You didn't warn me to expect such a very fetching young lady, Mr Rumbelow,' she said, and smiled at me. Her voice was low and attractive, and her distinctive accent made her seem to me exotic and a little mysterious. 'Come, Flotsam,' she continued, 'sit next to me while I finish telling Mr Rumbelow about my predicament.'

As I settled into the chair closest to hers, I noticed how smooth and unlined her skin was, like the complexion of a china doll.

'I do hope you understand, Mr Rumbelow,' she was saying, 'that it's really only on Mr Verity's insistence that I am here. My husband and I don't want to be any trouble to anyone. To tell the truth, Mr Rumbelow,' and here she raised her eyes to his a little shyly, 'I'm a little embarrassed to be taking up so much of your valuable time.'

'Not at all! Not at all!' the solicitor countered gallantly. 'Happy to be of assistance.'

'You see, although events at Broomheath Hall since we moved in have been peculiar, well, we feel perhaps Mr Verity is unduly flustered. After all, what can possibly happen to us, here in England, in these modern times? We Americans enjoy your old English ghost stories, but that doesn't mean we believe in the ghosts.'

Mr Rumbelow greeted this comment with a single, solemn nod, then began to rustle through the papers in front of him.

'Now, let me see . . . Ah, yes. I understand from Verity that Broomheath Hall is rather a remote establishment. Tell me, Mrs Summersby, how did you come to choose such a place?'

'It is certainly a long way from this great city of yours,' she agreed, 'but perhaps in our country we are more accustomed to great distances. And after all, Broomheath is less than a mile from Alston, which has the railway and is such a pretty little town, and of course we can send to London for all our little luxuries. The moors can be a little bleak, of course, but my husband's great passion is for antiquities and he's always wanted to make a serious study of your Hadrian's Wall. When we read that Broomheath Hall was vacant, it seemed ideal. Such a distinguished house and so well placed. The wall runs quite near there, you know, and the railway makes it all very convenient.'

She turned to me and gave me a little smile that made me somehow complicit in their adventure.

'Now,' Mr Rumbelow went on, his eyes returning to the papers on his desk. 'Verity says here that when you decided to take the house, it was already under a cloud . . .'

'Yes, sir, it was. The unfortunate Mr Baldwick . . .' She ran one gloved hand rather absently down the length of the other, as if instinctively smoothing out any creases. They were, I noticed, gloves of the very highest quality and they fitted her to perfection. 'Mr Baldwick, the previous tenant, was a very unhappy gentleman. Have you heard of him?'

Mr Rumbelow and I shook our heads in perfect unison and she laughed prettily.

'I fear few people have. I understand he was a gentleman with a great desire for fame but little in the way of talent to support his ambitions. He styled himself an archaeologist but it seems no one took him very seriously. Mr Verity says he had no particular training or expertise. By all accounts he was a very unstable character, given to moods of great bitterness and brooding.'

Mr Rumbelow looked a little embarrassed. 'I understand that eventually . . .'

'I fear so.' His visitor dropped her lashes, then raised them to reveal eyes full of sadness. 'During the months he spent at Broomheath it seems he slipped into insanity. They say he began to rage about being accursed, about being haunted by the ghosts of those he'd wronged, and about hiding from God's vengeance. He had trunks full of self-published pamphlets which he slept with at the end of his bed. And the servants reported that he was always *digging*.'

'Digging, madam?'

'They would find him digging in the cellars or in the grounds of the estate, babbling about needing to find a hiding place; that the devil was on his heels. And as you know, eventually he took his own life, out on the moors.'

'My word, Mrs Summersby!' Mr Rumbelow shook his head. 'Did you not find any of that off-putting? It is a disturbing tale.'

She laughed again. 'Oh, it was worse than that, Mr Rumbelow! It seems there is a local legend that no suicide can rest in peace on those moors. There is much talk of the dead man returning to seek companions. But I guess over in Boston we don't have too much time for all those old superstitions. Of course, we feel sorry for poor Mr Baldwick, but because of him we were able to take Broomheath at a much reduced rent, and the place suits us perfectly.'

She leant forward a little as if to emphasise the point. I noticed that the hem of her dress, although of a gorgeous and rich fabric, had been mended with invisible stitching at some point in the past.

'But strange incidents continue, I understand?' Mr Rumbelow looked very anxious on her behalf.

'Only little things.' She reassured him with a flutter of her hand. 'The townsfolk have spoken of Mr Baldwick's ghost abroad after dark, haunting the moors. And Mr Verity himself is adamant he has seen lights moving in the house at night. One local farmer swore he had come across the spectre digging by the ruined chapel, but later we heard the man had been at the inn in Alston for most of the afternoon, so that was probably the liquor talking.'

'Nothing else in the house itself?'

'Oh, no, Mr Rumbelow. At least, nothing *sinister*. Our butler has been up once or twice in the night to investigate noises, but really I think perhaps events have just made us all a little jumpy. I'm sure things will settle down soon, once Mr Baldwick has been forgotten about.'

She paused and looked her host directly in the eyes. 'Do you think, Mr Rumbelow, given that my husband and I are not at all upset or worried, that you might write to Mr Verity and say that it would be better to delay calling on Sherlock Holmes until there is something more definite to report? It seems such a drastic step, to trouble a famous detective over a few local rumours, and we'd hate to be seen as a pair of foolish Americans.'

Mr Rumbelow blushed a little under her gaze.

'Why, indeed, Mrs Summersby. Indeed. I understand your position perfectly, and anything I can do to help . . . It sounds as though this Baldwick business has upset Verity. All that raving and digging – very unsettling. But I'm sure he'll see that we can't bother Mr Holmes with a few rumours started by fanciful locals. What do you say, Flotsam?'

I nodded earnestly, and Mrs Summersby reached out to pat my hand.

'Then that's decided!' She rose from her chair, and Mr Rumbelow and I rose with her. 'Thank you so much for your time, Mr Rumbelow. It's a great comfort to know you are on our side. I'm sure you will be wonderfully good at calming Mr Verity. And my husband will get on very well if he's allowed a little peace in which to pursue his studies. Now,' she went on, casting a glance at Mr Rumbelow's grandfather clock, 'I am supposed to be meeting my husband in a few minutes' time. He has been at the British Museum, studying away, but tonight we are to dine with Sir Bulstrode Peveril. We met him in the South of France last year and struck up quite a friendship. A real English knight! I'm so looking forward to it! So I must say good day to you both. *So* lovely to meet you, Flotsam . . .'

And with that, Mrs Summersby was gone, ushered away by the pimply youth, leaving behind her a little silence and just the faintest trace of jasmine in the air.

CHAPTER FIVE

The Lost Gospel

Sir Percival Grenville-Ffitch returned to Baker Street two days later, his visit preceded by the most courteous note. In it he apologised for Mr de Lacey's abruptness and begged to be allowed to return in person. It was clear this missive caused Mr Holmes a great deal of satisfaction, for on reading it he allowed himself one of his broadest smiles and treated himself to a second pipe before bedtime. Mrs Hudson, on the other hand, welcomed the news with no more than a shrug.

'So, Flottie,' she sighed, 'perhaps we shall find out a little more about this Wrexham business after all. Though goodness knows, things are busy enough without the two gentlemen going off on another of their wild chases. Tell me, Flottie, how often do you read the Bible?'

I confess I looked at her in astonishment, for Mrs Hudson was not a religious woman and this sudden inquiry about my spiritual welfare seemed to bear no connection to anything that had gone before.

'Oh, no matter,' she chuckled on seeing my surprise. 'I just wondered if you were up to scratch on your Bible stories, that's all.'

Further discussion of the subject was interrupted by the arrival of Scraggs, the grocer's boy, an old acquaintance of mine and someone entrusted by Mrs Hudson with all manner of important commissions.

'Hello, Flot,' he chirped, putting his head around the kitchen door, 'I hear you've been playing Florence Nightingale to the fallen.'

'Now, Scraggs,' Mrs Hudson warned him with a growl, 'we'll have none of your cheek about that. It was not a pleasant incident.'

'Course it wasn't.' He stepped into the warmth of the kitchen with a winning smile on his face. 'That's why I brought you these, Flot. Thought you might need cheering up.' And he produced from behind his back a small bunch of bluebells. 'First of the season,' he added with some pride. 'Up from Cornwall, grown under glass. Mr Finchley let me take 'em in return for all that soap I managed to sell in Drury Lane.'

'Very well, Scraggs,' Mrs Hudson conceded. 'You may come in. And I daresay you'll find a biscuit in the tin on the dresser. Meanwhile, those flowers will need some water. Go on, Flotsam, jump to it!'

While Scraggs settled down at the kitchen table, I hid my blushes at his gift by busying myself with the little stems, arranging them prettily in a suitable glass.

'So, Scraggs,' Mrs Hudson continued, 'what's new?'

'Well, Mrs H, I spent over an hour down at Brown's Hotel

talking to all the cabbies round there, but I couldn't find one who remembered taking your bloke to King's Cross. They'd heard about the chap getting knocked down, and if it was someone who'd been in a cab that day, that sort of thing usually gets around.'

This lack of news didn't seem to disappoint Mrs Hudson at all, for her face was untroubled as she wiped away the crumbs from beneath Scraggs's chin.

'Thank you. That's very interesting indeed,' she told him. 'And if you want another biscuit, young man, you can eat the next one off a plate.'

'Sorry, Mrs H, no time. Got to be in Billingsgate sharpish,' he told her, jumping to his feet and flashing me a smile. 'Take care, Flot,' he said, 'and try to keep the old ogre out of trouble.' And before either of us could respond to this impertinence, he'd darted through the door and up the area steps.

On opening the door to our illustrious guest that evening, I found Sir Percival accompanied by a meek-looking man of vaguely clerical aspect, a man who did not actually wear a clergyman's collar but who had the look of one whose neck would fit such a collar very well. This gentleman was introduced as Mr Fallowell, and the way he twisted his hands in front of his chest suggested that the prospect of an audience with Mr Sherlock Holmes was one he found rather daunting.

His companion, meanwhile, greeted me with a courteous nod and, while I helped him from his coat, expressed a hope that I was a little recovered from the events I had witnessed a few days before. But for all Sir Percival's politeness, there was something in his grim air of purpose as I announced him that suggested weighty matters upon his shoulders. The last thing I saw before withdrawing was his hand being shaken vigorously by Dr Watson while the nervous Mr Fallowell cast a wistful look behind him, as if wishing he could, like me, slip quietly from the room.

I confess I had already determined that my evening should be spent in bringing every remaining item of silver to the most perfect shine. And from where I stood to do this, I could glimpse Sir Percival, his white mane illuminated by the firelight, in the process of introducing his companion, who appeared to be gulping rather a lot and making nervous, butterfly shapes with his hands.

'. . . Mr Fallowell's subsequent study of Aramaic parchments was brought to the notice of the Archbishop, Mr Holmes, and it is that same expertise which, indirectly, brings him here tonight.'

Mr Fallowell seemed to gulp again at that. He had a rather round face, and when Mr Holmes's sharp features were trained upon him he quivered slightly, like a dormouse in the presence of a hawk.

'I am sure Mr Fallowell's academic qualifications are remarkable, sir,' Mr Holmes replied dryly, 'but until you explain to us the nature of your visit, I fear neither Dr Watson nor I will be able to form any opinion as to their relevance.'

'Of course, Mr Holmes,' Sir Percival nodded. 'I am only too aware that I failed to keep my appointment with you two nights ago. I fear that my private secretary, Mr de Lacey, who attended in my place, may not have broached the subject as tactfully as I might have wished. But to be fair, he did not then have authority to divulge anything but the bare facts of Viscount Wrexham's disappearance. It was hoped that you would act for us within the boundaries of public knowledge. But of course I see now that it would be insulting to expect a man such as yourself to act without being entirely in his client's confidence.'

For a man of Sir Percival's stature to speak in such a conciliatory way struck me as highly unusual, and Mr Holmes acknowledged as much with a short but silent bow of his head.

'In my defence,' our visitor went on, 'I must plead the rare delicacy of the matter, and the many powerful elements with an interest in it. Not until today have they agreed to give me a free hand to act as I choose. And in stressing the importance of the case, I can honestly say it is one that threatens something fundamental to the fabric of our society, perhaps to the whole edifice of Western civilisation. Oh, I can see that you think I exaggerate, Mr Holmes. Perhaps this will alter your opinion.'

The old gentleman produced a document from his inner pocket and handed it to the great detective. I could see at once it had the desired effect upon him for as he read his eyes narrowed and his face grew suddenly more alert.

'The Archbishop of Canterbury, the Papal Nuncio, the Patriarch of the Orthodox Church . . .' He looked up, his eyes meeting Sir Percival's. 'An astonishing document, sir. You see, Watson,' he went on, handing the paper to his friend, 'a letter signed by the representatives of every significant element of the Christian faith, all stating that Sir Percival acts as their joint agent in this matter.'

Dr Watson peered at the pages thrust under his nose and pursed his lips in surprise.

'I say, this *is* quite something. For all those fellows to agree on anything at all is a miracle in itself, eh?'

Sir Percival eyed him a little coldly. 'I believe, sir, that once you have heard what I have to say, you will realise there is little room for levity in this affair.' Then, turning back to Mr Holmes, he went on. 'You are already aware of the details of Viscount Wrexham's disappearance. But my tale begins a long time before that, with his father, Lord Beaumaris. It is his lordship who is the key to all this. How much do you know of the man?'

Mr Holmes contemplated his pipe. 'Very little, I fear. His lordship's interests were not my own. He was devoted to biblical archaeology, was he not?'

Sir Percival nodded. 'That's right, Mr Holmes. He spent the last thirty years of his life in the Orient, in Jerusalem, Cairo, Damascus and other such places. To be honest, we know very little about what he was up to out there. All we know is that he poured nearly all his fortune into various archaeological ventures. For staff, he surrounded himself with a rag-tag collection of locals. Over the years he collected people from all over the Levant. And I'm afraid they have proved unable or unwilling to add very much to our store of knowledge.

'But one thing we do know, Mr Holmes, is that Lord Beaumaris wasn't interested in archaeology as a discipline in itself. As a subject of study it meant nothing to him. In all his projects he had one particular object in mind, something which came to dominate his life – a monomania, we might call it. An object in the pursuit of which he was prepared to squander his health and his fortune. Something for which he was prepared to tolerate a lifetime of ridicule.' Sir Percival paused again, and this time he looked over at Mr Fallowell. During that moment of silence I could sense the atmosphere in the room changing. Behind the shutters a rising wind was buffeting the windows, but the speaker showed no sign of hearing it. There was something in his manner that had captured the attention of his audience and when he spoke again his voice sounded dry and strained.

'Well, none of us are laughing at him now,' he went on. 'You see, gentlemen, Lord Beaumaris's life was spent seeking an object so mysterious, so precious, so highly prized, that perhaps only the Holy Grail itself surpasses it as an object of wonder. And my problem, Mr Holmes, is that it seems Lord Beaumaris actually found it. Yes, Mr Holmes, on the eve of his death, Lord Beaumaris announced his search was complete. He had found the Lazarus Testament.'

That night proved a stormy one. The clear blue calm of the day had been utterly vanquished, and the angry gale which followed drove the rubbish in the streets this way and that, throwing it high into the air with bursts of sudden fury. But indoors, where the fire still crackled and the lamps burnt as brightly as before, the room had fallen still. Sir Percival's last words meant nothing to me, but they were spoken with such gravity, such profound earnestness, that I felt a shiver run through my body. I found myself poised, motionless, with the big candelabra still in my hands, waiting for someone to break the silence.

To my surprise, it was Mr Fallowell who was the first to

speak, prefacing his words with a nervous and apologetic cough.

'Of course, gentlemen, the phrase "Lazarus Testament" probably means nothing to you. Outside certain ecclesiastical and archaeological circles it is not often spoken of. Indeed, it might be argued that it has been in the interests of the Church down the centuries to make sure it is a phrase that remains unspoken. Perhaps if I were to tell you a little about it . . .'

'That would be very helpful, Mr Fallowell.' Mr Holmes nodded impatiently. 'I think you can safely assume that neither Dr Watson nor I are close followers of the latest theological controversies.'

'Oh, no, Mr Holmes,' Mr Fallowell replied quickly. 'This is not a *recent* controversy. It is a very ancient one. The issues raised by the existence of the Lazarus Testament have been debated within the Church from its earliest years.'

'An ancient religious debate, eh?' Dr Watson cast a wistful glance towards the drinks tray. 'Not really our usual sort of thing, is it, Holmes? And forgive me if I'm being a bit slow, but what exactly is the Lazarus Testament?'

'The Lazarus Testament, Dr Watson, is an ancient Aramaic parchment said to contain the personal testimony of the man Lazarus who was raised from the dead by our Lord's touch. Of all the miracles, the raising of Lazarus is perhaps the one that resonates most loudly down the ages, representing as it does Christ's triumph over death itself.'

'Good heavens, Mr Fallowell!' Dr Watson stirred uneasily in his chair. 'You surely can't be telling us that Lazarus is supposed to have written his own account of the affair? Of what it's like to be dead? I've certainly never heard of any such thing!'

'And yet, Doctor, the first mention of just such a document can be traced back to within a very few years of Christ's life. St Opinus's eighth century commentary on Mark's Gospel refers to it as if its existence is undisputed. And so does the *Life of St Vespasian*, written five centuries earlier. Unfortunately the Vespasian document is only known to us from a later Arabic synopsis. But from that we learn that Vespasian travelled to Jerusalem from Antioch and was shown the original manuscript of the Lazarus Testament. Vespasian was much moved at the thought of handling a document touched by Lazarus himself, someone who had felt the touch of Christ upon him.'

Mr Fallowell paused and gulped. 'But that was before the contents of the documents were known to him. We are told that reading them provoked a strange reaction in Vespasian. He gave orders that the document was to be returned to its earthenware jar and sealed inside it, and that no one should look upon it again until Doomsday.'

At this point Mr Holmes felt it necessary to knock the tobacco from his pipe. 'An intriguing tale, sir, but surely little more than that? In these more rational times, such matters should not detain us for very long, sir. Even if we were to concede that this story of Vespasian could be trusted, there would still be no proof that the document he saw was genuine.'

'No, sir.' Mr Fallowell swallowed noisily. 'But the belief that Lazarus wrote down his story is surprisingly persistent.'

'Who'd have thought it, eh?' Dr Watson had quietly recharged his glass while Mr Fallowell was talking and was looking a little happier. 'Gospels, testaments . . . I must say, it's all a trifle confusing.'

'And then, sir,' Mr Fallowell went on brightly, 'there are all the other rumours attached to the parchment. One story has it that anyone who holds the parchment is touched by the miraculous power that once raised Lazarus himself.'

'Great Scott! You don't mean . . . ?'

'Yes, Doctor.' Mr Fallowell nodded meaningfully. 'We are talking about the power to return from the dead.'

'Oh, come, sir!' Sherlock Holmes's cool tones were something of a relief in that warm, breathless room. 'You cannot expect us to believe such superstitious absurdities. I don't say that the ancient accounts were not written in good faith, but their authors had none of the benefits of modern learning. They were a good deal more credulous than we are today.' He looked across at his other guest. 'Sir Percival, I am surprised that you, of all men, should concern yourself with this sort of nonsense.'

In response, Sir Percival rose to his feet and began to pace to and fro in front of the shuttered window.

'Mr Holmes,' he began, 'let me ask you to look at this in a slightly different way. Mr Fallowell and his fellow scholars are able to show beyond any reasonable doubt that at one point in the early history of the Church there existed a document purporting to be a personal account of Lazarus's death and resurrection. Let us not concern ourselves for the moment with its provenance, with whether or not this document was genuine, nor with any of the superstition attached to it. The fact is that such a document, whether genuine or not, did exist.'

He paused in his pacing and drew himself up to his full height.

'Now, Mr Holmes, can you imagine what would happen if

that document were to reappear tomorrow? Can you imagine the sensation it would cause? And then imagine that its contents were in some way controversial. For instance, imagine that it contained an account of Lazarus's experience after death that was not a comfortable or comforting one. Imagine if its message was lurid or shocking, and did not sit easily with the current teaching of the Church. Think of the consternation, Mr Holmes! Think of the implications! Millions of honest souls plunged into fear and confusion. The Church's teaching in ruins. A thousand renegade sects springing up to feed on people's fears. It would be no good then for the scholars to declare that the document was an ancient fabrication. The damage would be done and their voices would barely be heard above the cries of an anguished multitude. Why, the thing could prompt a crisis of faith on a scale unprecedented in Christian history. And this, Mr Holmes, is what we are seeking to avert.'

Mr Holmes simply gazed at his guest in surprise. 'Why, Sir Percival, I see it now! No one pretends to know what the document contains. All this anxiety is simply fear of what revelations it *might* contain. Am I right?'

Once again Sir Percival and Mr Fallowell exchanged glances and Sir Percival began to nod.

'Alas, Mr Holmes, that is correct. You begin to understand our predicament. It is crucial that such a document should be properly examined by responsible authorities before it is made public. Its publication would need to be carefully managed. Were it to be blundered into the public arena by a well-meaning amateur such as Lord Beaumaris – or worse, were it to fall into the hands of unscrupulous parties intent on stirring up trouble –

the results for the stability of the nation could be disastrous.'

'In other words, if you can get to it first, you have the option to suppress it,' Mr Holmes retorted impatiently.

'I give you my word, sir, that it is not the government's intention to allow the document to be suppressed or destroyed. We simply wish to manage its publication in an orderly way, and after proper academic scrutiny.'

'And there is nothing new in that, sir,' Mr Fallowell added hastily. 'It was realised as early as the Fifth Century that the document needed to be handled with extreme caution. It was kept firmly under lock and key in the library at Alexandria, apparently sealed in an earthenware jar ever since the days of Vespasian. But if we were to find it and put it in the hands of proper, responsible scholars, why the greatest mystery of all would be revealed to us! We would glimpse for the first time what it is like to pass over the Great Divide!'

Sherlock Holmes paused for a moment. 'Very well,' he said. 'I accept the document, whatever its provenance, still has some social and political significance. Now tell me, at what point in history did it go missing?'

'That was in the Seventh Century.' When speaking of his own subject Mr Fallowell seemed a lot more forceful. 'When Alexandria fell to the Arabs the fate of the document was unclear, but rumours have persisted down the centuries. In the Fifteenth Century, the Arab scholar Ibn-Kibrun reported that in Baghdad there was "a casket precious to the Christians". He said it contained the holy writing of one who had been blessed by the prophet Jesus. There are rumours of it after that in Damascus, in Jericho, in Jerusalem. It was said that wherever the parchment went, it was followed by a mysterious guardian, a dark-skinned stranger wrapped in a cloak – an angel, some said, or even Lazarus himself, doomed to live forever to watch over his work . . .'

'Only a story, of course,' Sir Percival added quickly, with a worried glance at Mr Holmes. 'And as you can imagine, none of this was of any interest to Her Majesty's government. Even when the Archbishop of Canterbury approached us last year, we were not inclined to take the matter seriously.'

'A-ha!' Mr Holmes's interest seemed to revive as the narrative returned to modern times. 'Now we come to the nub of it. Enter Lord Beaumaris, I take it.'

'That's correct, Mr Holmes. His lordship wrote to the archbishop saying that he had discovered the precise whereabouts of the ancient scroll and that he was returning to England to secure it. It seems that, against all probability, his search had somehow brought him to this country and that the document was to be found under our noses.'

Mr Holmes's eyes were bright again. 'Of course I should wish to see that letter for myself . . .'

'I have already taken steps to make it available to you, Mr Holmes. On receiving it, the archbishop passed it to the Cabinet, but there was no sense of alarm. Lord Beaumaris was known to be very old and very ill. To be honest, we dismissed his letter as the ramblings of a dying man.'

'But something has occurred since to change your mind?'

'It has indeed, Mr Holmes. We received – in great secrecy – high level representations from the Vatican. It appears that for some time rumours have been circulating in Syria about Lord

Beaumaris. Persistent rumours. It was said he was on the brink of an amazing breakthrough concerning the Lazarus scroll. The cardinals took it seriously enough to conduct their own investigation, and what they found unnerved them greatly. We don't need to go into the details here, but they uncovered a remarkable story of ancient clues and ciphers, the sort of tale that we should dismiss as risible nonsense were we to read it in a popular novel. But it was enough to convince the Vatican's investigators that Lord Beaumaris really *was* on the verge of a sensational discovery, and when his lordship returned suddenly to London they asked our help in . . . well, let us say, in *managing* the affair.'

'And what did happen when Beaumaris arrived in London?' Holmes was listening intently now, his eyes fastened on the speaker.

'I'm sorry to say that his lordship's health had deteriorated greatly during his journey, Mr Holmes. Even before he embarked he was a very sick man. By the time he arrived in Portsmouth, it was clear he had only a few days to live. There was no question of him continuing his search. Instead he was carried to his house in Randolph Square, too weak to even leave his bed. I visited him there, but he absolutely refused to divulge a word of what he knew. He had decided to take his secret to the grave, he told me. He said he trusted no one else with such a precious document. And that, Mr Holmes, appeared to be an end to it. We sent word to Viscount Wrexham that his father was dying, but the Viscount was examining bloodstock in Ireland and it seemed uncertain he could return in time.'

'But surely, with so much at stake, you took measures to

ensure that any last words would be taken down?'

'We did, Mr Holmes, although I am not proud of it. I installed a small group of officials in the house and closed the doors to all other comers. The group was made up of two Scotland Yard men to guard against intruders, our own nurses and a Home Office physician, a shorthand reporter to take down any last words, and Mr Fallowell here, as the archbishop's representative, the only one of the whole party his lordship was pleased to see.'

'You see, sir,' his companion explained, 'I had often corresponded with Lord Beaumaris over technical points of Aramaic syntax. He seemed pleased that at the last he was able to talk about such subjects, although he was very weak, and often incoherent.'

'But he said nothing about the Lazarus Testament itself?' Mr Holmes asked sharply.

'Not until right at the end, sir. Then he told me that if fate had given him just two more days of strength, he might have held it in his hands.'

'But he gave no indication of its whereabouts?'

'No, Mr Holmes. Only that it involved a journey out of London. I think I sensed that deep down he wanted to share what he knew. Otherwise his life's work was wasted, you see. But he told me I was safer not knowing. He said there were people out there who would kill to obtain the Lazarus Testament.'

Sherlock Holmes fixed a shrewd glance upon his visitor. 'But something tells me the matter did not rest there, Mr Fallowell?'

'No indeed, although it seemed certain that it would. His

lordship was beginning to slip in and out of consciousness, and the doctors were shaking their heads. And then, at that desperate moment, Viscount Wrexham made his entrance.'

'Remember, gentlemen,' Sir Percival put in, 'that the two men had not spoken for decades. No one had expected the Viscount to appear. Remember too, that Lord Beaumaris had bankrupted himself by his quest and that there was nothing but debt for the Viscount to inherit. So whether it was lingering filial affection that brought him, or rumours of a priceless treasure in his father's grasp, we shall never know.'

'And when the two met?' Dr Watson asked. 'A very moving moment, I imagine.'

'Certainly a dramatic one, Doctor,' Mr Fallowell replied. 'In fact I have never witnessed a more remarkable scene in my life. I was seated by his lordship's bed when the doors to the room were thrown open. The doctors and the shorthand writer were in close attendance too, but the Viscount ignored us all. He paused for a moment in the doorway, his eyes on his father, then strode quickly forward and knelt at the bedside.

'I shall never forget the powerful effect of that entrance, Doctor. Viscount Wrexham was no longer a young man, sir. He must have been sixty if a day, and his famous long golden locks were turned a striking shade of silver. But you felt the power of the man instantly. It was as if he filled the room with a new vigour and a new vitality. Even though I had heard many bad things about his conduct, it was impossible not to be impressed by him.'

'Very interesting, I'm sure, Mr Fallowell. But what did he actually *do*?'

'As I say, Mr Holmes, he kneeled by his father's bed and took his hand. He didn't say a word – not even a whisper – but I saw the old man's eyes open. For a few seconds he looked into his son's face and then with his other hand he beckoned him forward, until the Viscount's ear was almost against his lips. And then I saw him whisper. I say "saw" because, of all the observers, I was the closest, and I heard nothing. But I could see his lips move and could see the rise of his chest as he struggled for breath. And then he seemed to sink back, as if his last task were accomplished. His son nodded, and rose to his feet. I waited then, expecting him to speak, but the Viscount simply turned on his heel and walked from the room.

'I hardly had time to be surprised, for my first thoughts were for his lordship, who I feared had breathed his last. But when I had reassured myself that he still lived, I looked up into the ante-room, and I saw the Viscount at the writing desk in the corner. As I watched, he pulled out a pen and scribbled something on a sheet of writing paper. Then he thrust the paper into his pocket, and without once looking back, he strode from his father's apartments.'

'And was never seen again, Mr Holmes,' Sir Percival added in solemn, weighty tones. A silence fell upon the room then and all eyes turned to him. 'Well, actually I exaggerate a little. A maid downstairs saw him leave the house. But from that point on, from the moment he stepped into Randolph Square, he was gone. It was as Mr de Lacey told you. Nothing. Not a sighting, not a rumour, not a squeak.'

In the pause which followed, I became aware that the wind which had risen so suddenly must have blown itself out. Now the world outside was deadly still. It seemed to me, lurking in the shadows of the silver cupboard, that there was something eerie in that stillness, as though the night itself was hanging on the speaker's words. But then Dr Watson stirred and busied himself filling glasses, and the moment passed, allowing the reassuring comfort of the study to reassert itself. And I could see from the look in Mr Holmes's eyes that he was enjoying the mystery that had been placed before him.

'So Viscount Wrexham disappeared, taking with him the only information concerning the whereabouts of the Lazarus Testament. And now you believe him dead. From what we were told of the corpse found by the Thames, it seems you believe he died the day he vanished, or very near that time. Is that correct?'

'Well, Mr Holmes, that would explain our complete failure to find any trace of him. The Viscount was a distinctive looking man – that long hair of his – and a well known figure across the Home Counties and beyond. And we've had posters in every railway station. But not a word.'

'And tell me, Sir Percival, have you speculated about how he may have ended up in the Thames?'

Our visitor looked uneasy. 'Well, sir, there are various possible explanations. On his father's death, the family estates would be sold to pay the creditors. The Viscount would be left with nothing at all. After so many years of high living that would be a bleak prospect for the man.'

'So you suspect suicide?'

'It is one possibility, Mr Holmes. And we cannot rule out common assault. It was growing dark when the Viscount left

Randolph Square. If he had set out on foot for his destination, perhaps pre-occupied with his father's words, perhaps a little careless of his own safety, he might have been set upon by thieves.'

'And your other explanation?'

'It is the one we fear most: that the Viscount fell into the hands of persons intent on finding the Lazarus Testament. They may simply have considered him a useful hostage in extracting information from Lord Beaumaris. But they may then have discovered that he had information himself. He may even have volunteered what he knew in the hope of saving his life. In which case, Mr Holmes, I fear there are others out there, ahead of us in the chase . . .'

'And there is nothing else to report from the bedchamber of Lord Beaumaris? No other word was spoken about the Lazarus Testament?'

'No, Mr Holmes. Lord Beaumaris never regained consciousness, although he lingered on for a few days more. It seems he might have outlived his only son and heir.'

The great detective digested this silently for a moment. 'Thank you, Sir Percival,' he concluded. 'A very pretty puzzle indeed. We accept the case. There are unarguably points of unusual interest in it. And although we shall have many further questions for you in due course, I think for now it would be better if we were to step back and collect our thoughts.' He turned to Dr Watson with a smile. 'I fear your planned holiday in the Downs will have to wait, my friend. And now, gentlemen,' he went on, turning back to his guests, 'I perceive that the excellent Flotsam is on hand to show you out. You will excuse us if we do not accompany you to the door? We have much to consider.'

And with that the great detective turned his full attention to his pipe, while I, jolted by his words, almost dropped the big candelabra. For I had been thinking, not about Lord Beaumaris or Viscount Wrexham, nor even of how Mrs Hudson had known to ask me about Bible stories. I had been thinking of a man lying in the mud on Baker Street, and of his last words. *A dead man risen from the grave . . .*

Those words had been whispered to me that day, and they had been spoken so faintly I had barely been able to make them out. But somehow, it seemed, they were growing louder with every day that passed.

CHAPTER SIX

The Deathbed Clue

To my surprise, the evening did not end with the departure of Sir Percival and Mr Fallowell. Although the hour was already advanced, no sooner had I returned to the kitchen, where Mrs Hudson was repairing aprons by the fire, than a timid knock behind me announced that Mr Holmes had followed me downstairs. I had learnt already that it was not unusual for the great detective to visit Mrs Hudson's private domain when he had particular instructions to impart or when, in Dr Watson's absence, he required an audience for his brilliant reasoning. On this occasion he put his head around the door and coughed apologetically.

'Ah, Mrs Hudson,' he began, 'I wondered if I might disturb you for a moment?'

'Of course you may, sir.' The housekeeper roused herself from her seat and drew another chair up to the hearth. 'I daresay you and Dr Watson will be making an early start tomorrow, sir, in the light of Sir Percival's visit?'

'Very astute, as always, Mrs Hudson,' the detective smiled as he settled himself into the proffered chair. 'We have a great deal of work to do. Ah! Brown ale! Thank you. You know how much I enjoy a glass. It is a vice Watson insists on keeping from the readers of those little accounts of his. He says drinking brown ale is a habit devoid of all mystery.'

He allowed himself a private chuckle at his friend's folly and then leant forward to place the bottle by the grate.

'I confess the subject of our investigations is a rather esoteric one, Mrs Hudson. Dr Watson and I will need to learn quickly. Still, I fancy few people outside holy orders would know very much more than we do about this thing we seek – a document they are calling the Lazarus Testament.'

'Yes, sir,' Mrs Hudson replied calmly, returning to her stitching. 'Speaking for myself, apart from it being a lost text of uncertain origin, last recorded in Alexandria, I know very little about it.'

My eyes opened wide at this remarkable display of knowledge, but Mr Holmes simply smiled.

'Surprised, Flotsam?' he asked. 'Yet one glance around this room is enough to tell me that Mrs Hudson has been asking one or two questions of her own.'

When I looked around in bewilderment, the great man smiled again.

'If you raise your eyes a little, to that shelf yonder, you will notice a glass jar marked "saffron" among Mrs Hudson's herbs and spices. It is three quarters full. Yet if you look at the dresser over there, you will notice a small bag, similarly marked, still with its shop tag and ribbon. Now Mrs Hudson's efficiency is not in any doubt, so it is not by accident that she has bought spices she doesn't need. And since she made her purchase at

Pomfret's, and not at the much closer establishment on the Marylebone Road, it is tempting to speculate that it was information, not saffron, that was the principal reason for her visit.'

Mrs Hudson favoured her employer with an approving nod.

'It is true, sir, that Flotsam overheard a mention of Viscount Wrexham the other evening. And that put me in mind of old Mr Pomfret. Mr Pomfret, of course, was acquainted with the Viscount's father through Lord Ullswater.'

'And was Mr Pomfret informative, I wonder?'

'Only in his personal recollections of Lord Beaumaris, sir. Sir Percival will no doubt have been able to tell you a good deal more. Now, I imagine you and Dr Watson will be requiring an early breakfast, sir?'

'Yes, indeed. That would be most helpful. Really, Mrs Hudson, you wouldn't believe some of the nonsense we have had to listen to tonight. Cloaked angels standing guard over ancient artefacts. Dead people returning from the grave!'

Just then the heat of the fire popped the cork from his bottle of beer and the detective rose, clutching the bottle to his chest.

'Now, if you will excuse me . . . I have asked Dr Watson to be at the British Library as soon as it opens. I myself shall be at the Home Office for the first part of the day, and after that at Randolph Square, conducting my own investigations . . .'

With great difficulty I managed to restrain myself until Mr Holmes was out of earshot.

'But, Mrs Hudson, is that really why you went to Mr Pomfret's? I had no idea you were interested in Viscount Wrexham's disappearance!'

'Well, Flottie,' she replied with a low chuckle, 'I cannot deny a certain curiosity. And Mr Pomfret, of course, spent a great deal of time in the east with Lord Ullswater. He became very chatty indeed when I mentioned Lord Beaumaris. Mr Pomfret had known him well, and knew all about his lordship's fixation with the Lazarus Testament. Apparently it was always said in archaeological circles that there'd be trouble if it was ever found'.

She rose and returned her sewing carefully to its basket. 'Now, Flottie, I think it's bedtime. We have an early start tomorrow, remember . . .'

So much had happened that evening, and I had heard so much to wonder at and to ponder, that perhaps my imagination had become a little feverish from it all. At least that is what I told myself later on, as I lay in bed shortly after closing down the study for the night. Why else, I wondered, would I allow my eyes to play such tricks? No, I was an over-excited young girl, I told myself, and I tried to dismiss from my mind the moment when, in checking the shutters, I had caught a glimpse of the street below. It was dark outside and raining, and the gaslight was treacherous. Why else would I have imagined, fleetingly, at the very edge of my vision, a dark, shadowy figure, looking up at us? A figure in a hooded cloak, a man standing very still, with the air of one who watches and waits with infinite patience . . .

Mr Holmes was as good as his word and next morning, before I had even finished scouring the pans, he and Dr Watson had departed in pursuit of their investigations. However, any hopes

I had that Mrs Hudson might immediately whisk me away in pursuit of further information about the Lazarus Testament were quickly dashed; for although her visit to Mr Pomfret suggested she was not indifferent to Mr Holmes's new case, her demeanour that morning indicated she had serious work on her mind, and we set about polishing the furniture and shining the leather with all the urgency of storm-tossed sailors at the pumps. So great was our energy that by mid-morning our lengthy list of jobs was already much diminished, with the happy result that, when Miss Peters appeared in her uncle's carriage and begged for me to be allowed to accompany her to the bookbinder, Mrs Hudson relented and told me sternly that I was to keep Miss Peters out of trouble and thereby save a lot of work for everyone.

After a morning of such diligence, it was a wonderful thing to find myself in my best clothes, with my hair elegantly arranged, driving through the sunlit streets and feeling fresh air on my face. The Earl's brougham was slow and rather dark inside, but was very grand and comfortable, and Miss Peters brightened the interior considerably with a long story of how she had disgraced herself the previous evening at a fancy dress ball by congratulating the French ambassador for his impersonation of the Walrus from *Alice*.

The French ambassador, it turned out, had not yet donned his costume.

Fortunately for her peace of mind, the bookbinder in Dover Street turned out to be a most distinguished-looking old gentleman who, Miss Peters felt sure, would be able to pass himself off as a deacon at the very least when he called at

Bloomsbury Square. Equally fortunately, the old craftsman appeared very taken by Miss Peters and, I suspect, after a few minutes of her pleading would probably have agreed to call in the guise of a Hindu holy man had she truly desired it.

Our business quickly concluded, Hetty insisted that I accompanied her home, and it was as we dismounted from the carriage in Bloomsbury Square that I noticed a familiar figure advancing towards us unsteadily along the pavement. His arms were full of books, piled up to his chin, which tottered alarmingly whenever he attempted to raise his hand at a passing hansom.

'Why, Hetty!' I exclaimed. 'Isn't that Dr Watson?'

And Dr Watson it was, who at that moment saw us and directed at us a cheerful wave that threatened once more to undo his precarious balance.

'Flotsam! Just the person!' he cried, managing, after a little perilous groping, to raise his hat. 'I confess I am in need of some assistance. I've just had a message from Holmes asking me to meet him at the Beaumaris house in Randolph Square, but as you can see I'm rather over-burdened . . .'

'But what are all these books, sir?' I wondered, relieving him of those that seemed in most imminent danger of falling. 'I didn't know you were allowed to take books away from the British Library.'

'Quite right, Flotsam,' the doctor nodded gloomily. 'Unfortunately I got talking to one of the librarians there and it turned out he'd made a particular study of ancient religious texts. He insisted on going all the way home and bringing these from his personal collection. Very good of him, of course, but

I rather wish he hadn't. What am I to do with them all? I can barely lift them as it is. And if Holmes thinks I'm *reading* all these, he's very much mistaken!'

That is how, twenty minutes later, I came to be dismounting from a cab in Randolph Square alongside Dr Watson, my arms full of dusty leather volumes. The door to Lord Beaumaris's town house was opened to us, not by a maid as might have been expected, but by Inspector Mapperley of Scotland Yard, a lugubrious individual who always appeared rather disheartened by the criminality he encountered daily in the performance of his duties.

'Ah, Dr Watson, sir,' he acknowledged rather sorrowfully. 'Mr Holmes said to expect you. He's upstairs. Follow me . . .'

With no servant in evidence, Dr Watson and I piled our books onto a smart lacquered table near the door and looked around. It was a grand hallway, opulently finished in dark marble and decorated with a series of imposing, shoulder-height Japanese vases. But for all its opulence, there was a chill in the air that told us the house was not lived in, and we didn't think to remove our coats. The surfaces were clear of dust, it is true, and there was nothing obvious to the eye to suggest the house was not properly looked after, but there was a sense of emptiness in that hallway which the great vases and the grand staircase only seemed to accentuate. It seemed a house without a beating heart.

I looked around me and shivered. Inspector Mapperley was already leading Dr Watson towards the stairs and, as no one seemed to mind particularly what became of me, I scurried after them.

We found Mr Holmes pacing Lord Beaumaris's private apartments, listening again to Mr Fallowell's account of his lordship's last hours. We approached the pair through an ante-room, a splendid, high-ceilinged chamber furnished with ornate tables and chairs and a fine old writing bureau that lay open, ready for use. Beyond the ante-chamber, through the half-open double doors, lay a richly appointed bedroom where Mr Holmes was prowling. Mr Fallowell was sitting on a very high-backed chair watching him, a look of acute and painful concentration on his face.

'Yes, Mr Holmes,' he was saying. 'I was seated here, exactly as you see me. His lordship was on the bed. Everything is exactly as it was when Viscount Wrexham burst in.'

Just then the two gentlemen became aware of us for the first time.

'Ah, Watson!' Mr Holmes exclaimed cordially. 'You are just in time. So far today I have done little of any value. I have been talking to the inspector and Sir Percival about groups and factions which might have been organised and ruthless enough to seize the Viscount from a public street.' He arched an eyebrow in the inspector's direction. 'I confess I am none the wiser as a result. But now we come to the real business of the day and I am delighted to have you by me. So, Mr Fallowell, tell us exactly what happened when Viscount Wrexham left his father's bedside.'

'Well, Mr Holmes, I was looking down at the invalid, but I heard the Viscount cross the ante-room. When I looked up he was scribbling a note to himself at that bureau.'

'And he put that paper in his pocket, then left immediately?'

'He did, Mr Holmes.'

'Inspector, you are sure that bureau has not been touched by anyone since?'

'I'm certain of it, Mr Holmes. We've been very careful.'

The detective moved past us, purposeful and silent. Producing a magnifying glass from beneath his cape, he began the most minute examination of the desk and the objects on it, paying particular attention, it seemed, to the block of writing paper at its centre.

'Looking for an impression of the Viscount's message on the sheet below,' Dr Watson whispered knowingly, giving me a nudge.

'But it will do him no good, sir,' Inspector Mapperley replied morosely. 'We had already thought of that. There's nothing there.'

Before Dr Watson could make any further observation, Mr Holmes straightened and turned to the inspector.

'There appears to be no paper on the blotter,' he remarked icily.

'No, sir,' Inspector Mapperley replied mournfully. 'A great shame that. Had there been, the Viscount might have used it to blot his note, and we might have been able to make out an outline of what he'd written.'

'I think you misunderstand me, Inspector. I do not mention the fact to lament our ill fortune. No, the obvious question that presents itself to me is *why*? *Why* is there no paper on the blotter, Inspector?'

The detective began to look a little uneasy. 'I couldn't say, Mr Holmes. I suppose the old paper was done with, and someone forgot to put in clean paper. I can't really see as it matters, sir.'

'In a household such as this, Inspector, you think someone simply *forgot*?' He cast his eyes around the assembled group as if missing someone. 'Ah, if only Mrs Hudson were here! She knows these things. Flotsam, in her absence, tell me, do you think that's likely?'

'No, sir,' I told him, thankful for the many times Mrs Hudson had explained to me the routines of a great household. 'You'd expect a footman to replenish the writing paper every day. He would always put a clean paper in the blotter at the same time, I'm sure he would.'

'Thank you, Flotsam. Invaluable.' Still ignoring Inspector Mapperley, Mr Holmes turned to Mr Fallowell. 'I confess I find myself warming to Viscount Wrexham,' he smiled. 'He strikes me as a very cool customer indeed. Now tell me, there is something you have missed out, isn't there?'

At this accusation Mr Fallowell first blanched, then turned very red.

'It has certainly not been my intention to mislead—' he began rather stiffly.

'No, no, no,' Mr Holmes interrupted him impatiently. 'I'm sure you had no such intention. But you have told us the last thing the Viscount did before leaving was to place his scribbled note in his pocket.'

'That's right, Mr Holmes. And I stand by it.'

'Think again. Did he not perhaps reach down and remove something else from the desk? Did he not in fact remove the paper from the blotter as you watched? It might have been done in one simple movement as he turned to leave.'

Mr Fallowell gulped audibly. 'No, really, Mr Holmes, I'm

sure . . .' His frown of concentration deepened until he had succeeded in crumpling his brow into a shape not unlike a question mark. 'I was thinking about the note, you see. It was that which seemed so important. But I suppose it's just possible he might have . . . Yes, I suppose it's possible he *did* reach down for something else . . . I wouldn't have taken much notice of that. Yes, now you describe it to me, I think perhaps he might have done, Mr Holmes. I can almost see him reach out his arm a second time. I never really thought about it before. I was thinking so very hard about that note, you see . . .'

The detective straightened triumphantly.

'You see, Inspector! I've always maintained that logic is a far better witness than the human eye. And what does this tell us? Why, that even at such a time, and with scarcely a moment for reflection, Viscount Wrexham understood the implications of blotting his note. A sharp mind indeed!'

'You can't be sure of that, though, can you, sir?' the inspector objected. 'Mr Fallowell here isn't certain.'

But Mr Holmes was having none of it. 'From this we can deduce that when the Viscount left the room he carried the blotting paper with him, for it is not on the desk and the wastepaper basket is empty, and we know that nothing in this room has been interfered with since he left it.'

'Magnificent, Holmes!' Dr Watson exclaimed with fervour. 'It must be exactly as you say!' Then he paused as though a thought had struck him. 'But where exactly does that leave us? Surely the blotting paper is just as lost as the original note?'

His companion greeted this objection with pursed lips. 'Not necessarily, my friend. You see, there was a great difference, in the Viscount's eyes, between the two papers. Put yourself in his position, Watson. He has heard his father whisper to him instructions that are potentially worth a fortune. He immediately writes them down. That note becomes to him a document of almost incalculable value. But the other paper? No, that is merely something he wishes to remove from prying eyes. He simply wishes to discard it discreetly. Now, let us follow the Viscount's footsteps . . .'

With that he stalked from the room, his brows knitted in thought and the rest of us trailing behind him like cygnets behind a swan.

The door from the antechamber opened onto a gallery landing that looked down upon the main entrance hall. From there, Mr Holmes descended the main staircase with us on his heels, and paused in the great marbled hallway.

On hearing our footsteps, a small and timid-looking maid of about my own age appeared from a concealed doorway below the stairs and came forward to greet us.

'Is it your coats you'll be wanting, sir?' she asked cautiously.

'It will not,' Mr Holmes replied. 'You will observe that we are still wearing our coats. No, it is you I wish to see. Gertrude, is it not? Inspector Mapperley here tells me you were the last person to see Viscount Wrexham alive. Is that correct?'

'Yes, sir.' She seemed to quake a little in the face of such a terrible accusation. 'Least ways, that's what they tell me, sir. It was me what gave him his gloves and stick that day, sir.'

'Excellent!' Mr Holmes cast a look around the rest of us, like a conjuror contemplating the production of rabbits from unlikely places. 'And tell me, child, did he have anything in his hands as he came downstairs? A screwed up piece of paper, perhaps?'

'Why, sir, I don't think I could say, sir . . .' But even as she tried to elude the bright glare of Mr Holmes's gaze, we saw a thought strike her, halting her denial. It was with genuine surprise, and not a little awe, that she raised her eyes to meet his.

'Why, yes, sir,' she told him, 'now you come to mention it, I believe he *did* have something in his hand. A little ball of paper it was, sir, like you say. He was bouncing it up and down on the palm of his hand as he came down the stairs. It being such a little thing, I didn't really take any notice. If you hadn't mentioned it, sir, I'd never have remembered.'

Once again Mr Holmes turned to the rest of us, eyes bright, before turning back to the girl.

'And can you tell us what the Viscount did with that ball of paper? Did he put it in his pocket? Or did he discard it somewhere in this house? Think carefully. Your answer is important.'

We all watched in anxious silence as the girl considered this.

'Well, sir,' she began at last, and it seemed to me that everyone present leant towards her an inch or two in anticipation. 'He must've had it in his hand when I gave him his gloves. But then I turned round to get his stick, and when I turned back he was buttoning his gloves, so I suppose he must have put it somewhere by then, sir.'

Sherlock Holmes nodded encouragingly. 'Indeed he must. And have you any idea where he might have put it?'

But all the girl could do was shake her head and drop her eyes in disappointment.

'Must have put it in his pocket, Holmes,' Dr Watson concluded glumly. 'Otherwise someone would have found it. He probably tossed it into the gutter when he left. Damned rotten luck, I say.'

But I was barely listening to him. I was thinking of the way that Dr Watson and I had come in from the street that day with our arms full of books, and how we had discarded them onto the first table that presented itself. We had not *thought* where to put them. We had just put them down without thinking.

Which is why I found myself looking at the huge Japanese vase that stood to one side of the staircase, very close to the spot where Viscount Wrexham would have stopped for his hat and gloves.

It was a tall vase, at least five feet high, broad in the waist and narrow at the neck. Too large to move easily, it was the sort of object that simply stands in its place season after season, largely unnoticed, undisturbed save for an occasional dusting. Then I imagined the Viscount standing there with something in his hand that he wished to be rid of. I imagined the maid turning her back as he came to pull on his gloves . . .

Mr Holmes, I noticed, also seemed to be lost in thought, as if he too was imagining the Viscount's movements. And then, at that moment, he lifted his head and our eyes met, and we both turned to face the vase.

'Watson,' he said quietly, 'do you think yourself strong enough to pick that thing up?'

As it turned out, the vase proved a great deal too heavy for one person to lift. In fact, it required the combined efforts of all four men in our party to lower the fragile object to its side and then to tip it slightly, a process during which Mr Fallowell more than once declared himself faint and Inspector Mapperley twice expressed a mumbled contempt for 'blooming great jars with no purpose, not even a lid on them to keep biscuits'. Even these efforts did not succeed in completely up-ending the item in question, so while the four men held it at an angle, it was left to me to reach inside and feel for anything hidden within.

It soon became apparent that over the years many objects had been deposited in the accommodating depths of that vase, and from the multitude of old cigarette ends and chewed tips of cigars I quickly extracted a torn ostrich feather, the lid of a snuffbox and a copy of *The Times* dated December 1889. Lurking beneath those were two or three torn-up calling cards, an old invitation to take tea with the Bishop of Lichfield and, rather surprisingly, an ivory-handled grapefruit knife. Only on my third attempt did I feel something more promising against my finger tips, and I gave a little shout of triumph when my fingers closed around a crumpled ball of soft, fibrous paper.

'It is here, sir!' I cried. 'This must be it. The Viscount did exactly what you said, sir!'

But Mr Holmes made no reply. He merely took the paper from my fingers, opened it carefully, then turned it towards the ornate mirror in such a way that all of us could see its reflection. I could see at once that it was a clean sheet of blotting paper, used only once, with the Viscount's handwriting printed perfectly legibly across its middle:

Andover Teddington Prince Leopold

Tyrant ? Colonel Middleton

'By Jove!' Dr Watson blinked rapidly. 'What's all that about?'

In reply, Mr Holmes raised one thin eyebrow. 'Well, my friend,' he said softly. 'It is an answer of sorts. But I fear Lord Beaumaris and his son have not made it easy for us. It would seem we still have some work to do . . .'

We returned to Baker Street in triumph, a copy of the Viscount's note clutched firmly between Mr Holmes's fingers. The original was left in the care of Inspector Mapperley with instructions that he should communicate the discovery at once to Sir Percival Grenville-Ffitch. Then Mr Holmes had hailed a four-wheeler and had insisted that I should join him and Dr Watson in it, along with the large pile of learned books that now seemed to be of no interest to anyone. Although all of us were thinking of the message we had discovered, for a short time elation triumphed over curiosity. Mr Holmes and Dr Watson were both in high good humour, exchanging jocular views on Scotland Yard and its singular lack of perspicacity.

On our arrival home we were greeted by Mrs Hudson, who was immediately regaled with an account of our great achievement. Indeed, so general was the air of celebration as our employers took off their coats that she had some difficulty in explaining to Mr Holmes that a gentleman had called in his absence but had declined to wait.

'He did not leave a card, sir, but he said he might write to you.'

'I hope his need is not urgent, Mrs Hudson,' the detective

replied, 'for we shall be fully occupied with Sir Percival's case for a little while yet. Now, if you would be so good as to help us upstairs with these books, Dr Watson and I can get down to some serious work. There is not a moment to be lost!'

And such was Mr Holmes's eagerness to scrutinise the Viscount's note further that even before Mrs Hudson and I had finished piling up the books in his study, he had produced his copy and was reading it aloud.

'What do you say to that, then, Watson?' he asked. 'Now we have escaped the inspector, we can speak freely.'

'Well, Holmes,' the doctor muttered doubtfully, 'it's all a bit cryptic, isn't it? I mean, are these the places where the Lazarus Testament is supposed to be hidden? And are those the people who did the hiding? It all sounds very unlikely to me . . .'

'One moment, Watson. Let us consult out trusty gazetteer. Mrs Hudson, would you be so kind? It's the large green volume to your left . . . Now, let me see . . . Alfreton, Amberley, Amersham . . . Ah! Here we are. *Andover: Hampshire market town situated on the River Anton, 18 miles north-west of Winchester. Principal industries include dyes, dairy products and fancy goods.* Well, that sounds simple enough.'

With the same taut urgency, his fingers were already rifling through the volume for a second time.

'*Teddington: Middlesex village situated on the River Thames, 12 miles south west of London, chiefly notable for its navigable lock and for a footbridge linking Middlesex with Surrey.*' He looked across at Dr Watson. 'Nothing obvious there, my friend. And it would be wise to see if those paths are leading in the right direction before we follow them too far.'

He closed the book, placed his fingertips together and contemplated the ceiling.

'This is a very pretty puzzle, Watson. But not one beyond our capabilities, I trust.' He smiled again, then rubbed his hands as if relishing the challenge. 'And what about you, Mrs Hudson?' he enquired with a twinkle in his eye. 'Does the Viscount's clue suggest anything to you?' The housekeeper furrowed her brow in response. 'Do I understand, sir, that those words are intended to indicate the whereabouts of the lost document you mentioned?'

'That is correct, Mrs Hudson.'

'And that message was written by Viscount Wrexham?'

'It was. He wrote it immediately after his father had told him where to find the document.'

'I see, sir. Very interesting. Very interesting indeed. And do I understand, sir, that you intend to concentrate your search in the locations you've just mentioned?'

In reply, Sherlock Holmes simply raised an eyebrow and there seemed to me to be particular meaning in the look they exchanged.

'You can be sure Sir Percival will not wish to rule anything out, Mrs Hudson,' he told her with a smile. 'And he will no doubt wish to employ considerable resources in the search.'

Mrs Hudson nodded, then reached down to straighten the large pile of books we had placed on the floor beneath the window. That task complete, she wiped her hands on her apron.

'I'm afraid, sir, I couldn't suggest the precise meaning of such a message at present. But, of course, sir, if any location does suggest itself, I shall be sure to let you know. Now, will there be anything else, sir?'

The gentlemen requiring nothing further, Mrs Hudson took her leave with all the dignity of a battleship putting to sea, leaving me with no option but to follow, bobbing slightly, in her wake.

CHAPTER SEVEN

Too Many Colonel Middletons

The days that followed our discovery in Randolph Square were hectic with activity. Sir Percival Grenville-Ffitch mobilised the might of Scotland Yard and set it to investigate the clue left behind by Viscount Wrexham. If any citizens of either Andover or Teddington had even the slightest knowledge of the Lazarus Testament, Sir Percival declared, his men would find them out and extract it. And as for the military man in question, well, he made it clear to Inspector Mapperley and his men that he wanted every officer named Middleton, serving or retired, who had ever reached the rank of colonel, to be found and interviewed. 'Although I confess I am a little anxious,' he declared. 'That question mark – might it not suggest that Viscount Wrexham was uncertain of the man's rank? Or perhaps even of his name? Perhaps he couldn't hear his father's whisper. Perhaps the whole clue is flawed . . .'

Mr Holmes heard this with a smile. 'But, Sir Percival, might the question mark not equally refer to the word *tyrant*?' he asked. 'Perhaps the Viscount's doubt concerned this colonel's degree of tyranny?'

This sort of comment invariably made Sir Percival groan, and his distinguished face would contort in an agony of doubt.

'And what are we to make of the reference to Prince Leopold, Mr Holmes? I refuse to believe any son of our good queen is involved in this matter in any way. His Royal Highness died rather young, if you remember, and as far as I can discover at no point in his life did he show any interest at all in Biblical archaeology. I met him myself on more than one occasion. Hardly a tyrant. He was a most mild-mannered man . . .'

Despite these doubts, Sir Percival's efforts were unstinting, and even Sherlock Holmes confessed himself impressed by his energy and by the resources being brought to bear on the case. Perhaps in recognition of Sir Percival's determination, he charged Dr Watson with the task of reading through the very large number of reports being collected about various Colonel Middletons; and with interviewing in person those individuals he considered most promising. This involved a good deal of travelling, and very soon the task began to strain the doctor's temper. 'If I never drink another glass of dining-car claret again, it will be far too soon,' he declared to Mrs Hudson one evening. 'And it's not as if I know what to ask these chappies when I *do* meet them. It's clear from the first few words they say that none of them has ever had the slightest interest in the New Testament. They can't wait to tell me that they spent their best years in the army snoozing through church parades. Dash it! Most of them think Aramaic is what the Romans used to decorate their floors!'

An attempt to advertise for any undiscovered Colonel Middletons proved even less helpful, with a persistent stream of individuals arriving on our doorstep hungry for reward, very few of whom proved, upon investigation, to be either genuine colonels or genuine Middletons.

Mr Holmes viewed all this urgent activity with an air of detached amusement. While tolerating Sir Percival's investigations with a benign smile, he confessed openly to Mrs Hudson that he believed Viscount Wrexham's note had a less obvious meaning.

'After all, Mrs Hudson, the man who thought to remove the paper from that blotter had no common intelligence. He knew what he was about, and his brain moved quickly. We must ask ourselves what sort of cipher such a man might have adopted to disguise his father's meaning.'

With this end in mind, Mr Holmes confined himself to his study for long periods, with the words of the Viscount's message scrawled on a large blackboard which he had placed above the mantelpiece.

'You see, Flotsam,' he explained to me one evening when I interrupted his vigil with a plate of thickly-cut sandwiches, 'either these words are the *actual* message given to Viscount Wrexham by his father, with a meaning we can only guess at, or they are some sort of shorthand or code employed by the Viscount himself.' He brandished a sandwich at the blackboard as he spoke, but his eyes rarely left the cryptic words in front of him. 'If the former, then no doubt Sir Percival will get his man. But if the latter, Flotsam, well, the nation's hopes rest with us. And if you would like to crack the code, my girl, don't ask yourself what the words actually mean. Ask yourself what meaning they would have to a man such as Viscount Wrexham . . .'

Mrs Hudson, however, appeared unmoved by all this excitement. She observed the comings and goings of Dr Watson and Sir Percival with an indulgent shrug of her shoulders, then rolled up her sleeves to make sure that the smooth running of the household never faltered. In the days that followed, however unlikely our gentlemen's requirements for sustenance or clean laundry, we were never found wanting.

Only once did I see her show any interest in the mysterious message that was causing such consternation elsewhere. That was a full three days after its first discovery, when Mr Holmes had been summoned to the Home Office and we were taking advantage of his absence to dust and tidy the study. I was busy on my knees dealing with the skirting boards, and when I looked up I saw Mrs Hudson was standing deep in thought by the fireplace, studying the blackboard where the message was scrawled.

'What do you think it means, ma'am?' I asked her rather timidly. 'Mr Holmes thinks it might be some sort of code. If he's right, then I'm afraid Dr Watson might be wasting his time investigating people called Colonel Middleton.'

'Of course he is, Flotsam, and Mr Holmes is well aware of it,' she replied without hesitation. 'But I agree with him wholeheartedly that it's good for Dr Watson to be getting out and getting some exercise. Sitting here smoking all day with Mr Holmes would be very bad for him. He's a gentleman who needs to keep active.'

'But, ma'am,' I reproached her, 'how can you be so sure? It almost sounds as though you know what the message means!'

But rather than denying such a preposterous suggestion

instantly, as I had expected, the housekeeper frowned at the board for a few seconds more.

'Why *Colonel*, Flotsam?' Her frown deepened. '*Colonel*. It's very puzzling. You see, Flottie, there's only one element in that message I don't quite understand. But I can think of just the person to help us with it, and as soon as I get a moment in this upside-down household of ours, I shall drop him a line.'

'Dr Watson says all the experts on ciphers have already seen it, ma'am,' I warned her. 'And Sir Percival told him it's been circulated to any number of top professors too.'

'Has it really, Flotsam?' Mrs Hudson seemed unimpressed. 'Well, the person I have in mind is an expert, certainly, but I confess he is no professor.'

What became of Mrs Hudson's inquiry wasn't immediately clear, for the next day I heard no more from her about the Viscount's message. And the day after that, when she finally had an hour or two free, it became clear that the unfortunate Mr Swan was still uppermost in her mind.

'Perhaps you would care to join me, Flotsam?' she asked. 'It is my plan to call on Constable Dobson at the police station, to see if he can help us with one or two more questions. Since the day is mild and our two gentlemen are not at home, I think we would both benefit from the walk.'

It was certainly true that the day was a fine one. The pale sunlight of the week before had already grown stronger, and everything, from the deportment of pedestrians to the whistling of the bakers' boys about their rounds, spoke of a bright new season on its way. The tentative buds on the plane trees were already showing green, and around the ponds in the parks the crocuses were surprising last year's ducklings with their splashes of purple and of gold. As we walked, we talked of things unrelated to Mr Holmes and his mysteries, until we arrived at the police station where Constable Dobson was on duty and in excellent spirits.

Unfortunately, however, our optimism received something of a check at his hands. Mrs Hudson, it appeared, had hoped to persuade the constable to let us look at Mr Swan's personal effects, only to be told, to our great dismay, that everything Mr Swan owned had already been parcelled up and shipped to his heir in South Africa. And by the slowest class of shipment too, so it was probable that nothing would emerge from transit for many weeks to come.

'*All* his things?' Mrs Hudson asked with some asperity. 'Even the train tickets he carried with him when he died?'

'I'm afraid so, ma'am. It's *procedure*, you see.' Constable Dobson spoke as one paying reverence to a higher power. The only good news seemed to be that the silver watch which I'd seen in Mr Swan's hand had not been sent with his other possessions. The official view remained that it must have been dropped by a third party, and so it lingered, unclaimed, in the police station's lost-property room. Constable Dobson allowed us to look at it again, but apart from the sinister initials on its case, there was nothing about it to excite our curiosity. It was a relatively inexpensive object, perhaps the sort a prosperous shopkeeper might own, but it was solid, weighty, and in every way inscrutable. 'And tell me, Constable,' Mrs Hudson went on, changing the subject, 'that railway ticket of Mr Swan's . . .

Have you by any chance been able to recall the destination he was bound for?'

In his eagerness to help, Constable Dobson contorted his face and stared quite hard at the ceiling, but in the end he could only shake his head and explain that he hadn't really taken much notice of it.

'Was it Alnwick?' he asked himself, scratching his chin. 'Or North Allerton? Somewhere like that, I reckon. You see, I just remember thinking I'd heard of it. I didn't think at the time that the place was important, ma'am.'

And Mrs Hudson could do no more than accept his promise that if the name came back to him, he would let her know straightaway.

'It's all a great shame, Flotsam,' Mrs Hudson sighed as we stepped back into the street. 'I blame myself for not clarifying the point earlier, but it hadn't occurred to me that the authorities would be so prompt in their actions.'

She shook her head again and a little frown betrayed her frustration.

'You see, Flotsam, it occurs to me that Mr Swan might have been going to visit his Elsie on the day of his death. If we only knew where he was going, we might be able to look for her there. But now, I fear, we can do little but hope that Mr Rumbelow's advertisements will reap some reward.'

I thought this was an end to our inquiries that day, but as Mrs Hudson and I continued our wanderings, our path brought us close to the Albany, where Viscount Wrexham had once lived.

'And since we happen to be in the vicinity,' the housekeeper conceded, 'I can see no harm in us paying a call. The caretaker here is known to me, and it's never a bad thing to renew an old acquaintance, is it, Flotsam?'

This caretaker turned out to be a rather grizzled old man of piratical appearance, for he wore a patch over one eye and one sleeve pinned to his chest. He welcomed Mrs Hudson with a greeting that betrayed a slight Cornish accent, which only enhanced the suggestion of a retired buccaneer. However, he seemed to welcome our company and he ushered us into a tiny basement room where a kettle bubbled on the stove amid countless piles of old sporting newspapers.

'One moment and I'll have cleared a seat for you ladies,' he mumbled. 'It's been a few years since I saw you last, ma'am, and I'd be telling the truth if I said you don't look a day older. You'll find me sadly aged, I'm afraid, sadly aged. And as for my lumbago . . .'

Mrs Hudson waited until we were seated and supplied with tea before turning the conversation to Viscount Wrexham and his disappearance.

'Arr, that was a rum business, ma'am. He went out that morning like any other morning, he did, dressed impeccable, with those long silver locks of his all shining. *Horace*, he said to me, *Pauncefoot is planning to return some collars to the laundry. He may ask you to pack them up for him*. Now, I ask you, ma'am, is those the words of a man who expects to disappear?'

Mrs Hudson agreed they were not obviously indicative of such an intention.

'And who is Pauncefoot?' she asked.

'Pauncefoot's the Viscount's valet, ma'am. Been together for years, they had. When the Viscount disappeared, his man took it bad. Took to staying out all hours, he did, like he couldn't settle. I used to say to Mrs Hicks at the draper's, *he's pining, is Pauncefoot.* And he was, ma'am. All jumpy and anxious he became. Missed the Viscount something terrible, I'd say. Don't think he was being paid either, what with old Lord Beaumaris dying and the estate in the hands of the creditors. That's why he went. Took another job, he did. Went into service out of town, I think he said.'

Mrs Hudson nodded. 'I'd very much like to talk to Pauncefoot, Mr Trelawney. Did he leave a forwarding address?'

'I don't know that he did, ma'am. Least ways, not with me. Perhaps them solicitors who run things now might know where to find him.'

'And what do *you* think happened to the Viscount, Mr Trelawney?'

The old man considered for a moment. 'Well, like I say, ma'am, I don't hold with them that says he's running from his debts. He was never one to believe himself beaten, you see, ma'am. He always held that a good winner was just round the corner to put him back on his feet. Very resourceful was the Viscount. Nah, if he's gone of his own free will, it's because he's up to something. But after all this time, well, I fears for him, ma'am. I said to Mrs Hicks only yesterday, *there's skulduggery at work, Mrs Hicks*, I said, and she said straight back, *I think you're right, Mr Trelawney.*'

'And what has happened to the Viscount's things? Are his rooms still taken?'

The old caretaker shook his head. 'No, ma'am. After

Pauncefoot left, they kept the place on for a bit, in case the old fox reappeared. But there's nothing left to pay for such things now and the creditors kicked up a fuss. So three months after he disappeared, the solicitors had his things sent for and gave up the lease. If the Viscount came back tomorrow, ma'am, he'd find a young hearty just down from the Varsity sitting in his favourite seat. And much less cheery the place is for it, I'll tell you that.'

'Tell me, Flottie,' Mrs Hudson asked as we made our way homewards, 'have you noticed anything about the way people speak of the Viscount?'

'Yes, ma'am,' I replied promptly, for our meeting with the caretaker had set me thinking. 'It's as if everyone who's actually met him has a lot of respect for him, ma'am. And affection too. I mean, I know he's a rogue, ma'am, and I'm sure all those terrible things Mr de Lacey told us about him are true, but even he said the Viscount always showed daring. And Mr Fallowell spoke of him dominating the room . . .'

'Yes, Flottie. Somehow it's hard to imagine such a man being set upon in the street, isn't it? Not without him creating an uproar. And as for him being kidnapped, well, again you'd think such a resourceful figure would be a little ahead of his enemies, wouldn't you?'

'And I know it sounds stupid, ma'am, but I was thinking that once his father had whispered the secret to him, wouldn't he have to disappear?'

Mrs Hudson raised an eyebrow. 'Go on, Flottie,' she prompted.

'Well, I was wondering what I'd do if such a valuable piece of information came my way. I mean, he was desperate for money, ma'am, but he also knew that a great many other people were after the Lazarus Testament and they'd all be watching to see what he did next. I mean, he couldn't start searching for it without leading all his rivals to it, too, could he, ma'am?'

We had reached a little square where there were public benches beneath the trees and Mrs Hudson steered me towards one of them.

'I quite agree, Flotsam. He certainly couldn't.'

'But if he could somehow *vanish* so no one at all knew where he was . . . Well, ma'am, then he could go and find it in his own time, without giving anything away.'

Mrs Hudson clucked approvingly. 'I think that's quite right, Flotsam. The fox will always try to slip the hounds before returning to its den. And there's something else to consider, Flottie. Who is the rightful owner of this precious document? If Lord Beaumaris had traced it to a hiding place on someone else's land, for instance, then neither he nor his son had any legal claim on it. Now, I don't think ownership mattered very much to old Lord Beaumaris. He simply wanted to find it. But it would be the owner who reaped the financial rewards, and those mattered very much to his son.'

A pedlar had appeared in the little square selling brightly coloured sweets, but I was so excited I hardly noticed them. 'Of course, ma'am!' I exclaimed. 'He wouldn't want to hand over the prize to someone else, would he? He'd want it for himself. And if that meant stealing it . . . Well, he couldn't do that while Sir Percival and the police were dogging his footsteps. But if he could give them all the slip . . . Well, really, ma'am, he had no choice but to disappear!'

The trace of a smile played round the edge of Mrs Hudson's lips.

'Which is why it's a shame, Flottie, that the experts are so convinced the Viscount drowned some months ago. But even so, let us not be too downcast. As Mr de Lacey said, after so much time, one drowned body looks much like another. I've suggested to Scraggs that he looks up the man who handed in the Viscount's ring. I'd like to hear exactly how he came to find it. And there's one other question bothering me, Flotsam.'

'What's that, ma'am?'

'If it's true that the Viscount isn't dead, that he has simply engineered his own disappearance, we'll have to consider where he's been all this time.' She rose slowly to her feet. 'Yes, Flottie,' she concluded, 'I'd give a great deal to know how such a flamboyant and striking gentleman has managed to lie low for so long – and who has been helping him do it.'

Dark was already falling when we returned to Baker Street, turning the bright streets sombre and replacing the optimism of the daytime with the lingering menace of nightfall. The remainder of our day had been spent shopping for ribbons and buttons, and for other such dress-making necessities, but by the time we reached home we were glad of the warmth from the stove and the promise of a snug evening indoors. We immediately set about the task of lighting lamps and closing shutters, and had largely succeeded when we were surprised by the appearance of a liveried footman in the area outside our kitchen door. Sir Percival Grenville-Ffitch, he informed us rather coldly, as if reluctant to announce such a grand personage in so lowly a place, was waiting outside and was desirous of a short audience. He was also, we were told, eager to renew his acquaintance with a certain Mr Morley, if that were at all possible. His message delivered, the footman disappeared up the area steps and was replaced shortly afterwards by the gentleman himself, resplendent in evening dress, with a shiny top hat balanced upon his mane of white hair. However, it struck me at once that the rigours of the last weeks were beginning to take their toll on him. He looked a weary man as he sank into the seat Mrs Hudson offered him, and he accepted a glass of the Morley Madeira with a tired smile.

'I cannot thank you enough, Mrs Hudson,' he sighed. 'It is unforgivable to present myself like this and demand such a rare treat, especially when supplies are so scarce. But I arrived here early for an appointment with Mr Holmes and, to be frank with you, as I sat in my carriage, too enervated to stir myself, it occurred to me that I was probably in as much need of a glass of the Morley as any man in history. I trust you will find yourself able to forgive such impertinence. I assure you, the circumstances are most unusual.'

'I understand that these are trying times, sir,' Mrs Hudson acknowledged with a stately nod of her head. 'And if you would not consider it a sacrilege, perhaps I might recommend a slice of our Dundee cake to accompany the wine? There are very few problems that do not appear less daunting after a slice of Dundee cake . . .'

While I administered this restorative to him on a piece of our best china, Sir Percival took his first sips of the Madeira and closed his eyes for a moment in wordless appreciation.

'The very thing,' he told us contentedly when he opened them again. 'I will confess to you, Mrs Hudson, that my spirits had sunk rather low. No doubt Mr Holmes has told you something of our difficulties. I have had half the policemen in the south of England knocking on doors in Andover and Teddington to no avail, while the finest Biblical archaeologists in the country are still attempting to work out exactly what it is they're looking for. And all the time there's the very real danger that someone else might get their hands on the blasted document first. And if *that* happens, Mrs Hudson, I'm afraid not only my own reputation, but also Mr Holmes's, will be in absolute tatters. Half a century of loyal service, worthless, just like that.'

'Oh, I'm sure things aren't as bad as all that, sir,' Mrs Hudson reassured him, and I could see that his anguish had touched her. 'It may be that Mr Holmes is already closer to solving the problem than you think. In fact, that might be him now, sir. When you have finished here, I shall show you up.'

But it turned out that the new arrival was Dr Watson, returning from another of his fruitless expeditions.

'Three more Middletons,' he sighed as I helped him out of his coat, 'and not a thing to report. Any callers, at all?'

He received the news that Sir Percival Grenville-Ffitch was drinking Madeira in the kitchen with surprising equanimity.

'Is he, by Jove? That's a rather rum thing, Flotsam. But I suppose these great men must be humoured. I'd better go down and pay my respects, I suppose.'

The arrival of a second gentleman in her kitchen seemed to take Mrs Hudson no more by surprise than the arrival of the first. In no time at all she had supplied Dr Watson with Dundee cake and had settled him by the fire, although I noticed that when his eye fell on Sir Percival's glass she was quick to steer him away from the Madeira and towards a large glass of whisky-and-soda-water instead. Sir Percy, clearly concluding that such surprising domestic arrangements must be usual in the households of eminent detectives, accepted a second glass of the Morley with evident satisfaction.

'Any luck, sir?' he asked Dr Watson.

'None at all, I'm afraid. What's worse, a fellow I spoke to today said he'd once met a Colonel Middleton in the *American* army, which made me think that perhaps there are hundreds of colonels we haven't even considered. After all, why stop at America? There are British fighting men all over the world. Ours might have been a mercenary in Chile or in Mexico. He could even be French! No, I'm beginning to think this task is beyond us . . .'

'Courage, my friend!' None of us had heard Mr Holmes return, but there he was in the doorway of the kitchen, smiling at Dr Watson with that air of amused toleration we had all come to recognise. 'There remain other outlets for your energies, and for Sir Percival's too. No, thank you, Mrs Hudson, no Dundee cake for me.'

He came further into the room, waving Sir Percival and Dr Watson back into their seats.

'I hate to see you despair, Watson. So let me suggest a rather different way of looking at the Viscount's clue. Sir Percival, if you heard two costermongers planning to visit the Prince of Wales, what would you conclude?'

Sir Percival looked a little bewildered. 'The Prince of Wales? Well, they would hardly be visiting his Royal Highness, would they? I suppose they must be speaking of some public house . . .'

He tailed off, realising the implications of his reply. 'My word, Holmes!' Dr Watson exclaimed. 'The Prince Leopold! A tavern! Of course! But tell me, is there any such establishment? It is not a traditional name for an inn.'

'My thoughts precisely, Watson,' Mr Holmes declared, producing a slip of paper from his coat. 'But what if I told you that, not only does such a public house exist, but that its address places it near Warminster, only some thirty miles west of Andover?'

Sir Percival was on his feet by now. 'By George, Mr Holmes, I believe you are on to something. We must act at once . . .'

He paused, his mind apparently racing.

'My word! It doesn't stop there, does it? *Teddington* might not be a reference to the place in Surrey after all. There might be a Mr Teddington. Even a Mrs or a Miss Teddington. And a family of Andovers! Why, Dr Watson, if we concentrate our searches on Warminster for a spell, we may even be able to narrow down the number of Colonel Middletons for your inspection . . . !'

Mr Holmes's arrival, and this new suggestion of his, had transformed the atmosphere in the room. Gone was the melancholy that had prevailed earlier, dissipated completely by the surging energy of men intent on action. Plans for transport and accommodation were discussed while glasses were still being drained, and by the time the three gentlemen quitted the kitchen, Sir Percival seemed convinced that the recovery of the Lazarus Testament had become little more than a formality.

Mrs Hudson watched them go and then turned to me in the silence that followed.

'Mr Holmes is a very shrewd man, is he not, Flotsam?'

'You mean that idea about the public house, ma'am?' I considered this for a moment. 'I suppose that *might* be the answer . . .'

'Goodness me, Flotsam, it wasn't the country tavern I was referring to. I'd no more expect to find the Lazarus Testament in that Warminster pub than I'd expect to find the Archbishop of Canterbury in an opium den on the Isle of Dogs. But Dr Watson and Sir Percival are men of action, and men of action are only happy if they are rushing about a lot. Mr Holmes, having unleashed the straining hounds, will now have some peace and quiet in which to consider the real problem of the Viscount's clue.'

'But Mrs Hudson, ma'am, didn't you say that you already knew someone, some expert, who might be able to decode it?'

The housekeeper frowned slightly. 'I did indeed, young Flotsam, but it appears he is out of town. If he hasn't returned by tomorrow, I shall think of somebody else.'

And with that she turned and began to clear away the Dundee cake with perfect equanimity, as though there was no more important task in the whole of the world.

That night, when I came to close up the study, I was in no mood for imaginings. My mind was firmly on the matters in hand, and I barely looked into the street below. And if a tiny movement disturbed one patch of darkness, well, I wasn't going to imagine the shade of Lazarus watching from the gloom. Lots of gentlemen wore cloaks at dusk on chilly spring evenings. Some of them wore hoods too. If I'd seen anything at all, it was probably one of them, hurrying home to his fireside. It was absurd to imagine otherwise. I hurriedly dismissed it from my mind.

CHAPTER EIGHT

Miss Blenkinsop Remembers

The following day, a strange peace descended upon Baker Street. Dr Watson and Sir Percival were absent, the focus of their investigations having shifted to the area around Warminster, and, with the exception of one or two stray Colonel Middletons, we had few callers. Mr Holmes barely left his room, consuming a great deal of brown ale and the better part of a Chatsworth ham, while sending out for volumes which included, if I remember correctly, *A Beginner's Guide to Boxing Slang, Recollections of a Hare-Coursing Man, Forgotten Card Games of the Regency* and a book that arrived in discreet brown-paper covers entitled *The Rake's Lexicon.* Mrs Hudson meanwhile directed our daily household routines with her usual vigour, and took advantage of Dr Watson's absence to begin one or two larger cleaning projects of the sort generally impossible when both gentlemen were in residence.

Nevertheless, I was aware that, for all her serenity, she too was growing impatient, and that afternoon she took the step of waiting on Mr Rumbelow, who had been tasked with locating Pauncefoot, Viscount Wrexham's former valet. While she was gone, I set off, in rather sombre mood, to my next lesson in Bloomsbury Square. On arriving there, it was some consolation to find that Miss Peters refused to be downcast.

'Nonsense, Flottie! Of course Mrs Hudson will sort it all out. She always does. Rupert says the talk at his club is all about the Viscount having been kidnapped by Nihilists who want to convert him to their views. Are Nihilists like Methodists, Flottie? If so, it can't be much fun for him, with nothing to drink and having to listen to all those hymns. Now, do tell me, what news about that haunted house of yours?'

Miss Peters, who took a great deal of interest in the clothes of other young ladies, had been much taken by my description of Mrs Summersby, the young American lady, and frequently inquired after her, even though I had heard no new bulletins from Mr Rumbelow about the situation at Broomheath Hall. It was Miss Peters's belief that Mrs Summersby required rescuing. She found it impossible to believe that an attractive young lady with good taste in matters of feminine attire could possibly remain in such a remote spot except under protest. Her husband, Miss Peters felt certain, was a brute.

'I'm sure he must beat her, Flottie,' she insisted. 'Or perhaps she has a dreadful secret, a dark stain on her past which means she must hide herself away from the world like a nun.'

This last remark was overheard by Mr Spencer, who had joined us in the library.

'Really, Hetty, for a young lady who has surely never got much beyond the cover of a Gothic novel in her life, you have a remarkably well developed instinct for horror. Please ignore her, Miss Flotsam. I hope you are well?'

My lesson that week was largely geographical, concerning the lines of the tropics and the significance of the Equator, and all about latitude and longitude. With the help of a very big globe, Mr Spencer showed me how the world could be reduced to a simple grid where any position could be expressed in terms of degrees, minutes and seconds, and he explained some of the difficulties in calculating longitude. He had a rare ability to convey these matters in such a conversational way that it never really felt like a lesson. And throughout he would smile so charmingly with those brown eyes of his that I felt sure, on more than one occasion, that Miss Peters had forgotten to breathe.

With all the other excitements in my life, I had rather forgotten the mysterious message Reynolds had asked me to convey to Mrs Hudson; but I was reminded of it later that evening when, as I came to depart, he slipped a note into my palm.

'For Mrs Hudson,' he whispered solemnly, and sent me on my way with the most elegant of bows.

I found the housekeeper at home on my return, busily engaged in chopping carrots.

'Ah, Flotsam,' she greeted me, 'grab a knife and join me. There's all the vegetables still to prepare, I'm afraid. I'm only just back from Mr Rumbelow's, and am a little behind as a result.'

'Did he have any news, ma'am?' I asked hopefully, but my inquiry was met with a shake of the head.

'I'm afraid not, Flottie. He has been in contact with the executors of Lord Beaumaris's estate and finds that no record was kept of Pauncefoot's new position. The valet simply worked two weeks' notice and went. No forwarding address at all, apparently.'

I digested this as I removed my coat and hung it carefully behind the door.

'Well, we don't know for certain that he'd have been any help to us, do we, ma'am?'

She lopped the pointed end off a carrot with some force. 'That's true, Flottie. But I would most certainly have liked to speak to him all the same.'

When I gave her Reynolds's note, she read it with a smile and then tossed it back to me.

'Well, that's some good news at least. Have a look, Flottie. You might find it of interest . . .'

The note was written in the butler's rather beautiful handwriting and the message was succinct.

'Turkish Delight unplaced in Lincolnshire Handicap,' it read. '*Cook and I most grateful for your warning. James, alas, could not be dissuaded.*'

'So *that's* what he meant by Turkish Delight, ma'am! A horse! I thought he meant something completely different!' But instead of laughing along with me as I expected, Mrs Hudson merely turned her attention to her chopping board. 'Indeed, Flotsam,' she agreed, 'it would be an easy mistake to make, wouldn't it?' And with that solemn utterance, she once again engaged with the vegetables.

Shortly after the last carrot had been dealt with, but before Mrs Hudson and I had finished with the parsnips, Scraggs arrived.

I had scarcely seen him since the day he presented me with

the bluebells, and I blushed a little on his arrival, but he gave me an affectionate grin and proceeded to help himself to some stray slices of carrot.

'Blimey, Mrs H, you've had me chasing all over the place,' he announced cheerfully. 'I've been hanging around the docks like a dose of the . . . Well, like a dose of something nasty. This man Smith who found the ring . . .'

'Yes, Scraggs?' she asked, drying her hands carefully. 'You've found him?'

'Nah!' he replied, unabashed. 'And d'you know why not? I'll tell you, Mrs H. Cos he doesn't exist.'

The housekeeper returned the towel neatly to its place and then lowered herself into a seat by the kitchen table. Only a twitch of her eyebrow betrayed her interest.

'Go on, Scraggs. Tell me more.'

And so we heard the full story of Scraggs's search for the man who had claimed the discovery of Viscount Wrexham's ring. His name and address had appeared in the large pile of police papers deposited by Sir Percival on the table upstairs. But when Scraggs had visited the address, a cheap boarding house in Shadwell, he had found no record of a lodger called Smith.

'Of course my first thought was that he hadn't wanted to give the police his real name. Perhaps he'd taken it in hoping for a reward, then got cold feet or something. So I went and looked up the bobby on duty at the time. I know him a bit. He's all right. Gave me a good description, he did. Said the bloke was tall, with a big bushy beard, and bald as a coot. You don't forget a man like that, he said. Spoke almost like a gentleman, he thought. So I went back to the lodgings in Shadwell with that description, but still no luck. Nobody looking like that had been staying there, nor at any of the places nearby. I checked 'em all, and nothing. I'm telling you, Mrs H, this man Smith is a sham. I don't care who looks for him. They ain't going to find him.'

To my surprise, this news was greeted by Mrs Hudson with quiet satisfaction. Far from despairing as another door closed in our faces, she seemed to take unusual comfort in this further proof of the problem's impenetrability.

'No Smith, no Pauncefoot . . .' she murmured when Scraggs had left us. 'Really, Flotsam, this grows more interesting by the day.'

And no Colonel Middleton either, it seemed, for the noises reaching Baker Street from Warminster were growing less and less encouraging. The following day, the gentlemen were back, disgruntled and weary, and in lower spirits than I had ever seen them. The Prince Leopold had proved a serviceable enough inn but nothing about it had suggested any connection to the Lazarus Testament. Neither the overt inquiries of the police nor the covert observations of Dr Watson and Sir Percival had succeeded in establishing any path for further investigation. No Colonel Middletons were known in the area. Teddington meant nothing to the people there, and Andover was known to them only as the place where the vicar had found his wife. The word *tyrant* simply made them think of Napoleon.

So the expedition returned, disconsolate. Sir Percival, it was understood, was expecting an extremely uncomfortable reception in Whitehall. Inspector Mapperley was grown so morose he barely spoke. That night Mr Holmes took up his violin and filled the house with another haunting melody.

Mrs Hudson, hearing it, shuddered a little, and sent me out to call on Mr Trelawney, the caretaker at the Albany, to ask him for a description of Viscount Wrexham's valet. Who, it turned out, was quite a distinctive-looking individual, being both tall and bald, and given to sporting a bushy grey beard . . .

Next morning, spring returned to the streets of London, filling them with a brightness and a freshness and a promise of warmth that could not help but lift my spirits. I had already run an errand to Covent Garden and another to Regent Street, and Mrs Hudson and I were at work washing up the breakfast things, when we heard a tentative tapping on the kitchen door. There, at the foot of the area steps, stood a woman of about sixty years of age, tidily but discreetly clad in mourning. From the manner of her dress, she might have been the widow of a shopkeeper but there was a pleasant brightness in her smile that belied the melancholy of her clothing.

'Mrs Hudson?' she asked, stepping cautiously inside and holding out her hand. 'Mr Rumbelow sent me. My name is Elsie.'

Miss Elsie Blenkinsop turned out to be a woman of irrepressible good spirits, who, it seemed, had never allowed the reverses and the disappointments of her existence to alter her fundamental belief that life was as good as you made it, and that however bad things were, a person still had a lot to be thankful for. She perched on the edge of one of our kitchen chairs as lightly as a sparrow and filled the room with a warm breeze of good humour. And yet, her eyes were often full of tears, too, for the cause of her visit was a sad one. She lived in Brighton, she said, and she had seen Mrs Hudson's advertisement in a local newspaper. 'It came as a terrible shock to me,' she told us, 'because till then I'd no idea there was anything wrong with Bertie. I'd . . . I'd . . . Well, I'd been hoping that he might visit me . . .'

'You were in touch with Mr Swan, then?' Mrs Hudson asked gently.

'No . . . Well, not for many years . . . It cut me up something terrible it did, once upon a time, his going away . . . Still, you have to make the best of these things don't you? And I always knew he was doing what was right for him . . .'

Slowly and with great kindness, Mrs Hudson drew from her the full story.

Albert Swan and Elsie Blenkinsop, it emerged, had known each other as children. They were born in adjoining cottages in a village under the Downs and had been playmates from their earliest days. And they had been happy days, according to Miss Blenkinsop. The two of them were joined in their games by Bob, another child of the village, and the three of them were considered inseparable.

'Oh, what days we had!' Miss Blenkinsop sighed. 'Climbing trees and pinching apples, fishing in the stream with hooks we made from old nails . . .' She paused, as if to view again that sunny landscape. 'I thought life would always be like that,' she reflected.

But as the three children grew, they quickly found the world had other ideas. Elsie was found a place in service as scullery maid at the local manor, and Bob followed her there a few weeks later as boot boy. Albert, whose father had ambitions for him, was put to work as an errand boy with the local seed merchant.

'He was always the golden one, was Bertie,' Miss Blenkinsop remembered. 'Bob was cleverer, perhaps, and everyone knew he'd do well for himself, but it was Bertie I preferred. He was strong and ever so cheerful and you always felt there was nothing he couldn't do. He kissed me in the orchard one May Day and, you know, I thought I was the most blessed girl that ever lived.'

She laughed as she told us, but also dabbed at the corner of her eye with her handkerchief.

'Of course, it couldn't last. Bertie soon became a favourite with his boss and in the end got the chance to travel to South Africa. His boss knew someone there who could offer him a place. Oh, it was a great chance for him, no doubt about it, but I cried all night when he told me. He promised to write, and to be fair to him he kept his word for ten months or more. I still have the letters. But you know how these things go! We were only children really, and our lives were changing. First Bob left the village and went into service in a gentleman's house in London, and then a little later Bertie's letters stopped. I still wrote to him after that, but he'd moved lodgings and the letters all came back to me. A long time later I heard he'd done well for himself and married someone with money. And I was happy for him, I really was.'

Again she smiled at us, and Mrs Hudson reached out and touched her hand. 'And you, Miss Blenkinsop? You never married?'

'I've never had that happiness, Mrs Hudson. But I've had

a full and useful life, and a happy one. I count myself a lucky woman.'

'And recently you heard from Mr Swan again?'

Miss Blenkinsop nodded and gave a quick little smile. 'Last summer, it was. Out of the blue, and after all those years! Quite knocked me back, it did! It was a lovely letter though. He said he wanted to apologise for losing touch and said how he blamed himself for it, and asked me to forgive him. Oh, and there was other stuff too. He said he was wealthy and a widower. And he told me that he was going to write to Bob too, and that he hoped to travel home at some point to see us both.'

Mrs Hudson nodded. 'And that was the last you heard of him?'

'Oh, no, Mrs Hudson! He wrote regularly after that, telling me about his plans.' She blushed a little. 'Very friendly letters, they were, and he was most definite about coming home. He said he'd always dreamt of seeing France, and he had a mind to take it in on his way back. He wrote to me from there, too. Very grand notepaper it was, from one of those fancy French hotels. And then, the next thing I know, your advertisement . . . Mr Rumbelow tells me he was hit by a carriage, ma'am?'

A tear rolled down her cheek and I found myself slipping from my seat to place an arm around her. As gently as I could, I told her about Mr Swan's last moments and about his love for her. She cried in earnest then, and I think I joined her, and it was not until some time later, when tea and sponge cake had been served and Miss Blenkinsop's smile restored, that any of us were in a fit state to return to the subject. Even then

Mrs Hudson confined herself to a question about the other childhood friend, Bob, and where he could be found.

'Oh, Mrs Hudson!' Miss Blenkinsop exclaimed, and her lips trembled. 'Did I not tell you? Oh, I'm afraid my tale grows even sadder. You see, Bob is dead too.' I saw her tears well up again, but she went on bravely. 'Bertie wrote from the South of France and told me. He'd heard, while he was out there – quite by chance, you know – that Bob had found a new position. So he wrote to him at his new place, proposing to pay him a visit as soon as he got back to England. You can imagine his horror, ma'am, when he received a reply telling him that Bob had died of influenza within days of starting his new post. Bertie was terribly upset, I could tell. I think Bob must have seemed like a long-lost brother to him. He said in his letter to me that he planned to cut short his stay in France and to visit the grave at the earliest opportunity. But given what happened, I don't suppose he ever did . . .'

Miss Blenkinsop still looked tearful, but Mrs Hudson leant forward with another question and there was a note of urgency in her voice.

'Tell me,' she urged, 'was Bob's name really "Robert"? And if so, what were his other initials? Could it be that his surname began with "P"?'

'Why, yes, Mrs Hudson.' Our visitor looked surprised. 'It's true his name was Robert. And his initials – well, we used to joke about them, although just now the joke doesn't seem so funny. They were a bit sombre, you see. R.I.P, that's what they were. And I truly hope that him and Bertie both rest in peace.'

And then, while Mrs Hudson and I were exchanging looks of triumph, Miss Blenkinsop went further.

'Yes, R.I.P. That was his full name. They stood for Robert Inigo Pauncefoot.'

'So let's get this straight, Flottie,' Mrs Hudson began when we returned to the kitchen after helping Miss Blenkinsop onto a bus bound for Victoria. 'Viscount Wrexham disappeared last October. Not long afterwards, Robert Pauncefoot, his valet, takes up another appointment. We don't know where, but Albert Swan knew, for he wrote to him there.'

I nodded. 'What a shame he didn't mention where Pauncefoot had gone in his letters to Elsie, ma'am.'

'Indeed, Flotsam. Now, let's see . . . Mr Swan is wintering in France when he receives a reply to his letter telling him Pauncefoot is dead. And if that letter was accompanied by the man's watch, he would certainly not question the truth of such a claim. But who was that reply from?'

'I suppose it was from Pauncefoot's new employers, ma'am.'

'Except, Flotsam, that Pauncefoot wasn't dead, was he? Because someone closely matching his description was alive enough to hand in the Viscount's ring. And I'm sure Mr Swan caught sight of him that morning, on the way to the station. He was probably on his way to visit Pauncefoot's grave at the time, so it's hardly surprising he was a little rattled by it.'

'If only Mr Swan's things had not been sent back to South Africa, ma'am! If we could just see his papers . . .'

'Yes, Flotsam. They would make interesting reading. I'd particularly like to know who wrote the letter about

Pauncefoot's death. Did they really think he was dead? Or were they part of the deception? Unfortunately, all Mr Swan's things are likely to be in transit to the Cape for some time to come.'

'And in the meantime, ma'am, I just don't understand *why* anyone would make it up about Pauncefoot's death. I mean, we've worked out why Viscount Wrexham might want to disappear, but no one was looking for Pauncefoot. Why pretend *he's* dead?'

Mrs Hudson shook her head in mystification.

'These are shifting sands, Flottie. It seems certain that the Viscount is up to something, but are we any closer to working out what? Or, for that matter, where?'

These were questions I never answered because just then the second significant event of the day occurred: the arrival of Mr Rumbelow, red-faced and in some disarray, a telegram in his hand.

'Mrs Hudson!' he exclaimed. 'Thank goodness you are here! I wished to consult you . . . This telegram just in . . . From my friend Verity . . . Most urgent . . .'

Mrs Hudson and I put our heads together to peer at the scrap of paper placed before us. And what we saw was enough to assure us that, on this occasion at least, Mr Rumbelow's agitation was entirely justified.

GRAVES OPENED IN ALSTON STOP GHOST OF SUICIDE WALKING STOP ANCIENT CURSE UNLEASHED STOP FOR GODS SAKE SEND HELP

VERITY

CHAPTER NINE

The Viscount's Question Mark

The kettle was bubbling on the stove and the spring sunlight was etching pale diamonds on the kitchen floor by the time Mr Rumbelow was recovered sufficiently to complete his sentences. Alarmed at the urgent tone of his friend's message, and unable to find a hansom cab, he had come to us on foot, in a great hurry, and Mr Rumbelow was not a man built for speed over distance.

'You must excuse me,' he kept gasping. 'Such an intrusion . . . So melodramatic . . . And, oh dear me, such a warm day for the time of year, is it not?' And with that he would dab his forehead with his handkerchief, still perspiring slightly from his great haste.

But finally, refreshment having been administered and his breath restored, we were ready to discuss Mr Verity's extraordinary telegram.

'The thing is, Mrs Hudson,' our visitor remarked, 'I honestly don't know what to make of it. Either a genuine emergency has occurred, or else my friend Verity is simply going mad. Either way, I think it is imperative that his plea is not ignored. Would

Mr Holmes and Dr Watson be prepared to travel to Alston, do you think?'

Mrs Hudson looked grave. 'I fear, sir, that both are committed to this case of Sir Percival's.'

'Then I must plead with them, Mrs Hudson! At the very least, if Dr Watson could be spared for a few days . . . As a medical man, he would be ideally placed to decide if Verity's sanity should concern us. Do you think I should write to Mr Holmes at once, placing the situation before him and begging for his assistance?'

'As you see fit, sir,' Mrs Hudson allowed, 'but I understood that your interview with the young lady staying at Broomheath Hall had served to reassure you that Mr Verity's concerns were unfounded?'

The solicitor rubbed his nose where his spectacles pinched them.

'It had, Mrs Hudson, it had. Mrs Summersby seems a most composed and level-headed young lady. The idea of Mr Holmes travelling all the way to Alston on her account filled her with horror, didn't it, Flotsam?'

'Yes, sir. She didn't seem at all alarmed by the events Mr Verity described.'

'But now I fear I was wrong to ignore his entreaty. It is clear that he feels the want of my assistance most acutely. I would go myself without delay if my affairs here allowed it. But in the meantime, I shall definitely write to Mr Holmes . . .'

And with this intention still clearly at the forefront of his mind, Mr Rumbelow departed, leaving a very small frown on Mrs Hudson's brow.

'*Graves opened in Alston*,' she mused, quoting from the telegram. 'There's something there I can't quite put my finger on, Flottie . . .'

'It does seem very sinister, doesn't it, ma'am?'

'And I feel there is something I ought to be grasping, Flottie, something which persists in eluding me . . .'

And for the rest of the day Mrs Hudson spoke little, but went about her duties with a face clouded by thought.

After a day of such excitements, I might have expected the pace of life to revert to a more gentle rhythm, but the following morning brought Mr Rumbelow's letter. It happened that Mrs Hudson and I were both in the study, laying out the breakfast things, when Mr Holmes was opening his post. He did this seated in his armchair, smoking his first pipe of the day, and when we heard him utter a low exclamation, Mrs Hudson and I exchanged glances.

'Something interesting, Holmes?' Dr Watson asked, looking up from his newspaper.

'Very possibly, Watson, very possibly.' I saw he held a single sheet of paper in his hands and was scanning it intently. 'It may be nothing, of course, but I believe I should look into it. It might perhaps prove rewarding.'

Mrs Hudson coughed discreetly. 'Might it by any chance be from Mr Rumbelow, sir?' she asked.

Mr Holmes looked up at her.

'Not at all, Mrs Hudson. Mr Rumbelow's communication is this one here.' He fumbled amongst the other papers that had arrived that morning. 'His would seem to be rather less germane to the matter in hand. Nevertheless, we must do what we can to assist him. Watson,' he announced airily, 'you must go and see Mr Rumbelow at once. He has a friend called Verity who appears to be suffering from delusions, and a diagnosis is required. Somewhere out of town – his letter doesn't specify where, precisely, but it is unlikely to take you long, and I will be able to spare you for the next few days.'

'Really, Holmes!' Dr Watson protested. 'I'm sure there's any number of medical men Mr Rumbelow could approach, and I'm still up to my neck in this business of Sir Percival's. I like to believe I may still be of some help with it,' he finished rather stiffly.

'I'm sure you may, Watson, but we cannot let down Mr Rumbelow. And besides, this other note I have received will take me out of town for a spell. It concerns the Lazarus Testament and it represents something a bit more solid than the Viscount's peculiar note. Anonymous, I fear, and you know how I usually scorn such communications, but the writer appears well informed and we have little enough to go on just now. Yes, I shall make a point of investigating. Mrs Hudson, you should expect us both to be gone for a few days. I'm sure you will welcome a little peace and quiet in our absence.'

'And if I need to contact you, Holmes?' Watson asked.

'Then you must wait, my friend. I shall be travelling incognito as I have no wish to advertise my presence. You must rely on *me* to contact *you* when the time is right. And now, to work!'

And with this rallying call, he leant back in his armchair and, with evident satisfaction, drew deeply and languorously on his pipe.

It did not take long for Dr Watson to follow Mrs Hudson and myself down to the kitchen, his honest face betraying his distress.

'Sorry to intrude, Mrs Hudson,' he began, 'but I wondered if you happened to know exactly *where* it is that Holmes is sending me? A fellow would like to have some idea of his movements, after all. I sometimes think Holmes forgets that other people may have affairs of their own they need to attend to . . .'

He blushed a little at this uncharacteristic show of dissent, but Mrs Hudson merely nodded solemnly.

'Mr Rumbelow will explain everything, I'm sure, sir, but I believe his friend lives in a town called Alston in Cumberland. Rather a remote place, I understand.'

'Well, really! It's a bit much, isn't it, Mrs Hudson? I spend half my life on trains visiting retired colonels at Holmes's request, and now that there's finally some sort of clue to investigate, he keeps it to himself and dispatches me into the wilds without even bothering to ask where! And to rub it in, he won't give us a clue as to his own movements. Well, I tell you, Mrs Hudson, I've a good mind not to go!'

'Of course, sir,' Mrs Hudson assured him, 'no one could possibly blame you if you declined. And I'm sure Mr Rumbelow would not wish to put you out in any way. But it does appear that something a little peculiar *might* be going on, sir. And *Alston* . . . Tell me, Flotsam, have we heard that name in relation to something else? I feel sure someone has spoken of it.'

But however diligently I searched my memory, I could not find anything to support her in this belief. I was as certain as I could be that I had never heard mention of the place except by

Mr Rumbelow and Mrs Summersby. I felt sure that any other reference to it would have struck me most particularly.

Dr Watson, however, appeared to take some comfort from her words.

'Well, perhaps you're right, Mrs Hudson. If there really is some funny business to sort out, then it may not be a wasted journey. And I like to think that it's not beyond me to apply Holmes's methods in his absence. It would serve him right if I were to solve a mystery without him for once! I'd rather like to write up a case where Holmes is not the hero!'

Thus roused, Dr Watson's good humour returned and he resolved to pay a call on Mr Rumbelow without delay, while Mrs Hudson and I promised to attend to his packing. But first the housekeeper insisted that I should seat myself at the kitchen table and apply myself to a large and rather intimidating volume called *Osbert on Cartography*, certain passages of which had been chosen by Rupert Spencer as further reading after my latest lesson.

With so many mysteries in my head, I found it hard to concentrate. The examples of maps contained in the book seemed only to lead me into idle speculation about the location of the Lazarus Testament, and any mention of northern latitudes inevitably made me think of Mrs Summersby, surrounded by wild countryside, perhaps in danger from sinister forces. Mrs Hudson, however, kept me company, settling down beside me with her accounts, and soon an air of quiet application prevailed in the Baker Street kitchen.

With time, the subject of Mr Osbert's book began to grip me, and so engrossed had I become in my studies that a knock on the front door roused me with a start. Before I could recover myself, Mrs Hudson had pushed away her ledger and risen to her feet.

'I shall go, Flottie. You continue.' And it says something for Mr Osbert's command of his subject that before she returned I was once again buried in his book.

As a result, I didn't notice the change in Mrs Hudson at first, and it was only when I reached a natural break in my reading that I looked up and noticed the frown on her face.

'What is it, ma'am?' I asked, concerned. 'Who was that at the door?'

'It was a telegram, Flotsam. A reply to my letter about Viscount Wrexham's note. Here, take a look. As you see, I have my answer.'

> 1828 STOP MY FATHER WAS THERE STOP COLONEL ABOMINABLY TREATED STOP POPULAR OPINION ALL FOR HIM STOP BUT JUDGE AN INDECISIVE FOOL STOP INSISTED COLONEL TRIED AGAIN STOP VERDICT AGAINST HIM SECOND TIME STOP EXHAUSTED STOP TRAVESTY STOP

'But what does all this *mean*, ma'am? Is it about some old scandal? Does it mean the colonel was sent to prison?'

'Oh, no, Flotsam,' Mrs Hudson smiled. 'On the contrary, I think we can be sure he spent the rest of his days in considerable comfort.'

'And did he know where the Lazarus Testament was, ma'am?'

At this Mrs Hudson tutted.

'Really, Flotsam, surely you don't still subscribe to the theory that the Viscount was jotting down his father's *actual* words, do you? As Mr Holmes has pointed out repeatedly, he was far too clever for that. No, the Viscount was *translating* his father's words, putting them into a form that had particular significance for him. And that is why Mr Holmes has been at something of a disadvantage in this case.'

She favoured me with an affectionate pat on the head.

'You see, Flottie, Viscount Wrexham's particular areas of expertise, acquired over a lifetime of debauchery, loose living and rather looser morals, are not those shared by Mr Holmes. For myself, however, having worked below stairs in some very fine houses, dissipation holds few mysteries. As soon as I saw the Viscount's note, a good deal of its meaning was clear to me. But there was one part that confused me – the word *Colonel*. It didn't fit with the rest. This, however . . .' She indicated the telegram before us. 'This explains my confusion.'

I looked at her in astonishment. 'Does that mean you know what the Viscount's note means, ma'am?'

'Not at all, Flotsam. But I do at least know what message the dying Lord Beaumaris whispered to his son. Six numbers, Flotsam . . . Six numbers . . . How can six numbers be translated into a particular place?'

'Six numbers, ma'am?' I looked down at the book still open under my nose. Was *that* it? With my newfound knowledge fresh before me, the answer was simple. 'Do you mean degrees, minutes and seconds, ma'am?'

Mrs Hudson had followed my gaze, and as she looked up from the book she was beaming at me.

'Flotsam, what a wonder you are! Latitude and longitude! *That's* the answer. *That* was what Lord Beaumaris whispered to his son. He told him the precise co-ordinates of the object he was seeking!'

'But *where*, ma'am? Where was the Viscount told to look? Where will we find it?'

'You know, Flotsam,' Mrs Hudson replied, her satisfaction undimmed, 'I have absolutely no idea. But we can soon find out. Mr Spencer has a set of those government maps.'

She pulled pencil and paper from the table drawer and began to write.

'Quickly, Flottie, take these numbers to Bloomsbury Square and ask him if he can discover the place they refer to. I have one or two things I need to do, but I will follow you as soon as I can. And, Flotsam . . .'

'Yes, ma'am?'

She put her arm around my shoulder and gave me a squeeze. 'We make progress, do we not?'

The burst of bright weather had come to an end, and my route to Bloomsbury Square lay through streets made bleak by a cold and dreary afternoon. The skies seemed to reflect the grey of the pavements, and carriages creaked over the cobblestones as though the damp had crept into their joints and rendered every movement painful. But I moved light-footed through the mud, a sense of discovery buoying my spirits and Mrs Hudson's strange set of numbers running through my brain. *Fifty four, fifty one, sixteen. Two, twenty eight, twenty five* . . . What did they mean? What place were they pointing to? Soon we would know! Soon I would be the first person to hear the answer to Viscount Wrexham's riddle . . .

I arrived at the great house in Bloomsbury Square and was admitted by Reynolds, who appeared a little startled by the urgency of my knocking.

'Quickly!' I blurted out rather rudely, as soon as the door was open. 'I have a message from Mrs Hudson for Mr Spencer. It's terribly important! Is he at home?'

Reynolds reassured me with a stately nod of his head. 'Mr Spencer is in the library, miss. His lordship is also at home, having returned this morning from an extended visit to the country.'

'The Irascible Earl!' I quailed slightly. 'Oh, dear! Is he in the library too?'

'I believe his lordship is upstairs, miss. You should therefore be quite safe in the library for a short while.'

I admit I was relieved. Everybody, even Miss Peters, was a little intimidated by the Earl of Brabham, and his presence inevitably reduced me to a trembling silence. But instead I was welcomed into the library by Mr Spencer, who greeted me with a friendly grin.

'Hello, Flotsam,' he smiled, laying his book to one side and advancing to meet me. 'Hetty is out, I'm afraid, if it was her you were hoping to see. I believe she's shopping for bonnets, and therefore cannot be expected back for a very long time. In her absence, should I ring for tea?'

But I waved this offer aside while I tried to explain as coherently as I could that it was him I had come to see, and that we urgently required his assistance. As I was still a little out of breath, perhaps I was not very clear, for when I had finished he still looked a little mystified.

'So these numbers, you say, represent the resting place of the Lazarus Testament?'

'Yes, sir. At least that's what Mrs Hudson thinks.'

'And who are we to question that, eh, Flotsam? Come, let us place her note here while I look for the appropriate maps . . .'

While Mr Spencer browsed the shelves, Mrs Hudson's scrap of paper was propped on a rather grand lectern, from where the mysterious numbers looked out at me, their secret still obscure.

54 51 16

02 28 25

'Right, here we go!' Mr Spencer heaved a huge volume onto the table in front of me. 'It's a map of the extreme north of England. A very special one, drawn up as part of a government survey. It comes in ten parts, but from a first glance at the numbers, I think this is the one we want. So, where shall we start . . . ?'

He peered at the numbers again.

'That first line, they should be the northings, so we'll take them first. Let me see . . . Fifty four degrees puts us in the north of England . . . Fifty one minutes . . . Sixteen seconds . . . See, Flotsam, we end up on a line that runs from the Solway Firth to the River Wear.'

He paused and examined the next three numbers.

'It isn't explicit from Mrs Hudson's note, but I think we can assume these next numbers must be west of the meridian.

Otherwise they'd be landing us somewhere in the North Sea. So, if we find the line of two degrees west . . .'

He turned the great heavy leaves until he found the page he was looking for.

'Here we are, Flotsam. Now we move across to twenty eight minutes . . . and then twenty five seconds . . . And now we simply find where the two lines cross. Here. This is the place. According to Mrs Hudson, this is where we should be looking for the Lazarus Testament . . .'

I peered at the point where his finger had come to rest. From the dark brown colours it seemed to be a place of hills and mountains.

'Just here, Flotsam. See? A place called Broomheath Hall, near Alston in Cumberland. Does that mean anything to you? It looks a fairly remote sort of place to me . . .'

But I didn't reply. I simply wasn't able to. My mind was racing. Broomheath Hall! Broomheath Hall! I thought of Mrs Summersby and of the strange goings on that were terrifying Mr Verity . . . And now, the Lazarus Testament! There, in exactly that place! *What did it all mean*, I asked myself. *What did it mean*?

'Mrs Hudson, sir.'

Reynolds's cool tones shook me from my confusion, and there in the doorway stood the housekeeper herself, steady and calm and reassuringly ordinary.

'Your timing is perfect, Mrs Hudson,' Mr Spencer greeted her. 'Come and see. We have located your treasure!'

'And ma'am,' I gasped, still wide-eyed with bewilderment, 'you'll never, ever guess where!'

'Won't I, Flotsam?' she smiled, approaching the atlas. 'I think you may be wrong about that. You see, on my way here, just as I was crossing Bedford Square to be precise, the thing that has been bothering me for so long suddenly became clear.'

'And what was that, Mrs Hudson?' Mr Spencer asked, bemused.

'Something I should have seen a good deal sooner, sir. Flottie, do you remember when we visited Constable Dawson and asked him about Mr Swan's destination on the day of his death? He made a stab at recalling where Mr Swan's train ticket was made out for. *Alnwick*, he thought, or perhaps *North Allerton*. And he was so nearly right! That is why all this talk of Alston has been fretting me. Broomheath Hall, near Alston . . .' she continued calmly, following Mr Spencer's finger to the crucial point on the map, 'Yes, that makes sense. And so, Flottie, the two lines meet! Alston is where Lord Beaumaris was heading, and it's where Mr Swan was heading, too. And do you know, I find myself quite curious to pay the place a little visit myself . . .'

I must still have been reeling from the shock and surprise, for I passed the next ten minutes or so in something of a daze while Mrs Hudson explained to Rupert Spencer about the reports of peculiar events near Broomheath Hall. 'Of course, sir, there was no reason then to connect any of those things with the Lazarus Testament. But now there's every reason, and I'd very much like to hear a little more about Mr Verity's strange happenings.' Mr Spencer rubbed his chin pensively.

'But there is still one thing you haven't explained to me, Mrs Hudson. How on earth did you manage to arrive at these co-ordinates? I can't imagine what mechanism you used to tease them out of Viscount Wrexham's note.'

Mrs Hudson looked at him. 'Really, sir, you surprise me. A young gentleman like yourself. Of course, the word *Colonel* was confusing, but luckily I knew someone who could help me with that.'

'One of those cipher experts, Mrs Hudson?'

'Oh, no, sir. I'm not sure they could have helped. They seem rather to have missed the point. No, I turned to someone much closer to home. I asked your uncle.'

'My *uncle*?' I had never seen Mr Spencer more astonished. 'You mean, *my* uncle? The one upstairs? Lord Brabham? Him?'

'Of course, sir. And here he is now. You can ask him about it yourself.'

And sure enough, the door had opened to admit Rupert's uncle, the Irascible Earl. He was a short, impeccably dressed figure but his brow was marked by a deep frown that gave him an unmistakeably ferocious air, made worse by his habit of stroking his clipped moustache in a distinctly threatening manner.

'Eh? Rupert?' he grunted. 'What's going on? Reynolds said there were callers. At this hour? Pah! Blasted tea scavengers! Where are they skulking? Let's get rid of 'em so I can have a scotch. Ah, Mrs Hudson!'

To my surprise, on discovering his guest's identity the Earl's spirits seemed to revive.

'Didn't know it was you, Mrs Hudson. You won't mind me drinking some whisky. Always were a sensible woman. Reynolds! Bring the tray. Well, Rupert, don't just stand there like a blasted stuffed trout! Introduce me to this young lady.'

'This is Miss Flotsam, Uncle,' Mr Spencer explained. 'You've met her before.'

'Have I? Really?' He studied me through his eyeglass for a moment. 'Ah, yes. I remember. Bright girl. Doesn't chatter. How d'you do?'

Then, without paying me any further attention, he turned back to Mrs Hudson.

'Got your note this morning,' he told her. 'Been away. Sent you a telegram.'

'Indeed, sir. And very helpful it was, too. Once you'd jogged my memory, I remember that I'd heard of the incident before. Old Lord Dunwich complained about it well into his dotage. Very cross, he was.'

Mr Spencer coughed politely. 'Uncle, Mrs Hudson has been telling us that you've helped to decode a message which has defied the greatest cipher experts in the country.'

'Eh? What's that? Code? Cipher? Nonsense, my boy! You're babbling like an imbecile. Yes, that's right, Reynolds, just leave it there, and pour one out for me. Then line up a spare beside it, there's a good fellow.'

'Perhaps if you showed your uncle this, sir, he will understand . . .'

I watched Mrs Hudson pass Mr Spencer a copy of the Viscount's original message, which he in turn passed to the Earl.

Andover Teddington Prince Leopold

Tyrant ? Colonel Middleton

'Eh? What's this? Ah, I see! Some chap's been jotting down the names of old Derby winners. Let's see. *Andover* won it in 1854. I was at Epsom for that one. Kissed a damn pretty girl near the winning post. And *Teddington* won two or three years earlier. '51, it must have been. I remember I had a bit on the runner-up. The others were a bit before my time, of course. *Prince Leopold* is easy though. 1816, the year after Waterloo. How am I doing so far, Mrs Hudson?'

'Full marks so far, sir.'

The Earl's moustache trembled slightly in what might have been a smile and he returned to the list in front of him.

'Now, *Tyrant* goes right back. 1801, perhaps? No, must have been '02. Charles Bunbury's filly won in '01. And *Middleton* won it in '25. But the other one's a load of nonsense. Ludicrous! The chap who made this list must be an idiot, Rupert! *The Colonel* might have won the St Leger but he never won the Derby. I was making that clear to Mrs Hudson only this morning!'

Sensing that Mr Spencer was still confused, Mrs Hudson intervened.

'Perhaps I should explain, sir. You see, one doesn't spend as many years in servants' halls as I have without becoming familiar with the names of Derby winners, even very old ones. For a week or so every June the talk is of little else. So as soon as I saw the Viscount's note, I recognised five of the names. But I was also fairly sure no horse called *The Colonel* had ever won the race. And the Viscount clearly had his doubts too, which is why he preceded it with a question mark.'

Mr Spencer looked at her. 'Bear with me a moment, Mrs Hudson. You are telling us that the Viscount was using the names of *racehorses* to represent the numbers his father whispered to him?'

'Of course, sir. It must have seemed more discreet than writing down the figures, and probably easier for him to remember. But when he came to one of the numbers, his memory failed him. And for a good reason. You see, in 1828 the first running of the Derby ended in a dead-heat.'

'Ah! And that confused him?'

'Yes, sir. In the pressure of the moment he could recall the horses involved in the close finish – but he couldn't remember which one ended up the winner. So all I had to do, sir, was to write to your uncle and ask if he could recall which year a horse called *The Colonel* had come close to winning the Derby. His reply this morning supplied the year – and filled in the one missing number.'

'Terrible scandal,' the Earl added. 'My father always swore *The Colonel* won by a short head that afternoon, but the judge's nerve failed him and he called a dead-heat. Of course, under the rules of the race, a dead-heat meant a run-off the same afternoon, and *The Colonel* was beaten that time. My father said he lost a fortune because of it. Old Lord Dunwich too, by the sound of it.'

'And so, Flotsam . . .' Mr Spencer grinned. 'The code is broken.'

'Yes, sir, and now . . . Well, Mrs Hudson, ma'am, should

we not be telling Mr Holmes about all this? Quickly, before he leaves London?'

But Mrs Hudson waved her hand in a way that suggested my concern for the great detective was unnecessary.

'Mr Holmes set off this afternoon, Flottie. Before he went he scribbled a hasty message to Dr Watson on that blackboard of his. I saw it when I went up to clean the hearth, and took the liberty of jotting it down . . .'

Mrs Hudson fished another piece of paper from the depths of her bag. Beneath the Viscount's familiar note, Mr Holmes had added another – crisp and urgent, if somewhat cryptic.

Horses, Watson! Horses!
Dates in stud book
Follow where they lead you

I had just opened my mouth to respond to this curious message when the doors of the library were flung open and a whirlwind of pink silk flounced into the room.

'You beasts!' Miss Peters exclaimed indignantly. 'Reynolds says you've solved the mystery without me! How could you? I was only gone for a few minutes, just to pick up a few essentials, and this is what happens!' She paused in her advance to make a hasty adjustment to her bonnet, then returned to the offensive. 'You know, it will jolly well serve you all right if I solve some baffling mystery for myself one of these days. And when I do, you can be quite sure that I shall take all the credit for myself! So there!'

And with that she came to a halt and smiled radiantly at each of us in turn, the sky once again unclouded.

'Now, tell me, Rupert, don't you think this bonnet is simply the most divine creation ever? I think it's *so* beautiful that I may just have to go back and try on the one they had in blue . . .'

CHAPTER TEN

Alston

On the high moors that rise bleak and magnificent across England's northern border, spring comes late. Travellers from the south who leave behind them budding leaves and nascent blossom quickly put aside all thoughts of milder days as their train edges northwards and shows them with every new mile the barer branches, desolate fields and, finally, the empty majesty of the moors.

Amid the great sweep of these uplands lies Alston, a town shaped by rain and rock, and by the wind that sweeps from the north across the fells; an outpost of warmth and human welcome in the wilderness. My first sight of it came from the window of a third class railway carriage where Mrs Hudson and I, with blankets tucked around our legs, were the only passengers. Ours was the last train of the day and Alston, at the end of its own branch line, the final stop. A local farmer and his wife had left the train two stops before, and after that we'd been alone.

As we pulled into the little station, we found a town still in the grip of winter. Even in the fading light I could make out the church tower stark against the moors and snow still lying on the high fells beyond. My entire life had been lived in or near the streets of London. Here, the unforgiving emptiness of the landscape made me gasp. In all my life, I had never seen anything more beautiful.

'Alston!' the station master cried from one end of the platform. 'Last stop! Last stop!' and Mrs Hudson placed a reassuring hand on my knee.

'Come, Flotsam,' she smiled. 'We are finally here. Let us hope the porter has lingered long enough to help us with our bags. Otherwise we will face a rather strenuous walk to the inn.'

But to our great delight, someone was waiting for us at the station. Dr Watson, who had made the journey three days earlier, had taken the trouble to meet us in person and had borrowed Mr Verity's pony and trap for the purpose.

'Ah, Mrs Hudson! Flotsam! How good to see you! Pleased you could get here so soon!' he exclaimed with genuine warmth, and ushered us to his vehicle while a solitary porter hurried to see to our bags. 'There are rooms reserved for you at the Angel,' he reassured us, 'which Verity tells me is a very passable inn. I will take you there directly so you can rest after your journey. Mrs Garth, the landlady, is sending someone for your luggage. And with your permission I shall call first thing tomorrow and bring you back with me to Verity's house. I have explained to him that Holmes would not want me toiling here without assistance, and he is very much looking forward to meeting you. It seems the Duke of Buccleuch once mentioned your name to him in connection with the affair at Crailing Castle. As for me, it's jolly good to see two familiar faces. There's something about this place when the mist comes down in the evenings. You can almost feel . . .'

He broke off, and I thought his face looked troubled.

'No, it's not the time to be going into it just now. Much better to let Verity tell you the full tale tomorrow. But to be honest, Mrs H, to be perfectly honest, it would seem things up here have taken a nasty turn.'

Alston's railway station sits a short drive from the village, on the floor of the valley where a little river tumbles northwards, seeking passage through the hills. The town itself is built higher up and its main street climbs steeply towards the top of the fell. About halfway up, the street broadens into a pretty cobbled marketplace flanked by handsome buildings, and it was here we found the Angel Inn, where Dr Watson passed us into the care of Mrs Garth.

Our hostess seemed to take to Mrs Hudson at once and did her utmost to make us comfortable. We were shown to two small rooms at the back of the house and pressed to join her in the kitchen of the inn for our evening meal. Here she evinced a certain curiosity about our visit and Mrs Hudson, anxious not to attract attention to the Lazarus affair, told her a little uncomfortably that we had come to Alston to see her second cousin, a footman on the other side of Allendale, who was hoping to join us shortly. In the meantime, she was hoping for word of her cousin's friend, a man called Robert Pauncefoot, who Mrs Hudson thought might once have been in service somewhere nearby.

'Are you familiar with that name at all, Mrs Garth?' she inquired.

'Pauncefoot?' She shook her head. 'I'm afraid not, Mrs Hudson. It doesn't sound like a local name. But we get a lot of visitors here in the summer months, and some of the inns take on extra helpers. I daresay he might have passed through here one summer.'

'He's a gentleman of striking appearance, so I'm sure you would remember him, Mrs Garth. How did Mr Trelawney describe him, Flotsam?'

'Mr Pauncefoot is a very tall man, ma'am, with a bald head and a very bushy beard.'

'Who has been known to call himself Smith,' Mrs Hudson added, without explaining why.

But Mrs Garth simply shook her head.

'There's plenty of farmers in town on market day who are thinning a bit on top, of course, but I can't say as any of them has beards, Mrs Hudson. Not so as you'd notice, at any rate.'

'We've heard Broomheath Hall is a very distinguished property,' Mrs Hudson went on, changing the subject. 'I imagine you know it well. The staff must be mainly local people?'

Again Mrs Garth shook her head, but this time I thought she looked a little wary.

'That used to be the case, when the old squire was still here. But now that the place is rented out things aren't the same. It was empty for months, and then the last tenant went mad and blew his brains out. A Mr Baldwick, it was. A southerner,' she concluded, as though that explained everything. 'He didn't keep any staff at all, I'm sorry to say, just a woman from one of the farms who would go in once a week and do some cleaning.'

'But there are new tenants now, are there not? We heard the

place had been taken by an American couple.'

'American, are they? I really wouldn't know, Mrs Hudson. They haven't been seen in town since they arrived. As for their staff, the butler came from London and never shows his face down here at the Angel. Too superior, I suppose. And the cook and the maid are both girls from the outlying farms who sleep out, so nowadays we don't hear much about the Hall.'

Mrs Hudson's voice suddenly became jocular. 'And what about the ghosts, Mrs Garth? On the train here we were told all sorts of stories about ghosts!'

But Mrs Garth did not laugh. She looked at us both a little cautiously. 'That's just tales, Mrs Hudson. Stupid folk with a pot of ale too many inside 'em.'

She hesitated, then lowered her voice. 'I don't hold with that sort of talk, you see. This village needs its visitors, and it does the place no good to put them off with wild tales. But there's certain folk who aren't above snaring a hare or two in the grounds of the Hall who talk a sight too freely. Lanterns in the night, they say, and fresh graves dug in the woods between one night and the next. There's some who say it's the ghost of Mr Baldwick, him what killed himself, trying to find himself a peaceful place to rest. But I don't hold with any of that. Not when Mr Verity says the new tenant is one of them *archaeologists*. Stands to reason he'd be digging things up all the time.'

We learnt little more from her that night about events at Broomheath Hall, but later, as I lay in my little bed and listened to the incredible silence of the moors, it was not as hard as it should have been to imagine a lantern waving in a spectral hand and a lost soul roaming the heath in search of sanctuary.

* * *

Mrs Hudson and I were up promptly the next morning, and long before Dr Watson called for us we had explored the town from one end to the other. It proved to be a thriving and friendly place with a lively market, a fine church and a teashop that displayed a very promising array of cakes. Broomheath Hall, we learnt, was a mile or so out of the town, not far from the line of the railway that had brought us to Alston. Of those we spoke to, only the verger had met the Summersbys in person, when he called on them at Broomheath in the hope of raising funds for font repairs. No one seemed to have heard the name Pauncefoot and, as we expected, an inspection of the churchyard showed no grave marked with any such name. It was when we came to a row of cottages at the foot of the town that Mrs Hudson paused and pointed at something that clearly surprised her. Above the door of the end cottage was a neat little sign which read in small letters:

The Anthony Baldwick Archive

If Locked, Key Available From Rectory

It was hard to know what to make of such a thing and, although my companion felt it worth her while to cross the road and peer through the windows, she restricted her comments to one eloquently raised eyebrow.

Our interview with Mr Verity followed later that morning. Dr Watson collected us from the Angel and escorted us to the smart Georgian house where the solicitor resided. There we finally met the individual who had first brought the town of Alston to our attention, and he received us in his elegant drawing room with great warmth. At first, I confess, I found it difficult to reconcile the figure before me with the panic-stricken telegram Mr Rumbelow had shown us in Baker Street. Mr Verity appeared on the surface to be every bit as phlegmatic as Mr Rumbelow had suggested, a short, rather fleshy man with fine whiskers and eyes that bulged slightly when he spoke. He greeted us very cordially and said a few words about the Duke of Buccleuch. Then, having first made sure that both Mrs Hudson and I were comfortably seated, he planted himself firmly on the hearthrug and began to tell us the full story behind his urgent telegram.

'I should start, Mrs Hudson, by telling you a little more about Broomheath Hall and the legends associated with it. I beg you to bear with me, for although these tales might strike you as fanciful, I assure you that they are not without relevance to recent events. Broomheath, you see, although a fine dwelling, is not without stains upon its history. Indeed this whole area, until comparatively recent times, has been a lawless place, a region of feuding families and murderous cattle raids, of bloodshed and killings and kidnaps.

'In the middle of the last century,' Mr Verity continued, 'Broomheath Hall fell into the hands of a well-bred rogue who established a certain bloody peace in Alston and the surrounding fells. Squire Venterton was a handsome fellow, and in his middle years by the time he had established his fortune. Having achieved both wealth and security, he decided it was time to find himself a wife. And he didn't settle upon some local girl as was the custom, but found his bride in London on one of his rare visits there. Some say the squire won her at a game of cards. Whatever the truth, Lady Sylvia was never happy in these rougher climes of ours. They say her beauty and her youth faded quickly, and as time passed and her misery grew, she became subject to uncontrollable fits of weeping and explosions of great anger.'

Mr Verity cleared his throat, apparently uneasy about the direction his tale was taking.

'It is said in the end she descended into madness, Mrs Hudson, confined to her rooms at Broomheath, tormented by her solitude and by her husband's affairs. For Squire Venterton was still a good-looking man, and the acquisition of a bride in no way curtailed the wanton indulgence of his manly appetites. Furthermore, he made no attempt to hide his conquests, and with his wife confined to her sick quarters he would – quite blatantly – entertain his new paramours at Broomheath. It is said that on one such night, when the squire lay in bed with the daughter of a local farmer, Lady Sylvia burst into his bedchamber with a gleaming dagger in her hand, a weapon which she used, not to exact revenge upon her husband or his lover, but to end her own sorry existence. In short, she cut her wrists, there, in the bedchamber, and she died raving, vowing that no grave would hold her until the squire shared it with her, swearing that she would never rest until she had returned from the grave and dragged her husband with her back to hell.'

A slight warmth had coloured the solicitor's cheeks during parts of this story, but Mrs Hudson remained commendably unembarrassed.

'Do please go on, sir,' she prompted.

'Well, the story does not end there, I'm afraid, Mrs Hudson.

Lady Sylvia was laid to rest in the grounds of the chapel, now a ruin, which stands on the fells above Broomheath Hall. But it's said that her ravings proved prophetic, because seven nights after her death her grave was discovered opened and empty, apparently desecrated by some unknown hand. It was a great scandal, and the squire's men rode out at once to seek the culprit, certain the outrage must have been perpetrated by one of his enemies.

But that same night Squire Venterton thought he heard a voice calling him from below his window. He slipped from the bed he was sharing with a serving girl, telling her that he would be gone for no longer than a few moments. But the squire was never seen again. Only his blood-stained boots were found, out on the moors, not far from the old chapel. And to the amazement of everyone who saw it, Lady Sylvia's grave, which had been open and empty the previous day, was now seen to be filled in again, as though it had never been disturbed.'

Mr Verity paused to clear his throat again, apparently torn between enjoyment of the ancient tale and embarrassment at its supernatural nature.

'It is still widely believed in these parts, Mrs Hudson, that were the grave ever to be opened again, the remains of Squire Venterton would be found there, clasped in the arms of his wife. And a rumour has persisted to this day that no suicide will ever be able to sleep easily on Broomheath Moor. Like Lady Sylvia, they must return and claim a companion to lie with them for eternity.'

'Sinister stuff, eh, Mrs H?' Dr Watson, who had listened to this tale from a position very close to the sherry decanter, clearly felt the need to raise our spirits. 'But a long time ago, wasn't it, Verity? I like these old tales, but I don't think we should take them too seriously, eh?'

'And yet, sir,' Mrs Hudson replied evenly, 'Mr Verity assured us before he began that he is telling us this story for a reason.'

'Yes, indeed, Mrs Hudson,' the solicitor confirmed. 'Perhaps, though, I should now jump to more recent times, to my first dealings with Mr Anthony Baldwick, until recently the tenant of Broomheath Hall. You see, the current owner of Broomheath is a well-to-do farmer who, upon reaching the age of seventy, decided to follow both his sons to Canada, leaving responsibility for the hall – for its upkeep and for finding tenants – in my hands. And I should tell you, Broomheath is not an easy property to let. Its remote location is against it, and I daresay the tales told about it do not help its cause. When I first heard from Mr Baldwick, the property had been without a tenant for more than a year.

'I was at first overjoyed to receive Mr Baldwick's letter, for he told me that he was an archaeologist looking for a property within easy reach of the Wall and that a solitary location, where he could work undisturbed, was essential. We get many gentlemen of archaeological leanings here, Mrs Hudson, with the Wall being so close and because of the Roman Camp just across the river. They are quite frequently a little eccentric. But Mr Baldwick was different.'

As Mr Verity continued his tale, I found my eyes wandering from his honest face to the window beyond, and to the dark flanks of the moor that seemed to defy all the certainties of his neat Georgian drawing room. A dark cloud was passing, and the wind was whipping over the heather. To seek out such a place to hide, to reject all the comforts of cheerful company . . . It was hard not to wonder what could have driven Mr Anthony Baldwick to seek refuge in so bleak a place.

It had been the strange behaviour of the new tenant which had first begun to unsettle Mr Verity.

'He purported to be a gentleman, Mrs Hudson, but his bearing and manners were most erratic. He struck me as anxious for approval, very eager to please a person to his face, but behind a man's back he was a different person altogether. And there were other things, too. His luggage, for instance. He had brought with him to Alston a number of large crates and a profusion of smaller boxes which he said contained his papers, yet he appeared to have no other personal effects at all. On his first day here he purchased tweeds and an old-fashioned cape and from that day on was never seen to wear anything else. He required no staff. Indeed it seemed he lived on little more than bread and cheese.'

Mr Verity, who showed every sign of keeping a very good table, shook his head sadly before going on.

'He kept no company and received no visitors. Indeed I think I was his only confidant, and I found the role a taxing one. He would call on me frequently in the evenings and would talk at great length about his reputation as an archaeologist, about how one day he would be famous. He told me of the many pamphlets he had published and urged copies of them upon me. And then at other times he would appear pale and distraught, and would ask me my views about sin and punishment, and about the inevitability of God's vengeance on those who had transgressed. Well, of course, that isn't really my subject and I urged him to speak to the rector, but I don't believe he ever did.

'It was when word of Mr Baldwick's irrational behaviour became more widespread that I began to question whether he was a fit and proper tenant. First there were tales of him lurking in the ruined chapel at dusk, and then came reports of him digging: in the grounds of the Hall, out on the moors, even in the ruins of cottages on the fells, well beyond Alston. Like a ghoul, the local poachers said, all shrouded in that cape of his. Or like some sort of devilish beast, pawing at the ground with his shovel.

'Well, I made some further inquiries,' Mr Verity went on, 'and found that everything he'd told me about himself seemed to be lies or exaggeration. His father had made his money through railway speculation and had died when Baldwick was a child. The son had spent his whole life in an obsessive pursuit of fame. A pamphlet about folk tales that he published early in his career had proved popular, and for the rest of his life he endeavoured to repeat this triumph, inundating the public with an apparently endless torrent of pamphlets and papers, none of which ever achieved any success whatsoever. Far from being pre-eminent in the field, as he claimed, I discovered he had only turned his attention to archaeology a couple of years before arriving in Alston.'

Mr Verity swallowed nervously as he recalled the situation he had found himself in.

'Perhaps what I did next was injudicious. But I confess I felt angry and deceived. It appeared his references were forgeries and his word without value. So I rode out to Broomheath to confront him. It was a stormy day and there was thunder in the air when I arrived. I will never forget that interview, Mrs Hudson. I found him pale, shrunken and shivering, whining and raging in turns. He wept, and spoke of demons pursuing him and a messenger from God sent to drive him to the grave. He claimed he was a new Jonah, attempting to hide from his creator's wrath. He raved that eternal torment awaited him and that even if he lived forever he could not escape the clutches of hell, as hell would find him out in life *or* death. Well, of course, I recognised the ramblings of a lunatic and I tried to calm him, but so aberrant was his behaviour, so desperate his manner, that I decided to ride for medical assistance. And of course I was too late. That night, before I returned, he had died by his own hand.'

It was clear that Mr Verity was deeply affected by the anguish of that evening; clear too that the memory of it still filled him with horror. Perhaps the discovery that the dead man had named him as the executor of his will had made his guilt even worse, for he had performed his legal duties with exaggerated punctiliousness. Acting upon a scribbled note found near the body, Mr Verity had arranged for the dead man's remains to be interred in the grounds of the old chapel. As for his estate, it emerged that what was left of Mr Baldwick's fortune had largely been exhausted by his rental of Broomheath Hall. His will required that the remainder should be spent on establishing a public reading room for the display of his papers and pamphlets.

'I think he imagined a grand establishment on the Strand,

I'm afraid, but with so little to spend, my hands were tied. In the end I was able to secure the lease on a cottage in the village and moved his papers there. As far as I'm aware, its only visitor is the woman I pay to keep it clean.'

'And when you went through his things you found only papers? No artefacts of any kind?'

'No, Mrs Hudson, nothing of that sort at all, I'm afraid.'

Before our arrival in Alston, I had not given much thought to the previous tenant of Broomheath Hall, but it was clear from the concentration on her face as she listened to all this that Mrs Hudson took a great deal of interest in the late Anthony Baldwick and his career. Unfortunately Mr Verity had been able to discover very little about the man's activities in the months immediately before he arrived at Alston. The only information he had been able to garner had come from Mr Baldwick himself, and Verity considered him an unreliable witness.

'Even so, sir, I would be interested in hearing what he told you.'

'Very little, Mrs Hudson, and all of it the same boastful stuff. He claimed he had been leading archaeological expeditions in the Near East and in Palestine, and with great success.'

Mrs Hudson showed no emotion on hearing this. She merely nodded. 'Thank you, sir. That is very interesting. Now, since Mr Baldwick's death . . . ?'

'That is when things began to take a sinister turn, Mrs Hudson, although at first everything seemed to go smoothly. I was delighted to find new tenants almost immediately, the young American couple who are there now. They considered the property ideally situated for Mr Summersby's archaeological pursuits. The Summersbys engaged a London agency to find a suitably qualified butler, someone who would open up the house before their arrival, and an appropriate individual was sent up almost by return. I myself found two young girls from the outlying farms to act as cook and maid, two sensible young things who weren't in the least disturbed by the wild rumours that were beginning to circulate. And the following month the Summersbys arrived from the south of France, where they had been spending part of the winter.'

Mr Verity broke off and sighed, and when he continued, his face was troubled. It seemed that the first reports of strange events at Broomheath Hall had reached his ears shortly before the Summersbys arrived. Those early stories had mostly concerned lights moving in the grounds at night, but as the Summersbys attempted to settle in, the reports became more frequent, and extended from the Hall grounds to the moors beyond. Next came the discoveries of freshly turned earth: on the moors, near the ruined chapel, sometimes near the Hall itself; in fact, in all the places where the suicide had been wont to dig. Then, as rumour spread, the first sightings were reported – the caped figure of Anthony Baldwick, it was said, digging in the ground by night, just as he had done when he was alive.

'And then there was Crummoch.' Mr Verity's frown had deepened. 'It's hard to describe Archie Crummoch. Hard even to say how old he was. But he'd lived in a ramshackle cottage half a mile from Broomheath Hall for as long as anyone could remember. I think he worked on the estate once and had been allowed to stay on in the cottage, but that must have been a great many years ago, for Crummoch is eighty if he's a day, and no one round here can remember him working. He just keeps himself to himself in that cottage of his, and haunts the moors like some north-country Caliban, all long hair and beard and staring eyes. We don't see him down here in town very often, and people here tend to forget about him. But that changed when we buried Mr Baldwick.

'It was the rector who alerted me. The night after the interment at the old chapel there was a terrible storm. The rain lashed down all night. And in the morning, the rector found old Crummoch curled up on his doorstep, soaked to the skin. It seems he'd spent the night there. Of course by the time the rector found him he was chilled and feverish, but we managed to get a little bit out of him. He told us that he'd come to seek sanctuary because he knew Baldwick's ghost would be coming for him, that he would be dragged down to hell like old Squire Venterton. He begged us to let him sleep by the church altar – seemed to think that was the only place he'd be safe.

'In the end we brought him here. My cook is a distant relation of his, apparently, and Crummoch seemed to feel safe with her. Though not very safe. We put him to bed and she tended him with the doctor's help. At first it seemed certain we would lose him, for the fever had taken hold with a vengeance. For a week or more he was delirious, and for a month after that too weak even to lift his head. Not many men would have survived such affliction, but for all his years Crummoch was still strong. Gradually, as the weeks passed, he began to regain his old vigour.

'By then, of course, the stories of strange lights up on the moors were becoming frequent, but we took great care to keep them from Crummoch. We feared they would excite him and set back his recovery. He was calm and sane, and making good progress, when the unfortunate incident occurred. That was the day before I sent my second telegram, Mrs Hudson, the one begging for urgent assistance. It was the day when an old poacher, a strange and superstitious fellow, called here to tell me that he had seen a light moving around the ruined chapel, moving around the grave of Mr Baldwick. The grave was undisturbed, he told me, but he felt sure the curse was at work, that any day the dead man would force himself to the surface and come looking for a companion to lie with him in his grave. This conversation took place in the garden, within earshot of Crummoch's window, and by ill chance it seems the old man was awake and listening.

'Well, I tell you, Mrs Hudson, all the good work of the previous weeks was undone at a stroke. That afternoon, Crummoch was wild-eyed and raving again, convinced that Baldwick's ghost was coming for him. I assured him that the grave was undisturbed, that he had nothing to fear, but he wouldn't listen. So great was his hysteria that I confess I turned the key in his bedroom door that night, afraid that he intended to set out for the moors to reassure himself that the grave had not been opened. But I had not reckoned on the old man's strength. While the household slept, he forced the lock on the window and was gone, taking with him nothing but an overcoat and the Bible from his bedside.'

Mrs Hudson leant forward intently. 'But you searched for him, sir?'

'We did. I roused the village and a good many honest folk

came out to hunt for him. But we never found him, Mrs Hudson. Instead, when we reached the ruined chapel, we found that Baldwick's grave had been newly turned over, as though opened and refilled. And beside it, Mrs Hudson . . . I know this is hard to credit, but I saw it with my own eyes, I promise you. Beside it, Mrs Hudson, we found my missing Bible. And beside that, battered and worn, we found the blood-stained boots of Archibald Crummoch.'

CHAPTER ELEVEN

A Salute by Night

A short silence followed Mr Verity's narrative. Mrs Hudson, I saw, was rubbing her chin, apparently deep in thought, while our host dabbed at his brow with his crisp linen handkerchief. Dr Watson shivered, then poured himself another sherry. Outside, the dark clouds had thickened, and the flanks of the moor that rose above the town seemed to brood in their shadow.

'I confess, Mrs Hudson,' Mr Verity went on, 'that my immediate thought was to open the grave. A man was missing, the grave had been turned – I'd have set about it with a shovel there and then had the rector not restrained me. But the rector, I fear, is a very upright fellow of rigid views, who sees it as his mission to stamp out the old superstitions that linger in this place. He insisted that no action should be taken without the proper permissions, and certainly not until the matter had been placed in the hands of the police.

'I daresay he was right, of course, but I confess such restraint went against the grain. I felt certain something dreadful had occurred, and that no time was to be lost. It took more than a day for an inspector of police to make his way from Hexham, and although we continued the search for Crummoch throughout that time, no further traces were found. And the inspector, when he came, was a most unprepossessing individual, a rather weasel-ish man named Robinson who clearly thought himself a bit cleverer than we were. I urged him to pursue the search by exhuming Baldwick's remains, but this suggestion was greeted with the most supercilious disdain. I was made to feel little better than a superstitious old crank, the victim of pranksters who knew the old stories and were having a bit of fun at my expense.

'And I'm afraid Inspector Robinson also made the mistake of pursuing his investigations in the public bar of the Grapes. That's the rather rough tavern at the foot of the hill. It's barely respectable, not at all like the Angel, and the fellows who drink there don't usually care for outsiders. They want to be left to their own devices, and they were quick to persuade Inspector Robinson that Archie Crummoch was simply a crazed old man given to sudden disappearances, someone who thought nothing of taking himself off over the moors for days, even weeks, at a time.

'I'm sorry to say, Mrs Hudson, that the inspector seemed more than happy to take their opinion above mine, and after a couple of days he announced his investigation was at an end and that he was returning to Hexham. Needless to say, there has been no sign of Crummoch since then, and unless we pursue our own inquiries I feel certain the whole incident will remain a mystery.'

He straightened and I saw his eyes drift to the window. 'Old Crummoch was an honest fellow and he never hurt a fly.

He loved it up on the fells. But the moors are treacherous and unforgiving at this time of year,' he added, his voice growing quiet with sadness, 'and I'm afraid, Mrs Hudson, that they tend to keep their secrets.'

'So what do you think of all that?' Dr Watson asked as we stepped out again onto the Alston cobbles. Quite suddenly the dark clouds had parted, and a shaft of pale sunlight touched our faces. Above the town the open moor had turned to amber.

'Very interesting, sir. Very interesting indeed. Mr Baldwick's behaviour is intriguing, is it not?'

'Sounds like the fellow was simply a lunatic, Mrs Hudson. But what about those boots? That's the part of the story that worries me. A chap's gone missing and there's blood in his boots. Sounds like foul play to me.'

'Indeed, sir. But I have a suspicion that Mr Baldwick and the boots are not unconnected. What do you think he was up to, Flotsam?'

'Well, ma'am, Mr Baldwick claimed he'd travelled to the Holy Land. Perhaps he somehow discovered where the Lazarus Testament was hidden. Might he not have stumbled upon the same information as Lord Beaumaris? And I think he came here looking for it, ma'am. That would explain all the digging, you see. Perhaps it was not finding it that drove him mad.'

'Thank you, Flotsam.' She considered for a moment. 'Now, tell me, sir, what steps do you intend to take next?'

The question seemed to disconcert the good doctor. 'Well, I daresay we should talk to this Inspector Robinson . . . Dash it, Mrs Hudson, it's too bad of Holmes, disappearing like this! It was the same with that Baskerville business, if you remember. Barely a sniff of him for weeks. A bit thoughtless, I call it. Never seems to occur to him that it's confoundedly hard for a fellow to write up his cases in an interesting way when he takes himself off for weeks at a time!'

'Indeed, sir. Now, I think you're right to say you'll need to have a word with the police inspector at some point, but from what we've been told it would seem his investigations have been cursory at best. In the meantime, it occurs to me that the answer to all this mystery lies at Broomheath Hall. And Flotsam here has already met Mrs Summersby. Perhaps if the two of you were to call on her together, sir, you might find her more inclined to speak freely of the latest events on her doorstep?'

'Why, yes, of course, Mrs Hudson. Broomheath! An excellent idea. And always delighted to have Flotsam along, as you know . . .'

And with that, our plan was formed. It was decided that Dr Watson and I should call that very afternoon.

The old hall stood alone, over a mile from Alston, and proved a striking building, its foundations laid in the days when prosperous landowners built for security, fearful of the lawlessness of the times and of the gangs of Border reivers who would raid for cattle and captives and any sort of portable plunder. In those days, farmhouses were fortified like castles, with thick walls and small windows, and much of that original character could still be perceived in the fine old dwelling that greeted us as our trap skirted a flank of barren moorland to reveal the hall below us. As we drew closer, however, we began to notice the later additions and improvements that had followed and which had turned Broomheath Hall into a comfortable modern dwelling. By the time Dr Watson pulled to a halt on the gravel sweep, it was clear to us both we were in the grounds of a neat but attractive country residence that wore with comfort its great antiquity.

The door was opened to us by a young girl in a rather grubby cook's apron, who ushered us into a drawing room with hunting trophies on the walls and a fire blazing in the grate. Mrs Summersby joined us a few minutes later and laughed with delight on recognising me.

'Why, Flotsam! Imagine seeing you here! Mr Verity told us that Sherlock Holmes was sending someone, but I must say I never expected it to be you!'

Very hastily, I introduced her to Dr Watson and explained that he was Mr Holmes's closest colleague.

'Delighted to meet you, Doctor.' She held out her hand to him. 'I'm afraid my husband is not here to welcome you. Flotsam has no doubt told you that he's a fiend for Roman remains!'

Mrs Summersby, in a green day-dress that set off her pale skin, was looking every bit as beautiful as I remembered her, and Dr Watson was clearly impressed, mumbling a compliment and hoping rather incoherently that our visit was not inconvenient.

'Not at all, Doctor. Visitors are a rare treat for me!'

'I must say, Mrs Summersby, that this is a very remote spot. I'm surprised that a young lady such as yourself can be content in such a place. It must seem very lonely.'

'Oh, not at all! I love your beautiful English countryside,

and Broomheath Hall is the sort of building that the folks dream about back in Boston! So romantic! Sometimes I feel like a princess in a fairytale in this wonderful old house.'

'But with no visitors, and nothing in the way of entertainment . . .'

'I make my own, Doctor! I'm quite the bookworm, you know. A man in Charing Cross sends me five volumes a month. And there is sewing to do, and the house to manage, and it's my job to look after my husband's notes and diagrams. And when all that palls, I explore Broomheath! How could one possibly be bored in a mysterious old place like this?'

So bright was her smile that both Dr Watson and I found ourselves returning it. Then, remembering himself, Dr Watson pursed his lips.

'But recent events, madam . . . The disappearance of this poor fellow Crummoch . . .'

Mrs Summersby's pretty face fell into a frown.

'That poor man! I understand he was a little deranged. The police inspector who called here seemed to think he had taken it into his head to leave Alston for a bit. Apparently it is not uncommon for him to disappear in this way.'

'But his boots, madam! Those bloody boots of his!' Dr Watson paused and flushed slightly at this unfortunate phrase. 'I just meant to say, surely the police must fear the worst?'

'Oh, Dr Watson!' Mrs Summersby waved one delicate, gloved hand. 'Those boots are a prank, surely? Everyone says so. You cannot seriously believe that an old man has been dragged underground by a malevolent spirit?' She permitted herself the smallest of smiles. 'My husband and I feel sure that

Old Crummoch's boots represent a rather unpleasant joke by someone who wants to scare his new Yankee neighbours.'

'Well, I don't deny it's put the wind up me!' Dr Watson grunted. 'But what about all those mysterious lights on the moor that Verity has told me about. Seen any of those?'

But Mrs Summersby, in her pretty way, laughed away all rumours of supernatural activity at Broomheath, refusing to give them any credence at all.

'I'm sure the mysterious lamps are simply those of poachers, Doctor. As for the sightings of Mr Baldwick's ghost, well, one man in a cape looks very much like another. My husband thinks they are badger-baiters, and threatens to go out one night to see them off with his gun! I'm terribly afraid, Doctor, that you've come all this way on something of a wild goose chase.'

Dr Watson, however, for as long as he was sitting opposite her at the tea table, seemed quite content to have made the long journey.

'You say your husband is interested in antiquities, madam. Does he spend every day up at the Wall?'

'Oh, no, Doctor. Perhaps he will when the days grow longer. But for now he is making a study of the Roman Camp a little west of here, across the river. You will have passed it on the train. He is carrying out some small digs there, and in other places. Scratching around, he calls it, which sounds very American the way he says it.'

Dr Watson cleared his throat.

'It is only fair I should warn you, Mrs Summersby, that we have our own theory about these sightings. You see, it seems that some sort of ancient artefact might be concealed somewhere around here, and that some unscrupulous fellows are out to find it. I'd ask you and your husband to be very careful, and I daresay it would be prudent to keep your doors firmly locked at night.'

But instead of appearing alarmed at this warning, Mrs Summersby merely opened her eyes very wide.

'An ancient artefact! Why, that's just what our visit needs to make it perfect! Just like something out of a dusty old English novel! What sort of thing is it, Doctor? Would I recognise it? Perhaps we can help you find it!'

'Well I'm sure we'd be delighted . . .' Dr Watson began, before remembering himself. 'But of course it wouldn't be fair to involve you in any way. As I say, these are dangerous men. They are looking for some sort of old manuscript, and that's all we know. I suggest that you take great care about admitting strangers.'

'Why, of course, Doctor. Thank you so much for alerting us.'

In reply, Dr Watson seemed on the brink of further gallantries but was cut short by the return of Mr Summersby, still muddy from his activities on the moors. Perhaps it was wrong of me to have an idea of what an amateur antiquarian should look like, but I confess that Mr Summersby was not what I'd expected. He proved to be an unusually large man, ox-like in construction: broad where his wife was slight and dainty, unsmiling where she was full of laughter. To me, he looked more like a prize-fighter than an archaeologist, but without any of the secret kindness that sometimes lurks in the face of a man who fights for his living. He was very silent too. After grunting a greeting to Dr Watson and myself, he said very little, speaking only when his wife addressed him directly. If I was a little surprised that the vivacious Mrs Summersby had chosen such a sullen husband, it also struck me that perhaps in some ways their opposite qualities might make them a suitable pairing.

It was not until Mrs Summersby rang for the maid to show us out that Dr Watson asked the question I had been bursting to ask since our arrival.

'Almost forgot, madam. There was one other thing. We're trying to track down someone who might have come to Alston a little before you did. A man called Pauncefoot. We know he took a job in service somewhere, and we think it might have been around here. Probably not any more though. We think he might be dead.'

Mrs Summersby's face clouded with genuine astonishment.

'Pauncefoot? Dead? But that's absurd, Doctor. He brought us our breakfasts this very morning. Today is his afternoon off, or you could see for yourself. Why on earth are you looking for him?'

It was Dr Watson's turn to look thunderstruck. 'What? Pauncefoot here? At Broomheath?' My companion was clearly as startled as I was. 'My word! But that's remarkable news, isn't it, Flotsam? As for why we're looking for him, madam, I assure you it is nothing that should worry you. We simply wish to ask him some questions about one of his former employers. Would you happen to know when he will be back?'

'Not till after dusk, I'm afraid, Doctor. Pauncefoot likes to spend his free time tramping over the moors. We've always felt it was a very wholesome way for a butler to spend his leisure hours. But, of course, if you were to call again tomorrow . . .'

The light was fading when Dr Watson and I, having said our goodbyes, once again clambered onto Mr Verity's trap. In such treacherous light, Dr Watson had eyes only for the narrow road ahead, but I was free to look around, at the rising flanks of the moors that crowded upon us. As we left Broomheath Hall behind us, I felt sure I noticed a movement below the skyline. Was that a solitary figure descending towards the Hall? I felt sure it was, not least because the profile I glimpsed against the pale bracken was a striking one: with a luxuriant beard below its face and a smooth, bald pate above it.

Dr Watson and I returned to Broomheath Hall the following day but this time we did not call at the front door. Instead of borrowing Mr Verity's trap, we took the little train from Alston as far as Kirkhaugh, the first stop, a remote station used only by farmers and sportsmen and by visitors to Broomheath Hall, which lay about half a mile away down a rough track. We were determined that our visit should be an unofficial one, catching Pauncefoot alone, and not a formal interview in the Summersby's imposing sitting room.

The walk to the hall was a lonely one. Only once did we see another living creature, when Dr Watson exclaimed and pointed, but by the time I had turned to look there was nothing to see.

'Probably just a deer, Flotsam,' he decided. 'Looked a bit like a man in a cape for a moment. Just there, behind that outcrop of rock on the skyline. But these empty landscapes play tricks on you. I remember once in Afghanistan . . .'

He chattered on, but after that we both kept a keener

lookout. Even so, we saw no other sign of life until we reached the hall, not even a stray sheep grazing the moor. By arriving on foot we were able to approach the rear of the house unseen. Dr Watson rapped briskly at the servants' door with his walking stick and after a short pause the door was opened by the butler, an imposing figure, as bald and as bearded as the descriptions of him had suggested. He was dressed in his shirt sleeves, with a tea cloth over his shoulder.

'Yes?' he asked, his manner rather curt. 'Can I be of assistance, sir?'

'Indeed!' replied Dr Watson, 'I'm sure you can. My name is Dr John Watson and I am an associate of Mr Sherlock Holmes. Robert Inigo Pauncefoot, we have come to ask about your watch.'

Of one thing there could be no doubt: Mrs Summersby's butler knew how to keep his head. A flicker of surprise passed over his face at Dr Watson's question but he betrayed not one jot of fear or anxiety.

'My watch, sir? Very well. Perhaps you would be so good as to step inside?'

We were ushered into the butler's room, a small but comfortable retreat with sporting prints on the walls, littered with all the usual paraphernalia of a superior male servant, from boot trees and silver polish to back copies of sporting periodicals.

'I take it that you don't deny being Viscount Wrexham's former valet?' Dr Watson asked. 'Or that you were in his service at the time of his disappearance?'

'Really, sir, I can see no reason why I should deny any such thing. I am proud to have been in the Viscount's service. And, of course, when applying for my current post I furnished the London agency with full details of my former employment.'

He turned away for a moment to slip into his jacket and when he turned to face us he seemed the picture of a perfect servant.

'So how do you come to be here at Broomheath, then?' I could sense that Dr Watson was a little disconcerted by the fellow's perfect composure, but he was not yet ready to cede the initiative.

'I applied for the position shortly after the Viscount disappeared, sir.'

'And why was that? What was the attraction of Broomheath Hall? Come, man, tell us the truth!'

The butler looked slightly offended.

'Certainly, sir. It would not have occurred to me to do otherwise. You will appreciate, sir, that the Viscount's sudden disappearance left me in an awkward position. The death of Lord Beaumaris occurred almost simultaneously and it was unclear how the estate stood. Not to put too fine a point upon it, sir, it was far from certain that my salary would be paid, and if so, by whom. It was imperative to find alternative employment.'

'And you ask us to believe that you just happened to end up in Alston?'

Once again the butler looked a little pained by my companion's tone.

'It would be impertinent to make any such request, sir. But the truth is that this position was advertised at a very timely moment. And clearly, sir, the opportunity to move from the position of valet to that of butler is an advantageous one for someone who wishes to improve his prospects. I understood the Summersbys to be respectable employers, even if American, and although their establishment proves a rather unconventional one, I have hopes the post will lead to better things.'

Dr Watson looked unconvinced by this display of *sang-froid*, and I could see he still felt his hand was a winning one.

'Well, let me put things to you another way, Pauncefoot. The Viscount disappeared in early October. You replied to the agency's advertisement towards the end of that month. I telegraphed them last night and received a reply this morning. They tell me you provided an excellent testimonial from Viscount Wrexham himself. So tell me this*: if the Viscount had disappeared three weeks earlier, how was he able to provide you with a letter of reference at the end of October?*'

Dr Watson delivered the question with the air of a cross-examining counsel sensing a witness at his mercy. Unfortunately, instead of crumbling under this interrogation, the butler appeared utterly unmoved.

'I understand your confusion, sir. Perhaps it would help if I explained that I had already informed the Viscount of my intention to seek a new position *before* his unfortunate disappearance. He was good enough to provide me with a written testimonial at that time. I am confident that an examination of the date on the document would support this.'

'I see.' Dr Watson was beginning to look a little crestfallen at his inability to pin the witness down. 'And you just decided to leave, did you? Weren't you happy with the Viscount?'

'Most content, sir. But I had been his valet for many years. If I wished to advance myself, a change was inevitable.'

'And I suppose you'll expect me to believe you've never heard of the Lazarus Testament, either?'

The butler's face was innocence itself.

'The Lazarus Testament? I fear I am not familiar with anything by that name.'

'But confound it, Pauncefoot,' Dr Watson exploded. 'This is preposterous! What about all this pretending to be dead then?'

'Dead, sir?'

'Yes, dead! Your old friend Albert Swan wrote to you to propose a visit, and he received a reply telling him you'd died of a fever!'

'A fever, sir? I can assure you that was not the case. I have been in excellent health for many years. And I received no letter from Mr Swan. May I ask who told him such a wicked lie?'

Dr Watson turned a little pale and, if it is possible for a gentleman to gnash his teeth, I believe he gnashed them then.

'Well, we don't know that for certain yet. But someone did. Dammit, they sent him this!'

And with that Dr Watson pulled from his pocket the silver fob-watch we had obtained from the Marylebone police, an object he brandished under the butler's nose.

'I suppose you'll deny this is yours, will you?'

'On the contrary, sir,' Pauncefoot replied, taking it from Dr Watson and studying it closely. 'I was given this watch as a young man and kept it for many years. You will observe my initials on the back. I was most upset when it was lost.'

'Lost, Pauncefoot? Lost? When was that?'

The butler considered for a moment. 'Three or four months before I left London, sir. I believe the chain must have broken.'

'So how do you explain the fact that the watch was found on your old friend Swan when he was knocked down by a carriage?'

'I can offer no explanation, sir. I confess myself mystified.' He seemed to notice a mark on his cuff and began to examine it. 'Is Mr Swan not able to explain it, sir?'

'Mr Swan is dead, Pauncefoot.'

The butler clicked his tongue sympathetically.

'I am very sorry to hear that, sir. As you say, we were old friends.' But from where I was standing, watching him closely, the emotion that flickered across his face seemed closer to relief than to loss.

'And what if I told you, Pauncefoot, that we believe Mr Swan saw you in London on the day of his death?'

The butler raised an eyebrow. 'Most unlikely, sir. Of course, you have not been good enough to inform me on what day Mr Swan met with his end, but as Mrs Summersby will no doubt confirm, since taking up my post here last November I have travelled no further than Hexham, where from time to time I visit a goddaughter of mine.'

Dr Watson glanced across at me. The conversation was not unfolding as we had planned and I could see he was struggling to control his frustration.

'So tell me, Pauncefoot, am I to understand that you have had no contact whatsoever with the Viscount since his disappearance?'

'I regret to say I have not, sir.'

'And do you have any theory about what has become of him?'

'It is not my place to theorise, sir. But I am hopeful that some day the Viscount will reappear with his fortunes restored.

He is not one to allow life's trials to triumph over him, sir.'

'But what about his ring, Pauncefoot?'

'His ring, sir?'

'Someone handed it in to a police station saying they'd found it on the banks of the Thames. In fact, the person who handed it in bore a remarkable resemblance to you! The constable on duty remembers it most clearly.'

'Really, sir? How interesting. Of course, sir, one tends to find that, to many people, all tall, bald-headed men with beards look very much alike. It is a phenomenon I have often remarked upon.'

Dr Watson puffed out his cheeks.

'So that's your story, is it? You claim to know nothing of the Lazarus Testament, nothing of Viscount Wrexham's whereabouts, nothing about being dead, and you claim it is pure chance that you have ended up in Alston?'

The butler bowed respectfully. 'That describes my position with admirable clarity, sir.'

'Well, I must say I don't believe a word of it, Pauncefoot! And I've a good mind to tell Mrs Summersby that you are not to be trusted. Come, Flotsam! Let us find a more profitable way to spend our day!'

And with that we left the field a defeated force, making the long trudge back to the station with morose faces and the suspicion that we had merely put an enemy on his guard.

We retreated to the cosy front parlour of the Angel, where a generously laid tea tray awaited us, with Mrs Hudson sitting beside it.

'It cannot be coincidence that has brought him here, confound his impudence!' Dr Watson insisted, when the tea had been poured and the sandwiches shared. 'The fellow's lying, I'm sure of it! But we can talk to Mrs Summersby and see to it that he is sent away with his tail between his legs, Mrs Hudson!'

The housekeeper pursed her lips.

'I think we can assume that his presence here is part of a plan to recover the Lazarus Testament, sir. Presumably his plan is to locate the document discreetly, without alerting the Summersbys to his search.'

'Spade in hand and wearing a cape like Mr Baldwick's, ma'am?' I suggested.

'Precisely, Flotsam. He cannot easily search by day without attracting notice. So he goes about his business at night, assisted somewhat by the superstitious natures of Alston's poachers, who give him a wide berth. The good news, of course, is that Pauncefoot has shown no sign of leaving Broomheath, which means he is still looking. It is when he quits his position here that we have reason to be anxious.'

Dr Watson nodded thoughtfully. 'I see what you mean, Mrs Hudson. So all in all, you think we're probably better off letting him stay at the Hall where we can keep on eye on him? Yes, I can see that . . . Even so, I might have a word with the station master here and ask him to alert us if Pauncefoot buys a ticket out.'

'But, Mrs Hudson,' I wondered, putting into words the question that most bothered me, 'where is the Viscount in all this? Is he just leaving the whole thing to Pauncefoot? Or is he planning to take a hand in the search himself? Isn't it worrying, not knowing what he's up to?'

Dr Watson clattered down his tea cup. 'Good lord! You don't think perhaps he's dead after all? Perhaps his ring really was found by a stranger who just happened to look a bit like Pauncefoot?'

Mrs Hudson shook her head but I thought she looked troubled.

'That whole business of the ring and the body is all too neat, sir. If you wanted to persuade people you were drowned, it would not be difficult to wait until an unrecognisable corpse was discovered and then to arrange for an accomplice to place something of yours close to it.' Her frown deepened. 'I was *sure* in my own mind that it was Pauncefoot who handed in that ring. And sure it was Pauncefoot who Mr Swan saw in London. Could he *really* have been up here all the time?'

'There is one other thing, Mrs Hudson,' Dr Watson put in. 'Mr Verity was telling me that he met a birdwatcher on the moors the last time he drove over to Allendale. A dishevelled chap, he said. And it occurs to me that someone posing as an ornithologist would get to wander the moors unquestioned and spy on anything he wanted. Could that perhaps be the Viscount?'

'Who can say, sir? Now, if you will excuse me, I am eager to visit the shops here before they close. Will you accompany me, Flotsam? Why, whatever's the matter? You look very serious.'

'It's nothing, ma'am,' I reassured her, scrambling to my feet. But I was not being entirely truthful. Dr Watson's words had set me thinking about the hooded figure I'd seen in the shadows of Baker Street. A figment of my imagination? Or the vanished peer, keeping watch? Perhaps the latter . . . After all, I was not so foolish as to let myself imagine that the shade of Lazarus himself might really be standing guard over his last testament . . .

No, that was nonsense. I was safe with Mrs Hudson, and we were going shopping. Even if the Viscount was out there, watching us, there was nothing to fear. If I shivered a little as I followed the housekeeper out of the parlour and into the dark corridor beyond, it was merely the cold of the evening seeping in from the street.

If any sight was guaranteed to raise my spirits, it was the scene that greeted us in the little shop opposite the Angel Inn. Part drapery, part haberdashery, and in all other parts a purveyor of general goods, it was a cosy and welcoming place, its small counter dwarfed by the boxes stacked high around its walls, its displays presenting in tempting fashion everything from lengths of Indian silk to patent remedies against the hiccoughs. It was to this place that the townsfolk of Alston repaired for all manner of commonplace items and, as Mrs Hudson informed me, for all manner of gossip.

'Mrs Thimbly is something of a local oracle, it appears, Flotsam, to be consulted on every matter of importance in Alston and its surroundings. I spent a considerable part of yesterday afternoon winning her confidence, even though doing so involved the purchase of a rather garish length of purple ribbon and one or two secrets concerning Dr Watson's rakish past.'

'Goodness, ma'am! I didn't know Dr Watson *had* a rakish past!'

'Neither did Dr Watson. We shall just have to hope that he and Mrs Thimbly never compare notes.'

The purpose of our visit that afternoon was the purchase of certain embroidery materials required by Mrs Hudson to assist Mrs Garth with a new sampler for her parlour. At such a late hour, we found the shop empty but for the shopkeeper and a well-built young girl in a shawl who appeared to be coming to the end of a very long list of purchases.

'That's everything, ma'am, but for the shaving soap and another jar of styptic powder. He says the brands you sent last time will do very well for him. And everything to go on the Hall account, if you please, ma'am.'

To say that Mrs Hudson and I pricked up our ears when we heard this would not, anatomically speaking, be accurate, but it would certainly convey our quickening interest. We drew a little closer, and waited until the transactions of our fellow shopper were complete.

'Ah, good evening, Mrs Hudson!' Mrs Thimbly greeted her like an old friend. 'This must be your young travelling companion. Flotsam, is it not? Mrs Hudson has been telling me all about you, Flotsam.' And she gave me a smile so full of unspoken complicity that for a moment I was quite distracted, trying to imagine what wicked indiscretions Mrs Hudson might have ascribed to me.

'This is Martha Trotter,' the shopkeeper went on. 'Her father farms a few acres over at Deep Bottom, and Martha works as a maid at Broomheath Hall. Mrs Hudson is up from London, Martha,' she added proudly, as though such a metropolitan clientele reflected well upon her business. 'She hopes to meet her second-cousin here. He is a footman on the other side of Allendale. They haven't set eyes on each other for fifteen years.'

The introductions having been made to her satisfaction, she departed to search for the items Mrs Hudson required. Mrs Hudson was, I noticed, unusually specific about shades and specifications, therefore securing for us at least a minute or two of Martha's uninterrupted company.

'Broomheath Hall?' Mrs Hudson began. 'How do you like it there?'

'Very nice, ma'am.' Martha bobbed politely.

'They are kind to you there? I have been told they are very strict.'

'Oh, no, ma'am! Mrs Summersby is always very friendly. Very condescending, she is. Dad says it's her being an American and them not having any social higher-archery over there. But she's always very kind to me.'

'And the butler? His name is Pauncefoot, is it not?' The young girl blushed a little. 'Yes, ma'am.'

'I've heard he's a very mysterious character.'

'Mysterious, ma'am? Oh, no, not at all. I thought he was very grand at first, ma'am, but really . . .' She hesitated, clearly unsure how to proceed. 'Well, he's a terrible flirt, ma'am! And him older than my dad! Always teasing me, he is, and telling me I'm pretty. Mildred – she's the girl that cooks, ma'am – she calls him my admirer!'

From the manner of her blushing, it seemed that Martha did not find such badinage altogether unpleasant.

'Gracious me!' Mrs Hudson managed to sound suitably

scandalised. 'I confess I'm surprised. I'd heard he was a solitary fellow, much given to walking on the moors.'

Martha considered this. 'Well, ma'am, he does take a walk when he can. He calls it his constitutional. He sometimes asks me to go with him, but usually I have to stay back in case Mrs Summersby rings for something. Mildred gets very flustered by the bell, she does.'

'Well, well. And what about all these stories of strange goings on? Have *you* seen any ghosts there, child?'

'I wouldn't know about that, ma'am. I sleep out, you see. But my dad says it's an old poacher trick – telling scary tales so as no one respectable dares go out after nightfall.'

Mrs Hudson accepted this wisdom with a nod.

'He sounds very wise, Martha. Now, don't let me keep you from your errands. Do they bring you to Mrs Thimbly's very often?'

'Every week, ma'am. I likes it, ma'am.'

'Well, you certainly have a long list to get through. Do you draw it up yourself?'

'Oh, no, ma'am. Mr Pauncefoot makes the list, ma'am, him being the butler an' all, and there being no housekeeper, just me and Mildred.'

'I see. And no doubt Mr and Mrs Summersby ask for certain purchases too?'

'I don't think so, ma'am. Their things is sent up from London, you see. And sometimes even from America, too.'

Mrs Hudson nodded again. 'Yes, of course. They would be.'

'Well, if that's all, ma'am . . . Thank you, ma'am . . .' Martha bobbed again by way of leave-taking, before scurrying from the shop.

On Mrs Thimbly's return, Mrs Hudson seemed less inclined to chat but, even so, no polite retreat was possible until recipes for lavender jelly had been exchanged and the shopkeeper had revealed which local butcher could be best trusted for a good piece of tripe. When we finally regained the street, Mrs Hudson chuckled to herself.

'Well, Flotsam, I found all that extremely interesting. I think I begin to see the light.'

'Do you, ma'am?' I asked doubtfully, aware that I seemed to have learnt very little of any significance, other than Mrs Thimbly's special recipe for dumplings.

'Well, Flottie, let's just say that our meeting with Martha has made me think it's time I paid a little visit to Broomheath Hall. And, Flottie, I need to write to Mr Rumbelow at once. I am going to recommend he spends a few days in the South Downs. It is beautiful there in spring. I think he will find a short stay there very beneficial.'

That evening Dr Watson visited us in Mrs Garth's parlour, and between us we passed a happy evening. I crept into my bed that night full of happy and optimistic thoughts. And yet, although I fell asleep straightaway, there came a moment in the night when I stirred and found my body tense and my mind alert, charged with an overwhelming certainty that there was something I needed to do. I lay for a moment, confused by my strange surroundings, trying to bring my thoughts into focus. And then I heard something – the sound of horse's hooves – and I knew what it was that had roused me. The sound came from the street, I realised: hooves falling softly, as if the rider was loath to wake the town.

I slipped from under the blankets and reached for my shawl. The room I'd been given looked out over the rear of the inn but I remembered a window on the half-landing from which it was possible to see the road.

The door of my room creaked a little as I opened it but the sound made little impression on the heavy silence of the sleeping inn. When I reached the window, the scene below me was lit only by moonlight. I couldn't be sure of the hour but I knew it was the very dead of night, and Alston slept. Not a single window showed a light, not a curtain twitched, not one shutter stood open. The only moving thing was the horseman, picking his way down the hill, his face and form concealed by the folds of his cloak. But as he reached the Angel Inn and came to the point in the road directly below me, it was as if he felt the weight of my gaze fastened upon him. Slowly – so slowly – he turned his head and looked directly at my window. As he looked, his hood fell back a little and I saw his face: ancient, worn, wearied as if by infinite time; eyes dark, a proud nose, skin brown and deeply lined. It was a face of the desert, weathered by wind and sand, and scarred by suffering. Our eyes met. Then, with that same deliberation, he raised his hand in greeting. And before I could move or shrink away he had passed me and was gone, sliding back into the shadows.

A stranger, certainly. The watcher in Baker Street? I couldn't be sure. But of one thing I had no doubt: this solitary rider was not Viscount Wrexham, nor anyone like him. Whatever had brought him to Alston, whatever he sought, his road had been a long one. And it had begun in a land very different from my own.

CHAPTER TWELVE

The Watcher

I woke the following morning to discover that Mrs Hudson had risen early and had already left the house. The message entrusted to Mrs Garth proved a little cryptic as to her intentions.

'Now, let me see, Flotsam. What was it she said? Something about wanting to practise the piano. At least I think that's what she said, though it sounds a bit peculiar, doesn't it, dear? I mean, why should she need to? I told her that the rector has a very fine instrument but she just smiled and said she was setting her sights somewhat lower, and would I tell you to meet the gentleman off the ten o'clock train?'

'The gentleman?' I looked at her a little blankly.

'Yes, dear. He wired yesterday about a room. When I mentioned it to Mrs Hudson this morning she said you were acquainted with him. A Mr Spencer, is it? Yes, I think that was his name . . .'

And so it proved, for when the train pulled in that morning, Rupert Spencer was the first passenger out of it, his bag in his hand, a travel coat over his shoulder and a spring in his step.

'Hello, Flotsam!' he greeted me brightly. 'Well, here I am. I understand you have work for me?'

'Well, I'm sure we do, sir. But to be honest, sir, I didn't even know you were coming this morning.'

He looked apologetic. 'Of course. You must have been expecting me last night. In my defence, I set off almost as soon as I received Mrs Hudson's telegram, but I missed a connection, and I'd only got as far as Haltwhistle station by nightfall. I came on here straight after breakfast.'

'And what exactly did her telegram say, sir?'

'Only that she needed someone to go through a lot of old papers and pamphlets. Does that sound likely?'

With that, the light began to dawn.

'That would be the Baldwick Archive, sir. Mr Baldwick was the tenant at Broomheath Hall. He went mad and dug a lot of holes. And he left behind an awful lot of pamphlets too, I'm afraid.'

He grinned. 'Then let's hope they read well, Flotsam! Hetty sends her love, by the way. You can imagine how outraged she was when I told her I was coming up here! First she called me names for not bringing her with me, then she became all aloof and said she wouldn't be at all surprised if someone much cleverer than me didn't find the Lazarus Testament first. Then she told me she intended to wear that scandalous new Parisian dress to the Birtwhistles' ball, and what a shame that I was going to miss it because she would probably have to dance all night with the ambassador's nephew . . .'

It being a bright morning, we decided to walk the short distance into Alston so that I could point out the sights and show

Mr Spencer where the Baldwick papers were kept. As we walked, I gave him an account of all Mrs Hudson's activities since our arrival in Alston, and confided in him my fears that Viscount Wrexham must be lurking somewhere, ready to pounce when the time was right. Only when I came to the horseman in the night did I hold back: somehow, in the golden, wintry sunlight of the day, my reaction to the face I'd glimpsed in the darkness seemed melodramatic and absurd. A stranger on horseback, nothing more. I would keep my silly fancies to myself.

When eventually we reached the Angel Inn, we found Dr Watson waiting by the fire in the snug. He welcomed Mr Spencer with great enthusiasm and declared himself overjoyed at having an extra ally in the cause.

'Just what we need!' he pronounced, slapping the new arrival firmly on the back. 'It had already crossed my mind that someone might need to rifle through Baldwick's papers. The chap may have been unhinged, but we can't disregard him. Shouldn't surprise me if we found all sorts of answers in there, eh, Flotsam? Now, Mr Spencer, why not come and take a pew and I'll tell you all about my plan. I've been doing a bit of thinking, you see!'

I could tell from his exuberance that Dr Watson was feeling rather pleased with himself, and when Mr Spencer and I had settled down, he expanded upon his theme.

'You see, I was out on the moors earlier, having a look around, don't you know? And as I walked, I found myself wondering what Holmes would do if he were here. And do you know, it was like magic! I began to see the situation in an entirely different light! You see, the heart of this mystery is at Broomheath, if you get my drift. That's where Viscount Wrexham's clue led us, it's where Pauncefoot is, and it's where that mad archaeologist Baldwick ended up. It's even where the old man, Archie Crummoch, disappeared, or pretty close to it. So if Holmes were here, do you think he'd be eating an excellent breakfast at Mr Verity's house every morning? By no means! You know what he'd be doing? He'd be wracking his brains for some way of getting inside Broomheath Hall!'

'But, sir, haven't we been inside Broomheath Hall already?' I asked him. 'In fact we've been there twice.'

'Ah, yes, Flotsam! As visitors. But that wouldn't satisfy Holmes. You see, Mr Spencer, this Viscount chappie no doubt thinks he's been very clever, installing his man at Broomheath. But if we can keep an eye on him, his hands are tied. Can't get up to much if one of us is there, constantly ringing the bell for tea and scones and whatnot. And even if he did unearth this Lazarus thing, someone staying in the Hall would be the first to know about it.'

'It certainly sounds like a good plan, Doctor. But how do we get ourselves invited?'

Doctor Watson's face fell.

'Ah! There's the rub. You see, Mrs Summersby has made it very clear that she and her husband have come here for a bit of solitude. If only I could think up some excuse for another interview . . .'

But Dr Watson did not have to think very hard. We hadn't spoken for another five minutes before we were interrupted by the entrance of Mrs Garth, who was fanning herself with her fingertips.

'Please, sir, there's a lady called for you.' From the look on her face, I gathered that she felt this event reflected rather badly on Dr Watson's morals. 'A *foreign* lady, sir. I've put her in the parlour, if that's convenient. She says her name is Summersby.'

Dr Watson blinked in surprise.

'What remarkable timing! Now, Mr Spencer, you can take yourself off for a wash after your journey. Leave this to me and Flotsam. We'll arrange everything!'

We found our visitor reading a letter by the fire, a small frown marring the usual serenity of her face.

'Dr Watson! Flotsam!' she trilled when we entered. 'How pleased I am to see you both! I have just received a slightly surprising letter and I really felt I needed to ask your opinion of it.'

Dr Watson bowed and mumbled something about endeavouring to be of service.

'It comes from Sir Bulstrode Peveril,' she went on, 'a gentleman we were lucky enough to meet when we were visiting the South of France. He writes to say that an Italian *contessa*, a close friend of an acquaintance of his, is touring the antiquities in this area, and he feels sure we would like to meet her. She has a passion for archaeology, he says, and is very well connected in antiquarian circles. He says she may be able to assist my husband with some important introductions, and suggests we invite her to stay. Tell me, Dr Watson, would that be wise?'

Dr Watson examined the proffered letter for a few moments.

'It's from Sir Bulstrode, all right, and a very charming letter,' he concluded, 'and Sir Bulstrode is a gentleman who moves in the very best circles. The Countess Flavia of Mirandola, eh?

Never heard of her myself, but if Sir Bulstrode recommends her you can be sure she's highly respectable.'

'Then you think it's all right?' Mrs Summersby seemed a little distressed. 'I rather thought you'd advise against it. You see, after what you said yesterday about people trying to get into the house, well, I'm a little anxious about inviting someone I don't know. I hoped you would help me write a reply . . .'

'Your caution does you credit, Mrs Summersby, but someone recommended by Sir Bulstrode Peveril is certainly above suspicion.'

Our visitor continued to look a little put out, however. 'But I really don't think we're in any fit state to entertain, Doctor. My husband is not a sociable man, and he's so busy at present. And apart from Pauncefoot, our entire staff consists of two young girls who live out. And Sir Bulstrode indicates that the Countess will be arriving tomorrow night! I think perhaps it really would be better if we were to explain to Sir Bulstrode . . .'

Dr Watson returned the letter to her with a reassuring smile.

'On the contrary, Mrs Summersby, Sir Bulstrode goes to great pains to stress that the countess is travelling alone and very simply, and would not expect grand entertaining. Sounds like an eccentric old bird, doesn't she? And given that she is so close by, I'm sure Sir Bulstrode would consider it most odd if you did not take advantage of his introduction. The countess appears to be a very well connected woman.'

Mrs Summersby looked pensive and seemed far from reassured, but she did manage a brave smile.

'Well, Doctor, if you really think so . . . We must do what's right, mustn't we? And of course if we were just a little better prepared we would welcome such an introduction with open arms . . . And perhaps the *contessa* will not wish to stay for very long . . .'

I waited for Doctor Watson to seize the moment, then decided that perhaps waiting was unwise.

'Please, ma'am,' I piped up, 'if you're worried about entertaining, Mrs Hudson and I would be happy to help. She's been a housekeeper in all sorts of grand households, so the visit of an Italian countess wouldn't worry her at all.'

'That's a capital suggestion, Flotsam!' Dr Watson looked as pleased as if he'd thought of it himself. 'I'm sure Pauncefoot would be delighted to have the assistance of a woman like Mrs Hudson. And of course, madam, I'd feel greatly reassured if she and Flotsam were with you in Broomheath. Such a remote spot! With your permission, Mrs Summersby, I shall most certainly put it to her.'

But our hostess still seemed a little bewildered by the morning's rapid developments.

'Oh, no, Doctor. We couldn't possibly . . . No, it would be too great an imposition . . . We couldn't possibly cause so much trouble . . .'

'It's no trouble at all,' the good doctor declared gallantly. 'You'll be delighted, won't you, Flotsam? And as you say, ma'am, you are hardly equipped to look after visitors without some extra help. It would surely look most peculiar to set two country girls to wait upon the countess when you have one of the most sought after housekeepers in the country at your disposal!'

This logic was unarguable, and Mrs Summersby had little choice but to concede the point.

'Well, perhaps for a night or two, just until the countess moves on,' she decided. 'And we couldn't possibly ask you to stay overnight, Flotsam. No, that would be too much, I couldn't hear of it. But perhaps the father of one of the girls might bring the two of you back to Alston when he collects his daughter . . . Yes, I think perhaps my husband couldn't object to that . . .'

For all our urgings, Mrs Summersby would not relent on this, and in truth we did not press the point too forcefully, feeling that by establishing a foothold in Broomheath Hall for the greater part of the day we had achieved something of which Mr Holmes would greatly approve. Yet the arrangements did not seem to raise Mrs Summersby's spirits in quite the way they had raised my own.

'Oh, dear, Flotsam,' she murmured to me as she took her leave of the Angel. 'I do hope my husband won't be too unhappy with all this. He really is so shy. But a studious Italian countess cannot disturb him very much, can she?'

Perhaps it was the little smile with which she favoured me, but as she drove away, instead of any feeling of triumph, I felt a pang of guilt for imposing upon the good nature of one so trusting.

The rest of the day passed quickly. Dr Watson left almost at once to catch a train to Hexham, where he planned to interview Inspector Robinson about the disappearance of Archie Crummoch; and Mr Spencer expressed a desire to begin work at once in the Baldwick Archive. With no sign of Mrs Hudson, and no clear plan of my own, I decided to accompany him.

The Baldwick Archive, it turned out, was nothing more

than a single cottage room containing a collection of tea crates of various sizes, all packed, apparently at random, with papers of every sort: pamphlets, letters, diaries, drawings, memoranda – even, I discovered, some old receipts for gentlemen's undergarments from one of London's cheaper department stores. These crates had been pushed on top of one another into a large cupboard, and those that would not fit were piled three or four high along one wall. Amid this chaos, Mr Verity had somehow managed to fit two small tables and four very uncomfortable straight-backed chairs. Surveying the scene for the first time Mr Spencer paused, then let out a very long sigh.

'I suppose we just take things one crate at a time, Flotsam. Why don't you take this seat here, the one by the window? Let us start with a pile each and do nothing but sort them out. Anything that seems even vaguely relevant to this case – anything about archaeology or the Bible or about Alston, for instance – simply pile up in this corner here. Anything that seems utterly irrelevant, toss over there. So, let me see . . .' He fished out a pamphlet from the nearest box. '*Thoughts on the Huddlestone Mermaid and Other Maritime Mysteries*. Not relevant, surely? *Seducing the Muse – A Writer's Thoughts on Writing*. I'm not reading that, not even if you pay me. *Fairies – Fact or Fiction?* Oh my word, Flotsam, I feel this might be a very long day indeed!'

And yet, strangely, the time flew by. As the pile of discarded papers and pamphlets grew ever bigger, Mr Spencer and I seemed seized by a peculiar and ruthless determination, one that was made bearable by increasing quantities of laughter. I think the cause of this must have been Mr Baldwick's very painful earnestness. Otherwise it is hard to explain why, when Mr Spencer announced *A Short Paper on the Grocery Trade in Tooting*, I almost fell off my chair from laughing; nor why, when I countered with *Road Signs of Lisbon*, I swear that tears ran down my companion's cheeks. At lunchtime, we arranged for sandwiches to be sent from the Angel. We ignored tea time altogether. By seven o'clock, when we finally called a halt, we had examined the contents of five crates. A further thirty three remained. We had found nothing of any interest. And yet I felt strangely elated.

On returning to the Angel in search of dinner, we happened upon Dr Watson just descending from the station trap, weary and rather discouraged after his afternoon in Hexham. However the fine smell of cooking emanating from Mrs Garth's kitchen seemed to raise his spirits, and we agreed that we should eat together in the snug at eight o'clock to share accounts of the day. Of Mrs Hudson, there was no sign.

In the end, she did not return till after ten, by which time the gentlemen had enjoyed a bottle of Mrs Garth's best claret and were already talking of retiring. She entered the snug briskly, bringing with her a distinct smell of cheap tobacco smoke; and when Dr Watson asked her how she had spent her evening, she allowed a flicker of amusement to play around her lips.

'You may find this surprising, sir, but I have spent the last five hours in the public bar of the Grapes. And what a lot I've learnt! But perhaps, while I take off my gloves, you might tell me how you yourselves have spent the day?'

And so, as Mrs Hudson settled herself, Mr Spencer and I told her all about our efforts in the Baldwick Archive and Dr

Watson shared again the dismal story of his interview with Inspector Robinson.

'To be frank, Mrs Hudson, the fellow is little more than a mealy-mouthed idler. It's clear that he has no appetite for investigations that take him too far away from his own hearth, and he is adamant that there is no reason for further enquiry into Archie Crummoch's disappearance. Those fellows at the Grapes have convinced him that Crummoch was a half-crazed old man given to wandering, and Robinson seems to think he's probably just fallen down a mine shaft out on the moors.'

'And the boots, sir? How does Inspector Robinson explain those?'

'He considers them a hoax or a prank. Really, Mrs H, if they'd found Archie Crummoch lying with a dagger in his heart, I think Mr Robinson would have discovered an innocent explanation for it, if by doing so he could save himself some small degree of exertion!'

Mrs Hudson had joined us by the fire and for a moment or two her eyes remained fixed on the hearth.

'I see. Then we shall clearly get no help from that quarter. But one thing I do know, sir, is that the men at the Grapes were not telling our police inspector the whole truth.'

I sensed a quickening of interest in that small room and all three of us leant forward a little.

'Is that so, Mrs H?' Dr Watson seemed eager to be persuaded. 'What makes you think so?'

'Simply this, sir.' She settled herself a little more comfortably into her armchair. 'The clientele of the Grapes are a bunch of utter rogues. Poachers to a man, though not above a little sheep rustling in season. Suspicious of outsiders, suspicious of the police and for much of the time suspicious of each other. For them, lying to Inspector Robinson would have been almost a point of principle.'

'But were they not suspicious of you, ma'am?' I asked. I found it hard to imagine the stern and forbidding housekeeper of Baker Street mingling comfortably with such company.

'Not for very long, Flotsam,' Mrs Hudson assured me. 'You see, there is a dusty old piano in the public bar of the Grapes, so I went along and played it. Oh, I know, Flottie, you had no idea that I played, and why should you? After all, it is hardly the sort of accomplishment that a good housekeeper flaunts. And I'm certainly no expert. But I can bang out a fair *Lost Chord* and a passable *Maud*, both of which proved very popular, particularly with the baritone section. And in my experience there's nothing like a sing-song to form a bond. There was a ruffian there whose *Pretty Little Sarah* left scarcely a dry eye. After that his companions were only too happy to answer my questions.'

'And they confessed to misleading the inspector, Mrs H?'

'Oh, yes, sir. You see, most of them are doing very nicely from the Broomheath Hall estate, where there are plenty of birds and no one to stop them from trapping and netting as they please. That's why they're glad that Crummoch is gone. He knew their tricks, and from that little cottage of his he could see what they were up to. Now they can pilfer and poach from the estate with impunity. So the last thing they want is a party of policemen marching around the moors. They told Inspector Robinson exactly what he wanted to hear – anything that would send him happily back to Hexham. But after a couple of sentimental ballads and a pint or two of bitter-and-mild, it was a different story.' As Mrs Hudson spoke, a raw and wild gust of wind buffeted the window of the snug, stirring the curtain and reminding us all of the darkness that lay outside.

'It turns out there were two or three men at the Grapes who saw Archie Crummoch heading up to the moors on the night he disappeared, but no one saw him come down again – which surprised them, for they are used to watching the tracks by night without being seen. As for Crummoch taking himself off somewhere, it's true he was prone to that, but there was one piece of information they didn't share with the inspector. Apparently, you see, however far he roamed, he'd always be back in his cottage on rent day. It seems the old squire gave him the lease of the cottage for as long as he lived in it – all he had to do to retain possession was present himself there on rent day. Now, it's been years since anyone bothered to check, but Archie Crummoch never took that chance. In forty years the only rent days he'd ever missed were those when he was ill with the fever down at Mr Verity's house. But this time rent day fell three days after they found his boots, and there was no sign of him at the cottage. After that there wasn't a man at the Grapes who didn't think Archie Crummoch was dead. And for all their rough ways, I think they are afraid.'

Dr Watson cleared his throat a little uncomfortably. 'Afraid, Mrs H? Not of ghosts, surely? They can't really believe those old superstitions?'

'I don't think they do, sir. And that's why they're so scared. You see, if Archie Crummoch wasn't taken by an evil spirit then it was someone mortal who made him disappear. And that's why, when they talk of Crummoch's fate, there is always a moment when they look around the room, studying each other's faces. They think they know the moors. But not one of them can explain the evil that lurks there now.'

It was an uncomfortable thought, and in the silence that followed I don't think I was the only one aware of the angry wind outside. Dr Watson shifted a little in his chair then cleared his throat.

'So if Archie Crummoch's dead, Mrs H, do we have any idea who killed him? And even if we did, would that help us find this blasted Lazarus document?'

Mrs Hudson smiled and leant forward to warm her hands at the fire.

'There is no certain link between the two, sir. And yet it would be a strange coincidence if all the peculiar and unpleasant goings-on around Broomheath were not in some way linked. And the gentlemen at the Grapes were at least able to tell me one person who did not kill Archibald Crummoch.'

'They did? And who was that?'

'Mrs Summersby's butler. He may not be a familiar figure here in Alston, but those who frequent the moors know him well enough. His wanderings up there are common knowledge, and more than one of them have seen him set off from Broomheath at dusk carrying a spade. But he wasn't on the moors the evening Crummoch disappeared, because the landlord of the Grapes saw him that night in a Hexham tavern.'

'Visiting his goddaughter, ma'am?' I asked, remembering what Pauncefoot had said at our interview.

'I suspect his goddaughter is a convenient fiction, Flotsam.'

'My word!' Dr Watson exclaimed. 'Perhaps he was meeting up with Viscount Wrexham? That would explain it!'

But Mrs Hudson simply smiled.

'I think we can be sure, sir, that his visit had no such purpose. From what I heard at the Grapes, he spent the greater part of the evening drinking hard liquor and playing dominoes for money, with great success, before retiring to the rooms of a young lady known as Slip-Lace Polly with whom he had struck up a friendship. He was seen returning on the milk train the following morning. Now tell me . . .' She looked around questioningly. 'What about today's telegrams?'

'Telegrams, Mrs H?' Dr Watson looked bewildered.

'On the tray in the hallway, sir. Don't tell me that you didn't notice them? Why, they might be vital. There's one for you, sir, and there's one for Flotsam.'

'For me, ma'am?'

'Indeed. In fact, it has been quite a day for telegrams. I have received rather an interesting one myself. But perhaps . . .' She seemed to sense my eagerness. 'Perhaps you would like to read yours first?'

And of course she was right. It was the first telegram I had ever received, and it turned out to be from Miss Peters. Its contents, although cryptic, suggested that Mr Spencer was by no means forgiven for deserting her in London.

RUPERT UTTER BEAST DOES NOT DESERVE MY HELP STOP HAVE PLAN TO MAKE HIM SORRY STOP AM CERTAIN CAN COUNT ON

YOU STOP TELL HIM BEAST FROM ME STOP BLUE BONNET SIMPLY GORGEOUS STOP WALTERS BOY QUITE OVERWHELMED STOP REMEMBER AM RELYING ON YOU STOP VERY FONDLY

HETTY

Mrs Hudson's telegram was from Mr Rumbelow, and communicated rather more, with much greater economy.

URGENT NEWS SOUTH AFRICA STOP SWAN EFFECTS ARRIVED STOP LETTER RE DEATH PAUNCEFOOT SENT DECEMBER STOP SIGNED WREXHAM STOP QUOTE I ENCLOSE WATCH OF MY DEVOTED SERVANT UNQUOTE SIGNATURE BELIEVED GENUINE STOP

RUMBELOW

'But that's remarkable news, ma'am!' I exclaimed, waving the telegram excitedly. 'It proves that it was Viscount Wrexham who sent Pauncefoot's watch to Mr Swan. So it was the *Viscount* who was pretending Pauncefoot was dead. And Pauncefoot must have been lying to us too, because he didn't lose his watch at all. Not unless Viscount Wrexham stole it from him. And why would the Viscount do that?'

'It proves a little more than that, Flotsam. Think about when Swan received that letter . . .'

'It says in December, ma'am.'

'Precisely, Flotsam. And Viscount Wrexham was last seen

alive in October. It would seem that, six weeks or so after his disappearance, he was still alive enough to be taking an interest in his former servants, and even dealing with their correspondence.'

Dr Watson, however, was looking troubled.

'But why on earth would he be doing that, Mrs Hudson? Did they cook it up together? And whatever for? After all, Pauncefoot was respectably employed here at Broomheath – he wasn't doing anything wrong – so why pretend he was dead?' He shook his head sadly. 'If only we could lay our hands on the Viscount. Tell me, Mrs H, have you formed any opinion at all of where he might be?'

Mrs Hudson nodded briskly.

'Oh, yes, sir. I do have an idea about that. Now, that telegram of yours?'

It proved to be the shortest but most remarkable of the three.

URGENT PURCHASE PAIR OF SHOVELS

HOLMES

Dr Watson read this aloud three or four times, his bewilderment increasing with each reading.

'Well, I have to hand it to Holmes,' he concluded at last. 'He's a remarkable man. How he even knows I'm here beats me. I'm sure I never told him, but I suppose he must have got it from Mr Rumbelow. Yet I confess myself baffled as to the meaning of this message.'

'Well, Doctor,' Mr Spencer put in gently, 'I wouldn't like to guess exactly what Mr Holmes is up to, but the message itself seems clear enough. I would suggest that first thing in the morning we go out and buy some spades. And then, perhaps . . .' He shrugged and looked a little bemused. 'Then, perhaps, we should prepare ourselves for some digging.'

CHAPTER THIRTEEN

The Contessa

The following morning dawned bright, and for all the chill in the air, the moors above the town lay touched with gold, looking calm and oddly benign in the sunlight. We were up early, and before I had even breakfasted Mrs Hudson had already left for Broomheath Hall, to begin preparations for the arrival of the Countess Flavia, the Summersby's unexpected and not particularly welcome guest. I was to follow on later in the morning, when Dr Watson, having made the purchases stipulated in Mr Holmes's telegram, would drive me out to Broomheath in Mr Verity's trap. Before that I was to assist Mr Spencer in the Baldwick Archive.

This task proved considerably less amusing on a golden winter's morning than it had the evening before. Sequestered in the gloom of the little cottage room, surrounded by pamphlets that seemed both pointless and pompous, the slightly carefree hilarity that had previously made the work bearable somehow deserted us. Mr Baldwick's prose was leaden, his subjects mostly tedious and his sense of humour non-existent. Once, after I had excused myself for a few moments, I returned to find Mr Spencer sitting with his head in his hands in front of an unpublished paper entitled *Was Pontius Pilate British*?

After that, we agreed to avoid the pamphlets for a little, concentrating instead on the boxes of loose papers and jottings. The crate assigned to me contained a muddled collection of old notebooks and unpublished writings, and I confess there were moments trying to decipher Mr Baldwick's rather mean, self-pitying musings when I wondered if a morning blacking fireplaces in Baker Street might not have been greatly preferable.

Considerably more exciting was the prospect of the Countess Flavia's arrival at Broomheath Hall, and when Dr Watson called to collect me I joined him on the trap with undisguised enthusiasm.

'Lovely morning for a drive, eh, Flotsam?' he declared with fervour. 'But only if you're wrapped up warm of course. Perhaps if I were to place this rug over your knees . . . It being such a nice day, I thought I'd take a stroll on the moors myself this morning. I've a mind to go and see the ruined chapel where they buried Anthony Baldwick. That's where old Crummoch disappeared, if you remember. Can't help thinking I'd prefer to have a look at the place when the sun's shining, don't you know? Whoops! Almost hit that boulder . . .'

We were already on the moorland track which led to Broomheath, and the way was undeniably bumpy, but Dr Watson was a good driver who set a sensible pace. As we drove, he entertained me with tales of his Afghan campaigns, spiced up by a rather racy anecdote about his visit as a very young man to Lahore. We were skirting a flank of high, rolling moorland, bleak and beautiful in the early spring sun, and Dr Watson's gaze was directed towards this open expanse, when suddenly I saw his eyes narrow.

'Look there, Flotsam!' he urged. 'Just there, near the top of that spur!'

My eyes ran along the ridge, searching the heather for the cause of his sudden interest. At first I saw nothing but the sparse emptiness of the fells, and I was just about to turn away when a movement caught my eye. Only a hundred yards away from us, low in the heather and hugging the contours to escape our gaze, a figure was lurking. He was dressed from head to toe in brown tweed which provided an almost perfect camouflage against the winter colours of the moor. No sooner had I picked him out than he dropped out of sight, behind a fold of rock and heather.

'That fellow was watching us!' Dr Watson declared. 'I saw the sunlight flash on his binoculars.'

'And did you see his face at all, sir?'

'Too far away, Flotsam. But not for long! Listen, I'm going to try the old army bluff-and-double-back. We'll keep driving, as though we haven't noticed anything in particular, until we get round that spur and out of sight. Then I'll leave you with the horse while I double back behind him. Even if I can't lay hands on him, at least I might get a good look at the fellow!'

Without further exchange of words, the first part of this plan was put into action, and Dr Watson took to the moors. The first part only, I say, because of course I found myself incapable of staying meekly with the trap. Instead, seeing that our pony was perfectly content to graze the turf that fringed the road, I waited until Dr Watson was out of sight then hurried back on foot the way we'd come, to the point where I had first seen the stranger.

From there it was clear Dr Watson's quarry would not be easy to catch. He must have known himself observed, for he had already taken flight and was moving rapidly along the foot of the spur, staying low and close to the heather, away from the road and towards the higher reaches of the fell. Seeing that his path was taking him further from the line being followed by Dr Watson, I set off myself, holding my skirts high above the heather, in a direction that would block our quarry's line of escape.

I had no plan to conceal myself. On the contrary, by making my presence apparent, I hoped to divert the stranger back into the doctor's path. However, after a few dozen yards, I realised that the contours of the moor were coming between me and the fugitive and so, after I had hurried a hundred yards or more from the road, I had to alter course. I found myself clambering straight up a heathery slope.

This manoeuvre brought me to the top of a low ridge and, to my astonishment, there below me was the stranger himself, only forty yards away, making good speed up a shallow gully. I must have let out a cry on seeing him, for he changed direction, darting away from me until, for the first time, his figure was caught against the skyline.

In an instant he was gone again, dropping out of sight into some hidden hollow. Dr Watson must have seen him too, for I heard him shout and a moment later he too rose into view, cheeks puffed out and panting hard, but still going well. The two of us were converging rapidly on the place where our man had disappeared and in half a minute or so our paths had joined. With great caution, and perhaps a little trepidation, we approached the high lip of the hollow where the stranger had vanished.

The sight that met our eyes on cresting that ridge left me quite speechless. Even Dr Watson seemed lost for words, and I fear that, in truth, we simply stood and gaped at the figure below us. For instead of cowering from his pursuers, our quarry had settled himself comfortably on a tussock of heather and was in the process of lighting a pipe. The expression on his face was one of pure amusement.

'I congratulate you, Watson,' he announced. 'All those walks in Hyde Park are clearly keeping you in fine physical condition. For a moment I thought you would be upon me before I reached this spot.'

'Holmes!' Watson spluttered. 'But how on earth . . . ? We had no idea . . . ! How in the name of heaven do you come to be here?'

'I understand your mystification, my friend. But all in good time. First, I beg you, come down from that foolish vantage point where you can be seen for twenty miles or more. Down here you will be out of sight and out of the wind. When the sun shines there's not a better place to rest anywhere on the moor. I find it an excellent place for lying low, and I would be more than a little peeved should you draw the attention of the whole world to it.'

'You mean to say you led us here deliberately, Holmes?'

'Obviously, Watson.' The detective clicked his tongue, as if disappointed by the question. 'I've been eager to speak to you for the last couple of days, but I had no desire for our meeting to take place in public. So when, just now, it became clear you had finally noticed me and intended to give chase, it seemed prudent to make for somewhere suitably discreet.'

'But, sir,' I asked in wonder, while Dr Watson was still standing open-mouthed, 'however do you come to be here in the first place?'

He raised an eyebrow in my direction, his enjoyment of the situation evident from the smile playing over his lips.

'There is no mystery about that, Flotsam. That letter I received in London, remember? It was anonymous but very informative. It suggested that Lord Beaumaris had been heading to this area when he died. It also suggested that the late Anthony Baldwick was the person he was following. There was enough detail in the letter to persuade me that it was worth taking a look.'

Dr Watson still looked a little stunned. 'You must have been pretty taken aback when I arrived, eh, Holmes! For all your powers, I don't suppose you saw that coming!'

'On the contrary, my friend. I rather expected it.' Mr Holmes paused to draw on his pipe. 'After all, if my anonymous informant was telling the truth about Lord Beaumaris's destination, then the Viscount's horseracing code, once you had filled in the co-ordinates, would inevitably lead you to the same spot. And if for any reason you failed to decipher the Viscount's note, well, there surely can't be many lawyers in this country who go by the name of Verity and who wear the same old-school tie as Mr Rumbelow. I was not many minutes in Alston before I realised the connection.'

'You've got to admit that was a remarkable coincidence, eh, Holmes? Like something out of a novel!'

In reply, Mr Holmes merely raised one eyebrow. 'Possibly, Watson. But as I have observed before, when a number of disparate events are linked only by their apparent peculiarity, more often than not they prove to be parts of the same puzzle. So come, take a seat on this excellent heather – Flotsam, you can sit here beside me – and then, Watson, perhaps you would be good enough to let me hear your report!'

This the doctor attempted to do, telling Mr Holmes everything from the Earl of Brabham's explanation of the Viscount's message to our encounter with Pauncefoot; from our interviews with Mrs Summersby to the impending arrival of the Italian countess.

'Excellent!' his friend declared when everything had been laid before him. 'An admirable report. Just tell me again about Mr Swan's childhood in the Downs. It was there he became acquainted with Pauncefoot, was it?' The great detective's eyes seemed to cloud over for a moment. 'Strange . . . You see, in the course of my vigil here, I have had the opportunity to observe Pauncefoot more than once. There is something about the way he holds a spade—'

'But tell us, Holmes,' Dr Watson broke in. 'That letter you received. What exactly did it say?'

'Well, I don't carry it with me, Watson,' his friend replied tersely. 'But as well as linking Lord Beaumaris's name with Broomheath Hall, it contained details about his lordship's activities in Syria that convinced me the author was more than the usual time-waster. So I disguised myself as an ornithologist and took lodgings at one of the more remote farms, from where I have been able to observe the Hall most effectively.'

'Can't tell much just from looking, though, Holmes,' Dr Watson suggested. 'I'd have thought that you'd have been in Alston, asking questions.'

The great detective clicked his tongue impatiently.

'Clearly, Watson, I have not remained rooted on this heath. I've been every bit as active as you suggest, and if you doubt the efficacy of my investigations, let me supply you with three pieces of information that may change your mind. Last night, before dinner, you wrote a letter to your London broker, a letter that you have not yet posted. After dinner, you smoked one of Mr Spencer's cigarettes instead of your customary pipe. And this morning you purchased a small tin of peppermints from a shop near the Post Office. Am I correct?'

The doctor looked thunderstruck.

'Good lord, Holmes! Have you been spying on me? I think that's a bit much! But wait a moment . . . How could you know about the letter? It's as you say, I did write it, but it's gone no further than my jacket pocket. You couldn't possibly have seen it!'

'No, my friend.' Mr Holmes drew contentedly on his pipe. 'But I did see you, last night, on your way back into town on the station trap. You were filling your pipe and you had an evening newspaper under your arm.'

'A newspaper? Why, yes, I did. I'd been reading it on the train. But I fail to see what you could have learnt from that.'

'Ah, Watson! It's so simple. The leading item in last night's paper was another story about this gold seam in Australia. Now, I remember your excitement when that story first broke. It took me all of ten minutes to persuade you that the day after such a headline was the very worst time to invest. It stands to reason that a second headline would reawaken that enthusiasm for the venture, and your instinct – unless I'm mistaken – was to turn to your broker without delay.'

Dr Watson nodded a little reluctantly.

'Well, Holmes, now you've explained it, that's all straightforward enough. I confess I did draft a note to my man in London. But how do you know that I didn't send the letter? Must have been keeping an eye on the postman, I suppose?'

'Oh, really, Watson! You must see that I have better things to be doing with my time than spying on postmen! Had you returned from Hexham in time to catch the last post, I'm sure you *would* have posted the letter. But instead you've had a night to sleep on it, and we both know that you are, at heart, a sensible man in these matters. So although you find it hard to read about fortunes being made in gold mines without feeling that perhaps you should be seizing your share, you also know that such ventures are highly speculative. By this morning, I imagine, more cautious counsels had prevailed.'

Dr Watson looked a little put out.

'Well, I like to feel I can take a risk as well as the next man, Holmes. But I did decide to hold back for a day or two, just to see how things develop. Might not be as much gold there as everyone says. But what about those other things? The cigarette and the mints? You couldn't have deduced those just from seeing my evening newspaper!'

'Yet neither is a great mystery. What do you think, Flotsam?'

I confess I flushed at this unwonted attention, but luckily I had already applied myself to the problem.

'Well, sir, you said that you saw Dr Watson filling his pipe. And last night he'd run out of his favourite tobacco, which is why he accepted one of Mr Spencer's cigarettes. So if you'd seen him emptying his pouch, sir . . .'

'Of course. Excellent work.' Mr Holmes seemed genuinely delighted. 'I happen to know that Dr Watson is most particular about his pipe tobacco, Flotsam, and the tobacconist, of course, would have been closed for business until this morning. And those peppermints . . . ?'

'I suppose the tobacconist sells peppermints, sir?'

'Very good, Flotsam! He sells them in small tins that he stacks temptingly on the counter – just the sort of temptation to which my friend here routinely yields. He has at least a dozen half-empty tins of peppermints in his bedroom at Baker Street, is that not true, Watson?'

'Well, I do like a peppermint, Holmes, and those little tins, you put them down somewhere and then you forget that you've got them . . .'

'Just so. My point here is not to make you feel spied upon, my friend, but to show you that I am every bit as active in Alston as you would wish. In a relatively simple disguise I have been able to come and go, and to ask a great many questions, without arousing any suspicion. I have made only one error of judgement, and that was in missing last night's music at the Grapes. I understand Mrs Hudson was in excellent form. The fellows setting snares under High Top this morning are still very full of it.'

'So what now, Holmes?' Dr Watson asked, ignoring this

impressive display of local knowledge. 'Have you a plan yet for getting to the bottom of this Lazarus business? Because, apart from keeping an eye on Pauncefoot, I can't really see what's to be done.'

'Our next step is very clear, my friend, but it does not relate directly to the Lazarus Testament. While I'm prepared to exercise some patience in the pursuit of ancient scrolls, Watson, I cannot admit any such restraint when there's murder afoot. An old man has disappeared, and judging from the blood found at the scene, has been horribly slain. We cannot allow such a matter to rest. No, Watson, we must act at once. You have those shovels? Excellent. Then tonight we shall meet on the moor. It will no doubt be a macabre business but we have no choice. It should have been done long before this. There may well be an outcry, but Sir Percival will stand by us. Yes, Watson, tonight you and I are going to exhume a corpse. Or, more likely, a pair of corpses, for I feel certain that we shall find more than one when we open Anthony Baldwick's grave. What do you say, Flotsam? Care to join us for a spot of moon-lit disinterment?'

'Yes, please, sir.' The thought of being present at such an event filled me with utter horror. But the thought of not being present was even worse.

'Midnight then, Watson. We meet at the chapel.' He knocked his pipe against a stone, then rose from the heather. 'Bring the spades and a good storm lantern, and see if Rupert Spencer and Mrs Hudson will join us. The more witnesses the better. Now, if you will forgive me, I have a report to write for Sir Percival Grenville-Ffitch. Sir Percival is threatening to flood the county with troops if there is no sign of progress soon. An illegal exhumation will be just the thing to keep him occupied for a day or two!'

We said our goodbyes, and half an hour after first discovering him, Dr Watson and I watched Sherlock Holmes strike out across the moor, his long strides quickly carrying him out of sight behind a spur of grey rock. Then, as we made our way back over the heather, a cloud moved over the sun and a chill breath of wind accompanied it. To my great relief, our pony was still cropping the turf where we had left him.

If Mrs Hudson noticed my slightly tardy arrival at Broomheath Hall, she showed no sign of it. I stepped into the servants' hall to find her seated calmly at the table with Martha and Mildred, the two young girls who acted as cook and maid for the Summersbys. A large pile of cutlery lay in front of them and Mrs Hudson appeared to be explaining to them the difference between the various knives, forks and spoons. The faces of all three brightened when I entered.

'Ah, Flotsam,' Mrs Hudson greeted me. 'Just the person! You can continue here. These two young ladies are very quick learners. We've already covered bed-making, laundry, bathrooms and napkins, and we're about to move on to polishing. But first I should like to have a little chat with Mr Pauncefoot. He has been busy all morning with deliveries – I took the precaution of ordering in quite a substantial quantity of supplies – and I have barely spoken a word to him yet. However, it is high time he and I did a little planning . . .'

I had fully expected Pauncefoot to resent our intrusion, as

our presence at the Hall must surely hinder him in his searches for the Lazarus Testament; but to my surprise, when he emerged in his shirt sleeves from the pantry-cellar, he greeted my companion very warmly.

'If I may say so, Mrs Hudson, it is a great pleasure to welcome such a distinguished member of your profession to Broomheath. I believe your assistance will prove most beneficial. The two girls here at present are honest enough, and perfectly willing, but they have never seen service in a *proper* establishment. I fear the correct entertainment of a countess would prove quite beyond them.'

Mrs Hudson ran an appraising glance around the servants' hall. 'Thank you, Mr Pauncefoot. I daresay we can bring some helpful experience to the situation. Now tell me, what are your arrangements for the silver?'

'Arrangements, Mrs Hudson?' He looked a little awkward and shook his head as if in sorrow. 'I fear formal arrangements have not been necessary until now. The Summersbys live very simply. But I will of course be very happy to adopt whatever system you think most fit.'

The housekeeper nodded briskly. 'Yes, I understand. Very well. As for dinner, I have a menu in mind, and the various comestibles delivered this afternoon should all be of excellent quality. Let us hope the kitchen is capable of preparing them! And while I see to that, perhaps you would consider the wine, Mr Pauncefoot?'

This was a subject that seemed to cheer the butler considerably and, while Mrs Hudson took charge of affairs, he retired with a bow to the wine cellar in order to consider his options.

By mid-afternoon, the atmosphere in the servants' hall had been transformed. Martha and I were bustling in all directions with Mrs Hudson's instructions ringing in our ears, while Mildred, the young girl employed as a cook, was being given an emergency introduction to culinary arts hitherto quite unknown to her.

'And Flottie,' Mrs Hudson warned, 'the countess is travelling without a maid, so you will have to dress her. I'm sure you will cope admirably. Meanwhile, Mr Pauncefoot will no doubt be grateful for some help with the table settings. I will be through to check things presently . . .'

For all Mrs Hudson's confidence, I was rather daunted by the prospect of acting as lady's maid to an Italian countess, and as the hour of her arrival drew closer, I grew increasingly nervous. Even so, I could see at a glance that Broomheath Hall was nearly ready for her. Previously I had always felt that the house was not truly lived in, that the Summersbys were merely occupying the space within its walls. Yet somehow, in the course of a few hours, Mrs Hudson had changed all that. It was as if the spirit of the old house had come alive again and was smiling in anticipation of guests.

And Mrs Hudson's helpers rose to the occasion too. While one of us was sweeping the stairs, another would be polishing door handles or opening the door to a delivery of eggs, while someone else would be outside beating carpets. Pauncefoot, who had quickly surrendered himself entirely to Mrs Hudson's authority, appeared to be simultaneously decanting claret and arranging candelabra, while occasionally also checking the countess's bedroom for specks of dust. The effect of so much activity was to make Broomheath once more breathe a welcome, and despite my nerves I found myself humming cheerfully as I worked.

With so much to do, there was little time to worry, but when the hour finally arrived and we heard the sweep of the trap upon the gravel outside, I found all my anxieties returning. After so much hard work, such sterling efforts by all concerned, the prospect of my ruining the countess's welcome through some terrible error seemed almost too much to bear, and when Mrs Hudson signalled with a nod that I should follow Pauncefoot into the hall to greet our guest, I believe my legs were actually trembling.

I heard the *contessa* before I saw her. Pauncefoot had flung open the great doors in welcome and had advanced to assist her from the trap. Outside, thick clouds had made the afternoon murky, but rising from the gloom I heard musical laughter and a voice bubbling with excitement.

'*Bellissima*! *Bellissima*!' it trilled. 'Such walls! Such stones! Like the great bastions of Livorno, no? But so English too! Already I am happy to have accepted your so kind invitation!'

And with that conversational flourish, delivered in an Italian accent as robust as it was exotic, Miss Hetty Peters strode up the steps of Broomheath Hall.

I fear I can provide only a very limited account of the welcome given by the Summersbys to the Contessa Flavia. Such was my state of shock that I cannot be sure who said what, or what politenesses were exchanged, although I do remember that Pauncefoot at one point, seeing me dumbfounded, had to pinch my arm to prompt me into some particular action.

Only when I heard the *contessa* announce that she would like to rest for a little was I reminded of my duties.

'This preety girl is to help me, yes? *Eccellente*! Now I go and when I have rest, then I hope you will be so kind as to tell me all your archaeological adventures here. Archaeology! It is my passion! But first, I dress.'

On hearing this cue, I scurried about my business, and Miss Peters joined me in her smart guest bedroom only a few minutes later, her face radiant and her accent quite forgotten.

'Oh, Flottie!' she enthused. 'Isn't this just too wonderful? You and I together like this! I really feared I was going to have the most frightfully grim and lonely time here. But of course I didn't mind, because it would be worth it just to show Rupert that he can't leave me out of things, and can't leave me sitting in London with no one to dance with. After all, Flottie, Rupert may be a very average dancer but he's *so* much better looking than anyone else that it never seems to matter. And anyway, if I'd stayed in town I would have simply *had* to go to the Fearnleys' ball, and the Fearnleys would have expected me to wear my new duck-egg gown because I've been going on about it for weeks, and of course it would be a terrible waste of all that French stitching if Rupert wasn't there to see me in it! I just can't tell you how beautiful it is, Flottie! I know people go on and on about the *Mona Lisa* and the Taj Mahal by moonlight and things, but I honestly don't think there can be anything more beautiful in the *whole world* than one of Madame Lafitte's silk gowns.'

She paused for breath, but only for a fraction of an instant.

'Anyway, now Rupert will jolly well see what happens when he treats me so cruelly. He said in his letter that he was cooped up in a library all day. Well, for all I care he can stay there till he's as dusty as the books, while I'm tucked up all nice and warm in a lovely house, looking for treasure! It's true, isn't it, Flottie, that I'm in a *much* better position to find things out than he is? And how very dim of him not to think of something like this himself! Though he probably thinks it's *manly* to do something very boring in a good cause. Why is it, Flottie, that men always think suffering is noble when mostly it's just really, really stupid?'

She paused to take another breath and this time I was waiting for it.

'But, Hetty,' I put in, 'how do you come to be here at all? What has happened to the real *contessa*?'

She gave a little gurgle of pleasure.

'Why, Flottie, my angel, didn't I say? I made her up.'

I looked at her in astonishment. 'What? You mean there is no Countess Flavia?'

'Well, I suppose there must be one somewhere . . .'

'But Sir Bulstrode Peveril has vouched for her. I saw his letter!'

Miss Peters nodded a little sadly.

'*Dear* Sir Bulstrode! He's such a very kind and good man. When I told him that an old friend of my uncle's needed an introduction to the Summersbys, he was a bit dubious at first. But he's known me since I was a tiny girl and is ever so fond of me, and really I only have to pout a little and plead for a bit and he always gives in. It used to be rag-dolls and lollipops, now it's introductions. I felt quite guilty about it for a moment or two, until I realised that of course it was really *me* he was recommending to the Summersbys, and he'd have been very happy to do that if I'd asked him to. Only somehow I don't think even nice, trusting Sir Bulstrode was going to *quite* believe that I'd developed a burning passion for the archaeology of the Roman Empire.'

'But how did you even know that Sir Bulstrode was acquainted with the Summersbys?' I asked, still mystified.

'Oh, it seems that Mrs Summersby mentioned it to Mr Rumbelow when she went to his office. And when I told Mr Rumbelow how afraid I was that Rupert might be mixing in doubtful company, he was only too delighted to reassure me that the Summersbys were acquaintances of Sir Bulstrode. Well, after that it all seemed simple! Sir Bulstrode used to dandle me on his knee, you know. Not that I remember it, of course, but he speaks of it very warmly. Oh, what a wonderful view!'

The setting sun had burst through the clouds and was touching the high fells with an orange flame. For a moment we watched in silence, until the clouds closed again and left the great flank of the moor wrapped in night.

'There's something so excitingly *brooding* about these moors, isn't there, Flottie?' Miss Peters went on, her voice a little hushed. 'You feel sure that a strong-jawed Mr Rochester must be about to ride across them at any moment. And this is such a lovely room! I do hope my visit hasn't put anyone to too much trouble.'

'Well,' I confessed, 'we have been *rather* busy. There was a lot of dusting to do, and the prospect of feeding a countess caused all sorts of consternation in the kitchen. When I last looked, Mildred the cook was getting quite tearful over the blancmange . . .'

I might have continued for some time with a catalogue of that day's dramas, but Miss Peters looked immediately so very remorseful that my words trailed off.

'But it's wonderful to have you here,' I concluded truthfully. 'And having someone here to keep an eye on things must be a good thing, I'm sure. But you need to be careful. There's danger here too. A man has disappeared. Mr Holmes and Mrs Hudson are sure he's been murdered.' I was about to mention Mr Holmes's scheme for that very night, but realised just in time that Miss Peters would insist on coming too, and I was not at all sure, when Mr Holmes had spoken of the need for witnesses, that he had envisaged anyone quite as talkative as Miss Peters.

'Murder!' she shuddered. 'How appallingly gruesome. Do sit here next to me and tell me all about it . . .'

To my utter astonishment, Miss Peters's impersonation of an Italian countess with archaeological interests seemed to survive the evening; neither the Summersbys nor Pauncefoot seemed inclined to question Sir Bulstrode's recommendation and, after a period of initial exuberance, Miss Peters's Italian accent settled down into something a little less outrageous. Even so, it seemed to me inevitable that she would come to grief when the conversation turned to archaeology, for I was sure a serious enthusiast must see through her pretence in an instant.

But Miss Peters proved very deft at avoiding any traps. Indeed, she seemed in her element, asking her monosyllabic host all sorts of things about his work and filling his silences with such generous amounts of charm and enthusiasm that for the most part she avoided any questions about her own experience. And when Mrs Summersby did make polite enquiries, the *contessa* embarked upon a sequence of rather racy anecdotes about an Italian antiquarian called Corelli and his work in Pompeii, all of which, I rather suspected, were entirely invented.

'Most certainly, when I tell him of the magnificence of the remains here – of your Great Wall and . . . and of all the other ancient remains here, then surely Signor Corelli will be in haste to abandon Italy for this town of Alston. Only I fear it is the pretty girls of Napoli that Signor Corelli admires, quite as much as its antiquities,' she sighed, 'so perhaps he will not come. And the *Accademia*, perhaps they will not let him. But, of course, Signor Summersby, I forget that when you publish the results of your work here, then there will be nothing left for my dear friend Corelli to discover! Your work will be, how do you say, the *last word*. Is it not so?'

As always, Mr Summersby looked a little startled to be addressed directly and it was his wife who replied on his behalf.

'My husband has more modest aims, Countess. A short paper, perhaps, if all goes well. Now, do tell us more about Naples. We came over by way of Marseilles and spent some time in the South of France. That's where we met Sir Bulstrode, you know. But we had no time to visit Italy. Is it as beautiful as they say?'

'Ah, *Napoli*!' Miss Peters breathed, enraptured. 'Its blossoms! Its vineyards! Its great mountains! It is the most beautiful place on Earth!'

And the rest of the evening was given over to Miss Peters's

descriptions of an Italian landscape much populated by lithe young goatherds, innocent shepherdesses and handsome archaeologists, an Arcadia that appeared to beguile the teller every bit as much as it beguiled her audience.

Mrs Hudson, who had not been present at her arrival, greeted the news of the countess's true identity with a raised eyebrow and the trace of a smile.

'Well, well, Flotsam. A very spirited young lady. Let's hope she comes to no harm here.'

The Summersbys, it seemed, kept early hours. By ten o'clock the party had broken up for the night and I had escorted Miss Peters back to her room, where she celebrated her triumphant deception by jumping up and down on her bed in a French nightdress so exquisitely fine it was hardly there at all. By the time I left her, Mrs Hudson and her well-marshalled forces had already turned much of the kitchen chaos into good order. When Mildred's father arrived to collect us, at a little after eleven o'clock, the bulk of the work was done, and Mrs Hudson was happy to call a halt.

'Time enough to finish off tomorrow,' she declared. 'The Summersbys' demands are remarkably few, and I predict that the countess will be no trouble at all.' She turned to me and added, below her breath so that only I could hear, 'At least if she knows what's good for her! And anyway, Flotsam, I believe you have an appointment to keep . . .'

Mrs Hudson, to my surprise, had declined to join Mr Holmes's nocturnal expedition, arguing that it was a cold night and that she for one had plenty to do the following morning.

'Which isn't to say,' she conceded, 'that the job doesn't need to be done. Mr Holmes is perfectly right about that. But whether it has to be done by night, this very evening, I'm not so sure. If Sir Percival were to use his influence with the Home Office, an official exhumation could surely be arranged in two or three days at most.' She sighed. 'But boys will be boys, Flotsam, and I daresay you will learn a great deal from watching them in action. Just make sure you wrap up warm.'

'But, ma'am, don't you want to be there too? Aren't you just a little curious about what they might find?'

But at this she turned away a little sadly.

'I fear, Flotsam, that I already know exactly what they'll find.'

I have read many ghoulish tales in my time, many accounts of macabre goings-on in graveyards. Always the ingredients are much the same: swirling fog and flickering lanterns, a dread wind moaning between the graves, pale faces growing grim as the ghastly truth is uncovered. Very often a heroine swoons.

But there was no fog that night by the ruined chapel, high up on the moor. No fog, not even any wind, and certainly no swooning. Just a terrible stillness and a sky so cloudless that the diggers could work without lanterns. Their hunched profiles made dark, awkward shapes against a backdrop of stars. Around us the silver moor stretched empty on every side. And I don't remember feeling any fear, just terrible loneliness; as though we four were the only living souls left in the world. Mr Spencer took one spade from the start and refused to relinquish it. Mr Holmes and Dr Watson shared the other. Gradually all attempts at conversation were abandoned. The three men worked in silence.

I remember too the terrible cold; a cold moon, cold stars and frozen earth beneath the shovels. A frost was falling. I have seen graveyards in London crammed between slums, overgrown by weeds and strewn with waste; graveyards with broken headstones, dwarfed by high walls, lost beneath the smoke of factories. But that midnight on the moors, none of those terrible places of burial seemed as lonely or as lost as the grave where Anthony Baldwick lay. I promised myself that, when my time came, I would be laid to rest in warm earth, close to others, close to busy streets and jostling hansoms, somewhere where the world never slept; where I would never be so alone.

The grave was not deep – there was too little earth to allow for that. After the initial labour of breaking through the frosted ground, the gentlemen worked quickly, and it was not long before Mr Spencer's spade struck something hard. Then they worked more carefully, scraping and poking. Only at that point was a lantern lit, so that the diggers could more clearly see the sorry object they unearthed.

Archibald Crummoch lay on his side in the black earth, without casket or wrapping of any sort, without even a blanket to cover his face. He wore – grotesquely – pin-striped pyjamas with an old overcoat pulled over them. Perhaps the cold had preserved him, because his body was little decayed. One grey-white hand seemed clenched in a fist. The back of his skull had been stove in as if by a terrible blow.

'Something flat,' Mr Holmes suggested. 'A spade perhaps.' They were some of the first words anyone had spoken.

'What now?' Dr Watson asked.

'We can't move him. Not over the moor by night. Tonight

we'll alert the authorities. It can be done properly tomorrow.'

'So we'd better cover him again?'

'I think so, Watson. A foot or so of earth should be enough.'

'One moment, gentlemen.' Rupert Spencer unbuttoned his overcoat and stripped it off, then laid it over the dead man's face. None of us spoke. We watched while Dr Watson scraped some earth back into the grave, then we gathered up our things and turned away, leaving Archie Crummoch once again alone on the moor. A foot or so beneath him, the coffin of Anthony Baldwick lay undisturbed. That, at least, was some consolation.

It was half past one in the morning before I finally regained my room at the Angel. The town of Alston lay asleep outside, and the inn itself was silent. Mr Spencer and I had parted in the hallway, and the look in his eye as we said goodnight suggested that he felt every bit as unsettled by our adventure as I did. I would have given a great deal to be able to share the full story with Mrs Hudson before I slept, but when I passed her bedroom door I saw that her light was out, and when I pressed my ear to it I could hear the rise and fall of her breathing.

Alone in my room, I did not undress. There had been no ghosts in the ruined chapel that night, no ghouls or evil spirits. And yet I was strangely haunted by what I had seen there, and however hard I tried to blink it away I could not escape the image of Archie Crummoch's body, twisted and mud-stained, the stars bright above him. So lonely. So cold. So lost.

Beside my bedside was a small Bible, left there by Mrs Garth. It was a small, inexpensive volume, but it reminded me of what Mr Verity had told us about Old Crummoch's last night. He had escaped from Mr Verity's house through a window. He hadn't even paused to dress, taking nothing with him but an overcoat to cover his pyjamas. And a Bible. He had taken a Bible with him, a companion to face the fate that awaited him. They had found it by the freshly turned grave. They must have taken it away with them.

I have never been a church-goer. My early days at the orphanage did nothing to encourage it, and Mrs Hudson's households had always been run on unusually secular lines. But that night, for reasons I don't fully understand, I found myself wishing Archie Crummoch had been buried with his Bible.

I think my idea took a few minutes to take hold of me, and I am not proud of it. Writing from the distance of old age, I can barely credit the rashness and recklessness of my youth. Yet there is something in the impetuosity of the young girl I once was, something in her fearlessness and her determination, which I cannot help but admire. In her defence, I can only say that, alone in a silent bedroom, looking at Mrs Garth's Bible, it did not seem such an absurd idea to venture outside again. It was no more than half an hour's walk to the ruined chapel, it was a clear, bright night and the path was easy to follow. I could take the little brown Bible to Archie Crummoch, rest it on the soil that covered him, and be back in my room in no more than an hour. I had a warm coat and I would be walking fast: I would scarcely notice the cold. And there'd be no sleep for me were I to stay, restless in my room, thinking of that grave beneath the stars.

What could possibly go wrong?

No one heard me leave the Angel, and as I passed through the silent town no curtain stirred, no window showed a light. My enthusiasm for the task carried me along at a cracking pace and I was three quarters of the way to the ruined chapel before the loneliness of the moors began to press upon me once more. Even then I strode on, undeterred, and when I rounded a spur of hillside and saw the old chapel ahead of me in the moonlight it was as still and deserted as when we'd left it.

I'd thought of saying a few words over Archie Crummoch's grave, some sort of prayer, perhaps, but when I stood there looking down, no words came. Instead I knelt and placed the small volume softly on the newly turned soil, and felt pleased that I'd come. This time when I turned away, I felt the old man was not entirely alone. Then, as I dropped down from the high top of the fells, in a section of my journey where the moor rose high above me on both sides, a bank of cloud passed across the moon and the silver ribbon of track was lost in shadow.

I don't know if it was the sudden darkness that caused me to look around just then or whether a movement on the edge of my vision caught my eye. But it was then, just as the moonlight disappeared, that I noticed a light – a tiny flicker moving high above me on a flank of the heath. How far it was from where I stood I could hardly tell. Judging distance on those high fells was hard enough by daylight, and the sudden darkness had robbed me of perspective. Was it a small light quite near, perhaps only a hundred yards away? Or was it a great lantern made small by distance, somewhere on the far slopes that lay above the town?

For a full five seconds I stood still, torn by indecision,

remembering the tales of Pauncefoot digging by night, searching for the hiding place of the Lazarus Testament. If the light really was close by, there would be no harm in venturing a little closer, just to see. If, upon investigation, it proved to be a great distance away, I would simply make a note of its direction and return safely to the path. And so, with some trepidation, I stepped from the familiar track and into the deep embracing darkness of the heather.

At first I moved tentatively, feeling my way with cautious feet, but the heather was low and I found I could make good progress. I tried to keep my eye on the flickering light as I advanced. If it had been moving before, now it seemed to be stationary. Surely it was only a short distance away? If I could advance another fifty yards without mishap, I might discover for myself the identity of its bearer . . .

Of course, at the very moment I had that thought, the heather tripped me and sent me stumbling to my knees. I was swiftly on my feet again but, when I looked around, the light was gone.

Had someone heard my gasp as I fell? Had the lantern been extinguished? Or had it merely passed out of sight behind one of the folds in the heath? Either way, I pushed on, instinctively, certain that I was near my goal. After a few more strides and another stumble, the ground beneath me began to rise steeply and I scrambled forward using hands and feet until I gained the summit of a ridge and looked around.

Sure enough, there was the light again, a little to my left and some distance away. The cautious part of me knew that this was the time to retrace my steps, to retreat with dignity, but my blood was up and the fever of the chase had me in its grasp. Instead I moved forward, tripping on the down-slope and falling once more, but up again instantly, my momentum barely broken.

I had heard stories of travellers lured to their doom by the will o' the wisp, but this was no spirit flame and I had no fear of counting myself among their number. So I pressed on, faster and faster, while the light came and went in front of me. As I went I knew that retracing my steps would be far from simple, but the thought only made me more determined to succeed. I don't know how many minutes had passed, nor how far I had travelled, when I lost sight of the lantern for the last time. To this day I do not know who I was following so blindly that night: Pauncefoot most probably, on one of his nocturnal expeditions, or perhaps a simple poacher checking his snares. There came a point, however, when I stood still and looked about me and accepted that my quarry was lost. And very quickly after that came the realisation I had very little idea in which direction the track to Alston lay.

Above me, the sky that had been so remarkably clear was now three quarters obscured by cloud; it was as though a thick, black blind was being drawn over the stars. Although my eyes were already growing accustomed to the darkness, I could make out no feature to guide me. I shudder to think how many circles I might have described in the hour that followed. I only know that the cold, which had been held at bay by my rapid motion, began to advance as my energy waned. First my fingers and then my toes began to lose sensation, and I realised I was both damp and shivering. Only then did the seriousness of my plight begin to dawn on me. I was lost on the moors on the bitterest of March nights, with no one likely to find me and no idea which way to go. And I was already beginning to succumb to the cold. Then, when I thought my predicament could become no worse, I stepped forward onto softer ground and felt my feet begin to sink beneath me.

Of course I struggled to step back. The urge was too instinctive to resist. But in the panic of the moment, my sudden twist made things worse and I over-balanced and fell backwards. For a moment I felt my hands pressing through the thin layer of sedge into the slime beneath it, but I righted myself instantly. By doing so, however, I threw my weight heavily onto my feet, and found myself planted more firmly than before. And then, as I forced myself to stand still and think, I felt myself beginning to sink.

If I had read many tales set in graveyards at the dead of night, I had probably read an equal number that featured a character trapped in sinking sand. Never once had I taken them seriously. They were, I knew, a literary device to punish the evil and unwary, or to try the resolve of readers by threatening their hero with a hideous demise. In such cases, I knew, an innocent protagonist was always rescued, albeit at the very last moment, their deliverance such a formality I had never paused to imagine the actual feelings of a character so caught: the prickling flush of panic as understanding dawns; the disbelief, then desperation; the frantic pleading with fate; the raw despair that follows. And finally the choking, nauseating horror as imagination takes over and begins to paint with slow, inexorable strokes every detail of the fate that awaits – the last gasp of air, slime filling your mouth, then your nose; your last desperate breath drawing in the mud . . .

That night I don't think the idea of rescue ever seriously occurred to me. The possibility was too remote, too far-fetched. But that did not stop me shouting at the very top of my voice for help, shouting for as long as I had breath to do it.

'Here!' I cried. 'I'm here! Help me! If there's anyone out there, please help me!'

Even as I paused to refill my lungs I could hear my cries dying in the darkness. 'Help!' I tried again, determined above everything that while I still had life I would not go quietly.

It must have taken only a minute or two for me to sink almost to my waist in the mire, but at that point I felt the sinking motion begin to cease. It seemed I was no longer being drawn downwards with such terrible speed but was merely held fast, and for a time this knowledge gave me new hope. It seemed my fate was not, after all, to be the gruesome death I had imagined, and I redoubled my cries. Only as exhaustion began to take hold did I see that I had simply exchanged one dreadful fate for another, for the cold would surely succeed where the mud had failed. How long could I survive, shivering and wet, on such a cruel night? Could I stay alive till dawn, when perhaps some wildfowler or sportsman might hear my cries? Did my best hope lie in silence, in conserving my strength and energy?

I grappled with these questions for what seemed like hours, despairing and crying out by turns; and yet, when the clouds finally parted, the stars were bright in the night sky and the moon was still high. And by the light of that moon there was revealed to me the most impossible, the most remarkable sight. There, on a ridge above me, picked out in silhouette against the deep blue of the night sky, was a lone horseman, his cloak billowing behind him. As I watched, he turned and scanned the hollow where I struggled, then turned his horse and began to pick his way towards me, down the escarpment. As he drew nearer, the wind blew back his cloak and the moonlight fell on his face, revealing flowing white robes and the gnarled, ancient face I had seen once before by moonlight.

CHAPTER FOURTEEN

The Arabian

My memory of the rescue is too blurred and too fragmentary to take much telling. I must have swooned before he reached me, but whether from relief or from exhaustion I cannot be sure. I have a dim recollection of the rider urging his mount into the bog and I remember fearing that he too might become trapped. Then a strong arm came round me and I was pulled upwards. As I drifted in and out of consciousness, I heard a voice speaking in a language I didn't understand, a voice deep and somehow soothing. I remember marvelling that one so old had such strength in his arms, and after that I remember nothing until I found myself lying across the front of his saddle like a sack of corn, as his horse made its way softly under the archway of the Angel Inn.

How the rider knew to rouse Mrs Hudson, I have no idea. Perhaps she was already awake and fretting at my absence, for she was fully clothed when I first remember seeing her, and the next morning I found traces of mud on her boots. When the light fell on her face, my rescuer spoke to her in English.

'Madam,' he said softly, setting me lightly on my feet, 'we

have met before. You were so courteous when I waited at the great house in London.'

'I remember, sir. Mr Ibrahim, is it not? I see that I am greatly in your debt.'

'It is my pleasure to be of service. Your little friend wandered from the path. Fortunately, I was there to hear her cries.'

I felt Mrs Hudson's arm go round me and clasp me very tight.

My rescuer bowed again, as if preparing to depart. Even when very close to him and with the light of Mrs Hudson's lamp to assist, I found it hard to guess his age. My confused fancy that he was the ancient guardian appointed to watch over the Lazarus Testament had vanished with my fit of fainting and seemed foolish to me as I stood in the reassuring shadow of the Angel. But nevertheless, his face seemed somehow timeless, shaped and altered by the years like driftwood by the ocean.

'My pleasure,' he repeated, and began to turn away.

'It would be a terrible disgrace, sir, if I did not offer hospitality to one who has done us such a service. Perhaps you would take some tea against the cold? One who rides the moors so late is seeking something, and searching alone is not easy. Perhaps we can offer you our help in return.'

The man eyed the inn dubiously and I thought he would refuse, but at the last moment he seemed to change his mind.

'Tea I can accept,' he said softly. 'And your assistance also. I am a stranger here, and friendless.'

And that is how we came to hear the tale of someone who was also, in his way, on the trail of the Lazarus Testament. The church clock was striking four o'clock in the morning when, slightly cleaner and swathed in blankets, I was permitted to perch by the fire in Mrs Garth's front parlour and hear his story. Within a minute I was gripped, for his voice was rich for all its roughness and carried me far away from the chills of Alston to an antique land, as hot and dry as it was exotic.

'My homeland is Arabia,' he told us, 'a poor land of many deserts. My people are not blessed with the riches of its neighbours. The merchants of Cairo or Damascus carry more gold in their pockets than many of my people will see in a lifetime. Perhaps one day God's bounty will make my people rich also, but until then many young men must leave their ancient lands and seek their fortunes in Egypt or Syria or in the cities of the Maghreb. My nephew Abdullah was one such man. He was blessed with quick wits and a gift for study, and had he lived I feel sure he would have been a great man. To achieve his fortune, he travelled, in his fifteenth year, to Damascus . . .'

Tired as I was, I listened entranced as my rescuer described for us the great city of Syria, its covered markets and great mosques, its scholars and its holy men, a meeting place for people of every creed and colour. The fragrance of its courtyards drifted out to me as I listened, carrying me to secret places where fountains played and jasmine draped the archways.

To this ancient city, two years before, Lord Beaumaris had come. Then in his seventy-eighth year, his lordship's search for the Lazarus Testament had taken him from one great city of the east to the next, from Alexandria to Isfahan and back again, each time prompted by new rumours or following clues that crumbled to nothing in the dry sands of the desert. Many scores of times he had conducted digs without success, from Ararat in the north to Aden in the south. Finally, it was to Damascus he returned. And this time, he announced, he would not fail. His information was unimpeachable. The Lazarus Testament would be his.

Precisely when young Abdullah had joined the Beaumaris retinue, his uncle was unsure. But he had proved a quick and able learner, deft and skilful in the field, and ravenous for knowledge. Lord Beaumaris had warmed to his enthusiasm and, little by little, Abdullah had become his favoured protégé and his most trusted lieutenant.

It seems the two had been together when the crucial clue was found. In a caravanserai east of the Caspian they had run to earth a dying man, the grandson of a disgraced governor of Antioch, who claimed that he alone was privy to the secret. His grandfather had heard it from a condemned man, a renegade scholar turned spy, who had used it to bargain for his life. The condemned man's grandfather had been told it, in turn, in a *madrassa*, or holy school, by his tutor who was mourning the death of an only son. In despair he confided that a secret entrusted to his family for generations must now die with him. Two hundred years before, he said, during times of great upheaval, his ancestor had been ordered by the sultan of the day to hide a valuable Christian relic somewhere safe from where it could be easily recovered when the dangers had passed. This ancestor had taken the sealed urn he was given to a certain dwelling in Damascus, on the street that was called Straight, where he had placed it in a stone casket and buried it in the cellar. It was the naming of that house that had brought Lord Beaumaris and Abdullah to Damascus, certain that a great discovery awaited them. But others had got wind of their hopes, and to Lord Beaumaris's consternation he found his situation in the city fraught with difficulty. The Ottoman officials would certainly consider any significant discovery to be the property of the Sultan; and worse than that, there were unscrupulous parties who would not think twice before ransacking any site in which the Englishman showed an interest.

Faced with these obstacles, Beaumaris and Abdullah formed a plan. The old aristocrat set about applying for permission to conduct a major excavation on the outskirts of Damascus. The dig he proposed would be extensive and lengthy, and therefore it was only sensible for him to seek a house to rent for the duration of his stay. And, he had procured the lease of a house in Straight Street that would suit him very well indeed . . .

This cunning plan had one fatal drawback. Setting up the diversionary dig was an expensive business, and it was at precisely that time that his lordship's funds ran out. His estates were mortgaged, his bank account empty. He was, effectively, bankrupt.

'This English lord,' Mr Ibrahim told us sadly, 'even sent my nephew out to beg on his behalf. Abdullah came to me and asked for money, but what little I had I would not give him. I cannot believe it is God's will that we should disturb the relics of the dead. But now I regret my decision. Perhaps if I had helped him, Abdullah would never have met the man called Anthony whose fate was so entwined with his.'

It was not clear from the old man's tale exactly how Lord Beaumaris came to meet the man known in Damascus as Mr Anthony. He could only tell us that this man was an Englishman, a traveller with an interest in antiquities who for many months had been hanging around the fringes of archaeological circles in the Holy Land. He was known to have private, if limited, means, and to Lord Beaumaris even those must have seemed enviable. What agreement was reached between the two men is not clear, and it seems hard to believe his lordship would have shared his secret with a stranger, yet what is certain is that the lease for the house in Damascus was paid for by Mr Anthony and taken in his name.

And yet, despite the necessity of this unwelcome alliance, everything seemed to be going well for Lord Beaumaris and Abdullah. The decoy excavations had succeeded in capturing much attention, as frequent attempts to bribe his workers there confirmed. Meanwhile, hidden from view, the two friends were steadily excavating the cellar of the house in Straight Street. Abdullah did the digging, Lord Beaumaris supervised. It seems the ingratiating Mr Anthony was kept at arm's length. Perhaps the two archaeologists believed him completely ignorant of their plans.

Finally, with only a tiny part of the cellar floor still undisturbed, Abdullah's tool struck something solid. Some breathless moments later, the two men realised they were looking at the corner of an ancient urn. After a lifetime of searching, it seemed Lord Beaumaris had succeeded in his quest.

Given the circumstances, it seems incredible that the two confederates did not continue digging with even greater fervour. But, as Lord Beaumaris later explained to Abdullah's uncle, the night was well advanced and the streets were falling silent, and both men were terrified of making any noise that might draw attention to their activities. In searching so diligently and for so long, they had learnt patience. With quite remarkable restraint, they agreed to continue again the following day, when the streets would be loud and bustling.

But the next day brought a summons for Lord Beaumaris to attend the governor's palace. Such formalities were not uncommon and the elderly peer knew he might be detained for some hours, so it was agreed that Abdullah would continue the excavation alone, until the urn could be lifted. It was a large object and awkward to manoeuvre. Both men agreed that they would open it together.

It was not till many hours later that the terrible events of that day were known to Lord Beaumaris. On returning to his house, he found it apparently empty, until he entered the cellar and found the body of Abdullah lying crumpled in one of the holes he had dug. The young man had been pierced through the temple with one of his own chisels. To Lord Beaumaris, overwhelmed with horror though he was, the motive for the attack was clear: the excavations were empty, the precious urn gone.

While our visitor told his story, the streets outside the Angel Inn lay still. Inside, in the warmth of Mrs Garth's parlour, Mrs Hudson and I sat in silence, our faces flushed by the firelight. When he came to the episode of his nephew's death, I saw the old man's eyes grow dim with tears.

'I cannot tell you how I grieved,' he told us, 'for Abdullah was special to me. I held him on the first day of his life. I saw his first steps. When the news of his murder reached me, I left my home and travelled the long road to Syria, the pain of my loss like hot coals inside me. In Damascus, I met the English lord and saw at once his grief and pain were as great as my own. Indeed, he seemed broken by his loss, without purpose, without health, without hope. I could see in his eyes that he would not live many months more.

'He told me much about Abdullah and about the circumstances of his murder. He was certain the criminal must be one of a handful of villains who had in the past made threats against them. He gave me their names, and for three months I tracked these individuals from town to town across the Levant. One by one I came to look them in the eye. I am an old man, I know, but grief makes me strong. When I held their faces close to mine, I could see the fear in their eyes. Yet I could see no guilt. These, I knew, were not the men I sought.

'Finally, I returned to Syria, to the house of Lord Beaumaris. But on arriving there I discovered that the English lord had returned to his own country. He had left me a simple note. *Your nephew's murderer is fled to England, he told me. I shall ensure justice is done.* That is all he wrote. I think he feared my anger, feared that my thirst for vengeance would bring me to the gallows in this land of yours.' The old man sighed. 'But he was wrong. I felt inside me, not hatred, but an age-old sorrow and perhaps weariness too, for I would never rest until the fugitive had been brought to justice.'

With those words he fell silent, and Mrs Hudson let him pursue his own thoughts for a few moments.

'And so you still seek your nephew's murderer, sir?' she asked at last.

He nodded slowly, as if his head weighed heavily upon his shoulders.

'I do. It is this that has brought me here.'

He looked around at Mrs Garth's homely bric-a-brac, as if in wonder at the strangeness of it all. Then, with a shake of his head, he resumed his tale.

'Shortly after my return to Damascus I received word that Lord Beaumaris was dead. He had sent me no further message about the identity of my nephew's murderer. That is when I began my own inquiries. One name remained on the list the English lord had given me. The name was Anthony, and I tried to find out more. Those who had known him in Damascus told me there was something in his eyes, a strange light, which caused cautious men to shun him. Then I received a letter from England. I carry it with me still. It had been posted months earlier, and since then it had followed me from city to city in my travels. It was simply signed *Anthony*.'

It proved a remarkable document, written throughout in a scrawl that was by now familiar to me but which in parts was barely legible. The writing sloped erratically across the page: desperation made manifest in ink.

Alston, Cumberland

To the man I have wronged

Sir, I do not know if this will ever reach you. I believe you to be the guardian of the man I have slain. Believe me, I beg of you, by all heaven's saints, I did not intend to take his life. I cannot expect forgiveness, I know. An eye for an eye, that is the way in your country. Perhaps it is the only way.

Why did he die? Because the fates had decreed he stood between me and the thing I most desired, the key to all fame and all fortune – even, they say, to everlasting life! Only think of it! Just think! Imagine a man insignificant in every way, one who has always been a meagre, mean-faced attendant at the table of others' greatness, tasting glory only in their crumbs. And there before me, an object to raise me above them all! With one blow, respect and greatness would be mine! I would reveal to the world a treasure beyond price! Sir, there lurks in me a devil of dark moods, an angry cur that lashes out at the achievements of others. It was this beast that made me strike, and now I am lost forever. I felt a black anger seize me as I saw another hold the great prize and, before I knew it, my hand was raised. Never fear, sir, I shall not live to see it washed clean. I cannot escape punishment. The hell in which I burn each day makes my life a torment to me. I can only pray my blood will atone for my sins. When you read this, I shall have paid for my crime with my life.

The Lazarus Testament is by me as I write, still in its ancient urn. I have never dared to break the seal lest the rumours be true and its touch imparts eternal life. For me, no curse could be greater. This very night I have written to Lord Beaumaris to tell him where I am. Once here, he may find it if he can. I smuggled the urn from Damascus in a shipment of old but unremarkable ceramics and it sits amongst them still, inconspicuous among the many. I know myself to be like that plain vessel – ignored amongst the mass of men, yet bearing inside me an undiscovered brilliance!

The works I leave behind me shall be my memorial. Those who read my writings shall be my witnesses, and shall prove themselves worthy of my gift.

With these words, my life is over. You may sleep in peace knowing this letter is the penultimate act of the miserable wretch known to you as

Anthony

Mrs Hudson nodded as she returned the letter to its owner.

'Thank you, sir,' she said. 'This note explains a great deal. And it was this, I assume, that brought you to Alston?'

My rescuer nodded. 'Before I could rest, I wished to be sure this letter was not simply a device to elude justice. But I knew nothing of the man other than his name, so I determined to travel to the city of London to ask the assistance of your British officials. In London, however, I am only a poor Arab and the officials have no time for me. There are so many people, so many inquiries. After a while I began to despair, for London is expensive and I am not rich. Then I met by chance an Englishman known to me from the consulate in Baghdad. He was a kind man and he helped me. He said he'd heard a rumour that a very great man called Sir Percival was charged with finding the Lazarus Testament, and that he planned to consult Mr Sherlock Holmes.

'This news gave me hope. Even in my country, Mr Sherlock Holmes is famous for his cleverness. So I go to the office of Sir Percival and ask to be allowed an audience. But he is so busy he cannot see me, although I wait many days. So then I come to the place called Baker Street. I watch, hoping for a chance to approach Mr Sherlock Holmes and beg him for his help. But he too is busy, and always in the company of others. So one day I knock at his door and you invite me inside and are kind to me, but the great detective does not come. I know a little of your English manners so I do not wait too long. Instead I decide I will write to Mr Holmes, and the next day I travel to this town of Alston.'

'And you did write, but you did not sign the letter. Is that right, sir?'

The old man bowed courteously. 'I was afraid Mr Holmes would not read the letter of one such as I, *a dirty black*, as I am called in London. And I know that here in Alston also such a one as me will arouse suspicion. So I leave the train before I reach the town. I ask and find where I may sleep, from where I may hire a horse. The people there are rough but not unkind. They believe me to be Spanish, as if to them all people of dark skin are Spaniards. And now, at night, when I will not be noticed, I ride the moors and visit the villages. I study the graves, looking for the name of the man I seek. But I do not find it. And my hosts, who ask on my behalf, tell me that no Mr Anthony is known here.'

With these words our guest fell silent, his tale complete. I think the telling of it had helped him in some way, for when I looked at that weathered face, it seemed to me a certain heaviness was gone from his eyes. Perhaps it was a weight of loneliness that had lifted from him, for he seemed to me now less stern, less pained, than I had thought him earlier.

The silence was broken by the chimes of the church clock, and it raised our visitor from his reverie.

'It is time for me to go,' he said. 'My hosts rise early. I must be back before daybreak.'

But Mrs Hudson raised her hand.

'Please, sir, a moment longer if you will. In return for your story, let me tell you what we know. You see, I sincerely believe the man who killed your nephew is indeed dead by his own hand. Anthony was only one of his names. Here he was known as Anthony Baldwick, and he came here to hide from his pursuers.' Mrs Hudson paused for a moment, as if wondering how best to reassure the old man beside her. 'I can arrange for you to speak to Mr Verity, who was one of those who found his body. He can tell you something of the fellow's last days. It would seem he did indeed write to Lord Beaumaris, because we know his lordship was bound for Broomheath Hall when he died. But the Lazarus Testament is still not found. I suppose it is still where Mr Baldwick hid it.'

Our visitor listened very carefully as she spoke.

'Then I shall see this man you mention and hear his story. And then, perhaps, I shall go home – for the fate of your document does not concern me. I would only say to you that there are certain secrets hidden for a reason, and these it is better not to know.' He rose to his feet with great dignity. 'Home!' he said again. 'Even in a foreign tongue, how sweet that word can sound.'

That night was the last time I ever saw him. He turned and waved at me as he guided his mount beneath the archway. He had come to me in the night, in my hour of need, and then faded into the shadow. Like a dream, perhaps, or an hallucination born of fever. Or perhaps like a weary angel, recalled for one last act of mercy.

CHAPTER FIFTEEN

The Missing Box

The next day, I overslept. Neither the crashing of Mrs Garth's pans below me, nor the trundle of the market barrows outside, made the slightest ripple upon the smooth waters of my sleep. Only when Mrs Hudson hefted onto my bed a pile of papers so huge that they made the springs creak did I finally sit up and blink. Somewhere a clock was striking ten and my room was full of light.

'Golly,' I cried, and made to throw back the covers, only to be thwarted by Mrs Hudson seating herself firmly upon them.

'A young lady does not say *golly*, Flotsam,' she reproved me, 'although I confess I have heard one or two say worse. These,' she went on, pointing at the papers, 'are some documents I've brought you from the Baldwick Archive. I'm expecting you to stay here in bed and rest a little until we're sure you've recovered from last night's adventures. And, in case you get impatient, I thought a little reading might help pass the time.'

I must have grimaced because she added quickly, 'If you're feeling quite well this afternoon, you can come with me to the Hall and help keep an eye on Miss Peters. I dread to think what she's getting up to, and presumably it cannot be very long before the Countess Flavia is unmasked. If you cannot persuade her to pack her bags before that happens, you might at least help keep her out of the way of the Summersbys for an hour or two. Not that your little escapade last night says a great deal for your judgement, young lady.'

I accepted this rebuke with a blush, then pretended to study the pile of papers she'd brought me.

'How are things going at the Baldwick Archive, ma'am?' I asked. 'That's where we've got to look, isn't it? Mr Baldwick said so in his letter.'

'Ah!' Mrs Hudson nodded approvingly. 'So you noticed that too? What were the exact words?' She raised her eyes to the ceiling and recited a line we had both read the night before. '*Those who read my writings shall be my witnesses, and shall prove themselves worthy of my gift.*' She shook her head sadly. 'I was rather reminded, Flottie, of those manufacturers of soap powder who promise that one box somewhere contains a golden sovereign. It would seem Mr Baldwick's method of persuading people to read his writings is much the same.'

'But, ma'am, if there really is some clue in his papers about where to find the urn, shouldn't we all be down there looking as hard as we can?'

'Patience, Flottie, patience.' She pushed me gently back against the pillow and placed a hand on my forehead. 'Dr Watson has joined Mr Spencer at the Archive and Mr Holmes is at Mr Verity's house, so perhaps he will join them later. At the moment, though, Mr Holmes is extremely busy explaining last night's events to all the relevant authorities. Telegrams have been flying to and fro all morning. The local coroner is on his way, as well as the High Sheriff, and I believe someone high up in the Home Office is coming from London. A different police inspector has been sent out from Hexham, and his men are guarding the grave now, and there's talk of Scotland Yard. Your discovery last night changes everything, you see, Flottie. No more unobtrusive observations now. Mr Holmes says it is only a matter of time before Pauncefoot is charged with the murder.'

'But wasn't he seen in Hexham the night old Crummoch died, ma'am?'

'He was, Flottie. And by no means keeping a low profile. I imagine there will be no shortage of witnesses to his successes at dominoes. But a great many people have seen him on the moors at night with a spade in his hand, and in the eyes of the police nothing could be more damning. So I expect there will be a lot of questions in Hexham in the coming days about precise times and places. The thing is, Flotsam, whoever it was who committed the murder, we don't really know *why*.'

'Could Crummoch have known something about the Lazarus Testament, ma'am?'

'I'd have thought that was a better reason to keep him alive, Flotsam.'

'Then he saw something he shouldn't have seen, ma'am. Out there at the chapel. Someone opening the grave, perhaps?'

'And that brings the police back to Pauncefoot, whose tiresome habit of digging at night has been widely noted. Yet to kill, Flottie . . . To take a human life, someone needs to be extraordinarily desperate or extraordinarily angry or else a little unhinged. Is that how the Summersbys' butler strikes you? And either he found a way of getting back from Hexham unobserved on the night of the murder, or . . .'

'Or it was someone else, ma'am.'

'Indeed. But is there anyone else who knows that the Lazarus Testament was brought to Broomheath?'

'Viscount Wrexham, ma'am!'

The housekeeper's forehead creased into a frown.

'If the Viscount knows, Flottie, it's only because Anthony Baldwick wrote and told Lord Beaumaris. And Mr Baldwick told Mr Ibrahim also. I wonder how many other letters he wrote that night, Flotsam, and to whom?' She paused and rested her hand on the box of documents that still lay on my bed. 'Perhaps none, perhaps a dozen. Who knows? The answer to the question, my girl, if there is an answer to it, probably lies in Mr Baldwick's interminable archives . . .'

'I really must get up and help, ma'am.'

But Mrs Hudson laid a restraining hand upon my shoulder.

'There's plenty here for you to be getting on with, young lady. And this afternoon, while I sort out dinner with Martha and Mildred, I rather thought you and Miss Peters might bring some fresh eyes to the business of looking for hiding places at Broomheath. I don't like to denigrate the opposite sex, Flotsam, but I've generally found that men are a lot less cunning about hiding things than they think they are.'

It was with those words still very much in my mind that I went looking for Miss Peters that afternoon. On arriving at Broomheath Hall, we had found Martha and Mildred hard at work in the servants' hall, already grappling with that night's dinner. Neither seemed to know Pauncefoot's whereabouts, but the *contessa*, they assured us, was walking in the grounds.

I found her in the little sunken garden at the rear of the house, and her face brightened when she saw me.

'Ah, Flotsam! At last! I thought I'd been abandoned here for ever! Because, to be perfectly frank, looking for priceless ancient manuscripts isn't quite as much fun as I'd thought. I mean, it's so hard to know where to start! No one hides that sort of thing under a flower pot or up a tree, do they, Flottie? And even if I did start looking up trees I'd be bound to attract the attention of the Summersbys, who would know at once that I wasn't an Italian countess, because Italian countesses surely don't look up trees in person. They will always have dark and handsome gardeners to do that sort of thing for them.'

She paused for breath, but before I could interrupt, another thought had struck her.

'Actually, Mr Summersby isn't here, so that's one piece of good news. He has taken himself off to the place everyone calls the Roman Camp, which I suppose I ought to know all about, but which sounds so incredibly dull that I really can't make myself try. But Mrs Summersby is lurking in the house, so we can hardly search there, even though it's much warmer. As for *outside*, well, Flottie, there's quite a lot of outside at Broomheath, isn't there?'

'Mrs Hudson says we should be looking for somewhere warm and dry,' I explained, 'and big enough for quite a lot of old urns all at once. She thinks the only places big enough inside the house would be in the attics or the cellars, but Pauncefoot will presumably have searched those already. That's assuming there are no boarded-up cellars or bricked-in rooms that he hasn't found yet.'

'You know, Flottie, I don't think there are. I looked very carefully last night, you see. I think I really must have tapped on every wall in the whole house, and I didn't come across anything that sounded hollow or odd. It took ever so long and I got frightfully dusty. If I'd known how grim it was going to be, I'd never have started.'

'But Hetty, how could you possibly have done that? Didn't the Summersbys think it strange?'

'Well obviously I waited till they were asleep, Flottie! And just in case they woke up and caught me, I made rather a song and dance about how I walk in my sleep. It seemed such an obvious thing to do. It means that at night I can go anywhere I like, and tap on all the panels I want, and always have quite an innocent explanation! Not that I'll need one, of course, because if anyone catches me I shall simply look through them very dreamily and go back to bed. My cousin Clarissa used to sleep walk all the time when she was a child, you know. At least, that's what her parents say, although I've always wondered if it's something they just made up to explain the time she came to be found outside the bedroom of a captain of dragoons at three in the morning wearing nothing but a peignoir embroidered with very exquisite, pink silk lilies.'

As I could think of no sensible reply to any of that, Miss Peters hurried on with barely a pause.

'Now, if we're looking for somewhere big and dry, Flottie, I suppose we should start with the outbuildings. If I was going to hide a big collection of ancient pots, I wouldn't want to carry them too far. And nowhere too muddy or too smelly, either. Why make things less pleasant than they need to be?'

In the course of our stroll that afternoon, Miss Peters and I quickly established that there were nine different outbuildings in the vicinity of Broomheath Hall, not counting a derelict glass-house so full of brambles that we deemed it impossible for anyone to have hidden anything there in recent times. Of those nine, the nearest to the house was the Home Barn, an enormous and ancient stone structure, and it was there we decided to begin.

We entered cautiously, Miss Peters warning that there would definitely be spiders. Personally I was more worried that the Summersbys might observe us and consider our behaviour rather strange, but Miss Peters assured me that it had been mentioned at dinner that some of the barns were older than the house itself, so that it would be perfectly natural for a guest with such unbridled antiquarian passions as she possessed to investigate them at the earliest opportunity.

And the barn did seem very old, its roof high and its beams open like the vaulting of a church. The only light came from three narrow windows, also vaguely church-like, which, from the way they cut through the patterns of the stonework, seemed to have been added at a later date. At some point the barn had fallen into disuse, for now it was empty but for a decrepit-looking farm cart and some discarded pieces of sacking. Its stone-flagged floor must once have been very fine indeed, like the floor of a medieval hall, for even now the stones lay smooth and even, and offered very little scope for the concealment of treasure. Even so, we examined each flag closely to see if there was any sign that any had recently been raised.

This was a procedure that we repeated through various outbuildings. In many of them the floors were of beaten earth and these we examined carefully for any sign of disturbance. The last building we attempted to search was an ornamental belvedere positioned on the edge of the moor, a summer house that harked back to a different era, when Broomheath played host to house parties and when laughing young ladies and gentlemen would have picnicked there, or lingered in its shadows at dusk in the hope of a swift, illicit kiss.

Now it was notable only for its neglect. Its windows were all shuttered but in one place the shutter had worked loose, revealing two cracked panes of glass. The door was shuttered too, held fast by a rusty padlock and chain. It gave the impression that no one had entered there for many years, but of that it was not possible to be certain.

'Who keeps the key, do you think?' Miss Peters whispered, her voice hushed in the presence of such dereliction.

'I don't know. Pauncefoot, I suppose. If not, the Summersbys.'

'Oh, but we should find that out, Flottie. I'm sure mad Mr Baldwick would have found his way in here. But it's getting late, and perhaps I ought to be going to dress for dinner. An Italian countess probably spends a very long time dressing for dinner, don't you think? The funny thing is, Flottie, it's much easier to impersonate an archaeologist than I expected. I thought the Summersbys were going to talk about nothing but bones and flints and dead centurions, but in fact they only talk about the weather, just like everyone else. Mrs Summersby must be frightfully bored, sitting around here all day. I mean, her husband is quite the most silent man I've ever met. And not in a good way, either, Flottie. I'm sure I can't imagine how she came to marry him. Even Rupert is never *quite* such a dullard.'

'And yet he seems very devoted to her,' I mused. 'But then she is so *very* pretty and charming . . .'

A small frown appeared on Miss Peters's brow.

'Well, you know, Flotsam, I'm really not sure I share all this admiration for Mrs Summersby. Rupert says it's a hidden knowingness beneath the charm that makes such women alluring, but I'm not sure Mrs Summersby *has* any hidden knowingness. Not very knowledgeable knowingness, at any rate. I mean, she seems to know even less about Naples than I do, and how many people are there in the world you can say that about?'

'Why, Hetty, I do believe you're jealous!'

Miss Peters coloured a little at this charge.

'Not at all!' she retorted. 'Really, Flottie, how could you think such a thing? I simply don't warm to Mrs Summersby as much as everyone else, that's all. Now, I really am going to change, and then I'm going to write to Rupert. I'm still very cross with him, you see, and need to make sure I tell him so.'

On returning to the servants' hall, I found Pauncefoot still absent and the two girls so busy that I was able to give Mrs Hudson a full report on my afternoon's activities. In return she told me that Rupert Spencer had sent a note up with the butcher's boy.

'It seems they are making no progress with Mr Baldwick's papers, I'm afraid. Mr Spencer is still working through pamphlets and Dr Watson has found a box of manuscripts written by Mr Baldwick on a visit to America. According to Mr Spencer, he's been making very slow headway through a document entitled *Did the Romans Reach Philadelphia*? She chuckled a little to herself. 'I'm afraid it's not entirely the doctor's cup of tea.'

'And do they have any news of Mr Holmes, ma'am?'

'Apparently he has spent the afternoon in Alston, Flotsam, exchanging telegrams with Sir Percival Grenville-Ffitch. It seems Sir Percival feels that the Viscount, if still alive, is being given far too much rope. He is eager to obtain a special warrant allowing him to requisition Broomheath Hall on the grounds of national emergency. He seems to feel that two dozen policemen armed with crowbars and pickaxes would prove more effective in finding the document than any amount of waiting and watching.'

'Well, ma'am, I suppose that way he could at least be sure that no one else would find it.'

Mrs Hudson pursed her lips slightly. 'Only if his men were successful. But he couldn't requisition Broomheath Hall forever, Flottie, and if his men didn't find it then every treasure hunter in Europe would descend on the place in their wake. The owner would be free to sell the estate to whoever bid the highest. No, Flottie, I fear Sir Percival's plan may be a little rash. Take a look at this.'

She handed me a telegram that I saw had arrived only an hour earlier. It was sent by Mr Rumbelow, but to my surprise it appeared to be purely personal in nature.

EXCITING NEWS STOP MOTHER PAID VISIT TO WORTHING STOP RETURNED WITH NEW HAT STOP

RUMBELOW

'But what does this mean, ma'am?' I cried, further confused by this strange communication. 'I didn't even know that Mr Rumbelow *had* a mother. He certainly never speaks of her.'

Mrs Hudson's eyes fluttered very slightly. 'No, Flottie. More of that later, but now I hear footsteps. Let it never be said that we spend our time here gossiping . . .'

And so we returned to our duties, and dinner that night passed off without incident. The food was excellent, the service commendable, the *contessa* outrageous. Mrs Summersby smiled, Mr Summersby sulked and Pauncefoot appeared his usual unfathomable self, continuing to treat Mrs Hudson and myself quite cordially, as if delighted by our company. If anything he was even more affable than before, and took more than usual care with the napkins. My only interesting discovery came during dinner, when I was hurrying down the narrow corridor between the servants' hall and the dining room. I had passed that way umpteen times before but had never previously paid any attention to the large board on one wall, from which hung a collection of keys in various shapes and sizes. This time, with my afternoon expedition still prominent in my mind, I paused to examine it.

Of all the keys on that board, the largest and most noticeable was right in the middle, and its handwritten label clearly declared it to be the key to the belvedere. Hanging in such a place, I reflected, it would most certainly have been available to Mr Baldwick when he was looking for a hiding place. And, indeed, since then anyone at the Hall with a mind to look for keys would find it with the greatest of ease. I made a mental note to return to that ramshackle building the following day.

But before I could put this plan into action, events had overtaken me. And, looking back, I realise that the starting point for those events was not a dramatic discovery or a startling revelation but something much simpler: the arrival the following morning at the Baldwick Archive of Mrs Meakins, a local widow, armed with a feather duster and a small stool for standing on.

That morning I had risen early, determined to put in a good share of work at the Archive before returning to Broomheath Hall. Mr Spencer, Dr Watson and I had all been at our posts for a full hour before Mrs Meakins made her appearance. Our painstaking examination of Mr Baldwick's papers was progressing well, but nothing in either the turgid prose of his pamphlets or the bitter ranting of his diaries and notebooks had yet given any clue as to the whereabouts of the Lazarus Testament. Dr Watson had just finished a pamphlet about the goddess Diana which had caused him to blush a great deal when Mr Holmes himself made an appearance.

I had not seen him since that night of digging out on the moors and it was clear to me at once that the guise of innocent birdwatcher had now been completely discarded. Here was Mr Holmes in all his London glory, his eyes bright with excitement and his movements full of that urgent, impatient energy I knew so well.

'Good morning!' he greeted us crisply. 'I trust things go smoothly?' He paused and appeared to study Dr Watson for a moment before continuing. 'Mr Spencer, I should warn you to keep an eye on Watson's work today, for he clearly has other things on his mind. What's it to be, Watson? Urban Electric or the railways? I understand that Great Western shares are considered a safe investment.'

Dr Watson blinked in amazement.

'Good lord, Holmes! How on earth could you tell?'

The great detective allowed himself a smile of amusement and then turned back to Mr Spencer.

'You see, sir, Dr Watson's share dealings are rarely as secret as he thinks. It's obvious to me that he has made arrangements to sell the handful of shares he holds in Western & Oriental, and as a result has a small sum to invest. Is that not correct, Watson?'

'Absolutely, Holmes! But how the deuce could you possibly know it? The Australian gold was one thing, but this is quite another. I only decided to sell the Western & Oriental shares a couple of hours ago, and I wrote to my broker just before leaving the house. I'm prepared to swear no one could have caught sight of that letter as I wrote it!'

'And I'm sure you are right, my friend. You did not seriously think my deductions were based on the tittle-tattle of servants? On the contrary, Watson, it took no more than one glance at you for your share dealings to become apparent to me.'

Mr Spencer and I peered carefully at our companion, and even the doctor seemed to be studying his own person in search of a clue.

'Think about it, Watson! Is that not your pipe I observe, peeping out of your coat pocket?'

'Yes, Holmes, it is. But I can't see . . .'

'Of course not, Watson! But remember, my friend, you are a creature of habit, and it is invariably your custom to smoke a pipe after breakfast. When you have finished, it is equally your custom to leave your pipe on the mantelpiece, as you do not imagine you will smoke again until later in the day, when you have returned to your own hearth. So the fact that today you have chosen to bring your excellent briar with you tells me that something occurred this morning that has forced you to postpone your first pipe of the day.'

'That's very true, Holmes. But the rest of it – the letter, the shares. How could you possibly deduce all that?'

Mr Holmes looked a trifle smug. 'Very simply, my dear fellow. You have told me yourself that Mr Verity's household runs like clockwork, so it was unlikely to be any domestic drama that upset your usual routine. But I have observed that the morning post is delivered at about the time you take breakfast, so it is a reasonable deduction that the postman was the bearer of some item of correspondence that struck you as so urgent that you felt you must forego your pipe and reply at once.'

'My word, Holmes! You have it exactly!'

'And when I read yesterday that Western & Oriental were rumoured to be in difficulties, it occurred to me that you would shortly be receiving advice from your broker. The rest is obvious, of course. Having read his warning you replied at once, and being an essentially cautious fellow, you have instructed him to sell. And now you cannot fully concentrate on the task in hand for wondering what to do with your capital. I suspect that same streak of caution will lead you to opt for railways.'

And with that the great detective fished out his own pipe and, making no attempt to light it, began to chew on its stem with evident satisfaction.

'Well, that's the most remarkable thing, Holmes,' the good doctor concluded. 'Urban Electric, eh? I confess I *had* been leaning towards the railways. You know where you are with the rail companies. Tell me, Holmes, will you be joining us here this morning?'

The detective shook his head.

'I fear not, Watson. Sir Percival has a bad case of the jitters and I fear I must travel to London to prevent him from doing anything too precipitous. The Lazarus Testament has managed to elude its searchers for a thousand years, so I'm sure I can be spared for the day without missing anything momentous. Wire me if you need advice, Watson. Otherwise I shall assume all's well.'

The detective's departure was followed by another period of quiet as we continued to wrestle with Mr Baldwick's labyrinthine prose. The arrival of Mrs Meakins hardly disturbed us at all, for she came to the Archive every day to dust and tidy, and we had become accustomed to her working around us. She was a small, rosy-cheeked woman, round yet somehow *shrunken*, like a very old apple. It was purely by chance that she happened to be standing behind Dr Watson when he slammed closed a document box and growled with frustration.

'Really, this is too much! Whenever I think I'm getting

anywhere, the scent goes cold. That last box ended with some interesting papers written by Baldwick when he'd just arrived at Broomheath. They were mainly his thoughts about redemption, and rather crazed they were too, but I thought they might lead to something. But now I'm damned if I can find the next box. It must be here somewhere, but all these seem to be full of older papers. I don't suppose either of you have spirited one away, have you?'

Both Mr Spencer and I were busy denying any such thing when Mrs Meakins chimed in.

'You'll forgive me for interrupting, sir,' she began, 'but perhaps the box you're looking for is the one taken by the other gentleman?'

We all looked up at her sharply.

'The other gentleman, Mrs Meakins?' Dr Watson asked, as calmly as he could. 'Do you mean Mr Verity?'

'Oh, no, not Mr Verity, sir. I know him well. My cousin's daughter used to do his laundry. No, I mean the other gentleman.'

The three of us looked at each other in alarm.

'What other gentleman do you mean, Mrs Meakins? Is it someone we know?'

'The gentleman who used to come here before you started coming, sir. Every afternoon he would come, sir, just for half an hour or so. He used to call it his daily constitutional, although I can't see how sitting here amongst these dusty old things could do very much for his health. I think he must be staying up at the Hall, sir. A balding gentleman, sir, with a very fine beard.'

My eyes opened wide at this, and I looked across at Mr Spencer.

'Pauncefoot!' he murmured, while Dr Watson suppressed a spluttered oath. 'Tell me, Mrs Meakins, you say he took away a box. When was this?'

'Why, yesterday afternoon, sir. I was just popping down here to fill up the inkwells, if you remember, and I saw him at the bottom of the hill. Smoking a cigarette under a tree, he was, looking all cold and miserable. When he saw me he said hello, and I said something about him not coming here anymore, and he said it's a bit too busy for me nowadays, Mrs Meakins, or something like that. So when I was coming away and he was still there, I said something about you two gentlemen having gone off for some tea, and he said in that case he might just nip in as there was a particular thing he wanted to look at. And a little later, I was putting on the kettle when I happened to look out of my window, and there he was, walking away with one of those boxes under his arm. He looked a lot more cheerful for visiting, sir, so I'm thinking perhaps it's true about coming here being good for his health. I had a cousin once . . .'

Mrs Meakins seemed inclined to elaborate further on the beneficial effects of study, but Mr Spencer was already on his feet.

'This changes everything!' he declared. 'We had no idea that Pauncefoot had ever been here. But if that box contains something significant, we could be in trouble. Dr Watson, you're on calling terms with the Summersbys. Perhaps you could drive up to the Hall to check that Pauncefoot is still at his post? And, Flotsam, if you could go too, perhaps you might find a way of communicating all this to Hetty? It would be very helpful indeed if she could take a peek inside Pauncefoot's room . . .'

I nodded quickly, although I knew the difficulty would not be in persuading Miss Peters to search Pauncefoot's room, but in restraining her from doing so at an unpropitious moment, when discovery was inevitable. But there was no time to worry. Dr Watson was already pulling on his coat.

'We'll take Verity's trap,' he decided. 'We should be there in a quarter of an hour. What about you, sir? What will you do?'

'Well, I thought I'd see if I could catch Mr Holmes at the station. And I might also have a word with the station master, to see if Pauncefoot has shown any signs of leaving. After that, well . . .'

Mr Spencer looked at me, and I nodded.

'Yes, sir. You should try to find Mrs Hudson just as soon as you can.'

Five minutes later, I was wrapped in a pink tartan travel blanket on a rattling trap, and Dr Watson was shaking the reins with unusual impatience as we sped out towards the open moors.

CHAPTER SIXTEEN

The Butler Waits

I'm not entirely sure what I thought we'd find at Broomheath Hall. I think I half expected uproar and confusion, a scene of devastation in which the Summersbys, having been overwhelmed and bound, lay helpless in the cellar while their treasured English butler, crazed by lust for treasure, demolished the oak panelling in search of a secret chamber. But no such drama was evident from my first glimpse of the Hall, and when Dr Watson brought us juddering to a halt on the gravel sweep I was taken aback – and perhaps even a little disappointed – to see Pauncefoot opening the great double doors to greet us, as calm and as neat as he had always been.

I think Dr Watson was disconcerted too, for he looked decidedly sheepish as he dismounted and asked if Mrs Summersby was at home. On being told that she was, and that the butler's instructions were to show callers straight through, we followed Pauncefoot's stately progress in silence, and were ushered into Mrs Summersby's morning room still looking rather crestfallen.

Our hostess greeted us with her usual smile, however.

'How lovely!' she enthused. 'It seems so long since your last visit, and I was hoping you would call soon. I do so enjoy some company every now and then, you know.' She hesitated for a moment then, as if realising what she had just said. 'Of course, I know I have the *contessa* for company, but she is so very . . . well, so very *Italian*, I suppose, and I'm afraid I don't find her company altogether restful.'

I was all too willing to believe this, and felt again the pricking of guilt at my role in deceiving her. To compensate I gave Mrs Summersby my warmest smile as she took my hand and led me to a seat near the fire.

'And is the countess at home today?' Dr Watson asked cautiously, still standing. He seemed to be waiting until he was sure Pauncefoot had retired before broaching the subject that was on both our minds.

'She is lying down in her room,' Mrs Summersby replied. 'She had a very disturbed night, I'm afraid. The countess is prone to walking in her sleep, and last night we twice discovered her in the library, apparently quite oblivious to our presence.' As Mrs Summersby spoke, I noted a shadow cross her face. Perhaps she was wondering if it was indelicate of her to have made such a revelation. 'We heard a noise, you understand, and came down to investigate. Such an awkward affliction for a young woman to suffer from!'

Apparently satisfied that the coast was clear, Dr Watson joined us by the fire and rubbed his moustache for a moment rather anxiously.

'Madam,' he began, 'I hope you will forgive me for speaking frankly. Always the best thing, frankness, don't you think?

Anyway, I think it is time we took you into our confidence. As I told you, it seems very likely that your predecessor at Broomheath left something rather valuable hidden here. Well, the thing is, we rather think that Pauncefoot might be searching for it.'

'Pauncefoot?' Her eyes grew round with astonishment. 'But he came with such excellent references! And he seems, well, so very dignified. That's exactly why we insisted on a *London* butler. Everyone knows that they are the best.'

'I fear, madam, that Pauncefoot may still be in the pay of his former employer.' Dr Watson puffed out his cheeks as if to demonstrate the enormity of such behaviour. 'Now, I beg you do nothing hasty, my dear Mrs Summersby. You see, it rather seems that the fellow might be privy to a clue that no one else has.'

'Then we must demand that he shares it with us! Surely, Doctor, you won't allow a mere butler to stand in your way?'

Dr Watson held up a pacifying hand. 'No, no, no. Quite the opposite, in fact. You see, if we can all keep a very close eye on him, we rather think he might lead us to the treasure of his own accord.'

I could see understanding dawning on our hostess's face. 'Like a dog to a bone, you mean?'

'That's it exactly! And it occurs to me that it might be helpful if I were to join you here as your guest for a few days . . .'

I saw her face fall.

'Or failing that, ma'am,' I put in quickly, 'perhaps if you were to allow Mrs Hudson and me to take one of the rooms in the servants' quarters, just for a day or two? Travelling back to Alston so late, well, I can't deny that with all this going on we'd both feel a lot safer if we didn't have to cross the moors by night! You wouldn't know we were here, I promise. And of course it would mean we were on hand to help with breakfast! Mrs Hudson's breakfasts are famous . . .'

As I had anticipated, however jealous she might be of her husband's solitude, a plea made on such grounds proved tricky for Mrs Summersby to deny, and it was therefore agreed that when we returned to the Hall that evening, Mrs Hudson and I would bring with us such things as were necessary for a short stay. Then, as Dr Watson said his goodbyes to Mrs Summersby, I scribbled a quick note for the sleeping countess and congratulated myself on my cleverness. For surely, with Mrs Hudson and myself focused entirely on Pauncefoot and his movements, nothing could go wrong . . .

It was an opinion that, within the next two days, I would have good reason to revise.

That morning was a raw one and, as we drove back over the moor with the fells bleak and wintry all around us, my mind began to turn to thoughts of the warm fire at the Angel. But on arriving at the inn, we found Mr Spencer waiting for us by the doorway, pacing to and fro with a restless, troubled air. Dr Watson hailed him cheerfully, and suggested a warming drink in the snug.

'No time for that, sir, I'm afraid,' Mr Spencer told him briskly. 'There have been developments!'

'Developments?' Dr Watson started like a warhorse to the bugle.

'Yes, Doctor. As soon as you left I hurried down to the station to see if I could catch Mr Holmes before he left. I'm afraid he'd already departed for London, but while I was there I had a word with the stationmaster. It seems that a man answering to Pauncefoot's description was there yesterday evening. He bought a ticket for tomorrow morning, Dr Watson. A one-way ticket to London!'

Dr Watson whistled. 'Tomorrow, eh? So it must be tonight he intends to make his move. Well, the game's afoot! But at least we know when, and from where, he plans to escape!'

'Please, sir,' I asked Mr Spencer. 'Did you find Mrs Hudson at all?'

Mr Spencer frowned. 'I did, Flotsam. I found her writing letters in her room.'

'And what did she make of your news, eh?' Dr Watson asked. 'Pretty shaken up, I imagine!'

'Well, that was the strange thing, Doctor. She just carried on writing letters.'

'Surely not! Really, she must have said *something*.'

'She just listened very carefully, then nodded. Then she asked whether we'd told the Summersbys and I said you'd gone over to explain matters, and she just nodded again and said she'd have thought as much. And then she went back to her writing.'

'Remarkable!' Dr Watson looked utterly perplexed. 'Then I can only imagine she trusts us to get on with the job. After all, it shouldn't be beyond us, should it? We'll watch him like hawks tonight, and nab him if he tries to get away. Flotsam, I think you should reassure Mrs Hudson that she can leave matters entirely in our hands!'

* * *

That opportunity arose a few minutes later. Rather to my surprise, I found Mrs Hudson alone in Mrs Garth's kitchen, plucking a chicken. This activity was in such contrast to Dr Watson's urgent plotting and planning, and her air as she undertook it so serene, that I could not but wonder at her calm.

'Yes, Flotsam,' she reassured me, 'I believe I understood Mr Spencer's message very well. I imagine that he and Dr Watson are thoroughly enjoying themselves. Why, I confess I almost feel sorry for that butler. He is so very much outnumbered and surrounded by parties determined to part him from his prize. I'm rather looking forward to what he does next.'

'Then you don't think there's any chance Pauncefoot might get away with the urn, ma'am?'

For a fraction of a second her eyebrow flickered upwards. 'Pauncefoot? I'm sure he's the least of our worries, Flottie. Now tell me, how were things at the Hall?'

With some trepidation, I told her how I'd persuaded Mrs Summersby to allow us to make our home at Broomheath for a few days. To my relief, rather than protest, the housekeeper paused in her plucking and smiled at me fondly.

'Really, Flotsam, that's most resourceful. I had been thinking that some such arrangement would suit us very well. I must tell Mrs Garth at once. There's bound to be all sorts of nonsense going on at the Hall tonight and I confess I'll feel a little easier in my mind knowing we can keep an eye on things. Now, I have some letters to post . . .' She indicated a little pile of envelopes on a tray by the door. 'When I've finished here, we'll take them down to the post office. But I promised Mrs Garth I'd give her a hand with this, and as I don't foresee anything very urgent happening just yet, we may as well make ourselves useful while we can. You could start by helping me clear up these feathers.'

And help I did, but not before I'd taken a surreptitious peek at the addresses on the envelopes. Letters to Mr Rumbelow and to Scraggs did not particularly surprise me as Mrs Hudson was always a very assiduous correspondent, but I looked up in surprise when I saw that the third letter was addressed to Mr Bertram Peeves, Esq.

'Isn't he the famous diplomatist, ma'am?' I ventured to ask, forgetting that I was supposed to be helping with the chores. 'The one they've just recalled from Washington? Dr Watson said he was coming back because he was destined for a peerage.'

'That is indeed the gentleman, Flotsam,' Mrs Hudson confirmed. 'Now, about these feathers . . .'

I hastened to equip myself with Mrs Garth's brush and pan. 'Do you know Mr Peeves then, ma'am?' I asked after a pause, sweeping diligently as I spoke.

Mrs Hudson rose and began to unpin her apron, shaking the feathers neatly into the path of my broom.

'Oh, I wouldn't say that, Flottie. But some years ago, when Mr Bertram Peeves of the Diplomatic Corps was still young Bertie Peeves of the Rip-Roar Club, there was a little incident on Boat Race Night after his fellow club members had found him guilty of some breach of their rules. Very fortunately I was able to furnish him with a cloak to cover his modesty and to call for a locksmith before the bishop's wife arrived. It is, I believe, an intervention he remembers gratefully. Now, when we have finished helping Mrs Garth, we may take a stroll to the post office. And after that, since the afternoon is our own, I suggest we take up the Rector's invitation to view his collection of historical curios. I daresay they will prove educational and it will most certainly please the Rector, who is having a difficult time with his bunions.'

For all Mrs Hudson's urgings I was in no mood for curios that afternoon, and the Rector's gentle observations on local history were, I'm afraid, sown on fallow ground. My mind was entirely occupied with thoughts of the Hall and its occupants, and my imagination was running wild. What was Pauncefoot doing? What was he planning? Was it wise for Miss Peters to search his room? And where exactly *was* the urn?

The afternoon was a slow one and the Rector's insights into Neolithic settlements seemed to me to last almost as long as the settlements themselves. An age passed before I was back at the Angel, hurriedly stuffing a bag with everything I would need for my stay at Broomheath Hall. We were driven to our destination by Mrs Garth's son, a taciturn young man whose features seemed to have taken on some of the weathered inscrutability of the moors themselves. But he drove carefully and delivered us at the servants' entrance a little before four o'clock, in plenty of time to prepare for dinner.

I fear I was of little help to Martha and Mildred that evening, for once again I was unable to settle to the task in hand. I could not help but watch Mr Pauncefoot's every move, all the while marvelling at his calm. For the butler seemed as relaxed as ever, and even engaged in some rather avuncular flirtation with Martha over the state of her wardrobe, promising her that if his luck in life ever took a turn for the better he would be sure to remember the green muslin dress she'd set her heart on.

Such light-hearted comments set my mind racing, for it seemed to me that the butler's thoughts were turning towards a happier, wealthier future. But if he had really discovered where to look for the Lazarus Testament, it seemed impossible that he could remain so calm; impossible also that Mrs Hudson could continue about her business with such unflinching single-mindedness. I was reminded of Sir Frances Drake and his famous game of bowls. Mr Pauncefoot, it seemed, would not have been one to flinch at the approach of a mere Armada, and it would have taken more than an enemy fleet, guns blazing, to deflect Mrs Hudson from preparing dinner. But I was not of their stamp: by the time the meal was over and the dishes washed, my nerves were so tightly wound that I was certain they must snap.

It was perhaps some relief to me that Miss Peters shared my restlessness. Just before bedtime, with the excuse of helping her undress, I made my way to her room and found her pacing up and down by the window, a pillow hugged tightly to her chest.

'How can everybody possibly be so *calm*, Flottie?' she wailed. 'It's as if tonight was just another night, with Mr Summersby gulping his soup like a convict and Mrs Summersby asking me endless polite questions about Italy until I just wanted to *scream*. And there was Pauncefoot, gliding around with his yes-madams and his no-madams as if none of us had ever heard the words "hidden treasure"! And I'm sure he must know that someone searched his room today, because I wasn't the least bit careful about putting things back in the right place, but he doesn't look at all concerned about it, does he? When he served my soup tonight, part of me felt like grabbing his hand and biting him and shouting "*tell us where it is, you odious man*!" In fact, I rather wish I'd done just that, Flottie. Anything would be better than this terrible waiting!'

'You will be careful, won't you, Hetty? Pauncefoot is probably a desperate man.'

She seemed to brighten at this. 'Do you really think so? That's what they always say in the papers when prisoners escape from jail! I do hope Rupert knows that I'm about to wrestle with a desperate man. Is it true that he and Dr Watson and Mr Verity are all keeping watch on the house from the moors tonight? Well, if so I hope it's very cold. It will serve Rupert right for being such an utter beast.'

'And Mrs Hudson and I will be staying here tonight,' I reminded her. 'But somehow Mrs Hudson doesn't seem very interested in keeping watch on Mr Pauncefoot. Whenever I talk to her about it, she just mumbles about the trap not chasing the mouse.'

'Does she? Well, that's probably just her being wise again, Flottie. Mrs Hudson is so *very* wise that sometimes I don't really understand her at all. And I don't know much about mousetraps, except that they seem to involve a lot of cheese. Daddy always used to say the longer the chase, the sweeter the fruits, which strictly speaking doesn't make sense, of course, because you don't really chase fruits, do you? You just order them from the green grocer. And I rather think Daddy meant something slightly improper by it, because Daddy usually did, but even so, I intend to chase Pauncefoot absolutely as hard as

I can. And do you know, Flottie, I'm absolutely *certain* it will be me who gets hold of the Lazarus thingy first! I just feel sure of it.'

Buoyed a little by her confidence, but certainly no less on edge, I left Miss Peters trying to make towers on her wash-stand out of bars of soap and returned to the small bedroom at the back of the house where Mrs Hudson had laid out my things. There I found the housekeeper, still-dressed, putting clean slips around the pillows.

'Now, Flotsam,' she began sternly. 'I know that you don't expect to sleep a wink tonight, but I think a little lie-down won't do you any harm. I've aired the sheets and put on some good warm blankets, and I'll be downstairs if you need me.'

Of course I knew that rest of any sort was quite out of the question, but hearing the iron firmness in Mrs Hudson's voice I agreed to follow her advice, while secretly determining to lie down fully dressed beneath the covers, so as to be ready for prompt action should events require it. To pass the time, and to keep myself from fretting, I picked up the heavy pile of papers from the Baldwick Archive that I had brought with me from the Angel. They seemed to be part of an account of his journey to America, though whether they were intended as a journal, or an aide memoire, or as a polemic for public consumption, it was hard to tell. The writer seemed to switch from one to the other at random intervals, at times recording his observations, at others railing against the wrongs he perceived had been done to him. At no point was his style anything but leaden, and the tediousness of his complaints and grievances soon began to have the effect they always had. After thirty minutes of forcing myself to concentrate, the words were beginning to blur a little in front of my eyes; after forty, for all my determination, I was fast asleep.

I only became aware of this, however, when I was woken by a gentle shaking of my arm. The room was dark but for a faint haze of silver light from the window. Some of the papers on my chest had spilled onto the floor and my head was resting on the pillows at an awkward, crooked angle.

'Quietly, Flottie,' Mrs Hudson's voice whispered. 'It seems the promised excitement is beginning. From here we should have an excellent view of it.'

Blinking slightly, I followed her to the window. Outside, the grounds of the Hall lay in darkness, and beyond them the great flanks of the moor rose black and brooding. There was a very thin covering of cloud but the moon behind cast just enough light for me to make out the shapes of trees and outbuildings. From its position, I guessed I'd slept for an hour or more.

Mrs Hudson was also looking at the faint outline of the moon. 'A good night for our butler friend,' she murmured. 'Light enough to find his way, but dark enough to hide in. Now! Here he goes . . .'

Our window was almost directly above Broomheath's back door. Looking down, I saw the bald and bearded figure of the butler emerging, his cape drawn tight around his shoulders. To my surprise he held a bright storm lantern in his hand and made no attempt to conceal it.

'Now, watch carefully, Flottie,' Mrs Hudson whispered unnecessarily, for I don't believe any power on earth could have made me take my eyes from the figure below us. As I watched, he made his way at a steady pace to one of the outbuildings, but he made no effort to enter. On reaching its door he seemed to change his mind, and headed instead for an old glasshouse that stood just beyond it. But again he didn't go in, continuing in the same manner from one building to another, gradually inching further from the house and closer to the edge of the moor. Finally he came to the locked and shuttered belvedere that Miss Peters and I had been unable to examine.

'So that's the place!' I breathed as he approached it, but to my surprise he made no effort to gain entry. He merely skirted around it to reach the old wall that lay beyond, where a stile took him out onto the moor itself.

The brightness of his lantern made it easy for us to follow his progress, and at first I had eyes for nothing else. But as he began to ascend the flanks of the heath I became aware of two other figures moving in the darkness. The first must have been watching from somewhere within the grounds and was clearly following in the butler's footsteps. As I watched, that figure disappeared behind the belvedere, only to re-emerge by the stile, some thirty or forty yards behind his quarry. The other figure was even harder to pick out, camouflaged as it was by the blackness of the moor itself. This person had been stationed much further from the Hall, presumably on some helpful vantage point. Now, as the butler took to the fells, the watcher set a parallel course, keeping pace with him as he climbed but careful to stay well beyond the reach of his lantern.

'Mr Spencer and Dr Watson,' I concluded.

'And Mr Verity too,' Mrs Hudson added, gesturing towards a place where a third shadowy figure was making haste around the Hall's perimeter, apparently desperate to catch up with the others. As we watched, he stumbled once or twice and then fell completely, disappearing from view behind the dry stone wall. 'I fear he is not really cut out for this sort of work,' she added sadly.

It was then, as my eyes were moving back to the lantern, that I caught sight of a movement just below us.

'Miss Peters, if I'm not mistaken,' Mrs Hudson pointed out, 'apparently heading for the potting shed.'

'She must have seen Pauncefoot's light too, ma'am,' I decided. 'Will she be all right, do you think? Shouldn't we be going with her?'

'Oh, I think she'll be fine, Flottie,' Mrs Hudson declared with confidence, as Miss Peters sped after the distant lantern. 'She'll probably get very cold and very damp and I imagine she'll rather enjoy herself. And by the look of it she'll soon catch up Mr Verity so she'll be able to make sure he doesn't come to any harm.'

Left alone, I too would undoubtedly have rushed down and given chase, but Mrs Hudson showed no urge to move whatsoever. Instead we stood and watched as the butler's lantern, gaining height all the time, grew steadily smaller with distance. The various pursuers followed it, all well spread out, until their outlines became invisible to us against the heath.

In such circumstances, time can be difficult to measure. It seemed to me that we must have remained at that window for a full ten minutes, until the light from the butler's lamp was no more than a tiny pin-prick of light. And then, without warning, the lamp went out.

'He's gone!' I cried, and turned to my companion. But Mrs Hudson's eyes continued to scan the darkness. 'Of course it could be that he has simply dropped out of sight, into a hollow or something,' I added lamely.

'I don't think so, Flottie,' Mrs Hudson replied with enormous calm. 'I think he has put that light out quite deliberately.'

'But why, ma'am? Has he reached the spot where the treasure's hidden?'

'Hardly, Flottie. Surely that would mean he needed more light, not less. No, I fancy his sole object so far has been to lead his pursuers a long way away, and now he intends to leave them there. Because, of course, the object he is seeking is much closer to home. Now, if we are curious about that urn, I suggest we take a little walk. We don't have a great deal of time before our butler friend gets back.'

'The urn, ma'am? I don't understand! Do you mean you actually know where the urn is?'

There was enough moonlight for me to see a very faint smile play across her lips.

'Not at all, Flottie. But what we've seen tonight has certainly given me something of an idea.'

'What we've seen tonight . . . ? I *still* don't understand.'

'Come, Flotsam, put yourself for a moment in the butler's shoes. Ever since Dr Watson confronted him and accused him of being in league with Viscount Wrexham, he must have known that his actions would be closely observed. Now, what did you notice about his behaviour tonight?'

As she spoke, she was already helping me into my coat. 'Well, he wasn't really trying to hide himself, was he, ma'am? I mean, his lantern was very bright, and the way he was waltzing about between outbuildings, it was almost as if he wanted to make sure everyone had seen him.'

'Excellent, Flottie!' Mrs Hudson had pulled on her own coat and was busy wrapping me in a woollen muffler. 'He certainly did seem to be inviting attention, didn't he? Now, if you'd hidden something, Flottie, and people were watching your every move, what would you make sure you *didn't* do?'

I considered this as Mrs Hudson hustled me down the stairs.

'Well, I'd be very careful not to lead them to the hiding place, ma'am. That's what they'd want me to do.'

'Very sensible! And where did the butler lead them tonight?'

'To the moor! So it can't be hidden out there, can it, ma'am?'

Mrs Hudson clucked impatiently. 'Of course it isn't! Why would anyone go and hide it out there when there are so many good hiding places that are much handier? I know Mr Baldwick was unbalanced, but I don't believe he was as crazed as all that. So, Flottie, where did the butler go *before* he stepped out onto the moors?'

'Practically everywhere, ma'am! He made a great big circle around the grounds.'

'Everywhere, Flotsam? Are you sure?'

Suddenly it struck me. The strange route that Pauncefoot had taken had passed all the outbuildings except one. The oldest and largest of the barns had not been on the butler's route: indeed, I realised, he had deliberately contrived to give it as wide a berth as possible.

'The Home Barn!' I exclaimed. 'That's the one place he avoided! He must think . . . No, he must be certain! Mrs

Hudson, *that's* where we'll find the Lazarus Testament!'

Mrs Hudson nodded and held open the back door. 'Now keep to the shadows, Flottie. You never know who might be watching.' Together we slipped into the knife-sharp coldness of the night.

'But, ma'am,' I whispered as we walked, 'Miss Peters and I have searched the Home Barn. There's nothing in it but an old cart and some sacks, I'm sure of it.'

'You may well be right, Flottie. But that day you were searching a number of different buildings. Tonight we only have one to search, which is quite a different thing.'

We hurried on, my mind racing. I could see my breath in the air in front of me, but I was too excited to worry about the cold. Then another thought struck me and I looked around in fright.

'Mrs Hudson, ma'am! Might Pauncefoot have been clearing the way for someone else to come to the barn tonight? An accomplice, ma'am! Viscount Wrexham, perhaps!'

I heard Mrs Hudson's familiar, low chuckle. 'I shouldn't worry too much about the Viscount just yet, Flottie. I think we have a little time.'

She held up her hand and listened for a few seconds before we hurried on.

'So, ma'am, if the Lazarus Testament isn't hidden on the moors, what about all Pauncefoot's night-time expeditions? Was he just trying to lead us astray?'

'I suppose that's possible, Flotsam. More likely he really thought the hiding place was out there. After all, he'd have heard the stories about Mr Baldwick's digging. Without some definite clue to guide him, he knew no more than we did.'

We had arrived at the door of the Home Barn, and to my relief it opened smoothly, without squeaking. Inside, Mrs Hudson struck a match and lit her lantern, casting a pale, flickering glow that didn't quite reach into the corners. But there was enough light to see what I had seen before: a bare, stone-flagged floor and a rickety old wagon. Nothing else. Nothing had changed.

Even so, I followed Mrs Hudson closely as she paced each line of flagstones, her eyes never leaving the ground, until, having covered two thirds of the barn without incident, we arrived at the old cart. Mrs Hudson held up her lamp and studied it.

'Nowhere to hide anything in that,' she mused. 'But take a look at the wheels, Flottie.'

I looked, but could see nothing very striking, just some missing spokes and flaking paint.

'Just here.' She bent very low and pointed to some detail of the axle. 'See how it has been kept well greased? Here, help me . . .' Applying her shoulder to the rear of the cart, she began to push.

It proved surprisingly easy for the two of us to roll the vehicle forward a few feet. No sooner had we done so than Mrs Hudson was down on her knees, examining the section of the floor that we'd revealed.

'Look, Flottie! Progress at last!'

Crouching next to her, I saw at once what she meant. Set into the flagstones, in a place previously hidden by the cart's broad rear wheel, was a metal ring of the sort used to lift a trapdoor. Our eyes met, and Mrs Hudson's, I saw, were full of mischief.

'So, Flotsam, what is it to be? We could stand guard here,

ward off all intruders and wait for the gentlemen to join us before investigating further. Or we could behave like two silly and over-excited young girls and press on regardless, purely because we are unable to contain our own curiosity.'

I hesitated. 'Yes, ma'am. And we wouldn't want to do that. Although, of course, I suppose there may be nothing at all down there. And we wouldn't want to waste everyone's time if it turned out there was nothing to show them, would we, ma'am?'

The housekeeper nodded solemnly. 'Of course not, Flotsam. We certainly wouldn't want to waste the gentlemen's time. So perhaps it would be better if we took a very quick look after all . . .'

Mute with excitement, I could only nod, praying that she wouldn't change her mind. The look in my eyes made her smile and without another word she positioned herself above the iron ring and pulled.

CHAPTER SEVENTEEN

The Brides of Quietness

The trapdoor, though heavy, yielded to Mrs Hudson's urgings without great resistance, and swung upwards with a mournful groan to reveal a dark void below. By the glow of the lantern I was able to make out a narrow wooden stair leading down, but before I could see more, Mrs Hudson had raised the lantern high above her head and was studying the barn as if in search of something. She seized upon a short plank of wood that lay discarded beneath the wagon and, handing me the lantern, took it firmly in her hands like a club. Then, without a word, she advanced towards the opposite wall, where the three narrow windows looked out towards the Hall.

To my utter astonishment, and with a crash as resounding as the discharge of a cannon, my companion proceeded to smash the plank into the first of the windows, sending a shower of glass onto the paving stones beyond. In the quiet of the night the noise seemed catastrophic, but even more startling to me was the shock of seeing Mrs Hudson behave with such reckless abandon. Perhaps aware of my bewilderment, and pausing only to throw the plank out after the glass, she came quickly to my side and gave my shoulders a squeeze.

'No point in secrecy now, Flotsam,' she explained, 'and I don't intend to find myself down there with the trapdoor closed above me and the cart pushed back in place.'

'But the window, ma'am . . . !'

'I'm just letting people know where to look for us in case anything happens, Flottie. We'll send the bill to Sir Percival. Now, will you go first, or shall I?'

I will never forget the sight that met my eyes as I tiptoed down the narrow steps into the cellar of the Home Barn. The lamp revealed a long, low chamber, no more than twelve feet wide, but running the whole length of the building above it. At first I thought it empty but for an old shovel and one of those huge wicker baskets that peat-cutters strap to their backs to carry home their sods. These items were lying untidily beneath the wooden steps and around them I could see nothing but bare stones and a dusting of old straw. But then, as I descended further, the rest of the cellar was illuminated and I saw before me a sight of the sort that treasure-seekers down the ages have yearned for.

Positioned at the far end of the chamber, a little like skittles across an alley, stood an array of earthenware vessels – old jars or urns, stoppered and sealed, all of them about two or three feet tall, and all grey in the pale light. For a moment they looked a little absurd, like the wine flagons beneath some ancient Roman tavern, lined up for the attention of the cellarer. But as I grew closer and began to see in more detail the texture of their surfaces, the cracks and blemishes of unguessable age, I found myself moved by their simple, unadorned dignity. In their presence I felt a great solemnity begin to descend upon me, a sudden, awkward reverence that wiped away my smile and urged me to be still. I was standing face to face with the truly ancient, and something about them – something in their patience or their stillness – touched my soul with a sort of awe.

Treading very softly, Mrs Hudson joined me where I'd halted.

'I begin to understand Lord Beaumaris,' she whispered. 'Such things have a power of their own, don't they, Flotsam? Perhaps his obsession was not altogether the ridiculous thing people have thought it.'

'But which one contains the Lazarus Testament?' I asked, also whispering, as if out of some barely understood respect.

Mrs Hudson shook her head. 'What was it Mr Baldwick said in his letter? Something about hiding it among other vessels that were old but of less rarity. But which the rare one is, I cannot guess. To the untrained eye, they all look remarkably similar. But I'm sure Mr Fallowell will know.'

'So what now, ma'am? It doesn't seem right for us to start opening any of them. It would feel like . . . Well, somehow *wrong*.'

My companion placed her hand on my shoulder. 'How right you are, Flotsam. I begin to wish the whole collection could have rested here undisturbed. But I'm afraid it's too late for that now.'

A thought occurred to me. 'That basket under the steps. Do you think Mr Baldwick brought them here in that? If we wanted to move them to the Hall, ma'am, I think it would be just the thing . . .'

Intent on investigating, I stepped away from our discoveries, leaving Mrs Hudson to contemplate them in silence.

With the lantern still at the other end of the cellar, the space beneath the stairs was shrouded in gloom and my sober dress and coat must have merged into the darkness. It was that, I think, which saved me. That, and perhaps also the instinctive caution which made me shrink deeper into the darkness when I heard a footstep on the rungs above me.

The Summersbys' butler had returned a good deal quicker than we'd expected. I recognised his long legs and dignified carriage even before he had descended the steps and stepped forward into the light. But it was what I saw in his hand that made me freeze where I stood, with a cold sweat prickling my temples: a heavy, menacing revolver, its hammer cocked and ready to fire. And as Mrs Hudson turned to face him, I saw the butler slowly raise his hand.

'Please stand aside, Mrs Hudson,' I heard him say. 'I congratulate you for your remarkable astuteness in getting here before me, but now the game is over. I have not come this far to be thwarted now.'

Immediately it struck me that his voice seemed changed, richer and fuller than before, and certainly very full of confidence. But it seemed to have no effect whatsoever on the figure before him, for Mrs Hudson neither cowered nor quaked, she simply remained where she stood, very clearly in his path.

'Really, sir!' She shook her head. 'Please put down that ridiculous object at once, I beg you. Without it you will be able to walk away from here a free man. But if you persist in waving guns at people, all this must end very badly indeed.'

The revolver, however, didn't waver for an instant, and when the butler replied his voice was as steady as before.

'I applaud your courage, Mrs Hudson. In happier circumstances I would shake your hand. But you have no cards to play. Your friends are running around in circles on the moor. You are alone, between a desperate man and his treasure. You must see that you can expect no assistance.'

It is in moments of the greatest peril that we show our true mettle, and not for one moment did the housekeeper's gaze dart in my direction. I cannot recall my precise thoughts as I stepped out from behind the stairs. Perhaps I was recalling all the times Mrs Hudson had been the one to rescue me from danger; perhaps I was simply hoping I was brave enough. Perhaps I was thinking of the revolver, or of that bald pate before me. More probably I was thinking of absolutely nothing at all. I only remember feeling the shaft of the spade very rough and heavy in my hands. Then I hit him hard, on the back of his head, and as he crumpled a strange question flashed into my mind. *Sir?* I asked myself. *Sir? Why was Mrs Hudson calling him 'Sir'?*

To my great relief, he wasn't dead. He wasn't even unconscious, but he was certainly very greatly dazed. Mrs Hudson spent some time making him comfortable where he lay, but even then there remained a glassy look in his eye and no sound from his lips but for a low, pained moan. As soon as she was satisfied that he would recover, my companion gestured towards the revolver, which had fallen a little way from the prone figure.

'Flotsam, would you be so good as to bring me that? I don't want the others to see it.'

I watched her unload the weapon with surprising expertise, then slip both the gun and bullets inside the folds of her cloak.

'There, I think everything is now as it should be,' she concluded, and flashed me a warming smile. 'Thank you, Flottie. Yours was a very effective way of cutting that argument short. One day I believe he will thank you for it. Let us hope that when the lawyers have finished picking over the Beaumaris estate there will be enough left for him to buy you a very large bunch of flowers.'

'The Beaumaris estate?' I repeated, bewildered. 'You mean . . . ?'

'Yes, yes, of course. You have just assaulted a peer of the realm, Flottie. This is the much sought-after Viscount Wrexham himself. Or to be more correct, ever since the death of his father, the seventh Lord Beaumaris.'

'But Mrs Hudson, ma'am, are you sure? He doesn't look like the Viscount at all. In fact, he looks exactly like Pauncefoot!'

'Have you ever *seen* Pauncefoot, Flottie? I mean the real Pauncefoot.'

'Well, no, ma'am, but we've heard him described, haven't we? Tall and bald and bearded.'

'That's right, Flotsam. And, if you remember, that was also the description of the man who found Viscount Wrexham's ring on the banks of the Thames. But when the ring was handed in, this particular gentleman was already in post at Broomheath Hall. In other words, Flotsam, there were two tall, bald, bearded men at work in different places.'

'But isn't that a bit unlikely, ma'am? I mean, it's rather an unusual appearance . . .'

Mrs Hudson looked slightly exasperated. 'Surely you see it

is not a coincidence, Flotsam? On the contrary, the Viscount took great pains to make the resemblance as close as possible.'

'You mean he deliberately disguised himself as his own valet? I see! But how can you be sure which one is the Viscount, ma'am?'

'Oh, that's easy, Flottie. For one thing, this one was such a terrible butler. The real Pauncefoot would have done a much better job. This fellow might have fooled the Summersbys, but I've worked with one or two valets in my time, and believe me there isn't one of them who wouldn't have made a considerably better butler than he did.'

I found myself recalling Pauncefoot's confusion about the silver and his great relief at our assistance when an important guest was expected. His had been an imposing figure, but he hadn't really *done* very much.

'So you knew as soon as you met him, ma'am?'

'Oh, I knew before then, Flottie. Don't you remember when we bumped into Martha at Mrs Thimbly's shop? If you recall, the items on her weekly shopping list included shaving soap and styptic powder.'

I must have looked a little blank, because she paused to explain.

'Styptic powder is commonly applied to shaving cuts, Flottie. It staunches the bleeding. Now, since Martha told us that the Summersbys' personal purchases were sent from London, it must have been the bald and bearded butler who was consuming shaving supplies at such a surprising rate. Now, Flottie, he certainly wasn't shaving his chin, was he?'

'His head! Of course! Viscount Wrexham was famous for

his long, flowing locks, wasn't he, ma'am? It was the one thing about him that everyone remarked on. So if he wanted to alter his appearance . . .'

Mrs Hudson reached out and gave the dazed peer's pate a little rub.

'Very stubbly, you see. Of course, I don't suppose the Viscount had any such plan when he first decided to disappear. He just knew that he needed to escape the public gaze if he was to be free to seek out the Lazarus Testament. And of course he knew the loyal Pauncefoot would help him to hide. Then, when they saw from Mr Verity's advertisement that a butler was being sought for the very place the Viscount most wished to be, well, his way forward became obvious. He would impersonate Pauncefoot and take up the post himself.' Mrs Hudson shook her head a little sadly. 'It is surprising how many peers believe they could pass themselves off as butlers, Flottie. Most misguided! Although I've met one or two who might have made quite passable footmen.'

At this point the gentleman in question gave a groan. 'The urn . . .' he muttered. 'Lazarus . . .'

'Don't worry, sir. All's well,' Mrs Hudson reassured him. 'Just rest for now, sir. You've taken a nasty bump on the head.'

'So what happened to the real Pauncefoot, ma'am?' I asked as the Viscount subsided with a sigh.

'He's lurking in London at the Viscount's expense, Flottie, and sending regular postal orders to his ageing mother. Miss Blenkinsop told us that Pauncefoot had grown up on the South Downs, so I asked Mr Rumbelow to track down any family he might have there. Old Mrs Pauncefoot's extravagance with new hats suggested some additional source of income, and when Mr Rumbelow confronted her she revealed that Pauncefoot is in fact living above a slightly seedy pub not far from the old Woolwich Arsenal.'

'Goodness, ma'am! With all the excitement here I'd almost forgotten about Miss Blenkinsop! And about poor Mr Swan! But that's where all this began.' I paused for a moment as a thought occurred to me. 'Come to think of it, ma'am, I still don't really see why they pretended Pauncefoot was dead.'

Mrs Hudson leant forward and loosened the fallen gentleman's collar a little more. Around us the lantern was casting long shadows, and somewhere near us the ancient text of Lazarus himself rested quietly in the darkness.

'That was all because of Mr Swan, Flottie. Really, the Viscount was terribly unlucky. Mr Swan was in the South of France at the same time as the Summersbys, and we know from Miss Blenkinsop that it was there – quite by chance – that he heard about Bob Pauncefoot's new post. It isn't hard to imagine the charming and excitable Mrs Summersby telling people about the genuine English butler waiting for them at Broomheath Hall, is it, Flottie?'

'I see, ma'am! So Mr Swan wrote to Pauncefoot here at Broomheath, and the Viscount received the letter. And, of course, Mr Swan was suggesting he should visit, which would have meant the end of the Viscount's disguise.'

Mrs Hudson nodded. 'So the Viscount wrote back saying that Pauncefoot was dead, Flottie. He must have thought that would put an end to the matter. He even enclosed that watch for good measure. But there was no putting off Mr Swan. If he hadn't happened to catch a glimpse of the real Bob Pauncefoot on that fateful morning in London, he'd have arrived here anyway, insisting that the Summersbys show him their butler's grave!'

I had a great many further questions to put to Mrs Hudson but, before I could ask them, the heavy hush of the cellar was disturbed by the sound of voices above us. Hearing them, the housekeeper leant close to me, and there was real urgency in her whisper.

'Remember, Flottie, no mention of the revolver, nor of your excellent work with the shovel. The gentleman slipped on the steps and banged his head, that's all. It would be a terrible shame to see such a flamboyant career end with criminal charges. The Viscount will have problems enough as it is . . .'

I nodded hastily. Above us the voices were becoming clearer. I could hear Dr Watson's low rumble and Mr Spencer's lighter baritone and then, raised above both with clarion confidence, a familiar female voice.

'Frankly,' it was asserting loftily, 'I'm surprised you two think this is the right time for so much *fussing*. It was a very *small* pond, wasn't it, Mr Verity, and we hardly fell in it at all. Really we just sort of wallowed around at the edge for a bit. Now, *are* we looking for rogue butlers or *aren't* we? I'm *sure* I saw someone come in here . . .'

Miss Peters's further musings were cut short by Dr Watson.

'Look! A light!' he cried, and above us four sets of feet advanced stealthily across the barn floor. Then a silence fell and we saw the top of Dr Watson's tweed hat peeping over the edge of the trap door.

'Who's down there? Speak up!' he demanded. 'Whoever you are, come up at once. And I warn you, there are four of us up here carrying very stout sticks!'

'Those won't be necessary, sir,' Mrs Hudson called back gravely. 'But if you would like to come down, please do. There's plenty of space. It's just me, Flotsam, the new Lord Beaumaris and the Lazarus Testament. Do tread carefully on the steps. They are a little narrow . . .'

The explanations that followed went on long into the night. My principal memory of them is not of Dr Watson's honest astonishment, nor of Mr Spencer's generous congratulations – not even of Mr Verity's chattering teeth – but of Miss Peters's unbounded and heartfelt dismay.

'You beasts!' she kept exclaiming. 'I was so sure it would be me who found it! You know how sometimes you just have a feeling about something? Well, that's how I felt about this urn thing. And tonight, when I spotted Pauncefoot slipping out, I was *certain*. I really thought I was going to make a great discovery. How was I supposed to know that everyone else was following him too? Honestly, Flottie, it was busier than a Kensington church bazaar out there! I practically fell over Mr Verity in the darkness, which was probably a good thing because he ended up with terrible blisters and I really think he might still be limping around in circles if he hadn't had me to help him. But I so wanted to find it for myself, Flottie. I really did!'

The return to full consciousness of Viscount Wrexham was another memorable moment (I never *could* think of him as Lord Beaumaris), and I confess to a feeling of horrible nervousness as to how he might behave towards someone who had recently hit him with a spade. However it seemed the dashing peer had no clear memory of anything that had occurred since he'd served the burgundy at dinner. That being the case, he was considerably bemused to find himself lying with his head in Mrs Hudson's lap in a place he didn't recognise and in the presence of the object he had staked so much on finding for himself.

Ever the sportsman, however, the pain of this discovery showed on his face only fitfully. It is said that never, in his long career on the turf, had the Viscount greeted outrageous fortune with anything other than a shrug and a smile, and when it became clear to him that his identity was discovered and the Lazarus Testament secured by his rivals he became at once the easy-mannered and debonair gentleman we had heard so much about.

'By Hades, I shall certainly be glad to get rid of this!' he exclaimed, fingering his beard rather ruefully. 'I'm not sure any prize is worth such an infernal encumbrance. I can't think why Pauncefoot puts up with it. And I'll lay fifty to one against him ever finding a wife before he finds a razor! Now tell me . . .' He looked around, one eyebrow raised. 'Do you think there is any chance that my part in locating this thing might be recognised financially in any way? I only ask because my wretched father spent every penny of my inheritance searching for it. And you have to admit, in the end it was me who led you to it, wasn't it?'

'My word!' Dr Watson snorted with great indignation. 'I hardly think you can expect a reward, sir! You've led us all a merry dance, and the cost to the nation in searching for you when you went missing . . . Besides, we all know that if Mrs Hudson here hadn't got to it first, you'd have carried the thing away and had it up for sale to some unscrupulous collector in no time!'

'How very true, Dr Watson! I had planned to meet just such a one in Shoreditch in two days' time. The sum he was prepared to pay was simply staggering.' He looked across at Mrs Hudson. 'How unfortunate that I slipped on that step,' he added thoughtfully.

For a moment his eyes travelled to where I sat beside her, and his hand seemed to move instinctively to the back of his head. 'Yes,' he nodded, 'it seems I have been very unlucky. Still, there's no law against dropping out of sight for a while, and nothing to stop a gentleman becoming a butler if he fancies it. In fact, I'd recommend it. It seems to me the perfect solution to the problem of idleness amongst the upper classes. And I can't even be accused of falsifying my references. I meant every word I said about myself in my letter of recommendation.'

Once again Dr Watson spluttered with outrage, but the Viscount continued calmly.

'Tell me, Mr Verity, do I take it that my employment is now at an end? Or do you think I need to give the Summersbys formal notice? They are hardly a couple to stand on ceremony, I think. And just think how delighted that pretty Mrs Summersby will be to discover she has had a real British lord pouring her sherry. It will be quite the most exciting thing that has ever happened to her.'

'Really, sir!' Dr Watson retorted, 'your behaviour towards

the Summersbys has been quite despicable. To deceive them in such a way is unpardonable!'

'Oh, dear. Perhaps you're right . . .' The peer's gaze moved across to where Miss Peters was clinging onto Mr Spencer's arm. 'And I did it so much less prettily than our young friend here. Please allow me to congratulate you, my dear. I found your countess quite bewitching, if entirely bogus. Had I been in a position to invite her to spend a week at Hawthornden with me, I would most certainly have done so. I have always enjoyed the company of adventurous women.'

Dr Watson seemed to think it was time to change the subject.

'I suppose it's a bit late to start opening all these pots now, eh?' he wondered aloud. 'What do you think, Mr Spencer?'

'I think that is probably a job for an expert, Doctor. We'd probably do more harm than good by just blundering in. I suggest we wait until tomorrow, when we can seek out some advice about the care of ancient parchments.'

'If you'll forgive me, sir,' Mrs Hudson put in politely, 'isn't Sir Percival Grenville-Ffitch expected here tomorrow afternoon? And I believe he was bringing Mr Fallowell with him. Mr Fallowell is an expert in such matters. Also, since the ownership of these artefacts is something of a grey area, and since Sir Percival has official status, as it were, perhaps it would be better to wait for him?'

This suggestion was met with general approval, and it was agreed that the cellar should be resealed, and a watch kept on the barn until the following afternoon, when both Mr Fallowell and Sir Percival could be present.

'And Mr Holmes too, I hope,' Dr Watson added loyally. 'It's not often a mystery is solved in his absence. I know he would like to be here to see the conclusion of this one.'

It was, I think, almost the last thing anyone said before the gathering dispersed and Mrs Hudson shepherded me off to my bed. As no one could think of any reason to deprive Viscount Wrexham of his liberty, he returned to the Hall with the rest of us, still jaunty and unabashed but, judging by the way he kept looking at me rather thoughtfully, still nursing something of a headache. To be on the safe side, it was agreed that Mr Spencer and Dr Watson would both stand guard in the Home Barn until the local constable could be called out the following morning.

CHAPTER EIGHTEEN

Desperate Measures

Breakfast the next day was a most confusing affair. Martha and Mildred arrived at the usual time to discover several new faces at the breakfast table and an atmosphere decidedly strained. The Summersbys had been woken that morning by Mrs Hudson, who as well as bringing tea also brought the news that Pauncefoot the butler was in fact the seventh Lord Beaumaris, and had asked if he might join them at breakfast. And if that shock were not enough, the Summersbys were also informed that a number of other extra guests had spent the night at the Hall, that a collection of ancient ceramic vessels had been discovered beneath the Home Barn, and that Fred Arthurs, the local constable, was standing guard there with orders to allow no one to enter.

Perhaps a little stunned by all this, the Summersbys had accepted without demur the addition of Dr Watson, Mr Spencer and Mr Verity to the Hall's guest list, although their enthusiasm for these new visitors did not appear very great when they finally greeted them in the dining room. As I laid out extra bacon, even chatty Mrs Summersby seemed a little taciturn and her husband had retreated into one of his most morose and brooding silences.

Perhaps the atmosphere around the breakfast table was not helped by Miss Peters's absolute refusal to reveal to her host and hostess the deception she had practised on them. 'Please, no!' she had insisted. 'That would simply be too, too mortifying! I should never be able to look them in the eye again, really I shouldn't! I'd rather fling myself in the river right now!'

As Mr Spencer had appeared to give this offer serious consideration, she had then raised her chin defiantly.

'Well, Rupert, you may expose me if you wish, but I shall deny everything and shall probably become quite hysterical. But, of course, if you want a terrible scene over breakfast, that is entirely up to you. I do think it would be very selfish of you, though, after everyone has had such a stressful night! I know my opinion counts for nothing so you must do exactly as you please, but if poor Mr Verity gets another one of his headaches as a result, there will only be you to blame.'

The upshot of this was that the *contessa* reappeared at breakfast her usual serene and effusive self, and if Dr Watson and Mr Spencer eyed her a trifle coldly, Viscount Wrexham clearly relished the situation and made up for their *froideur* by flirting with her scandalously and insisting on exchanging tales of Italy.

'This discovery last night, Countess, will no doubt excite your friend in Naples. Professor Corelli, I think you said?'

'But indeed, my lord, he will be, how do you say, green to the gills when he hears of it! I shall return to Napoli in triumph, like Caesar himself! And, my lord, no doubt a gentleman such as yourself will have come across the professor in your travels?'

'Me? But of course! Dear old Professor Corelli! He's really something of a legend, is he not?'

Through all this, Mr Verity, whose placid existence had ill-equipped him for any activity more disturbing than the occasional hand of whist, seemed inclined to shut his eyes, as if in prayer. If he heard Dr Watson start to grind his teeth, he gave no sign of it.

Even Mrs Hudson did not seem to be entirely at ease, for later that morning I came upon her folding the laundry with her brow furrowed in thought.

Precisely what was worrying her, I wasn't sure, for with the cellar under guard and the Viscount identified and exposed, our business in Alston was drawing to a close. All that remained, tantalisingly, was to see the urns opened: then perhaps we might even hear, in his own words, the story of Lazarus himself!

With this momentous thought hanging over me, the morning passed with leaden footsteps and the afternoon brought nothing but a message from Mr Holmes saying that Sir Percival was delayed and would not now be able to reach Broomheath until the following day. This news was greeted with great dismay by the whole party, on whom the virtue of patience was beginning to take its toll. Dr Watson rolled his eyes and harrumphed and Mr Spencer looked anxious. Even Miss Peters's spirits seemed a little affected by the news.

'Really, Flottie,' she complained, 'it's a bit much, isn't it? A priceless treasure under our noses and we're expected to wait for some dull old official before we can look at it! I mean, really! That sort of thing never happens in pirate stories, does it? They just crack open the doubloons, run for their boats and anyone who complains is marooned on a barrel of rum! If Rupert wasn't so tediously law-abiding, he'd be down in that cellar putting us all out of our misery!'

Thankfully, Mrs Summersby's spirits seemed to have revived since the morning and she received the news of this delay with something akin to her old sparkle.

'My!' she exclaimed. 'You English are so patient! Back home we'd be at work on those pots just as soon as we got hold of them! But if waiting is the thing, I suppose we must just wait . . .'

As Constable Arthurs could not be expected to remain on duty indefinitely, and as it was too late in the day to summon a replacement from Hexham, it was agreed that Mr Spencer, Mr Verity and Dr Watson would watch in pairs, swapping in and out at various points throughout the night. Mrs Hudson was most insistent on this, absolutely refusing to allow anyone to stand watch alone, yet when Mrs Summersby offered the services of her husband as an extra guard, she declined on the grounds that Sir Percival Grenville-Ffitch himself had specified who was to keep watch. When I asked Mrs Hudson if it wouldn't be easier just to lock up the Viscount so everyone could get a good night's sleep, she looked slightly scandalised.

'One cannot just lock up peers of the realm, Flotsam. It is not considered hospitable.'

'But he did threaten you with a gun, ma'am. I'm sure that's reason enough!'

'I rather think that madness has passed now,' she replied, 'and I don't expect we'll see that sort of behaviour from him again. He strikes me as the sort of gentleman who knows when his hand has been played. And besides, we might yet have need of his assistance.'

'His assistance, ma'am?'

Mrs Hudson looked grave.

'You seem to be forgetting, Flottie, that although we have secured the urn containing the Lazarus Testament, there remains one crime unsolved. The Viscount might be disarmed, but somewhere out there the murderer of Archie Crummoch remains at large. That is why I don't want the gentlemen watching alone. There is still danger out there, Flotsam, and we must not drop our guard for an instant.'

And with that ominous warning, she turned her attention to matching the linen, an occupation that seemed to absorb her completely.

By four o'clock in the afternoon the light was fading and the shadow of the fells was falling over Broomheath Hall. After my conversation with Mrs Hudson, it was with some trepidation that I faced the prospect of nightfall, and when the honest face of Constable Arthurs appeared at the kitchen window to take his leave, his departure seemed to signal the end of all the day's bright certainties. He was relieved by Mr Spencer and Mr Verity, who seemed quite resigned to missing dinner for the sake of a long and chilly vigil.

Under Mrs Hudson's watchful eye, Mildred produced another fine meal that evening, but in truth it was little appreciated. Dr Watson appeared distracted and Miss Peters unusually subdued. Even Viscount Wrexham was more restless than I had ever seen him. To the relief of them all, the party broke up early, Mrs Summersby rising to announce that she thought everyone would benefit from an early night.

This suggestion went down well with her guests but it was not one I welcomed, for sleep was very far from my mind. Even when the dinner was cleared and the kitchen scrubbed clean I would have stayed downstairs keeping watch had it not been for Mrs Hudson's stern insistence that I rest. This, however, was easier to suggest than to achieve, and the significance of every creaking stair or groaning floorboard was amplified by my fretfulness.

In the end, out of pure desperation, I sought distraction in the pile of papers I'd brought with me from the Baldwick Archive. To my surprise, however, instead of lulling me to sleep as they had done the previous night, the section of the papers that I chanced upon proved rather more interesting than any I had yet discovered. They dealt with Mr Baldwick's visit to America, and my attention was quickly caught by the mention of a familiar name.

April 10th, Philadelphia

My visit to Mr Fazackerly was most successful. Put to him my plans re Sodom and Gomorrah. Impressed on him the scale and ambition of my plans. The Cities of the Plain – unseen since Lot – no greater archaeological prize! Explained to him my calculations, without of course revealing their result. Assured him that location of site a mere formality. Offered him a portion of the profit – and named my price. Fazackerly clearly struck by my vision. Promised to consider, but gleam in his eye betrayed his eagerness. Have written to my new friends to thank them for their assistance. Much moved by their support and solicitude. Will not accept a penny from them, but shall reward them when my fortune is made. As I took my leave of him, Fazackerly suggested possible introductions to notable figures in the field. Dalrymple, Le Blanc and Beaumaris were the names he mentioned.

Was this, then, how the fatal meeting between Anthony Baldwick and Lord Beaumaris had come about? In this casual encounter on a foreign shore?

After that, references to Mr Baldwick's ambitions in the Holy Land followed at regular intervals, and I began to see that the writer was setting great store in the prospect of assistance from the English peer.

May 17th, Boston

Visited Thomson, the museum curator, to answer reported criticisms of my Sodom theory. Laid the evidence before him and intimated that Beaumaris and Le Blanc likely to take an interest. Thomson impressed by mention of Beaumaris and seemed more inclined to listen. To my surprise, not acquainted with Mrs Kidd, despite her position in society. Makes me think less of the man – possibly not the well-connected figure I'd been led to believe.

June 5th, New York

Great developments! Mr Kidd out of town but waited upon Mrs Kidd at their apartments. To find acceptance with such a woman, so cultivated, so refined, so elevated in

American society, is a great joy to me – and sorry contrast with pride and contempt of British aristocracy. To my great surprise and joy, Mrs K intimated she had connections related to Beaumaris by marriage and would attempt to arrange introduction. So condescending! So generous and kind-hearted! No more was said of our small business transaction, but understood from her smile that debt now settled and creditor would not now be approaching Mr K. Has been my honour to be of assistance to such a one – a small price to pay for her friendship, especially as it offers so much in return.

June 30th, New York

No reply to Mrs K from Beaumaris. Aristocratic aloofness? English disdain? Comfort myself that correspondence may take time to find him in his desert camp. Meanwhile, my frustration is growing. Sodom scheme does not prosper as I had hoped. I find the people here less open to new ideas than I had imagined. Ignorance! I shall show them all! Only Mrs K proves the exception. Admire her more each day. So brave in her predicament! Called yesterday and found her in tears. The youthful indiscretion she confided in me still haunts. I consider it my great good fortune to be able to assist her. The new banker's draft should be enough to remove the danger for good. She has invited me to join them in the Hamptons should Mr K's business allow time for their annual visit. Optimistic things will be sorted with Beaumaris by then.

And so on! I read long into the night, tracing the failure of Mr Baldwick's plans to raise finance in America for his archaeological schemes, and his growing certainty that Lord Beaumaris's support was vital in achieving what he desired in the Holy Land. But strangely it was not these entries that eventually led me to sit bolt upright, blinking at my own stupidity. It was a much shorter note, scribbled quite hastily, one of the last Mr Baldwick made in America. By the time I read it my candle was burning very low, and perhaps by then weariness had slowed by brain, because it was not until that moment that understanding dawned.

September 2nd, New York

A most distressing night. I am lost, desolate! I will not be consoled. Truly this is a society of hypocrites, their evil greater for their pretended belief in democracy, in merit. That an angel should be cast out by their cruel hands and sneering pride! I scorn this place and shall shake its dust from my feet forever!

And in truth there is nothing to keep me here. She came to me tonight – so good, angelic in truth, to spare a thought for one such as me at such a moment! But already their things were packed, and they embark this very evening for Europe. There, she says, they will lead a humble life, set apart from those who would use her youthful folly to shame her name forever. For there is no way to escape disgrace if she stays, she tells me. Her blackmailer plans to expose her this very week and she has despaired of further attempts to purchase his silence. Not all her private fortune, nor all the sums I have made over to her, have been enough.

It is, I suppose, some comfort that her husband stands by her. For all his taciturnity it seems a good heart beats in that great frame. She tells me that he does not blame her, but shares her belief that ruin is certain if they do not fly at once. Of course I waived all consideration in this crisis. She owes me nothing, I assured her, for although the loss to me in money is considerable, kindness and friendship have no price – and when my great discovery is made I shall be a rich man. Yes, when my greatness is established, as I know one day it shall be, they shall be the first to benefit from my fortune . . .

Long before reading this entry I had formed my own suspicions about the kind-hearted Mrs Kidd and the mysterious indiscretion that seemed to require such a constant stream of funds to keep quiet. In none of the diary entries did the help she offered Mr Baldwick ever seem to materialise, nor did her introductions lead to any genuine advancement. Long before that entry for September I had been wondering if perhaps at some point the writer would find that both the Kidds and his money had disappeared from his life. But Europe! A well-built, taciturn husband and a charming, clever wife! Without a moment's hesitation I slipped from my bed and went in search of Mrs Hudson.

Even though the hands of the kitchen clock were a little short of four o'clock in the morning, I found Mrs Hudson still downstairs and still fully dressed, ironing linen by the kitchen range, with the air of one who intended to stay up all night. There was, I thought, a faint unease in her face, but the thoughts weighing on her mind were quickly put aside when I burst upon her, panting for breath.

'Why, Flotsam!' she exclaimed. 'Whatever is the matter at this hour?'

'Look, ma'am! Here! In Mr Baldwick's papers! I wondered . . . Well, see for yourself!'

She took the papers from me without further questioning and settled at the kitchen table to peruse them. Sitting beside her, I could see that her concentration was fierce, and from time to time her eyebrow flickered meaningfully.

'The Summersbys . . .' she breathed at last. 'Well, well! The pieces fit perfectly. Only yesterday I received a reply from Mr Bertram Peeves, recently of Washington, saying that he had never heard of them, and Mr Peeves is the sort of person who knows a great many people. But, of course, America is a large continent, Flottie, so such a telegram was hardly conclusive.'

'You already had suspicions of the Summersbys, ma'am? Even before this?'

She pursed her lips, as if pondering her answer. 'Well, Flotsam, Mrs Summersby strikes me as a much shrewder individual than those about her realise. She contrived to captivate Sir Bulstrode Peveril, for instance, and to win a place for herself in polite society in the South of France, with neither money nor a prepossessing husband to help her. And yet, when confronted with a dubious Italian countess, she appears completely taken in. Why is that?'

'Perhaps she hasn't met many Italians, ma'am?'

'There are plenty of Italians in New York, Flottie. No, for some reason she chose to avoid a fuss. It's as if she was deliberately trying to avoid the attention that would have accompanied the countess's exposure. In fact, she's been working very hard at avoiding attention, hasn't she, Flotsam? Look how anxious she was that Mr Verity should not summon Sherlock Holmes to Alston. Look how reluctant she was to entertain guests at Broomheath Hall. And then there's Mr Verity's evidence . . .'

'Mr Verity, ma'am?'

'Right at the beginning, if you remember, he reported lights moving around *inside* the house at night. But there were many more reports of lights *outside*, and it was those tales of ghosts and spirits, and all the reports of the butler's nocturnal expeditions, that tended to capture our attention. But what if the Summersbys knew about Pauncefoot's jaunts and took advantage of his absence to search the house at night? I don't think it ever occurred to him that the Summersbys might be playing the same game. I'm afraid he dismissed Mrs Summersby as a rather empty-headed American. And that, of course, is exactly what she intended.'

I paused to consider things in this new light. 'But, ma'am, we can't be sure that the Summersbys are *really* the same people as Mr and Mrs Kidd.'

'Well, Flotsam, we know from his papers that Mr Baldwick had vowed to repay Mrs Kidd for the kindness he felt she had shown him – even *after* she had parted him from his money. Don't you think he might have written to her in the South of France and told her that he had some great treasure in his possession?'

I nodded. From what I had read in his diaries that sounded like exactly the sort of thing Mr Baldwick would have done, especially once he had reached Broomheath and had grown so desperate.

'And then, of course, there is Crummoch. Mr Holmes says his skull was completely caved in by a blow from a spade. Well, Flottie, you know a little about hitting people with spades. To kill with one blow – and in particular to smash a skull so completely – would take unusual strength.

'And so,' she went on, rising to her feet and reaching for a storm lantern, 'as far as I'm concerned Sir Percival and his army of policemen cannot arrive a moment too soon. It was bad enough waiting until today, but another night in this old house worries me. If the Summersbys really are Mr Baldwick's American friends, they will not be sitting on their hands tonight. Until today they, like the rest of us, had no precise idea where to find the Lazarus Testament, but now they know exactly where it is. Come, girl. Dr Watson joined Mr Spencer on watch almost an hour ago. I think it would be wise to pay them a visit . . .'

The night was so still it seemed nothing could be awry with the world. As we stepped out into the darkness, the hall showed no lights at its windows and its grounds lay silent. There was so little wind that a light ground mist hung in small patches over the lawns, clinging to the dips and gullies and thickening ominously over the boggy fringe of the moor.

The only light other than ours came from the narrow windows of the Great Barn where, much to our relief, a lamp was burning just as it should. However, as we rounded the corner of the building, we found the doors of the barn hanging open, and instinctively we exchanged glances.

'Dr Watson?' I called as we approached. 'Mr Spencer?' But there was no reply, and when we stepped inside, the barn seemed empty. Apart from the absence of our sentries, however, nothing seemed amiss. Dr Watson's lantern was burning brightly by the wheels of the old cart, and nothing seemed disturbed. Only when we drew closer did we perceive that the wagon's position had altered, that it had been rolled forward a little, sufficient to allow the trapdoor to be raised.

'Dr Watson?' I called again, louder this time and with genuine alarm in my voice, and this time a reply came in the form of a muffled grunt that seemed to come from inside the cart. Peering over its boards, we were greeted by the sight of Dr Watson, curled up on a bed of sacking, eyes closed and a happy smile on his face.

'Sir!' I cried reproachfully. 'Wake up! You've fallen asleep!'

'Not just now, Flotsam,' he murmured happily. 'Five more minutes . . . Still very dark . . .'

Exasperated, I began to shake his prone form with some vigour, but Mrs Hudson reached out and stopped me.

'It's no good, Flotsam. Look.' And she held out to me a silver hip flask. 'Drugged, I think. And listen!'

From somewhere below the trapdoor we heard a low moan.

I'm not sure what I expected to find as I followed Mrs Hudson down the steps into the cellar. I think I was frightened that we'd find a chaos of broken pottery, with our hosts still amongst it – for I knew they had blood on their hands, and even between us we could be no match for the brute strength of Mr Summersby.

But instead, when I stepped onto the cold floor of the cellar and looked about me, the light of Mrs Hudson's lantern illuminated the groggy form of Rupert Spencer propped against the wall of an otherwise empty room. Where the rows of ancient vessels had stood, the floor was bare. No trace of them remained, no clue to indicate they had ever been there.

'Gone,' Mr Spencer muttered, attempting to point. 'Very tired. Watched them go. Summersby. Flask. Drank something. Watched them. Pots. Gone.'

'But why?' I asked, still looking around me as Mrs Hudson went to his aid. 'They only wanted the Lazarus Testament. Why would they take them all?'

But Mrs Hudson, having assured herself that Mr Spencer was in no immediate danger, was already hastening back up the wooden stairs. 'Quickly, Flotsam, I want you to alert the others. The Summersbys cannot have gone far.'

'I suppose they don't know which is which, either,' I decided, thinking aloud, 'and didn't think they'd have time to empty them all.'

'Precisely, Flotsam. I expect they've found out enough about ancient documents to know that the urn containing the Lazarus Testament must be opened with some care. So they have simply taken them all, to somewhere they won't be disturbed. Remember that huge peat-cutter's basket that was here before? Well, it isn't here now. They must have filled that and taken it off somewhere. Mr Summersby is just about big enough to lift it, I should think.'

'But where would they go, ma'am?'

'That's what we must find out, Flotsam. I don't think they came back to the Hall though, because I'm sure I'd have heard them. Could I ask you to raise the others? We'll need their help if we're to search the grounds . . .'

But raising the others did not prove easy, for it seemed Mrs Summersby was every bit as shrewd as Mrs Hudson had surmised. I roused Mr Verity by thumping very hard on his bedroom door, but when he tried to open it we discovered the door was locked and the key removed.

'But I don't understand,' he kept repeating, 'I know it was here on the inside earlier . . .'

Leaving him to try what he could to effect his own escape, I quickly found the situation to be the same for Miss Peters and Viscount Wrexham. Both were confined behind their heavy oak doors and no amount of hammering and shouting was likely to alter the fact, although very soon the whole east corridor was echoing to a cacophony of shouts and curses and heavy thumps, as chairs and other pieces of furniture were hammered against the locks to no avail. The confusion might have persisted all night had it not been ended startlingly by a loud explosion and the sight of Mr Verity stumbling into the corridor shrouded in smoke, waving in his hand an ancient-looking duelling pistol.

'Good lord!' he muttered. 'Good lord! It was hanging on the wall. I never really expected it to be loaded!'

Of course where there is one duelling pistol there is generally a second, and in this case there turned out to be not just one brace on display, but two. This was enough for both the remaining rooms, although the sight of Mr Verity, eyes bulging somewhat, discharging pistols into the doors of Broomheath Hall was not an easy one to forget. Nor was the spectacle of Miss Peters emerging from her smoke-filled doorway dressed in riding boots, a baggy pair of chocolate-coloured men's jodhpurs, a purple tweed hacking jacket and white silk gloves, with something resembling a Turkish turban wrapped around her head.

'I was expecting something like this,' she explained airily. 'And after getting so terribly cold and wet last night I decided to gather up all the warmest things I could find. Though I did draw a line at the pair of long-johns behind the fishing tackle in the boot room that are so itchy they must be made out of llama hair or something . . .'

It was only after some persuasion that Mr Verity was prevailed upon to shoot out the lock of the Viscount's bedroom. Indeed the honest solicitor might have refused altogether and was mumbling something about dangerous scoundrels when the roar of the peer himself decided things.

'The *Summersbys*, you say? The *Summersbys*! *They've* got the blasted document? By Hades, I'm not having that! I tell you, I'd rather present the thing to the British Museum than have myself beaten to it by that simpering girl and her oafish husband! Dammit, man! Blow the lock! Blow the lock! I give you my word that for this night at least you can count on me!'

Finally, after all these lamentable delays, we were ready for duty. Mrs Hudson must have heard us coming, for she greeted us at the front door, accompanied by a yawning and dishevelled Mr Spencer who appeared to have recovered something of his wits, but who nevertheless was leaning a little unsteadily against the wall. Her first step was to instil some order into our activities, reining in both the Viscount, who wanted to take to the moors with bloodhounds, if he could find any, and Mr Verity, who wanted to search the house for powder with which to reload his duelling pistols.

'We can't be sure where the Summersbys are,' the housekeeper admitted, 'but I daresay our first step should be to search the grounds. I don't think they can have any proper plan, as such. I think they've just seized the chance that presented itself. And now they've got the urns away, they'll be impatient to examine them and find the Lazarus Testament itself. With only that to carry, they have a chance of slipping away across the moors . . .'

'Very good!' Mr Spencer said it rather sleepily and stifled a yawn. 'Perhaps if Hetty and the Viscount and I form a party to go round the south side of the Hall . . .'

And so a plan was formed, and Mrs Hudson, Mr Verity and myself set off together in the other direction, approaching every barn or potting shed as quietly as we could, hoping to surprise the fugitives with their prize. But for all our care, we saw no sign of the Summersbys, and it seemed only a very short time before the two search parties met again, their rounds complete. However, I for one was not yet ready to give up.

'There is one other place, ma'am,' I pointed out. 'The old belvedere out on the edge of the moor. It's usually kept locked, but the Summersbys could easily have taken the key . . .'

And so we proceeded to the little summerhouse, our stealth and speed only slightly compromised by our numbers, but in good spirits and very determined. Even from a distance

I thought I could detect a gleam of light from the derelict building and, as we approached, this grew more distinct. Its effect on my companions was noticeable for I could sense their growing excitement, and without any instruction they began to move forward more quietly. Even Miss Peters followed without a gasp or a squeak. Almost twenty yards before we reached the belvedere, Mrs Hudson brought us to a halt and signalled for us to wait while she and Mr Spencer advanced towards the gap in the shutters from which the light was escaping.

It was here, perhaps, that the housekeeper misjudged the discipline of her troops, for no sooner had she and Rupert Spencer reached the belvedere than Miss Peters made an impatient hissing sound and began to follow them.

'Hetty!' I remonstrated in an urgent whisper, only to see the Viscount also breaking ranks, declaring beneath his breath that he was damned if he'd stand around like a lemon while the Summersbys squeezed his juice. That left Mr Verity and me, and we at least had the good grace to exchange guilty glances before we tiptoed forwards to see for ourselves what awaited us in the belvedere.

One glimpse through the wooden boards was enough to show me that we had the Summersbys at our mercy. The huge peat-basket stood in the middle of the room, with the various urns still neatly arranged within it. To move them all in one go must have been an immense effort for there were a dozen or more heavy clay pots, each of them more than two feet high. Even with the thick leather shoulder straps to assist him, Mr Summersby must have tottered under such a weight.

He now stood near the door of the summerhouse, facing

away from us, towards the moors. But for all his bulk, his was not the figure that dominated the scene. Closer to us, only a yard or so away, Mrs Summersby was pacing to and fro. The events of the night seemed to have wrought a change in her, or perhaps she had simply discarded a mask, for gone was the expression of light-hearted charm that had always characterised her, and in its place was the face of a strong and determined woman. She was no less handsome for the change: if anything, I thought, her beauty was enhanced by it. If there was menace in her face, it was the menace of a tiger – fierce, strong and utterly controlled. She appeared to be counting off options on her fingers, remonstrating with her husband as she did so. 'No, you great ox! Alston is out of the question. These people may be fools but they are not so stupid as to forget to guard the station. No, we must disappear without trace. Are the horses still in the place we arranged?'

From where I stood, behind most of my companions, my view of things was far from ideal, but another gap in the boards, a little to my right, seemed to hold out much better prospects. To reach it I had to clamber up a little and let one of the lower boards support my weight. From there I had an improved vantage point and was able to see the look of confidence on Mrs Summersby's face as she spoke of their escape.

'Very well,' she went on. 'I have our other papers here, so we'll have no trouble at the ports. And now to the Lazarus Testament. We'll smash all of these in turn until we find it . . .'

On my left, Mrs Hudson seemed to be whispering an instruction to Mr Spencer, but before he could act a terrible creaking noise interrupted her and, to my dismay, I felt the board I was peeping over begin to pull away from the wall. The nails were giving way beneath my weight and they were doing so with a hideous groan. I tried to jump off but I was too late: before I could escape, the whole board fell backwards, revealing to the Summersbys the startled faces of their pursuers.

Mrs Summersby cried out – in surprise, I think, rather than in fear. Mrs Hudson shouted something too, and I saw both Viscount Wrexham and Mr Spencer start immediately round the building towards the door. Then I heard Mrs Summersby's voice again, loud and clear and urgent.

'Quickly! Run! It is our only chance!' she cried, and as I leapt to my feet I was in time to see Mr Summersby once again pull the enormous basket onto his shoulders.

'Go!' she cried again, and with a roar Mr Summersby launched himself through the doorway, the basket secure on his back.

His great momentum was the undoing of Mr Spencer and the Viscount, for as they rounded the corner they came directly into his path. The charging American ran through them as easily as a rampaging bull through barley. Both men were taken off their feet and, as they tumbled backwards, Mr Summersby was past them, still running fast, his face towards the moor.

I think I heard Mrs Hudson shout again, but we were beyond instruction now, running past her towards our fallen friends, each of us lost completely in the thrill of the chase.

As we reached him, Viscount Wrexham was already on his feet and looking around him into the darkness.

'Which way did he go?' he cried.

'That way, sir!' I waved my arm towards the stile that led to the moor, and the two of us set off together with Mr Spencer a yard or so behind and Mr Verity in his wake. Miss Peters, showing a commendable turn of foot in her borrowed riding boots, was closing on the panting solicitor, and in that order we set out into the darkness of the fells.

It proved a difficult and confusing chase. Somewhere in the back of my mind I knew that first light was approaching, but on that particular night the darkest hour really did precede the dawn. Even with his burden on his back, the American proved hard to follow on the pitch-black moors, often vanishing from sight only to reappear, each time a little further off, a hunched silhouette against the paler sky. Behind him we floundered in the gloom. The terrain was rough and it was easy to trip and fall, but nevertheless we stuck to our chase, blundering forward with a will, certain that the weight on his back must soon begin to tell.

It quickly became apparent to me that Mr Summersby's line of flight was not a straight one. By cutting this way and that he confused his pursuers and scattered them across the hillside until, gradually, we became separated in the dark. Quite early on I realised I'd lost sight of Mr Verity, and a little later, after stumbling over a tussock of heather, I found that only Viscount Wrexham was still by my side.

'Quickly, girl! He's heading north-west. If he continues that way he'll come to the river and then we'll have him, for it's surely too full to cross.'

Too breathless to reply, I simply nodded and let the Viscount lead the way, reassured that Mr Summersby could not evade us much longer. At the same time I noticed that there was now a distinct light in the eastern sky. The night was nearly over and with it, surely, the thief's last chance of concealment.

But I had reckoned without the mist. Only when the Viscount and I reached the edge of the heath, where it fell away steeply to the river, did I realise that the mist we'd noticed at Broomheath was growing thicker with the advent of morning. Below us, the river valley was lost beneath an opaque shroud of fog, and somewhere in that grey cloud Mr Summersby had taken refuge.

'Which way now, sir?' I gasped, but the Viscount could only pull off his deerstalker hat and rub his bald pate rather ruefully.

'No idea!' he grunted, still breathing hard, then favoured me with an approving look. 'I'll say one thing, young lady, you're a game one! That was a fine chase. But all we can do now is hope for the best.'

'On the contrary, sir,' a voice contradicted him. 'I think, if you would care to follow me, we still have a chance of overhauling the gentleman.'

'Mrs Hudson!' I turned and saw her coming up behind us with Mr Verity in tow and, behind them, to my astonishment, a very pale Dr Watson, still groggy and glassy-eyed from his sleeping draught. Unlike the rest of us, Mrs Hudson seemed remarkably unflustered. Indeed, for all the urgency she showed, she might simply have been stepping out to post a letter or to buy a box of eggs.

'He's heading for the railway, you see,' she explained. 'He must have decided he'd no chance of finding his way in the dark to wherever it is they've hidden their horses. But Kirkhaugh station is about a mile away up the valley and if he can get there in time for the milk train he might yet escape us.'

'But there's a river between us and the railway line!' Viscount Wrexham countered. 'He'd have to go all the way back to Broomheath to find a crossing!'

Mrs Hudson nodded wisely. 'That's what I thought, sir. But Mr Verity here, who is a keen butterfly collector, tells me there's a shepherds' crossing a little downstream. Mr Summersby will know of it, of course, from his surveys of this area. But with the weight he has to carry, he can't be far ahead of us.'

With Mr Verity's help, we found the crossing fairly easily, despite the very dense fog. It consisted of some old planks laid from rock to rock, and offered a possible, if precarious, passage to anyone desperate to cross.

'If he managed to get over this with that burden on his back, it was an impressive piece of work,' Mr Verity mused as he wobbled uneasily in midstream. 'Why, I'm not sure it's even possible!'

'And yet he has done it, I believe.' Mrs Hudson had been the first to cross and was pointing to a mark in the mud near where she had alighted from the boards. 'His footprint, I think. See how deep it goes? That means he is still ahead of us.'

From the river bank it was but a small scramble up to the little railway that led to Alston. The fog, which had been at its thickest as we crossed the river, seemed to thin rapidly as we left the water behind us and I realised with a shock that for the first time since we had set out I could see the detail of my companions' faces. Morning had come and with it a very faint breeze to disperse the mist. Ahead of us, in the grey morning light, the railway stretched in a straight line towards Kirkhaugh.

'Look!' I cried, for there, perhaps a quarter of a mile ahead of us, was the bulky figure of Mr Summersby, his massive burden still on his shoulders. For him to have carried such a weight so far was a mighty achievement in itself, but to have done it through fog and mud, over heather and rocks, and all the time evading his pursuers, was almost magnificent. Yet it was clear his strength was almost spent, for we could see from the wobble in his gait that he was struggling to keep a straight course between the rails. Ahead of him, drawing him on, the outline of Kirkhaugh station was emerging from the mist.

'Quickly' the Viscount shouted. 'After him!'

But Mrs Hudson was pulling out her watch and shaking her head. 'I'm afraid, sir, however fast we run we won't be able to catch him before he reaches the platform. And if I remember the timetable correctly, the early train is likely to be coming in any moment now. From the progress he is making, I fear he'll catch it.'

'Then we must catch it too!' the Viscount declared and set off with renewed vigour. But for all his determination, I could see that Mrs Hudson was right. Mr Summersby's lead was too great, and I began to think that his escape was inevitable.

The Viscount had run only a few yards before a movement in the bushes a little further up the line captured our attention and brought him to a halt. As we watched, a gaunt figure scrambled into view between Mr Summersby and the station house.

'Look!' I yelled, suddenly excited. 'Look, ma'am! It's Mr Holmes! And he's not alone!'

Sure enough, we saw the detective turn and offer his hand to someone behind him on the slope, and first Mr Spencer, then Miss Peters, emerged into view. Both looked bedraggled, but nevertheless a great wave of optimism swept over me.

Their sudden appearance had a powerful effect on Mr Summersby too. The American stopped in his tracks and for the first time since setting out from the belvedere seemed to hesitate. He turned briefly, as if contemplating retreat, but the sight of Mrs Hudson's party spread out across the line behind him was enough to make up his mind. Very carefully he slipped the basket from his back and rested it between the rails, then turned to face Mr Holmes, rolling up his sleeves as he did so.

Strange to tell, for a moment my heart went out to the fugitive. As Mr Holmes and Mr Spencer advanced upon him, there was something splendid in his defiance. I saw Mr Holmes shout something, but Mr Summersby merely shook his head and then, with a roar that even we could hear, he threw himself upon his enemies.

Although too far away to intervene, we were close enough to appreciate the raw power of that charge as the big American caught both his opponents in his arms and hurled them backwards. How they withstood the impact of such a collision I will never know, but to their credit both Mr Holmes and Mr Spencer clung on to their assailant and, still locked together, the three combatants rolled in a tangled mass over the edge of the railway embankment and out of sight down towards the river.

'Goodness!' I gasped, but before I could move to assist them the Viscount let out another cry.

'Good God!' he exclaimed. 'Look! A train!'

CHAPTER NINETEEN

The Lazarus Testament

One glance up the tracks showed us he was right. At the very moment the three combatants tumbled out of view, a locomotive had burst from the mist at the far end of the valley and was heading towards us at full steam. It was clearly not a scheduled service, for it pulled behind it only one carriage and it travelled at such a speed that its smoke seemed black with urgency.

Even at first glance it was clear from its tremendous velocity that the driver had no intention of stopping at Kirkhaugh station. Perhaps our exertions that night had made us all dull-witted, perhaps we were simply bewildered by the rapidity of its approach, but for a few seconds we simply watched in awe, unaware of the implications. Then understanding came upon us with a rush.

'By Hades!' the Viscount exclaimed. 'The basket!'

'The urn!' I gasped.

'The pots!' Mr Verity added for good measure. 'The basket! The urn! The Lazarus Testament!'

For as we stared in horror, a single obstacle stood in the

path of the oncoming locomotive. The great peat-basket that contained the whole collection of ancient ceramic pieces remained carefully positioned where Mr Summersby had placed it, precisely and perfectly in the way of the oncoming train.

'Stop!' I shouted desperately and began to wave my arms, imagining the terrible carnage that must follow if the train hit those ancient vessels. But even as I gesticulated I knew it was useless. We were too far away to attract the driver's attention and too far away to reach the precious basket before its contents were destroyed forever.

'Great God! It's going to smash the lot!' The Viscount was also gesturing, a look of utter horror in his eyes. 'Stop!' he yelled. 'For goodness' sake, stop!'

But in our rush of despair we had forgotten that there remained one person who could reach Mr Summersby's basket before the train hit it. Miss Peters had disappeared from the embankment immediately after Mr Summersby's charge, presumably with the idea of assisting her companions. Whether our shouts had alerted her to the danger, or whether it was the sound of the train that brought her scrambling back, I couldn't be sure, but now she reappeared on the side of the track, her gaze jumping from the basket to the train and back again.

'The basket, Hetty!' I begged. 'Move the basket!'

We were all shouting now, even Mrs Hudson, as Miss Peters scampered onto the line and took hold of those great leather straps. With rising horror, I saw the huge locomotive come into focus behind her, still at full steam, looming darkly and horribly over her slight figure. And for all her efforts it was clear the weight of the basket was too much for her. Three times she attempted to heave it away from the line, tugging and pulling with all her strength, trying to topple it from its perilous position. But nothing she attempted moved it even an inch, and now the train was very close indeed, its brakes suddenly screaming.

'Get clear, Hetty!' I implored. 'Give it up!' Only seconds remained, I knew, and in despair I braced myself for the crash.

But instead of leaping away, Miss Peters released her grip on the basket and seemed instead to be peering inside, examining its contents.

'Jump!' we cried. 'Hetty! Please!'

I don't know if she could even hear us. The train was now only yards away, its momentum still barely checked. Twenty seconds, I thought. Fifteen. Ten. *Jump, Hetty! Jump!*

Just when her destruction seemed inevitable Miss Peters appeared to make a decision. Her hands darted out and selected just one of the dozen urns that peeped from the top of the basket. With a great heave, she raised it clear of the others and, part clutching it, part staggering beneath its weight, fell back from the basket and away from the quivering track.

The train must have missed her by no more than inches, for while she was still falling backwards the front of the locomotive struck the basket firmly in its centre. I remember the moment of impact with complete clarity – the sickening crack of those ancient jars as they exploded into fragments, the cloud of dust that billowed up from the tracks and, worse, the dreadful knowledge that the entire contents of the basket had been reduced in that moment to a thousand tiny pieces, or else lay utterly pulverised beneath the iron wheels.

I was dimly aware of activity in the locomotive, of a driver shouting, his voice drowned by the shriek of metal on metal as the train shuddered to a halt only a dozen yards from where we stood. The first figure to emerge from it was none other than Sir Percival Grenville-Ffitch himself, looking this way and that in alarm.

'What the . . . ? Eh? Mrs Hudson? Good lord!' he spluttered as he struggled to make sense of what he saw. 'Whatever are you doing here? As for us, we've come to secure the Lazarus Testament . . .'

But to our shame none of our party paid him any attention. We were already dashing towards the fallen figure of Miss Peters. As I hurried past the stationary carriage I glimpsed the nervous face of Mr Fallowell, the timid expert in Aramaic, looking down on us, accompanied, it seemed, by a great number of uniformed policemen, still unaware that their arrival had created the very havoc they'd been sent to prevent.

I think Mrs Hudson was the first to reach Miss Peters, although I was close behind her, and to my great joy I saw at once that she was alive and apparently uninjured, sitting upright and coughing in the dust with the urn she had rescued hugged tightly to her breast. The strange turban she had insisted on wearing was beginning to unravel and a loose end of fabric hung down between her eyes like a stray lock of hair in Paisley print.

'You see, Flottie!' she beamed when she saw me. 'I just knew it was going to be me who rescued the Lazarus Testament! Haven't I been telling you that for ages? And see, I have!' She broke off to cough a little more.

'But my dear young lady . . .' A voice spoke from behind me and I looked up to see Sherlock Holmes emerging from the bushes with Mr Spencer behind him. From the marks on their faces it was clear that their encounter with Mr Summersby had not been a comfortable one. 'There is, I fear, only a small chance that the pot you have saved is the one that contains the Lazarus Testament,' the detective continued. 'Although your efforts have been valiant, I fear they may yet prove futile.'

But Miss Peters scarcely seemed to hear this doubting voice. 'Rupert!' she shrieked. 'What has that brute done to you?'

'Just a scratch, Hetty,' Mr Spencer replied and I saw that a trickle of blood was escaping from his gashed forehead. 'I think I caught the edge of Mr Summersby's boot at some point. And I'm afraid to say he got away from us. We hung on to him for as long as we could, but he's built like a bear. In the end he escaped by plunging into the river. It's running pretty fast at the moment and I thought it would be the end of him but he made it across, and neither Mr Holmes nor I cared to follow him!'

'I hardly think it matters,' Mr Holmes assured him. 'He will surely not get far by daylight. And it was the contents of that basket that really concerned us.'

'But just look what has become of them!' I wailed, pointing to the debris scattered over the track. The Viscount was already sifting through it disconsolately with the toe of his boot, as if in search of anything that might resemble the remains of an ancient parchment. As he did so, Mr Fallowell and Sir Percival hurried up to us.

'Oh, dear! Oh, dear!' the smaller man lamented, surveying the scene. 'Mr Verity has explained to us what has happened.

I fear our arrival has not proved propitious. And it is I who must take the blame! It was I who urged Sir Percival to bring reinforcements by special train. With so many *villains* around, it seemed a sensible precaution.'

'Villains?' The Viscount looked up with a smile. 'How right you are! These archaeologists. You just can't trust them.'

'And who, pray, is this?' Sir Percival inquired, eyeing the bald peer with some suspicion.

'This, sir, is Viscount Wrexham. Or, to be more accurate, the seventh Lord Beaumaris,' Mrs Hudson explained. 'You will recall that you asked Mr Holmes to solve the mystery of his disappearance.'

'The Viscount? Him?' Sir Percival sounded incredulous. 'Good God, man! What has happened to your hair? You've aged twenty years! Mind you, we thought you were dead.'

Behind me, Dr Watson was clearing his throat, his eyes still bleary.

'But tell us, Holmes, how did you come to appear like that, just when you were needed? You should have seen it, Sir Percival! It was the most remarkable thing. Dashed if I can tell how he managed it!'

The great detective dismissed these plaudits with a wave of his hand. 'Ah, Watson! Once again I must disappoint you. The explanation is very simple. I came up from London ahead of Sir Percival and had planned to spend the night at Haltwhistle. But I found I could not rest, so in the early hours of this morning I set off to walk to Alston. It was not difficult. I knew I simply had to follow the rails. And it was purely by chance that I heard the shouts of Mr Spencer and Miss Peters as they sought a place to cross the river. Happily, with the knowledge acquired during my brief career as a bird-watcher, I was able to suggest a place where it might be forded. Our arrival in Mr Summersby's path was completely fortuitous.'

Dr Watson, however, was not to be talked out of his admiration. 'Well, I still say it was the most remarkable thing. I only wish, after all your efforts, that the outcome was a happier one.'

'But it is a happy one!' Miss Peters declared indignantly. 'And I keep telling you so. Really! After practically losing my head under that train, not to mention doing all sorts of damage to my nails, I do think a little gratitude would be in order! If it wasn't for me, your silly old testament would have been a lot of very choky dust like the rest of those pots. And, do you know, I almost think you'd have deserved it!'

'But, Hetty,' I asked, 'I know you were terribly brave, but how could you possibly hope to choose the right one from among so many?'

'Well—' she began, but was silenced by a strangled cry from Mr Fallowell.

'The urn!' he mouthed, pointing at Miss Peters's chest. 'The urn! It's a miracle!' And without another word he flung himself to his knees beside her and began to run his figures down the vessel's smooth curves.

'But surely, Mr Fallowell,' Sir Percival protested, 'you don't mean to tell us that the very urn we're after is the only one to have survived?'

'I certainly do!' the little man retorted, his eyes still full of wonder. 'It's a miracle!'

'No, it isn't!' Miss Peters put in crossly, but the scholar was not to be silenced.

'See here!' he went on, pointing. 'See the way the lip turns downwards? So characteristic of that precise period! And so rare! There cannot be more than a dozen complete specimens anywhere in the world! This *must* be the one!'

'Well, of course!' Miss Peters agreed, apparently a little mollified. 'And honestly, Mr Fallowell, if you'd seen the other pots you'd have known it was this one straightaway. They all had *rounded* lips, you see, so of course they couldn't be the right one, could they? They just weren't nearly old enough.'

She turned to the rest of her audience with an air of utter nonchalance.

'Probably late medieval. Not rare at all, you see,' she explained, dismissing them with a contemptuous shrug of her shoulders. 'I don't know *why* Mr Baldwick thought he could hide this one among them. To anyone with even the slightest knowledge of Mesopotamian funerary ceramics the difference is *glaringly* obvious.'

I confess this pronouncement was met with a rather stunned silence.

'But, Hetty,' Mr Spencer asked, blinking a little, 'you must forgive us for being just a little surprised at your grasp of the subject. It isn't an area of expertise for which you're generally known . . .'

'Well, really, Rupert!' Miss Peters raised her chin loftily. 'My life isn't *all* hats and dances, you know. And, of course, if you ever actually *looked* at any of those dusty old books of yours, you'd know all about it too. The one you need is about halfway up on the left-hand side, I believe. A very large volume. With a smart new binding. Now tell me,' and she looked around very sweetly, 'do you think this train might take us all back to Alston now? I'd rather like to take a hot bath before we open up this pot of mine.'

And noticing the loose strand of her turban for the first time, she frowned and then with great earnestness began to tuck it back in.

'Well, of course, Flottie,' Hetty confided after a lengthy soak in Mrs Garth's bathtub, 'I was absolutely as surprised as anyone.'

As well as a generous quantity of hot water, the landlady of the Angel Inn had also provided a plain but inoffensive set of clothes so that Miss Peters might discard her outlandish costume of the night before. She stood before me looking strangely demure in an old-fashioned dress and blouse, and most unlike an Italian countess.

'I just remember hearing that ghastly train coming,' she went on, 'and then realising I couldn't shift the great heavy basket, and suddenly it struck me that I could at least save one or two of the pots. And as I looked at them, all wedged in like beer bottles, and practically in the shadow of the train, a bit in that dreadful book suddenly came back to me. I've no idea *how*. I mean, I only read a few lines of it, and it really was the most tedious thing I'd ever come across. And then, just when I thought I was going to die, there it was, clear as crystal in my head! Can you imagine, Flottie? Moments from death, and instead of thinking about all the wonderful things that have happened to me, I'm thinking about ancient Mesopotamian pottery. It was too terribly gruesome! And, of course, the bit I'd been reading had gone on and on about the different lips on the wretched things, so that was what I found myself looking at, and, well, one of them was different from all the others, so *obviously* that was the one, and I just had time to snatch it out before *poof!* Everything was white and I thought I *was* dead, but then I started choking, and it seemed to me that if I was choking to death I must still be alive . . .'

She stretched blissfully and beamed at me.

'Oh, Flottie, I'm so happy! I've always dreamt that one day I'd actually *help* Mrs Hudson, instead of just getting in the way. And now there's going to be a world famous discovery, and it's all down to me! I think that nice French chef at the Mecklenburg ought to name a dish after me, don't you? After all, he named one after that frightful Johnson woman who saved her maid from drowning even though we all know that she makes her maids so miserable they'd probably *rather* drown. Of course, I don't believe her dish will ever really catch on, you know. I mean, Chicken Ethel just doesn't *sound* very nice, does it, Flottie? Anyway, the best thing of all is that Rupert will be forced to confess how utterly despicable he's been. I mean, he might know lots of things, but, really, he's never rescued a priceless biblical document from certain destruction, has he?'

I was spared having to reply by the appearance of Mrs Hudson with the news that Sir Percival and the other gentlemen had arrived at the Angel and were waiting downstairs for the opening of the urn.

'Mr Fallowell seems to think Mrs Garth's parlour will be a suitable place for the unsealing,' she told us. 'Dry but not too warm. There had been some talk of doing it at Mr Verity's house but of course I made it clear that you two had done enough gadding about for one day, and certainly weren't going out in weather like this.'

It was certainly true that the weather had taken an inclement turn, and in the Angel's snug the gentlemen's coats were steaming slightly in front of the fire. Everyone who had been involved in our Alston adventures was there: Sir Percival and Mr Fallowell, Sherlock Holmes and Dr Watson, Mr Spencer and Mr Verity. Even Viscount Wrexham was there, having won the respect of the entire company by the sporting way he'd accepted his defeat. When Mrs Hudson ushered us into the room, Sir Percival rose to his feet and bowed.

'Before we proceed to the main business of the day,' he announced gravely, 'I should tell you that I have just received word of Mr Summersby. He was apprehended earlier today trying to board a train for Newcastle. It turns out his real name is not Summersby at all, but Braddock, and under that name he is wanted in America for any number of acts of violence. He broke down completely when he realised his wife had escaped without him, and told us everything. It is as you said, Mrs Hudson, his wife cultivated Mr Baldwick's company when he was in the United States and fleeced him of a great deal of money. Such was her skill in the matter, they parted with Baldwick on good terms.

'The Summersbys relocated to the South of France, with the intention of preying on similar individuals, and it was there they received a letter from Mr Baldwick, a letter written only hours before his death. Baldwick told them that the Lazarus

Testament was at Broomheath Hall, but he didn't mention where. So they came here at once to find it and to make their fortunes, but after weeks of looking, they grew desperate. There had been a line in Mr Baldwick's letter about taking the secret to his grave, and they began to think he had meant it literally. Hence that gruesome business in the ruined chapel. But Archie Crummoch came across them as they dug up Baldwick's grave and declared he would denounce them to the rector. Summersby admits striking him, but claims that he never intended to kill. If he can convince a jury of that, he might just escape the noose.'

'And his wife?' Miss Peters asked. 'Flottie says Mrs Hudson locked her in the belvedere when the rest of us went chasing off onto the moors.'

Sir Percival appeared to flush slightly.

'Yes, that is true. Very quick thinking, I'm sure, Mrs Hudson. Unfortunately, the local constable was unaware of this. When he arrived at Broomheath this morning to resume his watch in the Home Barn, he found the house deserted and the treasure gone, but he *did* hear a knocking from the building you call the belvedere.'

'You don't mean he let her out?' Miss Peters gasped.

'Regrettably, yes,' Sir Percival confirmed. 'She told him such a very moving story about brigands and kidnappers that he even agreed to drive her to the doctor in Alston before raising the alarm. Of course she didn't visit the doctor. It appears she went straight to the station and took a ticket for London, but we don't believe she's travelled that far. No one noticed her changing trains at Haltwhistle and, to tell the truth, we don't really know where she is. But I daresay we shall pick her up shortly. A woman on her own like that . . . She can't get far.'

This prediction was met with a general nodding of heads but Mrs Hudson did not nod.

'A very clever and resourceful woman,' was her only comment, but something in the way she said it seemed to anticipate the young lady's eventual escape – although even Mrs Hudson could surely not have predicted the route by which she would achieve it, in a journey that was later to become notorious: by farm carts to South Shields, thence by collier to Aberdeen; by fishing smack to the Färoes; by whaler to East Greenland; by sled to West Greenland; on a sloop to Newfoundland amongst a cargo of seal furs; and thence by stages to New York, where under a different name she was to have such a glittering criminal career.

But although this was not the last time my path was to cross Mrs Summersby's, that day at the Angel Inn my thoughts were only of the Lazarus Testament and of the opening of the urn that had been sealed for so many centuries. And it was clear from the eyes of my companions and from the tense atmosphere in the room, that I was not alone in this. Mr Fallowell favoured us all with a few words about the history of the famous parchment and about the fragility of ancient documents in general, and then, finally, led us into the front parlour where we came face to face with the urn itself.

It had been placed on a small incidental table in a room full of chintz and china and prints of children holding puppies, but even these surroundings seemed somehow altered by its presence. I don't know how it came about, but in the parlour that day there was something of the long-fermented silence of an ancient cathedral, and I would no sooner have laughed or fidgeted there than I would have pulled faces in a chapel. Looking around, I saw Mr Holmes looking very grave. Dr Watson had discarded his pipe in a show of reverence.

'And now,' Mr Fallowell continued, 'I shall break the seal . . .'

We had formed a close semi-circle around him and not one of us made a sound as he went to work. I noticed that his hands trembled slightly as they neared the urn and more than once he stopped to wipe his palms against his waistcoat.

'The seal is likely to be a combination of beeswax and other substances. To be honest, we aren't sure of its exact composition. But I can vouch for its efficacy,' he went on, beginning to turn the stopper with some difficulty.

'There!' he declared at last, stepping back a little. 'It's done.' He looked around at our eager faces. 'When the elders of the Church caused this seal to be made, little would they have imagined the place or circumstances of its opening.'

'And its contents, sir?' demanded Sir Percival, his patience creaking under the strain.

'Let me see . . .'

Mr Fallowell reached into the urn until his arm disappeared up to its elbow. And as we watched, breathless with suspense, we saw his expression change from a frown of concentration into a look of puzzlement and then slow-dawning horror.

'I . . . I . . . There's nothing there!' he stammered. 'Only this . . .' And pulling out his hand, he revealed a fistful of ashes – pale grey, crumbling fragments that turned to dust at the touch of his fingers.

'Burnt!' he gasped. 'The document is burnt!' And thumping

down the ashes upon the table he began to search the urn again, pulling out handful after handful of the same dull substance.

By now our circle had broken and we were all crowding around him, anxious to see for ourselves. I reached out and ran my fingers through the light, flaky ash. On one fragment, a little less than half an inch across, I thought I could make out traces of an ancient script, but the whole thing, writing and all, dissolved into dust at my touch.

'This cannot be! It cannot!' Mr Fallowell was insisting. 'The seal was unbroken, I swear it!'

'So this cannot be Mr Baldwick's work?' Mr Spencer asked. 'We know he was very unbalanced . . .'

'No!' Mr Fallowell was adamant. 'The seal was unbroken, just as it would have been a thousand years ago!'

'In that case,' Mr Holmes observed, 'there can only be one explanation. It would seem—'

'Aha!' Mr Fallowell's fingers had touched something and very, very slowly he pulled his hand from the urn. Between his fingers rested a small rectangular tablet of clay, no more than an inch high and two inches across. From where I stood I could see there were words engraved on it, and these, I saw, were in a more familiar script.

'What does it say?' Sir Percival barked.

Mr Fallowell read for a moment before replying, then straightened and looked around him.

'It's in Latin,' he told us, 'and if I may translate, the message reads something like this . . .'

He cleared his throat.

'*In the name of God, our Father, and for the preservation of the divine mystery, Vespasian decreed that this document should be burnt. Thanks be to God.'*

In the silence that followed, Viscount Wrexham let out a low whistle.

'So it seems my old man was right. The Lazarus Testament really was dynamite, after all! I wonder what it said. It must have been pretty devastating for them to destroy it outright like that.'

'Wait!' Unnoticed by the rest of us, Mr Spencer had continued to search the urn while Mr Fallowell was busy with the tablet and now he pulled from it a handful of ashes in the middle of which, brittle and charred but still legible, lay one small surviving fragment of parchment.

The room fell silent at the sight of it and we watched Mr Spencer lower it to the table and lay it down with the most tender care. Mr Fallowell seemed almost too awed to approach it, pausing to clear his throat again before moving closer.

'Can you read it?' Miss Peters asked, her voice trembling a little, as if from the effort of holding in check for so long her natural exuberance. 'Goodness!' she added. 'Perhaps we're going to learn the secret after all!'

Mr Fallowell stooped to examine it but did not dare to touch it with his fingers.

'The writing is in Aramaic,' he informed us, 'and yes, I can make it out. Let me see . . .'

He composed himself for a moment or two, his face only inches from the scrap of parchment.

'Unfortunately the flame has left certain lacunae in the text,' he explained. 'That is to say, there are some gaps. But what I can make out reads thus.'

And in a slightly hoarse voice he began to read.

'*Yesterday I took dispute with the seller of fish. His goods are expensive and of poor quality . . . As I have repeated ten thousand times in these pages, manners are assuredly not as they were in the days of my childhood. The tax collector is a boy with pimples, his mother a . . . Young men respect not their elders, neither their experience nor judgement . . . I was forced to complain about the quality of the candles . . . the cost of mules . . . a good horse for that and money left over . . . When I was a youth . . .*'

The scholar's voice trailed off. 'I'm afraid that's all,' he concluded a little lamely.

'That's all?' Dr Watson looked bewildered. 'But that's hardly the stuff of ancient mystery! It sounds more like the ramblings of a retired colonel from Tunbridge Wells. And believe me, I've met a few.'

'Indeed, Watson.' Mr Holmes straightened and there was something in the manner of the movement that spoke of finality, of a chapter drawing towards its close. 'It seems we shall never know the full details of the reminiscences Lazarus committed to writing, nor why it was decided they needed to be destroyed. But from the fragment remaining to us, I should say there's a distinct possibility that Lazarus did not, after all, compose an explosive account that threatened the foundations of Christendom. Perhaps the elders of the Church simply found his diatribe something of an embarrassment. Who can say? Now, Sir Percival, I take it that you consider my work here done? This morning I received a telegram about a fascinating strangulation off Fleet Street and I rather think my presence is required.'

'Why, of course, Mr Holmes.' Sir Percival nodded. 'But first, perhaps Mr Fallowell and I might have a few words with you in private? You see, we shall be expected to produce a full report for the Prime Minister and we would value your thoughts . . .'

With a bow to the rest of us, the old gentleman took his leave and ushered Mr Holmes from the room. Mr Fallowell bobbed politely in our direction and scurried after them.

'So that's that, then?' Viscount Wrexham asked, his voice sounding rather indignant. 'My word, what an anti-climax! I'd been thinking all this would make a rather good drama for the stage. But an ending like that rather scuppers things, doesn't it? Not at all what the public wants. No sensational denouement, no ancient curse, no supernatural forces at work – only some rather grumpy memoirs about the price of fish! It's a pity. I'm told there's a lot of money to be made in the theatre nowadays.'

He reached out and touched the urn. 'In a way I'm rather glad my old man never did get his hands on it. It would have been a bitter disappointment for him. And now I think it's time I came up with a new plan to restore the family fortunes. There's a race meeting at Carlisle tomorrow, I believe, and a fellow has to start somewhere.'

He pulled a watch from his waistcoat pocket and I recognised the silver timepiece that Mr Swan had been holding that fateful day in Baker Street.

'Ah, yes,' he went on, noticing my reaction. 'Pauncefoot's watch. He'll be pleased to have it back. I had the devil of a time persuading him to give it up. The poor fellow! I understand he's terribly upset about his old friend's death. I think he rather blames me for it. What about you, Flotsam? Do you?'

So direct and frank was his gaze, that for a moment I struggled to know what to say.

'Well, sir,' I began, 'I suppose accidents do happen. All the time. But then again, if you hadn't tried to mislead Mr Swan . . . Oh, sir! I really couldn't say.'

A shadow seemed to pass over his face and he bowed his head.

'I stand condemned, Flotsam. Perhaps if I were to make it my mission in life to do nothing but good works from this day forward, you might learn to think better of me. Now that would be an end to the drama that would warm the audience's heart! Nothing like a bit of redemption, eh? But I fear I should only disappoint you. My spirit is willing but it is also famously weak, especially when faced with any sort of temptation. Perhaps it would be wiser simply to assure you that my offence was unintentional and my regret genuine. Now, if I hurry I may be able to catch the afternoon train and be in Carlisle by supper time. With the honest wages of domestic service in my pocket, I have some sort of stake to play with. And if I can't teach these north-country farmers a thing or two about horseflesh, things will have come to a pretty pass!'

He too left us with a bow. As he departed, a small eddy of air from the closing door stirred the ashes on the table and caught up the one remaining flake of legible parchment. Light though the draught was, it was enough to lift the fragment from the table, and in attempting to catch it, Mr Verity succeeded only in crushing the charred remnant into tiny pieces.

'My goodness!' The solicitor's face was the very picture of dismay. 'The only remaining piece . . . A priceless shard of history . . .'

Mr Spencer smiled. 'I don't think you need to be too hard on yourself, sir. It was too fragile to survive for very long. And besides, no one seems very interested in it anymore, do they?'

Rather huffily, Miss Peters began to scoop the little pile of fragments from Mr Verity's hand back into the urn.

'Well, I must say, Rupert, I think it's a bit rich of Sir Percival! Some of us have risked their lives to rescue these little bits because he was making such a fuss about them, and now he simply doesn't care! Just because old Lazarus wasn't writing about angels and things. And, really! If those fusty old bishops were going to burn it all those years ago, I do think they might have said so! Think of all the trouble they've caused. And anyway, if they *knew* the document was just ashes, why did they take so much trouble looking after the urn?'

Mr Spencer looked down at the traces of ash still clinging to one of Mrs Garth's lace doilies.

'I suppose in more religious times, even the remains of the document had some significance, Hetty. After all, they had been in the possession of Lazarus himself, which would make them a pretty remarkable relic in their own right.'

This aspect of things seemed to strike Mr Verity for the first time and he hurriedly brushed some grey smuts from his waistcoat.

'Dear me!' he exclaimed. 'I suppose that's true. And here's me, covered in relic, as you say. Most lacking in respect.' His attempt to brush it away had merely pressed the ash further into the fabric, and he began to look rather anxious. 'Yes, most disrespectful. Can't wander around like this . . . If we're finished here, perhaps you'd excuse me? I might just nip home and change . . .'

His departure left me with only Dr Watson, Mr Spencer, Miss Peters and Mrs Hudson for company. For a moment we all looked around at each other, and then Dr Watson began to smile; and with that, the room ceased to be a place of awe and silence and became once again Mrs Garth's homely and welcoming front parlour.

'So,' he began, 'here we are again. And if I may say so, I think we've all done jolly well. We've cracked the code and found the Viscount and seized what remains of the Lazarus Testament. What happens now, Mrs Hudson?'

The housekeeper straightened. 'Well, sir, Mr Holmes says he's dashing back to London, which means the house will need airing and the beds preparing and some supplies buying in. And whatever matter he involves himself in next, I'm sure he will want you by his side, sir. So I daresay we ought to be packing our bags and vacating Broomheath Hall. I suppose Mr Verity will need to find a new tenant now that the Summersbys have gone.'

Dr Watson looked thoughtful.

'I confess Mrs Summersby fooled me completely,' he admitted. 'Such a charming woman! When she took the trouble of bringing us out that flask of brandy, I don't mind telling you I flushed like a schoolboy.'

'Well, I never liked her,' Miss Peters declared. 'I always suspected there was something devious about her.'

'Nonsense, Hetty!' Mr Spencer spluttered. 'You insisted that she had no hidden depths at all! Besides, you were so busy making up preposterous tales of Neapolitan life that you could hardly have formed a proper opinion.'

'Yes,' Miss Peters sighed. 'I suppose I did rather lose myself in the role at times. Do you know, I keep thinking about dear old Professor Corelli. He sounds such a jolly man, if rather naughty. Then, of course, I remember that I invented him, and I'm terribly disappointed.' She shook her head very prettily. 'But now I should go and wire your uncle, Rupert. I told him I was nipping out to the shops, and that was nearly a week ago, although I don't suppose he's noticed yet. But think how cross he would be if he did! You know that mood when he goes purple and shakes with rage and talks about sending me to a nunnery? I do so hate it when he does that. So I thought if I sent him a telegram saying I was actually *visiting* a nunnery . . .'

'Great heavens!' Mr Spencer groaned. 'If you will excuse me, I had better go with her to see if I can prevent further carnage.' He nodded to Mrs Hudson and favoured me with one of his warmest smiles. 'As always, Mrs Hudson, Flotsam, it has been a pleasure.'

Dr Watson watched them go then cast an eye towards the window. The rain seemed to be getting heavier.

'They say it is breathtaking here in summer,' he mused, 'but, do you know, Mrs Hudson, right now I rather fancy being back in Baker Street again. Excitement is all very well, but there comes a time when a fellow likes to be by his own fire, with one of your hot whisky toddies in his hand. I daresay we could all do with a night or two under our own roof, eh, Flotsam?'

And as Mrs Hudson smiled and quietly began to wrap the long-lost urn in her shawl, I could only agree. But it was not the comfort of the fireside I found myself looking forward to, but to all the bustle and excitement that awaited me: to my lessons in Bloomsbury Square and my expeditions with Scraggs; to the shouts of the flower girls and the rumble of the carriages; to the busy markets and the thronging streets; to all the surging life and drama of the city; and perhaps best of all, to the thud of the knocker heralding a new visitor with a new story, and possibilities for danger and daring and love and adventure that seemed to me, that day in Alston, infinite and unending and impossibly wonderful.

Mrs Hudson and Flotsam return in

MRS HUDSON AND THE SAMARKAND CONSPIRACY

Read on for an extract of their adventures . . .

So much has changed since those days that sometimes I find it hard to believe I was ever such a young girl, dashing around Baker Street in so much haste, at the height of a sweltering summer. Hard too, in these different times, to imagine a desert city seething with spies, or the envoys of a great empire fleeing in disguise across steppes and seas and mountains, hunted by a ruthless enemy. All that belongs to another world, a lost world, the stuff of storybooks.

But sometimes, when the temperature in my rooms becomes unbearable, I slip on my sensible shoes and take a walk along the Serpentine, to a particular bench, where I sit and look out over the water and see, not ducks or toy boats, but the minarets of Samarkand and the domes of Tashkent, and the dust of horses galloping towards the shores of the Caspian Sea. And perhaps, sometimes, if I close my eyes, instead of the laughter of children, I hear a band playing, and then a whistle, and the roar of a shuddering locomotive as it plunges at speed into the gaping mouth of a coal-black tunnel . . .

And then I blink and stretch, and calm myself by watching the ducks' careless manoeuvres.

However warm it is, however sticky the season, it is never as warm as that one I remember.

PART I

Nothing Happens in Baker Street

CHAPTER ONE

It was so hot that summer you could have fried an egg on the pavement outside our front door. Or so Dr Watson declared, although I don't think anyone would ever have attempted it; the pavements were too thick with dust, whirled up from the cobbles by the passing hansoms and coating everything and everybody, from the wilting flower girls to the dispirited sparrows; it crept under the starchiest collar and eddied under ladies' skirts, so that by the end of the day, when you came to wash, you found yourself dirtier beneath your clothes than above them. It would have been a terrible waste of an egg.

Mrs Hudson, who believed in clean aprons even in the hottest weather, had me running errands to the laundry twice a day, and three times on Tuesdays when the coal-wagon made its calls. But despite the dirt and the dust and the terrible smells that sometimes rose from the gutters, our shady kitchen – so much lower than the street – remained cool and soothing, a little sanctuary from the fevered world around us. And we avoided the worst of the coal dust, for that summer, from the beginning of July to the middle of September, Mrs Hudson refused to light a fire.

'No need for one, Flotsam,' she assured me. 'With all our neighbours out of London and their houses all but empty, it would be foolish to heat up this house instead of theirs, wouldn't it, my girl? We made similar arrangements in St Peter's Square back in '68, and it worked very well. So Mrs Johnson, the housekeeper at 197, is going to provide boiling water for all of us at pre-arranged times. Mrs Turner and Mrs McFarland will provide baths for those of us left below stairs, and the gentlemen can bathe next door, in the Jenkinsons' rather grand porcelain tub. In return, we shall be generous with the iced white port, which all three of those ladies enjoy greatly, and come the autumn you and I will help with their airing and the parquet floors. And, as for cooking, well, Flotsam, fruit and salads are what's needed this summer. Bread and cheese, cold meats, good chutney, plenty of Derbyshire water. A chilled soup from Lamington's, perhaps, if the gentlemen wish it, and a good supply of light Moselle to wash it down. But I promise you one thing, Flotsam, whether Mr Holmes likes it or not, nothing hotter than a bunch of grapes is coming out of this kitchen until the weather breaks. And hopefully, before then, something will happen to distract our two gentlemen from this terrible heat.'

But in Baker Street that summer, apart from the dust-spirals and the grumbling victorias, and the reluctant pedestrians hugging the shade, nothing did happen. It was far too hot for crime. Mr Holmes complained that London's most significant villains had all left town, and that those who remained were too befuddled to be interesting. And Dr Watson, driven by days of sullen inactivity to brave the glare, reported that over in Scotland Yard, where the dust was even thicker, Inspector Lestrade and his colleagues had nothing to do but pore morosely over the documents of unsolved cases. Meanwhile, on the streets, our local bobbies spent their days perspiring into their uniforms and their nights breaking up the tavern brawls that sparked into life as soon as darkness fell.

Had it not been for a deranged sultan, a foreign spy and a peculiar piece of railway timetabling in a remote corner of Europe, we might all of us have gone mad before the end of August.

The morning Mrs Hudson sent me to St Pancras to ask about ice was as hot and breathless as any other. It was that part of the summer when the pace of the city slowed and the streets were less frantic, and I made my way to the station past grand houses closed up for the summer, and past shops that were barely less quiet, the shop-keepers leaning in their doorways with folded arms, or sheltering in deep shade beneath their awnings. By the time I reached St Pancras my crisp, new petticoat was limp and clinging, my summer skirt already streaked with grime.

There, beneath the station's thrusting tower, I found my old friend Scraggs, the grocer's boy, selling overpriced paper fans to desperate passengers. Business was brisk, but his face was flushed and his forehead dripping, although it was barely nine in the morning.

'Hottest day yet, Flot,' he told me cheerfully, 'or so I'm told by the lad who shines the station master's boots. And what brings you to this particular part of the furnace?'

'I've come to see the iceman,' I told him. 'And then I'm to go to Fotheringill's for raspberry syrup.'

'Ah! One of Mrs Hudson's summer punches!' He grinned

happily. 'Then I'll make a point of dropping in later on.' He paused to dab his brow with a shirt sleeve.

'What I don't understand, Flottie, is why you're all still here. Old Sherlock could afford to get out of town, couldn't he?'

It was a very fair question. Ours was, by now, the only front door on our side of Baker Street that had not been bolted for the season. But the great detective remained stubbornly at his post. Since his sensational triumph in the affair of the opera-singer's lizard, he had barely ventured beyond his own study, waiting in vain for the challenge that would rouse him from his torpor. Listless and out of sorts, he passed the hours staring at his fingertips or playing 'The Arab's Farewell' on the violin with such intensity of feeling that Dr Watson had to beg him to stop.

'I'm not sure Mr Holmes feels the heat,' I explained to Scraggs, 'and, besides, he says he needs to stay where he can be found.'

Scraggs didn't even attempt to reply to this. He merely shook his head in bewilderment and pointed out that, so great was the heat in Trafalgar Square, even the pigeons had left for the country.

And I couldn't blame them. By then, the long days of breathless, unstirred heat had turned London's streets into open ovens, the brick and stone still hot to the touch long after the sun had set. And the nights were worse than the days. People kept their windows closed to exclude the dust and the stench, and because the air outside was hotter than the air within. But the stillness of those sweltered rooms pressed down so heavily upon the occupants that, all across the city, sleep came and went in restless, ragged fragments. Nearly all the travellers who approached Scraggs for fans had about them an air of long-suffering weariness.

'So, Flot, if you're going to be here all through the summer, you could go to the Survivors' Ball. It's at the Mecklenberg Hotel this year.'

The Survivors' Ball! He said it very casually, rear-ranging the fans on his tray as he spoke, and he didn't look up when I laughed. Because the Survivors' Ball was, in those years, a hugely famous institution, and the grandest, poshest, most spectacular event that anyone in service could ever imagine attending. It was organised by old Lady Townsend, who never left London during the summer months, and took place every year on the last Saturday of August. It had begun as a simple thank-you dinner for her own servants, a reward for surviving summer in the city. Gradually it had grown to include the households of other aristocratic families, until it had become the stuff of legends, and the object of a thousand below-stairs fantasies. Its fireworks were spectacular, its orchestra the very finest, and the food was as sumptuous as the most lavish London banquet. All the grandest families subscribed.

'But, Scraggs,' I pointed out with a smile, 'I would never receive a ticket, and neither would you. We'd have to find employment in much grander homes first. I believe Lord Brabham's household all used to go, back when he used to stay in London all summer with the stud books. But now he closes down the house in Bloomsbury every August. And I don't know anyone else who ever goes.'

'Well, you never know, Flot . . .' Scraggs looked up from

his fans, and instead began to examine a locomotive that was building up steam on a nearby platform. 'If I thought you'd like to go . . . I'm very friendly with the boot boy at Lady Townsend's, you know. And ever since I helped him out with that bunion cream, old Perkins the butler thinks of me as a favourite son.'

'Really, Scraggs!' I laughed again. 'Last time I saw you and Mr Perkins together, he was throwing a rotten cabbage at you!'

He had no option but to smile at that. 'But fondly, Flottie. Very fondly.'

He turned back to me, and we grinned at each other. 'And he missed, remember, which shows his heart wasn't really in it. Anyway, think about it, Flot. Meanwhile,' he added, 'if it's true about Mrs H's punch, I'll be around about four. Unless the points melt before then, and all the trains get cancelled. But I don't think that will happen. Reliable things, railways.'

He paused and both of us considered the hissing locomotive in front of us – fifty tons of hefty, ponderous iron.

'Solid,' Scraggs pointed out. 'Predictable. A locomotive may run late every now and then, Flot, but you always know where you are with trains.'

And I smiled. I thought so too.

MARTIN DAVIES is the author of twelve novels, including international bestseller *The Conjuror's Bird* which was a Richard and Judy Book Club selection and *Havana Sleeping* which was shortlisted for an Historical Dagger award by the Crime Writers' Association. The Holmes & Hudson series was begun when Martin was at a loss for a suitable birthday gift for his father, an inspired teller of stories, who first introduced him to the household on Baker Street.

martindaviesauthor.com

@martindaviesauthor